LEVEL: UNKNOWN

By David Dalglish

Level: Unknown

Level: Unknown

Astral Kingdoms

The Radiant King

Vagrant Gods

The Bladed Faith
The Sapphire Altar
The Slain Divine

The Keepers

Soulkeeper
Ravencaller
Voidbreaker

Seraphim

Skyborn
Fireborn
Shadowborn

Shadowdance

A Dance of Cloaks
A Dance of Blades
A Dance of Mirrors
A Dance of Shadows
A Dance of Ghosts
A Dance of Chaos
Cloak and Spider (novella)

LEVEL: UNKNOWN

BOOK 1 OF LEVEL: UNKNOWN

DAVID DALGLISH

orbitbooks.net
orbitworks.net

This book is a work of fiction. Names, characters, places, and incidents are the product of the author's imagination or are used fictitiously. Any resemblance to actual events, locales, or persons, living or dead, is coincidental.

Copyright © 2025 by David Dalglish

Cover design by Alexia E. Pereira
Cover illustration by Alexander Gustafson
Cover copyright © 2025 by Hachette Book Group, Inc.
Author photograph by North Myrtle Beach Photography

Hachette Book Group supports the right to free expression and the value of copyright. The purpose of copyright is to encourage writers and artists to produce the creative works that enrich our culture.

The scanning, uploading, and distribution of this book without permission is a theft of the author's intellectual property. If you would like permission to use material from the book (other than for review purposes), please contact permissions@hbgusa.com. Thank you for your support of the author's rights.

Orbit
Hachette Book Group
1290 Avenue of the Americas
New York, NY 10104
orbitbooks.net
orbitworks.net

First eBook and Print on Demand Edition: January 2025

Orbit is an imprint of Hachette Book Group.
The Orbit name and logo are registered trademarks of Little, Brown Book Group Limited.

The publisher is not responsible for websites (or their content) that are not owned by the publisher.

The Hachette Speakers Bureau provides a wide range of authors for speaking events. To find out more, go to hachettespeakersbureau.com or email HachetteSpeakers@hbgusa.com.

Orbit books may be purchased in bulk for business, educational, or promotional use. For information, please contact your local bookseller or the Hachette Book Group Special Markets Department at special.markets@hbgusa.com.

Library of Congress Cataloging-in-Publication Data
Names: Dalglish, David, author.
Title: Level: unknown / David Dalglish.
Description: First print on demand edition. | New York, NY : Orbit, 2025. | Series: Level: Unknown ; book 1
Identifiers: LCCN 2024030407 | ISBN 9780316586825 (print on demand) | ISBN 9780316577373 (ebook)
Subjects: LCGFT: LitRPG (Fiction). | Novels.
Classification: LCC PS3604.A376 L48 2025 | DDC 813/.6—dc23/eng/20240712
LC record available at https://lccn.loc.gov/2024030407

ISBNs: 9780316577373 (ebook), 9780316586825 (print on demand)

*For Megan and Essa, who were there for every
question, every rant, every high, and every low*

Chapter 1
NICK

The sun was blinding on Nick's face. His head ached, and his confusion was made no better by the soothing feminine voice speaking within his skull.

Unique visitor cataloged
Level: Unknown

Visitor? Level? He glanced about, but nothing made sense. He was in a field of golden wheat, the stalks waving in a soft breeze flowing down from the mountains to the west. Their peaks were jagged and tilted, like shark teeth rising from the plains. Behind him was a small clearing, black soil surrounded by a circle of stones. The sky was a comforting blue, with nary a cloud. If only the sun wasn't so bright…

No. That wasn't right. Nick squinted. In the sky, there was a second sun, except it was black instead of yellow. Dark blue veins stretched out from its circumference, seemingly frozen.

Initial assessment commencing
Archetype: Unknown

Special Classification: Unknown
Statistical allocation determined by approximation of visitor's physical and mental self-definition

Nick flinched again. It felt like a spike was driving into his forehead. Stats? He didn't care about that. He didn't even know where he was. The last thing he remembered, he was... he was...

Where?

He glanced down at himself. His clothes were wrong. They were plain brown suspenders and a white shirt, the fabric surprisingly soft on his skin despite its thickness. A sort of farmer? That wasn't him, not him at all. He was a...

...researcher...

Nick dropped to his knees and clutched his head, fighting off a wave of pain so intense he feared he would vomit. He forced himself to breathe in and out, his gaze focused on the wheat before him. He watched its subtle movements near the roots, watched a little black bug crawl along the dark soil before vanishing beneath.

Again came the same soothing voice. It was female-coded, pleasant and calm, and with every syllable the ache in his forehead faded.

Assessment complete
Level: 1
Agility: 1
Physicality: 1
Endurance: 1
Archetype: None
Special Classification: None

LEVEL: UNKNOWN

Nick forced himself back to his feet. *Ignore the hole in the sky. Ignore the dwindling pain. Focus on what can be dealt with in the here and now.*

"Level one?" he tentatively asked aloud. He didn't know why, but instinct told him the voice would hear and respond.

Simplified estimations of overall caliber of being

"Fascinating," Nick said. Curiosity got the best of him, and he started walking through the wheat in search of where the field ended. "So, uh, do you have a name, voice, so I can call you anything other than 'voice'?"

I am Cataloger

"Nice to meet you, Cataloger. I'm Nick."

I am aware of that user attribute

He laughed, and it felt good to move. With the lifting of the painful fog around his mind, he grew more aware of his surroundings. The mountains to the west were beautiful, if distant. Their snowcapped tips rose in stark contrast to the flatness of the field before them. To the south, perhaps a half mile away, he saw a small stream whose water was siphoned off into little rivulets to water the field.

To the east, Nick could see a village, so he set off in that direction. Perhaps, once among people, he might get an explanation for whatever was going on.

"User attribute," he repeated aloud. Part of him knew it should be strange talking to a voice in his head calling herself "Cataloger," but at the same time, it felt normal. It felt... right. "I'm guessing you're not much for small talk, are you?"

I provide information and guidance for unique visitors

"And I am a unique visitor?"

Yes

Nick paused a moment. "Is that a good thing or a bad thing?"

Unknown

Time to get used to *that* response, he suspected. He waded through the wheat as if it were water that went up to his chest. Given how its golden glow continued onward for seemingly miles and miles to the west, it was like being lost in an ocean. Scattered throughout the field, he saw people in similar overalls hacking away with sickles that gleamed in the bright midday sun.

Nick thought to call out to them but decided against it. Let them work. He'd find someone in the village to talk to, someone who could explain what was going on. Maybe...maybe he was a farmer here and had passed out from the heat? He certainly felt thirsty. Perhaps dehydration? Given how much his head hurt, that could explain his difficulty remembering things, like where he'd been, or what the name of the village ahead even was.

Location: Meadowtint

Description: A small farming village, population one hundred and seventeen, largely dedicated to wheat production and harvesting

"Meadowtint?" Nick asked. It carried no familiarity on his tongue. If this was his home, there were no attached positive feelings or emotions. He pushed onward, glad to see the end of the field. The village seemed pleasant enough, about thirty homes arranged on either side of a main dirt road splitting through them. Their thatched rooftops were the color of the field, their walls wood and clay plaster. Beyond the village, from what little he could see, was a dirt road leading toward a distant little river; on the other side grew what appeared to be an oak forest whose contrast to the nearby field was stark.

Several people milled about the well in the center of the village. Nearby, an older woman sat in a rocking chair beside the door to her home, protected from the sun by a rickety awning. Nick approached, strolling over as if they were acquaintances... which they might even be, if he was suffering from memory loss.

"Hello there," he said. "I fear I might be a little lost and confused."

The woman hunched over in her chair, slowly rocking back and forth with the press of her heels. He thought she was busy sewing or crocheting, but her gnarled hands were empty when she looked up. Her silver hair was covered in a bonnet, her dress, a mixture of faded blues and pinks. Her eyes, though, were the color of night, as if the pupils had swallowed her irises.

"Lost?" she asked. "You've wandered off the beaten path, stranger. How does one lose themselves in Meadowtint, here where the west ends?"

"I somehow managed it," Nick said, doing his best to not recoil. The woman's tongue was a shade of black, as if she had spent the past minute licking tar. He smiled at her, trying to be disarming, while she stared at him until, suddenly, her eyes grew wide with terror.

"Vaan almighty, protect me," she whispered harshly,

shriveling into her chair. Her hands clenched into fists. "Though I am weak, through him I am strong."

Her voice was getting louder. Nick glanced about and saw others in the village, simple farming men and women, staring at him.

Several still held their sickles from the fields.

"Though I am frail, he is my iron. Though I weep, he dries my tears."

Nick retreated from underneath her awning, his hands up to show he meant no harm. Villagers arrived from every direction, surrounding him with unnerving silence.

"I give my heart to the Conqueror of Time, and in his hands, I am made safe."

The nearest man lifted his sickle. He wore the same clothes as Nick, only they were far more worn and faded. His skin was pale, too, pale and almost gray. Not tanned, like it should be for someone who spent their days in the fields. His eyes were the same as the old woman's—black.

"Demons in the village," he said, his tongue appearing as a void in his mouth. "Vaan be with us."

"What...what are you?" Nick asked, horrified by the pallid nature of the man's skin, the emptiness of his eyes, and the dark color of his tongue. Text appeared above his head, the black font faintly outlined in white to ensure clear legibility.

Cedric: Level 1 Human
Archetype: Villager

Sickles, rakes, and knives rose skyward as the other villagers readied their weaponry.

"Vaan be with us," they called in unison.

LEVEL: UNKNOWN

Nick chose a direction and ran, attempting to burst through the growing crowd. Shouts accompanied his sprint. When the people did not move, he tucked his shoulder and rammed through, saw open road, and then screamed as a sickle raked across his back. His vision flashed red, and then strangely, a red bar appeared in the upper corner of his left eye. Nick might have given it more thought if not for the pain flooding his body.

Thankfully his momentum carried him, and once free from the crowd, he dashed along the center road, eastward, toward the river and the oak forest beyond. As he ran, he noticed the red bar stayed firmly in place in the corner of his vision regardless of where he looked. It was like the little floaters one noticed if looking for them in one's vision, always there no matter where one turned.

This is insane. This is absolutely insane. This is a dream, or a nightmare, or, or...

Nick didn't see who fired the arrow, only felt it thud into his side. He gasped, and when his mouth opened, a faint spray of blood dribbled down his chin and onto his clothes. The red bar shrank, now half its original size.

Health, he thought as he ripped the arrow out. Only now did he see the archer lurking at the edge of the village, an older woman with a straw hat and a hunter's bow. *That's my health, isn't it?*

A graphical representation of your body's overall condition

Nick hated the idea of this Cataloger thing having access to his thoughts, but there was hardly time for that now. He had to run. He followed the road toward the river, and when he glanced behind him, he saw a huge group of people giving chase with crude weapons held at the ready. He'd no clue what he'd done to upset them, but he knew for certain he was no "demon," whatever that meant.

Now aware of that first bar, Nick noticed there was a second below it, similar in shape and simplicity, except slightly longer and filled halfway with solid green.

"What is that?" he asked Cataloger, and was disturbed by how weak and out of breath he already sounded, given the distance remaining to the river.

A graphical representation of your physical endurance

"And what happens when it runs out?"

You will need to rest—or to use a human colloquial term—"catch one's breath"

Nick eyed that little green meter in horror. With his every step, it emptied at a shocking pace. It certainly *felt* like he was about to drop from exhaustion. His legs ached, and his lungs burned when he gasped for air. But that made no sense; if he pushed on, if he forced himself to move, he should be able to run for so much longer...

The meter emptied, and it felt like Nick slammed into an invisible wall. He gasped in air, his chest tightening and his legs wobbling beneath him as he slowed to a walk. His every step felt like pushing through molasses. Pure stubbornness kept him stumbling across the grass toward the river.

Another glance behind him, one he instantly regretted. Still the villagers of Meadowtint gave chase... and they were so much closer than before.

"To the river," he muttered, resuming his sprint. "Just... cross the river."

Any attempt at running ended immediately. The damn green bar—it drained in seconds. His chest constricted, and even his throat felt narrowed in a way that reminded him of how his brother had once described an asthma attack.

...brother...

Again that searing pain in his mind, somehow worse than the ache of the arrow wound in his side and the cut on his back. Nick stumbled, dropped to one knee, and gasped.

"Just a dream," he said. "This cannot be real."

The world of Yensere is real by most definitions, with interactions, emotions, and events that are both consequential and long-lasting to the individuals who experience them

More answers unasked for. Nick pushed onward, refusing to argue with a voice in his head. After what felt like forever, he reached the river. Nick could practically *feel* Cataloger's presence hovering nearby, eager to tell him the river's name, but she blessedly remained silent. He pressed through the mud that formed the bank and then waded into the water. It only came up to his knees, which ruined his hopes of using its lazy current to swim away from his pursuers.

"Suffer not any demons to live!" a deep-voiced man shouted. Nick glanced back, saw the man leading the others, taller than them, his pitchfork raised above his head like a battle banner.

Nick waded onward as fast as he could while making sure he didn't push himself too hard, all so that damn green bar could steadily refill with his every exhausted gasp of air.

Surprise, though, had him momentarily stumble in the mud-slick water.

There, on the opposite riverbank, was the strangest woman he'd ever seen. Her skin was pale, her blond hair even more so, and cut short, just below her jawline. Her eyes were such a vibrant blue they seemed to glow despite the distance. She wore armor made of silver chain, yet azure fabric flowed throughout it, hiding the creases, covering her chest and waist, and coming together to form a sort of skirt that ended just below her knees. Her boots were of slender plate. In one gloved hand, she held a sword. Her other was bare, and she pointed its palm toward him.

Frost: Level \<hidden\> Human
Archetype: \<hidden\>
Special Classification: \<hidden\>

"Sorry about this," she said, "but we all have to learn eventually."

Blue mist coalesced into a sphere that hovered just shy of her palm and then shot across the river. It slammed into the water between Nick's feet but made no splash of impact. Instead, the water froze, ice stretching several feet in all directions and then locking together into one thick sheet.

Nick twisted, shifted, tried to move. Nothing. The ice had him trapped in place.

"What is this?" he shouted, baffled. "What are you doing?"

There was no hiding his panic—the villagers were right behind him. He heard the splashing of their steps. The woman grinned at him playfully, amused. It'd have been downright charming if he weren't afraid for his life.

LEVEL: UNKNOWN

"Everyone dies the first time they come here," she said. "Don't worry, Nick. You'll get used to it."

Nick's jaw dropped. "Get *used* to—"

Pain spiked through him as he felt the sharp teeth of a pitchfork stab his back. He gasped, his arms flailing to push them away, but he still could not move. The ice had him imprisoned. Another hit, a slash with a sickle across his side. Blood splashed to the river. The villagers surrounded him, muttering, murmuring, always that word on their black tongues, that same expression in their dull, hollow eyes.

"Demon. Slay the demon."

The red meter that was his life flashed just beyond the edge of the box. The pain was unreal. Nick awkwardly collapsed onto his side as the ice dissolved, releasing him. Above him, he saw only bodies, cruel in their aims, heartless in their words. The largest of them lifted his pitchfork and aimed it for Nick's throat. For once, Nick saw a bit of life and light enter the man's eyes when he spoke.

"Vaan be praised."

Down came the pitchfork.

Health: 0

Visit terminated

Chapter 2
NICK

Nick lurched in bed and immediately vomited.

"Easy there, deep breaths," his older brother, Simon, said as he grabbed him by the arm. Nick retched several more times, but nothing came out, just dry heaves that were painful to his abdomen.

"There you go. You're fine. Just take it slow, Nick."

Nick leaned back, his head resting on a pillow. He was in a bed. No, not just a bed. A med ward. There were wires attached to his wrists and a sensor on one finger. The world grew firmer around him, more real. The carefully chosen white of the station walls. His brother's blue eyes, staring at him with obvious worry. The stars shining from the room's lone window, as well as a tiny portion of the barren planet, Majus, around which Station 79 hovered in orbit.

The smell of the vomit across his chest and lap.

"Get this off me, will you?" Nick said, tugging at the blanket.

"Of course." Simon pulled it away, bundling it so the vomit

was trapped in the center. Nick noticed he wasn't wearing any sort of med gown. He must not have been here long.

Nick pulled off his shirt, dropped it to the tile, and then shivered as he lay on the bed. No sign of a doctor. Just his brother.

"What's going on?" he asked.

Simon opened a nearby shelf and pulled out another folded blanket and tossed it to Nick. He caught it and gratefully wrapped it about himself.

"Honestly, Nick, I was hoping you could tell me," said Simon.

Nick relaxed onto the pillow and closed his eyes. It felt like he had just emerged from a dream so deep it bordered on the absurd. His head felt light, and his heart heavy in his chest. All his limbs ached, too. What happened? Today had been special; he knew that in his gut. His brother's clothes, they were nicer than normal, formal attire, crisp blue fabric with gold trim. His brother... his brother was doing something special, something with...

The Artifact.

Nick pushed back up to a sitting position.

"What happened?" he asked. "The Artifact, what happened when you activated it?"

Simon's careful smile cracked.

"*What happened* is that my little brother had a seizure the moment I put my hands on it. Don't worry about the Artifact. Let's worry about you. Did you notice any particular irregularities? Hear unusual noises, maybe experience sensations you cannot explain?"

Nick felt memories hovering just outside his reach, refusing to come easily. The research station over Majus had originally been sent to Majus because of long-distance scans suggesting the possibility of life. Instead they had found a dead, barren planet. They continued their research, of course, collecting rocks and attempting to analyze the fate of the planet and discern why the scans had been so wrong…and that was when they found on the surface, seemingly waiting for them, the Artifact.

It was an octahedron, its surface as smooth as obsidian, its height thrice that of a man, and its weight, somehow a shocking fifty tons if placed under universal standard gravity. The researchers on the station had eagerly brought it aboard for study—this was potentially the most important discovery in all of humanity's long history. An actual piece of alien technology, the first ever found among the stars. Was it from a prior civilization, or the remnant of a spacecraft that had crashed? Whatever it was, the proof of life beyond humanity in the stars was exhilarating and frightening in equal measure. The scientists aboard the station did all they could to open it, speak with it, interface with it in any way. For a month, they accomplished nothing, but then the Artifact itself changed. Curved writing appeared upon the perfectly smooth surface, along with near-invisible grooves clearly meant to fit a pair of human hands.

Simon, Nick's older brother and the youngest station director of the Offworld Planetary Control organization, had been given the honor of tearing it open. There had been a grand ceremony earlier that day, with everyone on the station gathered in the curving observation deck overlooking the Artifact,

LEVEL: UNKNOWN

as Simon spoke aloud the words that had been painstakingly translated.

So far as everyone expected, Simon would be chosen for... whatever might happen. Simon, the charismatic director of Research Station 79, tall and handsome in his gold-trimmed blue OPC uniform, was the perfect person to make first contact with anything alien.

Yet when his older brother spoke the words, Nick had felt strange, like sharp needles were stabbing deep into his temples, followed by queasiness, a sense of vertigo, and then... then what?

Demons in the village.

"I did experience something unusual," he said. He swallowed. His tongue felt like sandpaper. "My head hurt, and then my stomach, too. After that, I think I passed out and went... somewhere."

Yensere.

"Went somewhere?" Simon asked.

Nick shook his head. "I don't know how to explain it, but I awoke in an entirely new place. And I don't mean, like, in a dream. It felt... real. Vivid. And very bizarre."

Simon grabbed a little rolling chair and slid it closer so he could sit. There was no hiding his excitement.

"Nick, you have to understand, this was our first significant reaction from the Artifact. For the briefest moment, its core lit up with faint violet light. At the exact same time, you collapsed, hundreds of feet away in the observation deck. This isn't a coincidence. If you had some sort of dream or encounter immediately after the Artifact's activation, it might be your mind's way of processing the information sent to you.

More importantly, all my colleagues think the Artifact influenced you, and they're demanding tests." Simon twiddled his thumbs. "Lots of tests. I understand if you want to refuse, but it's important that you—"

"Refuse?" Nick sat up straighter in his bed. "Are you kidding? I want to help, Simon. Everyone's considered me a freeloader for months now, so for me to have a chance to be useful, to actually accomplish something worth a damn?"

"Language," Simon said, and grinned.

"Fuck you," Nick said, and grinned right back. "I'm important now, aren't I?"

"To the detriment of all of us, yes, Nick, I think you are. But I'm glad you're taking it well."

Nick sank back into his bed, already starting to feel better. It was frightening, of course, to be linked to the unknown Artifact in ways he did not understand, but he would overcome that fear. When their father passed away two years ago, Nick had been shuffled from caretaker to caretaker on their home planet of Taneth until Simon pulled enough strings to bring Nick aboard Station 79 upon Nick's eighteenth birthday. Nick was technically a lab assistant, but he heard the whispers. Everyone considered him an unwanted helper, brought aboard through nepotism so Simon could keep an eye on his younger brother.

"I'm going to do what I can, but first, you need to do something for me," he said.

"What's that?"

Nick pointed past him to the med ward closet. "Grab me a shirt. It's cold in here."

LEVEL: UNKNOWN

Simon's mood immediately lightened as he walked to the thin med room closet and pulled out a clean shirt, tossing it to Nick. The shirt was basic white and short-sleeved, similar to a dozen in Nick's room. He slid it on though it was a bit too big for him, then settled once more into the bed.

"All right," Simon said, and he brushed his thumb over his watch twice, activating a recording program. "So after the physical discomfort, you said you experienced a vivid dream. Could you repeat everything that happened? Anything at all, no matter how strange or insignificant."

Nick closed his eyes and tried to think. It was all a bit hazy, as dreams often are when one wakes suddenly, but a few images stood out in stark contrast. The first was of an old woman, cowering in fear as she recited a strange mantra. The other was of being frozen in the middle of a river due to...

Well...due to magic.

"Remember, I'm not making any of this up," Nick said. "I exited a field of wheat into an extremely old-fashioned village, was chased by villagers wielding sickles and pitchforks calling me a demon, and died because a woman flung a ball of ice at my feet to freeze me in a river." He shrugged. "Told you it was bizarre."

"Perhaps," Simon muttered. He had no notes. Nick knew he would not write anything down, not yet. His older brother would transcribe everything by hand later while listening over the entire conversation. It helped him memorize things, puzzle through them at a pace that elevated him to a savant among his much older peers. "You say you died? How so?"

"As in I was stabbed to death and bled out," Nick said.

"And it wasn't like a normal dream, either. I didn't wake up just beforehand. It... it *hurt*."

Simon tapped at his lower lip.

"Strangely enough, I'm not surprised. Near the end of your period of unconsciousness, your heart rate rocketed to the 180s, and at times you were thrashing around like a wild animal. I almost bound your hands and feet to protect you. Whatever you experienced, it was traumatic, and your body reacted accordingly."

"But why am I encountering any of this at all?" Nick asked. "The people I saw were agrarian. They had no complex machinery, just pitchforks and sickles. I was wearing overalls, Simon. *Overalls*. It doesn't make any sense. Whoever made the Artifact were more scientifically advanced than we can yet conceive. Nothing about what I saw implied those people were the ones who made it. And they looked human." He squirmed uncomfortably. "Why would aliens look human?"

Simon rose from his chair and tapped the watch to click off his recording software.

"Remember, we don't know what we are dealing with," he said. "Perhaps you were shown what you could understand. Appearances might have been altered to be more acceptable. Perhaps you were introduced to a specific moment of the aliens' history, like a sliver of time before their space-faring began. If the Artifact is meant to initiate first contact between civilizations, they can't know what state of technological advancement the discoverers will be at unless the Artifact was purposefully positioned on uninhabitable worlds that required beyond light-speed travel to..."

LEVEL: UNKNOWN

"Hey, hey," Nick said, interrupting him. "You're rambling conjecture again."

Simon paused, then resumed that cocky grin of his.

"Right," he said. "Well. I've got enough to form some theories. Prepare for a barrage of tests, blood vials, urine samples, all kinds of fun."

"Can't wait," Nick said, and stared at the ceiling.

Simon left, and sure enough, the cavalcade began. Nick did as was asked of him, enduring the pricks of needles to draw seemingly dozens of vials of blood. Pupils were checked, pulse tracked. He recited the alphabet backward, twice, and proved his balance by hopping from foot to foot.

By the end of it all, Nick demanded a return to his room. Dr. Haley, the woman in charge of the med ward, had initially refused, until Nick brought Simon in to argue on his behalf. This resulted in a compromise, with Nick allowed to sleep in his own room instead of the med ward, but only if his sleep could be monitored. By the time the machinery switched rooms and Nick relaxed into his own bed, the ceiling lights had dimmed to signal the end of the daytime cycle.

"You here to observe my beauty sleep?" Nick asked the scientist sharing the room with him, a heavy-jowled man with a clean-shaven head and glasses so thick they seemed like an aesthetic choice. His name was Pagle, and Nick had never liked being around the dreadfully dull and serious man.

"I will be monitoring your vitals, yes," Pagle said, sliding an oxygen sensor onto one of Nick's fingers. Much of the machinery was stacked on his bedside table. The photograph he kept there of his mother and father had been swept aside to make room, a fact that annoyed Nick greatly. "This time, we will be ready if you experience another episode, and be able to properly track any stress-induced tachycardia."

Nick closed his eyes as the room darkened further. His stomach clenched. Had he eaten anything since he awoke? He didn't think so. What he'd give for a granola bar right now.

"So," he said, his eyes closed and his mind drifting. "You're going to be staring at me while I sleep?"

"Nothing so crass as that. And I will spend much of the time reviewing the results of your various tests, which are only now arriving on the shared server."

"Sounds great," Nick muttered. His eyelids were so heavy. It felt like it hit him all at once, a sudden exhaustion that made speaking difficult. "Have...fun."

Pagle responded, but Nick couldn't bother to spare the energy to make sense of his words. It felt so good to rest. His mind drifted further. Pagle's voice faded into nothing. Just silence. Darkness, mixed with a bit of color floating across his eyes.

And then.

A ring of stones.

Chapter 3
NICK

Nick stepped out from the barren circle of stones into the waving field of wheat.
Returning visitor cataloged
Level: 1
Agility: 1
Physicality: 1
Endurance: 1
Archetype: None
Special Classification: None
Welcome back

"Happy to be back," Nick said, squinting against the light. He meant it, too. To return so immediately only confirmed that his previous experience had been anything but a dream. He closed his eyes and slowly breathed in and out to gather himself. The dreamlike fog vanished from his memories of this place. He recognized Cataloger's voice. The field of wheat, the jagged mountains, the strange black sun; it was all coming back to him.

Including, of course, his unceremonious death.

"All right, let's take this slow," he said, opening his eyes. Judging by the yellow sun, it looked to be late in the day. No one was in the field, not that he saw, but he knelt down to hide within the flowing ocean of grain just in case. Hands to the dirt, he forced his mind to push through the fog to remember the previous day. The med bay. The Artifact. His real life, separate, unique, different from...

"Cataloger, where am I?" he asked.

You are outside the village of Meadowtint, which is situated in the western province known as Vestor

"I was hoping for a bit more information than that."

It is spring in Vestor, in the six hundred thirty-seventh Year of Vaan, seeing its second year of peace since Batal the Beast began his—

Nick shook his head and grinned despite there being no one to see it.

"Zoom out a little," he said, interrupting her. "Where is *here*? This whole world I'm in?"

Vestor is part of the world of Yensere, which is currently unified underneath the banner of the Alder Kingdom, ruled by God-King Vaan, Conqueror of Time and—

"Cataloger," Nick said, interrupting a second time and trying not to lose his patience. This would be information everyone on Station 79 would be dying for. "Please. Let's try again. Not Meadowtint or Vestor or Yensere." He gestured as broadly as he could, to the ground, the sky, the field of wheat, and the towering mountains to the west. "*All* of this.

LEVEL: UNKNOWN

The entire world. What is it? It's...it's virtual, right? A recreation, perhaps?"

A very long pause.

"Cataloger?"

I cannot answer that

"Can't, or won't?"

I cannot answer that

Nick sighed but abandoned the topic. At least that was information, in a way. If this was a virtual world, it might be designed to not let its inhabitants *know* it was virtual. Granted, the little red and green bars in his vision and the voice of Cataloger seemed to give that away. Still, best not to make any assumptions while still getting his footing. Gathering himself, he looked to the blue sky above.

It's so similar to Taneth, he thought. A momentary spinning sensation overcame him. It'd been so long since he'd stood in wide-open spaces instead of the cramped corridors of Station 79. Even the wind against his skin was a half-forgotten feeling. To ground himself, he thought of his home planet, its lush fields a mixture of flowers and blooming fungi. Taneth was one of the earliest terraformed planets, verdant and pure. For most of his life, it had been his home, and he used its memories to push away the disequilibrium. He had lived in a place like this before, walked open lands, and felt the heat of the sun upon him. He would do so again and relish it.

After about a minute, he felt significantly better. That he'd not experienced similar on his first trip into Yensere intrigued him. Did he need to clearly remember his real life for the difference to affect him?

Putting the thought aside for now, he peered at the nearby village of Meadowtint. A few villagers wandered the street, slowly, lazily, as if lost in a daze. No one in the field. Perhaps everyone had gone home? There was, however, that strange lady in her rocking chair. He shuddered as he remembered the way she'd cowered from him and prayed with her black tongue to Vaan.

The Conqueror of Time? An interesting title for her apparent god. Hopefully not someone Nick would run into anytime soon, especially if he was as friendly as these villagers.

"Think this through," Nick said aloud. "Pretend you're Simon. You're smart, confident, and actually know what you're doing. So we'll do what he would do, right?"

I do not know the Simon you are referencing; therefore, I cannot judge if his actions would be beneficial or detrimental to your visit

"I, uh, was talking to myself."

Understood

Nick groaned. As useful as Cataloger was certainly going to be, she also needed some lessons on privacy and the concept of "thinking aloud."

First things first: Based on his previous experience, it was probably best to assume everyone he met was a potential threat. That meant he was likely going to face a *lot* of threats, so he needed a method to defend himself. Violence wasn't his favorite answer to conflict, but he certainly wasn't keen to repeat the "death" he'd experienced last time. Dying from pitchfork wounds was both humiliating and horribly painful, and even if the pain was just psychosomatic, Simon had made it clear his physical body reacted negatively in the real world.

LEVEL: UNKNOWN

Curious, Nick patted his overalls. Nothing useful in the empty pockets. None of the Meadowtint villagers were likely to lend him a knife or a hatchet, so Nick instead scanned the ground, spotting the tip of a rock through the packed soil. He dug it up with his bare hands, revealing a stone roughly the size of his fist.

"At least it's something," he said, turning his attention to the village. The next question was, what to do? He could skirt its edges and make for the river, but the thing was, he didn't know where he was going. He barely even knew *why* he should be going anywhere. Granted, maybe someone with him did.

"Hey, Cataloger, is there a particular place I should be headed?"

Visitors are meant to explore the breadth of Yensere and experience all of its wondrous environs

"So...no?"

Correct

Nick was starting to think Cataloger was going to be the least helpful "helper" he'd ever met. He pinched his bottom lip, debating what to do about the villagers who seemed convinced he needed murdering.

"I just want to walk up, say hello, and ask some questions," he muttered. "Is that so terrible?"

Apparently it was, since he resembled some sort of "demon" to them. Perhaps he *did* look like a monstrous creature. Frowning, he glanced about the field despite knowing it was hopeless. Still, maybe if it had recently rained...

Are you seeking something? I may help you find it

"A puddle," Nick said. "Or even a mirror, if you've got one. I want to take a look at myself."

One moment

A little sheet of statistics flashed before Nick's eyes, neatly arrayed and matching what Cataloger had spoken to him upon returning to Yensere. In the top left corner beside his name, in a disturbingly accurate three-dimensional representation, was his own face. Nick stared at it, confirming nothing was out of the ordinary. Still had the same short brown hair, same long nose, same brown eyes his mother had referred to as her "two favorite pieces of amber."

Your eyes contain insufficient red and too much gold to be considered amber by most metrics—I would consider them hazel

Nick clenched his jaw.

"Cataloger?"

Yes?

"Please, stop reading my thoughts and respond only when I specifically address you. Can you do that?"

I seek only to be helpful

There was something almost plaintive in her voice, a shift in expression he had never heard from her before.

Had...had he hurt her feelings?

Nick tossed his rock up and down, catching it as if he were a pitcher in a ball game.

"Sorry, Cataloger, it's just a little strange having someone hear my thoughts."

Do not feel concerns for modesty, shame, or embarrassment—I am incapable of judgment

LEVEL: UNKNOWN

"Right, because you seek only to help."

Correct

Nick sighed. He had a helpful little voice in his head—so be it. As for the task at hand, he decided he needed supplies if he was to trek beyond the river in search of a civilization that would not try to murder him on sight.

Of course, that raised an interesting question.

"Do I need to eat?"

Silence.

Nick closed his eyes and felt a twinge of a headache as he approached the village.

"Cataloger, do I need to eat while I'm here?"

All living things must consume sustenance in some manner

"Are you upset with me, Cataloger?" he whispered upon reaching the edge of the wheat field. Though the black sun remained exactly where it had been, the yellow sun descended, casting long shadows across the village, sharp triangles stretching from thatched rooftops.

My advice is not influenced by emotions

"That's not a no."

Another long pause.

I seek only to help

Nick figured that was as close as he was going to get to a yes. And he felt hungry, just as he'd felt while falling asleep in the med ward. So, it seemed he had his heading—find food, then leave Meadowtint with haste. He eyed the nearby home opposite the lady in the rocking chair. So far as he could tell, there was no sign of life within the decrepit building. As for the lady, she was so still Nick assumed she was asleep, and her head tilted so most of her face was hidden underneath her bonnet. Nick waited a moment longer, searching for anyone who might be watching. Once convinced he was alone, he crept out from the field to the nearby window.

No glass, no mesh, just open air blocked off by curtains fluttering in the evening breeze. A small patch of flowers grew underneath it. They looked like buttercups, their healthy yellow a stark contrast to the apparent lifelessness of the rest of Meadowtint. Nick paused by the windowsill to listen. No sounds within, no creaking floorboards, no rustle of feet. Feeling a bit more confident, he climbed through the window headfirst and collapsed onto the floor.

The home was modest, to say the least. The floorboards were coated with a thin layer of dirt. Dust covered every inch of the walls and cupboards. To his left was a doorway blocked with a heavy curtain, and to his right, a sort of den leading to the front door. Nearby was a hearth, the fire currently out.

For Nick's purposes, the most exciting prospect was the closed cupboard nailed to the wall above a well-worn dining table. He hurried to it, wincing at his every footstep. It felt like the floorboards carried a vendetta against him, they made so much noise. Nick opened drawer after drawer, searching for anything edible.

What he found was a collection of wood plates and forks, all of them in deep disrepair. Some of the plates looked ready to crack in half, while others sported long streaks of black mold. Even if he did find food, the idea of eating any of it was losing its appeal.

LEVEL: UNKNOWN

The creak of the floorboard was his only warning before the sickle slashed his arm. Blood sprayed in a wide arc as the iron cut from shoulder to biceps. Nick choked down his scream with clenched teeth as his health bar flashed into view while also dropping by a quarter. He didn't want to alert the rest of the village with a cry of pain. Instead, he retreated while turning to face his assailant.

One of the villagers, an older man, his face covered with a white beard that stood in sharp contrast to the blackness of his tongue and emptiness in his eyes. He'd come from the room blocked off with the curtain, moving more quietly than Nick thought possible.

"Demon," the man said, his voice raspy and pained. He lifted the sickle for another strike. "Must you haunt us, demon?"

Nick readied the rock, slightly bewildered. "You attacked me!"

The old man charged at him. Nick had no combat training, so he leaned into what little he knew of defensive positioning. The sickle swung, but Nick was faster, easily dodging out of the way. But the villager was relentless, flailing with the sickle over and over again, so that Nick had to dodge again. In a panic, he swung the rock at his assailant, clubbing him across the jaw. A red bar appeared above him, similar to Nick's, and then it shrank a tiny bit.

The old villager staggered, blood trickling down his chin. Nick gave him no reprieve. He caught the man's wrist the next time he swung the sickle, holding its iron edge up high. A tug, and the man stumbled closer, his balance uneven. Nick beat him across the head twice more with the stone. Blood gushed from his broken nose, and more trickled from his teeth and across his black tongue.

Another pull, and the man fell to the ground. Nick dropped to his knees beside him, adrenaline taking over. He moved with a singular purpose. Teeth clenched, pain flaring from every movement of his injured arm, he smashed the rock into the man's face, again and again and again.

And then the bar was empty. No red left within it. No more movement. The old man lay still, breathless, limp, his face a mutilated mess. Nick collapsed onto his rear, the blood-soaked rock slipping from his fingers to roll across the dirt-covered floor.

A white bar flashed across the center of his vision, a bold number 1 at the far-right end. The bar filled halfway, then vanished.

"Not real," Nick whispered as his hands started to shake. The body, void of life, seemed to mock the assertion. The detail, the vacant eyes, the broken bones, the smell of blood; it was so real. So vivid. He began to heave, though there was nothing in his stomach to relieve the feeling.

Not real. Not real, not real.

"Cataloger, what... what was that?" he asked as he sat there and waited for his heartbeat to calm. Maybe talking would help, get him distracted by anything other than the growing foul smell of blood and shit.

Clarify

"That white bar or line."

A visitor's initial level and statistics are only an approximation—a more accurate assessment may be

obtained through comparison with existing known entities

Nick thought through the comment twice, piecing out the meaning.

"So...by killing that man, I proved I'm stronger than him?"

By comparison, yes—further improvements may also be made through lived experience to exemplify natural progression

"And the white line?"

Progress toward reassessment and improvement—please note visitors will receive accelerated experience growth for increased enjoyment and understanding

It made some sort of sense. If this virtual world was trying to replicate a real one, then someone would expect to see improvements after consistent practice. If Nick took to tilling these fields, he suspected his physicality score would improve. Sprinting around the village a lot might increase his...what was it...agility?

And it seemed if he wanted to become a stronger human, then he needed to kill.

The thought was a troubling one, and he didn't like the way it squirmed in his belly. Trying to put it out of his mind, he reached over the dead man's body for his sickle. The fingers were locked in a death grip, forcing Nick to grab it with both hands and pull it free.

"At least I have a real weapon now," Nick said as he clutched the sickle to his chest. "Better than a rock, anyway."

Approximately one hundred twenty percent better

Nick lifted an eyebrow. Though Cataloger was physically absent, it was hard not to imagine her hovering just to the side, able to see his every movement and expression.

"That's a weirdly specific percentage. You know this how?"

In answer, a little sheet popped into existence just above his sickle.

Item: Sickle
Quality: Tier 1 (Poor)
Classification: Farming Instrument
A single-handed agricultural tool known for its curved blade, typically used by farmers to harvest crops from fields

Nick reprimanded himself for being so ignorant. This was a digital simulation, after all. Of course there would be a statistical comparison in some manner between usable objects.

"Is that how you convert health to that red bar?" he asked, glancing again at the body. It was unnerving being next to it, even if he kept telling himself it wasn't a real person, but a simulation.

To reduce computational stress, the consequences of battle, such as the effects on muscle groups, blood flow, balance, and motion, are made with simplified methods of wounding and overall health based on one's physicality

It was exactly what Nick expected and yet still took twice as long to say. It also helped explain why the wound on his arm felt strangely... nebulous. There was a lot of blood across his sleeve, and it certainly hurt, but even when he focused on the injury, he couldn't quite tell how deep it went, nor see much beyond the surface of cut skin.

LEVEL: UNKNOWN

"But why do you need to save computational stress?" he asked. "This whole world, it's... it's incredible."

I cannot answer that

Nick shrugged in the fading light. "If you insist. But it also sounded like you admitted we are in a simulation, Cataloger."

A long, now familiar pause.

I cannot discuss that

Nick stood, sickle in hand, and looked once more to the corpse. The man was perfectly still, his eyes open, his black tongue hanging out the side of his mouth. Nick's stomach tightened, but he refused to look away.

"He's not real, is he?"

Clarify

Nick tucked the handle of the sickle into one of the deep pockets of his overalls, suddenly feeling much better. The old man wasn't real. *None* of this was real. It was a digital simulation, a fake world. This wasn't killing. It was the temporary removal of 1s and 0s. The people didn't die, no differently than how he didn't die when he was assaulted in the river.

Still, the way the man cried out, the way the blood flowed...

Nick started for the front door and then changed his mind. He wanted out of Meadowtint entirely now, but now he knew that running through the heart of the town wasn't going to make that happen. He peeked out the window and noted the forest in the distance beyond the stream he'd been "killed" in upon his first visit. That was probably as good a place as any to find some food, be it through foraging or hunting. He doubted he'd be any good at any of that, but perhaps Cataloger would have some tips on catching and cooking prey, if any of the fauna here were edible.

Survival advice is limited as to not diminish the benefits of acquired skills in hunting and foraging

"Well, never mind that," Nick muttered. He cast one last look at the dead man, then shook his head.

"Just a simulation," he muttered, and crawled out the window. He landed atop the buttercups, smashing them underneath his feet.

He forgot to look before doing so.

"Demon!" screamed the old woman from her rocking chair. She pointed at him from across the street, her bonnet falling from her head to land at her feet. "The demon has returned!"

"Happy to see you again, too," Nick said, waving at the old woman as several villagers ran toward him, farming tools in hand. This wasn't real. This was a game, one he could become stronger in. Perhaps that was even the expectation of visitors who came into the Artifact, like some sort of test? He didn't know, but what he did know was that it hurt so damn much when their weapons raked his flesh. Gripping his sickle in both hands, he braced his feet and held his ground. No running. Time to see how well he could fight.

A villager in ragged clothes and with ashen hair was the first to reach him, the man wielding a similarly old sickle. He slashed wildly, using frantic movements as if he were trying to strike a fly out of the air. Nick retreated several steps, waiting for an opening, and then seized it. He dashed in, striking with his own sickle directly into the man's chest.

LEVEL: UNKNOWN

The man screamed, and blood splashed across Nick's hand, wet and warm. A red bar appeared above, then immediately dissolved half of itself. As the villager staggered, Nick swung again, burying his weapon in the man's neck to release a bloody spray.

The man dropped, his own sickle falling to the dirt. Again Nick's white bar appeared, sliding from left to right to fill up and touch the bold 1. A surge of exhilaration filled Nick as that 1 became a 2, and the white bar emptied.

Reassessment
Level: 2 (+1)
Statistical Improvements:
Agility: 1
Physicality: 2 (+1)
Endurance: 2 (+1)
Archetype Changed—New Categorization: Vagrant

Nick's health bar extended, and weirdly, the sickle felt a little less heavy in his grip.

"Holy shit," he whispered. His body buzzed with excitement. It reminded him of when he and Simon had celebrated his eighteenth birthday with glasses of homegrown Station 79 beer made from fermented mushrooms. He'd been so giddy then that he'd challenged Simon to climb the entire rock wall in the station gymnasium without a harness, and despite his brother's slurred caution, Nick got halfway up before falling to the thick foam pad below, cackling all the while.

He grinned at the next two villagers hurrying toward him, their mouths open and their black tongues hanging low. The woman had a knife, and the man, a long shepherd's staff. Nick rushed them, abandoning any defense. He slashed at the man, except instead of hitting flesh, his weapon chunked into the staff. As Nick pulled his weapon back for another hit, the woman's knife cut across his left arm. He held back a scream as blood sprayed across them both.

His health shrank accordingly, dipping downward. Nick shifted his attention to her, swinging an overhead chop directly at her forehead. Her eyes widened, and though she tried to dodge, it took her much too long, her movements deeply sluggish. The curved end of the sickle buried in her forehead, pushing down through bone. Her health bar never even appeared. The instant death denied her a scream, but no such thing stopped the man with the staff.

"Clara!" he shrieked, the horror in his voice washing over Nick.

Don't think on it, he told himself as he ripped the sickle out of her body, feeling a little out of breath while doing so. His green stamina bar was shrinking.

"Come on," he said, swinging at the staff. It hit the wood twice more, and now that he was aware of it, Nick saw little chits of green stamina dissolve with his every attack. Not good. He had to finish this man off quickly. The entire village was coming. Already he saw the giant man with the pitchfork leading a squad of five toward him. All the while, the woman in the rocking chair howled out her warning.

"Demon! Demon! The demon returns! Vaan save us!"

Finally the man abandoned his defensive posture, his rage overwhelming him as he swung wide for Nick's waist. Nick did not try to block it, instead swiping for the man's neck in

LEVEL: UNKNOWN

an exchange of hits. The wood struck, and he gasped as his health dropped, but it was nothing compared to what he did in return. His sickle raked across the man's throat, gashing him. The man gasped with wide eyes at the hit, then pulled his staff back for another strike. Nick was faster, his sickle cutting twice more across the chest.

The body dropped. Nick's white experience bar filled by another third.

"That's right," he said. His heart thumped, and his exhaustion was more pronounced. There were so many of them now, approaching with their crude weapons held high. Too many to fend off by himself. Death was inevitable at this point, but he was going to go down swinging.

"Send all of you!"

He charged right into the center of them, his sickle flailing wildly. He clipped two of them, thin grooves into pale skin. Not enough to kill. Not enough to thin the numbers. A knife plunged into his abdomen. A hatchet smashed into his collarbone and buried deep down in his chest, releasing a stream of red blood. Last was the pitchfork, its teeth aimed straight for his eyes. He saw the metal, saw the grin on the face of the big man wielding it, and then saw only darkness.

Health: 0
Visit terminated

Chapter 4
GARETH

Sir Gareth gently pulled on the reins of his horse, Ladybell, to halt her trot. His golden chain mail rattled as he dismounted. Before him spread the tiny village of Meadowtint, and already he sensed a worsening of the blight since his last visit. Nearly every home was in a state of neglect. Curtains frayed. Doors hung from uneven hinges. When the people approached, they had an emaciated look to their flesh and bones.

"Gareth!" a young man shouted, the first to notice his arrival. Gareth came to Meadowtint rarely, for it was several hours' ride from his home in Greenborough. He was certain he'd met the boy before but could not recall his name for a proper response.

"Hello there," Gareth said. "I pray matters have not worsened since I received Baron Hulh's letter?"

The boy's already pale skin whitened further. Gareth pretended not to notice the black on his tongue when he spoke.

"They have, sir. The demon returned in the time it took you to arrive."

Gareth's hand fell to the sword belted to his waist. "Any casualties?"

The boy winced. "Yes."

Gareth hid his worries. They needed confidence, and sympathy. He put a hand on the adolescent's shoulder as more people of Meadowtint approached.

"Do not fear," he said. "Even in the outermost reaches of the world, Vaan watches over us and grants us his blessing."

"I'll stable Ladybell for you," a young girl said, rushing up to him. Gareth smiled at her.

"That's very kind of you," he said, offering her the reins. "If you have any snacks for her, she would much appreciate them. Just don't spoil her."

The girl, a freckled little thing maybe ten years old, beamed at him.

"Of course, sir," she said. No black on her tongue, full color in her irises. Gareth prayed the youth might be spared.

Ladybell taken care of, Gareth scanned the crowd.

"Where is Elder Malek?"

"I am here, still kicking by the grace of Vaan," a bearded man said, pushing through the crowd. His yellow shirt and brown trousers hung from his bony limbs. "Come with me, Sir Gareth. I would show you the bodies."

They went first to a ramshackle home at the edge of town, just shy of the beautiful flowing field of wheat. Gareth stepped inside and winced as the floorboards groaned from the weight of his armor. Dust covered every surface. It felt like no one had been taking care of the interior for weeks, if not months.

The body lay on the floor of the kitchen. It was an older

man, his face mutilated beyond recognition. A dozen flies buzzed about, swarming his exposed skin and open mouth. Gareth's stomach sank at the sight.

"How did he die?" he asked, careful to keep his voice calm.

"A monster beat him to death with a stone," Malek said. He pointed. "Body's still there. We were afraid to touch it."

Gareth picked up the stone, the rusty color of the dried blood a stark contrast to the graying floorboards. He tried to imagine the brutality, or perhaps desperation, that would cause a man to murder another with such a crude, simple tool.

"Poor Iver had done nothing wrong," Malek said. "Just living his life when that demon climbed in through the window and murdered him."

Gareth scanned the room, and he noted that nearly all the drawers and shelves were open and their insides disordered.

"He was looking for something," Gareth thought aloud. "But what, I wonder?"

Malek scratched his leathery cheek. Unlike most everyone in Meadowtint, he still had sunbaked-tan skin.

"Didn't think to check," he said. "The stories I heard as a child, they said demons are a resourceful lot and steal without hesitation. But what did he think poor Iver would have worth taking?"

Gareth dropped the rock to the floorboards.

"If I were to guess, a weapon," he said, and gestured to the body. "We'll dig a grave for him and pray for Vaan's blessing. Were there any other casualties?"

The mixture of anger and sorrow in Malek's dull brown eyes told Gareth the answer before the man even spoke.

"Two more," he said, and gestured for him to follow. He talked as they exited and curled around the side of the home.

"Happened late yesterday. One of our own, Julie's her name, spotted the demon as he was climbing out Iver's window and called out a warning to the village. We readied our weapons and hurried to defend our homes, but... but some of the youngsters, they didn't listen. They didn't wait until we were all gathered."

Gareth slowed to a halt upon arriving at the scene. This was worse somehow, the blood upon the ground more vibrant and plentiful beneath the gaze of the two suns. A pair of bodies lay side by side, together in death.

"Clara and Gerard Carpenter," Malek said. "Iver's son and his wife. They had a kid of their own, too, a kind lad named Matthew. I've taken him into my home, for now."

Gareth knelt to examine the bodies. No blunt trauma here. Instead, their corpses sported clear signs of being slashed and stabbed. Clara's forehead was cracked open, a slit across her brow. Her eyes were open, and they stared lifelessly at the blue sky. A fly buzzed around her mouth and then settled upon the black iris. Gareth shooed it away.

"The demon armed himself," he said, turning his attention to her husband, Gerard. "A knife, perhaps?"

"A sickle," Malek explained. "He wielded it when we killed him the second time."

Gareth clenched his jaw shut to prevent saying things he might regret. He had never fought a demon before, but during his instruction into knighthood, he had learned about them from his master, Lord Frey. Demons were often weak and feeble when they were first born, but their supposed immortality meant that they had the ability to become unstoppable monsters. They needed to be murdered quickly, and consistently, until their will was broken and their desire to walk the lands of Yensere extinguished like a candle in a storm.

For this demon to die so easily on the first day, and yet murder three villagers on the second, was a horrifying development with foreboding consequences.

"It's been a long ride," he said, standing and stretching. The motion pushed the lowest ridge of his shield, strapped to his back, uncomfortably against his spine. "Might we rest a moment at your house?"

"Of course," Malek said, and guided him there. It was the largest home in the village and was well kept, unlike many of the others, its curtains washed and its floor cleanly swept. A young kid sat at the kitchen table, a sheet of thick yellow paper in front of him. Matthew, Gareth assumed. The boy held a stick of charcoal, his fingers stained from using it to write.

"Go on and play for a bit outside," Malek said. "We adults need to talk."

Matthew politely nodded and hurried outside, though not before staring up at Gareth with big, teary eyes. Gareth's heart squeezed in his chest. He couldn't imagine the nightmares that boy would face knowing how his parents met their end. But there were still more pressing matters than a demon in their midst.

"I would hear of Meadowtint." Gareth's voice lowered. "How fares the blight?"

Malek rested his elbows on the table, clasped his hands as

LEVEL: UNKNOWN

if in prayer, and then pressed his forehead against his fists. He stared at the table, peering into nowhere.

"I try," he said softly. "I do, sir, I do, but it's like pissing into the wind. I'd say half the village has it bad, and the other half, they're just waiting their turn. I help feed the worst cases, but it all feels pointless. They seem so...hollow. So lost and gone. The people I knew, my friends, my loved ones...they aren't in there anymore. They've been replaced by slow, sluggish, forgetful impostors. It makes it so hard to trust in Vaan's light to save us."

Each word was a burning coal heaped atop Gareth's head. When Gareth achieved knighthood, Lord Frey Astarda had assigned him to work alongside Baron Hulh to govern and protect Greenborough and her surrounding villages. These were his people to care for, yet he came to the far west reaches of Vestor so rarely. Here they were, suffering, needing a glimmer of hope, and yet it took a demon's murders to bring Gareth riding.

"Do not despair," he said, putting his hand atop Malek's clenched fists. "The god who conquered time can conquer all of Yensere's trials, if only we keep our faith in him."

Malek lowered his fists. He was crying, albeit silently, maintaining control, with just the twin trails of tears down his cheeks to betray him.

"You're a good man, Gareth."

"Careful now, elder. It's a sin against Vaan to tell lies."

Their laughter was broken by a sudden, piercing scream. A single word, but enough to startle Gareth to his feet and drop his hand for his sword.

"Demon!"

He sprinted out the door, his long white cloak billowing behind him. Villagers rushed to their homes for weapons, and he dashed past them, his legs churning. Every second mattered. The scream came from the western edge of the village, the demon having once again emerged from the field of wheat. As Gareth neared, he slowed, the sight shocking in its brutality.

What appeared to be a young man with short brown hair stood before a rocking chair underneath an awning. He wore clothes similar to those of Meadowtint's villagers, only his shirt was startlingly white, or at least the parts of it that weren't stained with blood were. He carried a sickle, and its edge was wet from murdering the woman in the rocking chair.

Fury burned hot in Gareth's chest. *Julie.* The demon had sought out and murdered Julie as retribution for spotting him after last night's murders. The vindictiveness of it added an edge to Gareth's voice as he addressed the demon. He hadn't just killed her. He'd hacked her head clean off her shoulders.

"Murderer of another realm," Gareth said, drawing his sword and pointing it. He kept his shield in reserve, feeling no need for it. "I am Sir Gareth Anoc, knight of Greenborough. Hear my name, and look upon my face, for I will be the slayer of all your lives, from now until the dark sun sets."

The demon turned, his head tilting to one side. He looked so... normal, so like everyone else, but there was no denying the sense of *wrongness* that emanated from his presence. Just looking at him felt like jamming a tiny needle into the back of Gareth's neck. He was separate from Yensere. Different. Obscene.

LEVEL: UNKNOWN

"Nick," said the demon. "Just Nick."

And then he charged straight at Gareth, despite wielding only a rusty sickle and lacking any armor compared to Gareth's finely constructed chain mail. The confidence was unnerving, but Gareth refused to let it shake him. He planted his feet and let the demon close the distance.

Nick lifted his sickle just before his arrival. A clumsy swing. Brutish. Simple. Gareth stepped into the attack, his sword sweeping upward. Upon striking the sickle, he easily smashed it harmlessly away. His shoulder, meanwhile, collided with the demon's chest, bashing him several feet backward. The demon let out a cough, the wind knocked out of him.

Gareth gave him no reprieve. He pulled his sword back and extended a gloved hand with the palm facing outward. He didn't just need to kill the demon; he had to break his spirit. Words of prayer flashed through his mind, and he called upon the blessings of the god-king.

"Be still, and know your fate," he said as golden light flashed from his fingers. The light washed over Nick, burning into his skin. His movements slowed. His eyes widened. His every step was lethargic, time itself betraying him so that it moved at a snail's pace. His sickle, swiping in mid-swing, was child's play to dodge.

Gareth pressed his sword to the demon's neck. The magic would last only a few seconds, but it would be enough.

"There is no hope here," he told Nick. "Only death."

One press, and he rammed the sword straight through the demon's throat. His intention was to bury it all the way up to the hilt, but he never had the chance. As the sword ripped open his windpipe and snapped the bones of his neck, his entire body turned translucent and then burst apart like vapor. Nothing remained of him in the aftermath.

It was that strange disappearance, first witnessed after his death in the nearby Rattling Creek, that confirmed his status as a demon to the villagers and caused Elder Malek to write a letter to Baron Hulh pleading for aid. Gareth sheathed his weapon and looked to the rocking chair. No blood from the demon, not even a drop to wipe off his blade, but so much to clean from the murdered old woman.

Murmurs behind him. The rest of the village, arriving. They were staring, confused, frightened, and upset. Another dead loved one, and after Gareth's arrival. They might now doubt the safety he offered. He turned to them, and he let them stare into his blue eyes and see his resolve, his determination to save them from this nightmare.

"Tonight, we dig graves for four souls," he said. He lifted his left hand and summoned the magic of his god. Light shone from it, mastery of time at his command, as it was for all lords and knights sworn in service to the Alder Kingdom. Within that holy glow, he made his vow, one he would hold until the setting of the dark sun.

"But I swear to you, tonight's is the last grave you will dig. Let the demon come. Let him fight. Let him die, people of Meadowtint. Let him die, die, and die again until naught is left of his mind but dust and ruin, and you suffer his presence no longer."

Chapter 5
NICK

Nick jolted awake, his sweat-soaked clothes sticking to his body. The room was dark. He was not alone.

"Easy now," Simon said, his older brother gently pressing his palm against Nick's chest. "Deep breaths. Slow it down."

Nick lowered to the bed, glad to find his brother waiting for him instead of Pagle. It had been two days since the incident with the Artifact, and he'd already had a handful of visits into Yensere. After the second time, he relented and told Simon more details about what he'd been experiencing, how tactile, how real, this world felt. Especially the killing.

He brushed a bit of hair from his forehead and was surprised by just how wet it was. His body had the feeling of having just recently broken a fever.

"I'm fine," he said, and it was mostly true. There was no lingering pain from any of the "wounds" he'd received in the artificial world, but he did feel incredibly tired. His brother sat blocking his view of the clock, so he couldn't guess the time, but he suspected it was the middle of the night cycle. The last time he woke up, it had been midday, and he'd been so hungry that he only had the strength to stuff himself full of rations before falling right back to sleep.

"How can you be fine?" Simon asked. "Your heart rate keeps skyrocketing, and you're caked in sweat. Your whole body acts like it's in the middle of a race, yet so far as we can tell, you're only sleeping."

Nick closed his eyes. "I'm telling you, don't worry. It's only bad when I'm dying, but I'm getting used to it."

"What do you mean, 'getting used to it'?" Simon asked. The chair he sat in rattled. "Hey, no falling asleep on me; you just woke up. Talk a bit and alleviate your big brother's nerves."

Nick exaggerated his groaning as he sat back up and rubbed a bit of sleep from his eyes.

"All right, I'm here, I'm awake," he said. "What do you want?"

Simon looked honestly taken aback.

"What do I want? Nick, you're making contact with an alien artifact. The best we can tell, you're interacting with the only remaining traces of a civilization that could be millennia old. This interaction is happening without any proper supervision, study, or understanding of how it is affecting your body. I am *worried* about you."

The honesty forced Nick out of his own thoughts and to acknowledge the status of his older brother. Deep circles rimmed his eyes. His hair, usually carefully trimmed short and kept stiff with a prohibitively expensive gel that came with every food shipment, was unkempt and sticking up on his left side. Likely caused by falling asleep in his chair, Nick assumed, his head resting on the pillow that had now dropped behind his lower back. The top button of his uniform was undone, and his name tag was missing. The light of the beeping heart monitor shone green upon him, giving him a slightly sickly look.

"I can tell you're worried," Nick said, and grinned. "You look awful."

Simon punched him in the shoulder, all show and no force.

"I see whatever the Artifact is doing to you hasn't changed what a brat you are."

Nick clutched his shoulder anyway.

"You wound me," he said, and then shrugged. "But there's not much to tell. I arrive there with some jagged mountains in the distance and a field of wheat around me. Up ahead is a village, full of sickly people. When they see me, they try to kill me. Succeed every time, too, but I'm getting better, especially as my level increases."

Simon looked torn between fascination and a desire to vomit.

"Levels?" he said. "Like...in a game?"

Nick shrugged. "Make all the faces you want, but yeah, a little like that."

Simon rubbed his bloodshot eyes. "Forget it. I've been meaning to ask you something after going over notes of your first visit. You said you are in a field of wheat? You're certain it's wheat?"

Nick didn't immediately understand what his brother was getting at.

"Yeah, it's wheat. I know what wheat looks like."

Simon stood from his chair and immediately began pacing. "Are there other things equally familiar? Grass? Flowers? Trees? Insects?"

"The flies look like flies," Nick said. "As does the grass. And I saw flowers that I am pretty sure are buttercups. The people look like people, too, of course. I...I should probably have realized this was odd, wasn't it?"

"Odd?" Simon shook his head. "Try borderline impossible. For the Artifact to host remarkably similar evolutionary outcomes as Eden, as well as all our subsequent terraformed worlds...that's not happenstance. That's not coincidence."

The implications made Nick squirm in his bed. "What do you think it means?"

Simon bit at his thumbnail as he looked away, a tic of concentration he'd tried hard to bury when taking on the role of station director.

"There's the possibility that what you see has been adapted to be familiar and accommodating," he said at last. "A way to lessen the jarring culture shock, perhaps. And if the world is being made for you, tailored by information the Artifact is extracting from your mind, then there has to be a reason." He crossed his arms, hands clenched into fists. It was how he forced himself not to bite his nails. "Are you certain you cannot discuss matters with the people you find within this world? Introduce yourself, perhaps, and see if they will explain what is happening?"

Nick fought hard not to laugh at his older brother's sincere request.

LEVEL: UNKNOWN

"Yes," he said. "I have tried."

"But have you recently? You were disoriented and confused during your first arrival. Perhaps now that you're better adjusted, you can properly make contact."

"You want me to try to be friends *after* killing several of them?"

Simon shrugged. "Yes?"

It seemed there'd be no shaking him off this idea, so Nick relented.

"Fine, I'll try," he said, laying his head down on his pillow and closing his eyes.

"You can fall asleep that quickly?"

The incredulousness in his brother's voice would have been insulting if it weren't so heavily tinged with jealousy.

"Yeah," Nick said, his tongue feeling heavy in his mouth. "If I relax and let my mind go blank, I've found it's gotten easier and easier. I can just...close my eyes and..."

Nick trudged toward Meadowtint, his sickle tucked into his ratty trouser leg. He lifted his hands above his head, the best sign of universal peace he could think of.

"Hey," he shouted, not wanting to sneak up on anyone. "Hey, it's me, Nick Wright. I just want to talk. My brother thinks that'd be a good idea, for us to talk. So can we?"

A door from one of the houses burst open, and two villagers wielding machetes approached, walking shoulder to shoulder. Their eyes were wide and fearful.

"The demon," one said.

"No, not a demon, just a friend," Nick said, smiling wide. "We can be friends, right?"

Health: 0

Visit terminated

———————•———————

Nick sat up in his bed, wiped a fresh layer of sweat off his forehead, and then grinned at his brother.

"How long was that?" he asked.

"Five minutes," Simon answered. "Your heart rate only hit 160 that time."

"Nice. Died again, by the way. I feel very strongly that the people of Meadowtint are not interested in being friends."

Simon slumped in his chair and glanced aside, clearly deep in thought. His eyes flitted over the photo of their parents, now back in its proper position on the side table. The same photo was in Simon's room as well. It was of their mother and father, arm in arm, celebrating their mother's promotion to lead scientist. Both had been distinguished researchers, and it was a legacy that hung heavy over their sons.

"Look, when it comes to the Artifact, I will always be completely open and honest with you," Simon said, still staring at the photo. "We've been monitoring not just you, but the Artifact as well. It's clearly activating when you're sleeping, in ways we don't yet understand. Our theory that it is connected to you seems to be sound. What we don't know is *why*."

"Lucky me," Nick muttered.

LEVEL: UNKNOWN

"Maybe, maybe not," Simon said. "But I refuse to believe you were chosen just to play some strange game set in their far, far past. Nor do I think the inhabitants within, the flora and fauna, are being made to look familiar to you, not entirely. The theory most of us on the station are leaning toward is that you are in some sort of time capsule, a re-creation of an era set upon Majus. But if that is true, and their world is shockingly similar to ours, their own bodies and forms equally similar..."

He scratched his neck.

"Then we can't rule out a connection between this Artifact world and our original evolution back on Eden. We may not have found an alien race, Nick. We might have found our ancestors." He laughed, tired and bitter. "Our space-faring ancestors, who, according to you, are sickly-looking farmers wielding knives and pitchforks convinced you are a demon."

Nick pulled his blankets a little tighter around him.

"Never meet your heroes and all that," he said. "Maybe the same goes for our ancestors?"

Simon laughed, all exhaustion and surrender.

"Who knows," he said. "But I trust you to get to the bottom of it, Nick. For whatever reason, perhaps because you were the youngest in the vicinity, perhaps pure dumb luck, but you're it, the only one the Artifact is interfacing with. You're our excavator. Our plucky young archaeologist."

"You make it sound like I'm exploring a dead land," Nick said. "But Yensere...it feels very much alive, at least when I'm in there."

"Dead worlds," Simon muttered, then shook his head. "Forget it. Do what you can, Nick, but please try to be careful. You may not be noticing it at the time, but these trips are stressful on your body, especially your repeated... deaths."

Nick lay back down on his bed, his older brother adjusting the lower blanket so it properly covered his feet.

"No promises," he said as the darkness took him.

Chapter 6
NICK

Returning visitor cataloged
  Level: 3
  Agility: 1
  Physicality: 3
  Endurance: 2
  Archetype: Vagrant
  Special Classification: None
  Welcome back

Meadowtint's villagers were getting smarter. They stayed in clusters in their homes, and patrols looped the city limits, but the people spread out when working their field. That was his opening. One acre in particular seemed due for harvesting, the stalks tall and thick, and Nick lurked within the depths of it, the golden wheat swaying in the wind with a satisfying rustle. Nick brushed his fingers across the stalks, studying each individual strand and the way it felt upon his fingertips.

It's so real, he thought. *So perfect. How advanced were its creators?*

Whoever they were, they certainly weren't these vacant-eyed villagers. Nick lifted his sickle as a woman in a white blouse half-stained black by her own sweat and filth slowly made her way toward him. Her back was bent, her sickle swaying left to right.

"Cataloger, who made this world?" he whispered as the woman neared. Might as well try for answers while he waited. Simon would be disappointed with him otherwise.

I cannot answer

"Who built the Artifact hosting it?"

I cannot answer

"What is this world's purpose?"

To foster life

As expected, he'd have to get his own answers elsewhere, and that meant escaping Meadowtint. To do that, he needed to get past Sir Gareth, which meant getting stronger. Every trip to the village, he did just that. He sneaked through windows into homes, spilling blood, gaining progress toward reassessment. What did his deaths matter if those he killed stayed dead, while he grew in experience with his every attempt? He'd increased his level again, to three, but he knew he needed to be much higher than that to defeat the mighty knight.

"One more thing, Cataloger—why do I still have this sickle?" he asked, realizing how odd it was that he'd kept it upon dying. "Same for my clothes. How do I keep everything after they... well... kill me?"

Your possessions remain yours upon termination of your visit

LEVEL: UNKNOWN

Which meant they couldn't take any of his items off his body. Which, he also suspected, meant he didn't leave a body behind at all when he died. He certainly never saw one across his repeated trips to Meadowtint, as disturbing a thought as *that* was. If he didn't leave a body, it also meant, from the villagers' point of view, he was abnormal, if not supernatural.

"I guess that sort of explains that whole 'demon' thing," he said, though not quite. They'd known something was different about him from the very first moment he spoke to the elderly woman in her chair. One look in his eyes, and she shrieked and labeled him a "demon."

Something more must be at play.

Nick finally saw what he'd been waiting for, as Sir Gareth walked by on his patrol. He didn't bother with stealth this time. The villagers didn't frighten him anymore. In time, and with enough attempts, he could bring them low. Gareth was the real problem, and so Nick had decided during his last leveling to confront that problem immediately.

"Let's go, Gareth," Nick shouted, holding his sickle out wide as he approached the village. "You and me, one on one, a duel to the death. We'll keep it nice and fair."

The knight strode out to meet him. As always, he kept his shield on his back, and he pointed his enormous sword. His blue eyes narrowed.

"Fair, says the monster that defies death itself," he said. "But I accept your challenge, Nick. No other innocents must die between the time of your arrival and the time I banish you to your temporary grave."

"Not a grave," Nick said. "More like small but cozy bedroom."

Gareth lunged, his sword aimed straight for Nick's chest, and only a panicked dive kept Nick from being speared. He landed on his shoulder, rolled, and then burst out of the roll with frantic energy. No thought to tactics or discipline, just a slash with his sickle at Gareth, who looked caught off guard when Nick avoided the thrust by coming closer instead of retreating.

His sickle struck Gareth's breastplate and bounced off with a loud clang of metal. Nothing happened. The knight's health bar didn't even budge.

What? he frantically thought as he fled a swing that would have cleaved his head off his shoulders if he were the slightest bit slower. *Why?*

For simplification, armor values are flat reductions against potential damage

Nick retreated several more steps, buying himself a breather while staring at Sir Gareth's shining gold chain mail. His stomach sank.

How good is Gareth's armor?

The brief summary flashed in the corner of his vision, this time modified with additional information.

Gareth: Level 13 Human
Archetype: Knight
Special Classification: Deity Blessed (Vaan)
Armor: Augmented Chain Mail, Quality Tier 7

"Tier seven," Nick muttered. "I'll assume that means I need to hit him where he's not wearing armor."

"Who are you speaking with, demon?" Gareth asked. He hopped forward a single step and then swung in a wide arc

LEVEL: UNKNOWN

Nick had no hope of dodging. He flung his sickle in the way and braced himself. The metal collided, Nick's arms gave in against the overwhelming force, and then he went flying into a hard, bouncing roll across the dirt. When he came up to his knees, he saw an almost insultingly tiny amount of red float off his health bar from being thrown like a ragdoll.

"Just talking to myself," Nick said. "Since no one else seems interested in a chat."

"We need not heed the words of heresy."

Nick spat a bit of blood as he stood. "Heresy? I barely know where I am, and you think I'm here to spout *heresy*?"

Gareth frowned, apparently uncertain how to respond. Nick tried to seize that confusion for his own gain, closing the distance between them while slashing for Gareth's armpit. The knight's hesitation was not enough to make up the enormous gap between their raw skill and speed. His sword batted away Nick's sickle, and then he extended his off hand.

Spell: Time Slow

Gold light shimmered about his fingers as he cast his spell, slowing all Nick's movements so that he felt maddeningly sluggish.

According to Cataloger's rapid spew of information, **<time slow>** lasted a mere three seconds. It was amazing how long three seconds could feel as Gareth planted his back leg and swung, his sword smashing into Nick's ribs. Nick gasped, blood spewing from his lips as the weapon ripped free, taking with it a staggering amount of health. He stumbled, his momentum ruined and his vision turning dark as the effects of the spell faded. Gareth caught him by the throat and effortlessly lifted him into the air. The tip of his sword pressed into Nick's belly.

"The same fate as always," Gareth said, and thrust.

Health: 0
Visit terminated

───────────●───────────

Nick groaned and rubbed at his temples. His forehead ached as if a spike had been thrust into the center of it.

"You're certainly improving," Simon said, seated in the chair beside the bed. He checked his watch. "It only took you four minutes to die that time."

The beep of the heart monitor seemed to laugh along with him.

"Asshole," Nick said, and closed his eyes.

───────────●───────────

Another duel in the center of the village. Gareth showed even greater patience than before, which made Nick wonder if he was choosing the wrong tactic. The knight wanted these duels. He wanted Nick focused solely on him.

"Let's go," Nick said, shifting to the left to avoid being cleaved in half down the middle. "Come on, faster. Hit me, Gareth. Hit me!"

The knight did his best to oblige, and regardless of whether or not it seemed cowardly, Nick weaved and retreated from each strike. Only rarely did he try to swing his sickle, for he was too busy studying Gareth's movements. With each successful dodge, he better understood the world he found himself in: Levels were important, but Gareth still had to hit him with his sword to actually leverage those levels. Nick could avoid, engage, and strike whenever necessary. The odds were horribly stacked against him, but the outcomes didn't seem to be a purely numerical decision. Skill mattered.

The problem was, Nick was not exactly overflowing with skill in swordplay, either, whereas his opponent had what seemed like a lifetime of training.

"Is your goal to tire me out?" Gareth asked after yet another failed swing.

"The thought had occurred to me," Nick said, and grinned.

Gareth chopped, a half-hearted attempt to gain a bit of space, and then yanked his sword to his side.

"Enough of this."

The knight extended his hand. His fingers shifted, moving into shapes, but now Nick knew them for what they were—magic—and he had a theory about how to stop the casting of the spell. He lunged in, his sickle swiping for the moving digits. Gareth screamed as the curved blade sliced alongside his hand, cutting his thumb and forefinger deep without severing them. The red bar of his life shaved off a sliver at the end.

To Nick's glee, the spell halted. No freezing time. No slowing his movements to an agonizing degree.

"Sorry, no magic," Nick said. "We'll have to see how good you are without it."

Gareth pulled his shield off his back. A shadow fell across his handsome face.

"That magic also ensured you suffered a quick death," he said. "But that is not your way, is it, demon? Everyone must suffer, even yourself."

Nick swung his sickle twice, and each time the shield batted it away with insulting ease. The third, he pretended, but Gareth never fell for the feint. He only smirked, his knees bending, his elbows flexing.

"Foolish creature," he said. "Do you think I need my magic? My armor?"

He lunged forward with terrifying speed. Nick had no idea how to react, no real training to rely upon. He backpedaled while flailing with his sickle, dimly aware of how similar he was to the villagers he'd so recently slaughtered.

Gareth's sword pierced right through his stomach and sank halfway up the hilt.

"When will it be enough?" Gareth asked as Nick collapsed to his knees. He couldn't breathe. The pain flooding through him was far beyond what he'd ever suffered before. His health—he had a single point left. Since the hit wasn't fatal, he wasn't freed from it, wasn't spared the sensation of the steel sliding within the folds of his stomach.

"So many dead," the knight continued, ripping the blade free in a shower of blood. "So many innocent lives lost, and for what, demon Nick? Your pleasure?"

He pressed the tip of the sword underneath Nick's chin.

"Don't come back," he said. "I am no torturer, but against your cruelty, I will ensure your next death is lengthy and full of pain."

The blade thrust.

LEVEL: UNKNOWN

Health: 0
Visit terminated

"All right, new plan," Nick said as he stepped out of the ring of stones. The black sun remained firmly set in the sky as always, but the yellow sun was just starting its descent. Late afternoon, then. He could work with that.

Nick snuck through the wheat, keeping his back bent so his mode of travel was a sort of crouch-walk. It made his muscles ache, but he endured until reaching the end of the field. Meadowtint spread out before him, a shell of itself compared to when he first arrived. He didn't know how many he'd killed across his many visits, slowly whittling down the population. Fifteen? Twenty? They were blending together in his mind, a blur of bloodshed and agonizing pain before he jolted awake once more in his bed aboard the research station.

"There's no answers for you here," Nick told himself as he watched a patrol of two men and a woman curl around the outside of the village. "It's time to run."

Going through the village was out of the question, so he skirted Meadowtint's exterior as closely as he could without leaving the field. If he was quick, he'd need only worry about the rare patrol that wandered the outer perimeter. Nick remained patient, watching and waiting, until he saw that exact patrol. Two men, one of them holding a torch. He grimaced. Were they trying to burn him alive now?

Nick certainly had no desire to experience that particular

death. He watched them slowly curl around from the south, plodding along. They did not speak with each other but just walked, their black eyes the only alert part of them. It gave him shivers studying them so closely. Something was clearly wrong with this village, some disease or sickness.

Do you know what it is? he silently asked Cataloger.

The people of Alder call it the blight

Yes, but what do you call it? *What is it truly?*

The affliction is not cataloged

Nick was starting to wonder just how helpful this voice in his head would be if she kept finding ways to not answer his most intriguing questions. Then again, he suspected a lot of what he asked was beyond her purpose. He was doing the equivalent of asking philosophical and metaphysical questions to an AI tour guide.

Once the patrol was curling around the western edge of the village, Nick burst out from the wheat. He ran across the grass toward the nearest home. He'd thought about giving the village an extra-wide berth, but he feared the open space would only make him easier to spot. Instead he dashed from home to home, keeping in their shadows, always ensuring he could not be seen from the main road. Perhaps he could have shown more caution, but once his pulse was pounding, he found it hard to slow down. A whole world awaited. He just needed to get past Meadowtint.

When he was a few hundred steps beyond the borders of the village, Sir Gareth's voice broke the tense silence.

"Demon Nick!"

Shit shit shit shit shit!

LEVEL: UNKNOWN

He refused to look at his green stamina bar as he sprinted, just focused on breathing in and out. It helped to pretend it was his actual body running—*keep those arms and legs swinging*. The sprawling forest beyond the creek was near. He just needed to cross it, that place of his very first death.

Nick half expected the mysterious woman in silver to be waiting to freeze him in ice again. Instead, he found just the shallow flow of the creek. He splashed straight on through without stopping. Beyond were the thick trunks of apparent oak trees, and he dashed into them without a care for direction, bobbing and weaving among the trunks. His stamina was almost 0, but he dared not slow down. Just a little bit farther, a little bit...

Once he suspected Gareth could not see him through the dense trees, he hooked an immediate right and ran parallel to the tree line. Outrunning Gareth was impossible in Nick's current state, but if he could get a moment to catch his breath and watch that stupid little green bar refill? Then he'd have a chance. He sprinted until his meter hit 0, when his entire body locked into spasms, his ability to run utterly annihilated.

Nick collapsed behind a tree, his back pressed to the trunk and his legs pulled up to his chest. There he sat, gasping for air as quietly as he could manage, while Gareth barreled into the forest at a distance, sounding like a rampaging bull smashing through underbrush and low-hanging branches. Nick closed his eyes, daring to crack a smile. The juke had worked.

Won't find me over there, Nick thought as the sound of the knight's frantic searching grew more distant.

While he was hardly safe, Nick suspected it would take

mustering the whole village to catch him in a search. Perhaps they would, perhaps not, but Nick had no plans to wait to find out. Once he felt like he'd recovered, and his heart wasn't hammering hard enough to punch out the front of his chest, he stood and stretched his arms.

"All right, forest," he whispered. "I have no idea what's in you, but it can't possibly be worse than what's waiting for me back at Meadowtint."

Perhaps this was untrue, but Nick pushed the thought away as he jogged deeper into the woods at a southward angle away from where Sir Gareth chased. He did his best not to fret or feed the anxiety settling into his belly at entering this unknown stretch of land.

At least if he got killed, it'd be by something new.

Chapter 7
SIMON

"Was there any warning?" Simon asked as he joined his communications expert, Curtis, in the control room. The pair were alone, everyone else having gone to sleep hours earlier when the night cycle began. "Perhaps a message I failed to notice?"

Curtis frowned. He was a small man, the top of his head bald and his face long and angular, the length of his nose exacerbated by his thin oval glasses. The frown pushed those glasses up the tiniest bit.

"No, you didn't miss anything," Curtis said. A flick of his fingers, and the screen before them expanded its image of the world gate powering down. At its five-mile-wide center, just a speck in the distance, was a shuttle headed in their direction. "Nothing from OPC, nor any word from Salus. This is... highly unusual."

Simon crossed his arms, mirroring Curtis's frown. Salus was the planet connected to the world gate, and where the bulk of their supplies came from every week. According to the hailing data, the shuttle carried Planetary Director Jakob Lemley. From what little Simon could look up in the OPC database, Lemley led terraforming efforts for the planet Vasth, two jumps away. They'd never interacted once. For a director to arrive on another station, unannounced, and in the middle of the night...

"Do you think he's here about the Artifact?" Simon asked.

"I think there's a very good chance the answer to that question is yes."

Simon's stomach was an acid-filled pit at the best of times, and it clenched tightly now.

"Let the director know I'll be there to greet him in the docking bay," he said. "Also, send an alert to Daksh. I want him nearby until we're sure nothing is amiss."

"Will do," Curtis said. "And I'll make sure he knows it's your order, not mine. You know how cranky Daksh gets when his sleep is disrupted."

It was meant as a joke, Curtis trying to break the tension. Daksh, while a brilliant mathematician, was also the research station's lone security officer. There were exactly two weapons on the entire station. One was locked inside Simon's office. The other, in a safe inside Daksh's room.

Simon exited the control room and walked the main corridor through the station, guided by the faint white lights marking the intersection of the wall and floor. There was no need to branch off or change direction to reach the docking bay. The station was one giant ring, set to rotate at a precisely calculated speed so that, as long as one was in one of the rooms attached to the main outside corridor, one experienced

LEVEL: UNKNOWN

gravity akin to that on Taneth. Two elevators could take you from one side to the other, if you were willing to endure a bit of stomach-churning shifting into weightlessness and then the switching of what felt like up and down.

The docking bay was close enough that he could be spared that discomfort. Simon passed by the closed doors of various laboratories, the windows across their fronts all dark. A month ago, they would have been buzzing with life even at this late hour. The discovery of the Artifact had driven everyone to extremes, but after two weeks of that, Simon had forced strict sleep schedule protocols to prevent his best and brightest from burning out.

Simon paused before the docking bay door and hesitated. It was one of the few locations with restricted access; a near-invisible camera located above the door scanned his face and unlocked it automatically. A faint little light just above the door handle switched from red to green, and Simon pushed it open and entered.

Within was a small, secure room with reinforced walls and a circular opening. Clamps on the outside of the station would have grabbed onto sturdy bars built into the shuttle, holding it in place as the docking tube extended and their pressure was equalized. Simon stood before the tube's exit, watching the numbers on a screen beside it slowly shift from red to orange to green. Pressure fully equalized. Tunnel connection secured with zero leaks. The entrance deemed safe, it opened, and in stepped Planetary Director Jakob Lemley.

"Welcome to Research Station 79," Simon said, extending his hand. "Where's your pilot?"

"I flew the shuttle here myself," Lemley said, accepting the handshake with a firm grasp. He was an older man, the white of the stubble around his mouth and the curls around his ears in stark contrast to his black skin. He was dressed in his OPC finest, dark blue trimmed with gold around the wrists, belt, and heels. Attached to his vest was a pin bearing four crimson bars underneath a silver orb, establishing him as a planetary director, one of the highest ranks available within the organization.

"Is that so?" Simon said, the unusual nature of a planetary director traveling alone further heightening his worry. "Well, I suppose that is one less room we need to allocate. I wish you'd given us word of your visit ahead of time so I could give you a proper welcome."

"Your words are chastisement dressed as a greeting," Lemley said. "Do better, Director."

The man's deep voice cracked over Simon like a whip, hard and commanding despite his pleasant smile.

"Forgive me," Simon said. "My pride as station director would have me present a fine first impression, something the late hour and unexpected arrival make difficult. I'm sure you understand, as a fellow director, the desire to showcase your work in its best light."

"I do," Lemley said, walking past Simon toward the door. "But I arrived when I did for good reason, Director. I do not want pomp and circumstance, nor the greetings of every scientist aboard."

He stopped at the entrance to the main corridor and turned.

"What I want," he said, "is to see the Artifact."

LEVEL: UNKNOWN

The holding area of the Artifact had taken a week to convert from a conference bay into alien tech housing. Given how every scientist on the station was now dedicating their work to deciphering its glyphs, studying its surface, and scanning the strange, elusive signals it fired out, they needed a large, open space for easy access.

The Artifact was set in the center of the room. Despite its octahedral shape, there was no need to brace it with any supports. Somehow, despite touching the floor with the sharpest of points, no thicker than a needle, it remained perfectly balanced and able to support its fifty tons. From tip to tip, it was twenty feet tall, its surface seemingly a polished, unblemished black. It was only when it was carefully examined that the myriad swirls, glyphs, and markings became visible.

Dozens of sensors, detectors, and paper-covered desks formed a circle around the Artifact. It loomed within them like an object of worship. To a few of the scientists here, Simon suspected it was nearing that level of dedication.

Lemley approached the Artifact confidently, without any of the hesitation and awe that overcame most people who first encountered it. The director put a hand on its surface, slowly running his fingers along one of the sharp edges of the octahedron.

"It's beautiful, isn't it?" he said softly.

Simon cleared his throat.

"The work we've done here has been highly classified by the OPC," he said. "What have they shared with you of our investigations?"

"Oh, I've known everything since you first found this beauty buried in Majus's dirt," Lemley said. "I've wanted to look upon it ever since, but I'm sure you understand how the burdens of managing a planet prevented that."

Simon nodded, trying to appear calm while studying every reaction Lemley made, wary about what had brought the director here. Multiple members of OPC had tried to steal control of the Artifact from Simon, insisting he was too young and his facility too poorly staffed. They wanted the Artifact transported to their stations and worlds instead. Simon had used the smallness and distance of his outpost to his advantage. If the Artifact was dangerous, then it was best to keep it where it was, away from any populated world and with a small, controlled group to interact with it.

The argument had succeeded so far, but Simon suspected he was working on borrowed time. Lemley's arrival seemed to confirm that.

"There are scientists on Eden who would offer up their own children to place their hands on something so strange and wondrous," Lemley said. He shook his head. "But tell me, have you discerned how to activate it? Or has someone discovered a way to interface with it?"

Simon was glad the director's back was to him. It made lying that much easier.

"So far, we have made a single attempt to fully bring the Artifact to life," he said. "To poor results."

Lemley withdrew his hand from the immaculate surface that was so hard, so deep, it resembled onyx. It wasn't onyx, though. No one knew what it was. It was impossible to chip for a sample, and the vast majority of scans, from thermal to radiation to ultrasound, were all utterly rebuked, to the madness of many of Simon's scientists.

"Is that so?" Lemley said. "A shame. The mysteries of the universe seem forever locked to us, do they not? Perhaps that is for the best. There is no promise that the truths we find will not blind our eyes and burn away our bodies."

"Strange words for a scientist," Simon said, and he forced a false smile. "Are we not dedicated to uncovering the truth, however harsh it may at first seem?"

"I am not a scientist...not anymore." Lemley turned away from the Artifact. "I am a builder of worlds and protector of life."

Despite being severely outranked, Simon could take the suspense no longer.

"Now that you have seen the Artifact, I ask that you forgive my impertinence," he said. "But might you explain the purpose of your visit?"

Lemley hesitated.

"Tomorrow," he said. "I will explain tomorrow, I promise. Until then, the trip was long, and I seek a bed to rest."

Hardly satisfying, but at least there was hope for an explanation.

"Of course," Simon said, leading them to the main corridor. "This way, please."

The occasional visitor was expected at a research station, and so a single room was always prepared for guests. It wasn't much, barely more than a closet with a bed and a washroom. A planetary director deserved far better, and it was expected of Simon to offer up his own room during the director's stay, but Simon risked the appearance of rudeness and chose not to do so. The way Lemley had looked upon the Artifact left Simon unsettled.

"Sleep well," Simon said as the door to the guest room slid shut. That done, he quickly hurried down the corridor, past the personal rooms of other scientists and workers. Three doors down, he found one open, and Daksh waiting within. He was a burly man, his dark hair cut short, his brown eyes professionally wary. His uniform was wrinkled, likely the one he'd worn earlier in the day, hastily donned. His firearm was holstered at his hip, a slender device that would fire multiple needles connected to electric wires to stun and pacify as needed. No bullets, not when a single puncture could spell doom for an entire research station.

"What's wrong?" Daksh asked. "Curtis told me about our unexpected guest, and I don't like the look in your eye."

Simon glanced over his shoulder, toward the exit.

"Nothing yet, but I sense trouble coming. I want you stationed outside Lemley's room at all times. I don't care about his rank, and I don't care about any excuses he offers. I want him going nowhere alone, is that clear?"

Daksh's hand drifted to the handle of his stun gun.

"Understood," he said. The pair exited the room, and Simon watched the security officer take up position with his back against the wall beside the guest room door. It should have made him feel better.

It didn't.

Or has someone discovered a way to interface with it?

LEVEL: UNKNOWN

Simon returned to his office and the little safe kept in a corner, a false argentea plant resting atop it. A five-number combination later, he pulled the safe door open and withdrew his own stun gun.

That done, he returned to his younger brother's room, settled into the chair beside the bed with the gun resting on his lap, and let the steady rhythm of the heart monitor lull him into an uneasy sleep.

Chapter 8
NICK

Location: Aurora Woodlands
Description: A twenty-eight-acre deciduous forest, consisting mostly of oak trees, separating many of the westernmost farming villages of Vestor from the nearby town of Greenborough
Average level: 3

Nick had never experienced hunger like this before as he scrambled beneath the thick canopy of the forest, pushing through the thin, yellow-leafed brush that scraped at him with its scraggly branches. Life on Station 79 was highly organized and regimented. He ate when it was time to eat, with a carefully portioned meal designed to make him feel just shy of full. Yet here in Yensere, he had no such provisions, and his clenched stomach was furious at him for the lack.

"Hey, Cataloger," he said, pausing before one of the oak trees to glance behind him. So far, no sign of anyone giving chase, particularly the terrifying knight in golden armor.

LEVEL: UNKNOWN

Yes?

"Why am I so hungry? This is all a re-creation. I shouldn't need to eat."

Sustenance is a required aspect of life

"But why? Who made this world and decided to keep in starvation? Why not just remove that whole thing?"

I cannot answer that

Nick sighed and kept moving. He had to get farther away from Meadowtint. Anywhere in this world had to be better than that strange village with its black-tongued residents and time-warping guardian. Even without Cataloger giving an answer, Nick had a strong guess as to the reason why hunger remained. You had to eat because, well, that's what you did in the real world. And so far as he could tell, all these various re-creations of animals and people were unaware of the nature of their digital existence.

"Hey, Cataloger, you're meant to help me, right? Is that only with information, or can you change the world around me?"

Why would I be able to change the material world?

Nick paused his walk to feel the bark of an oak tree. At least, that was what his mind called it when he looked at it. He'd never seen an oak tree in real life, but he swore its bark shouldn't be quite so dark, nor smooth.

"Because this world isn't real, and you're a computer program run by it. Why *couldn't* you change what is around me?"

Visitor's insistence on the unreality and illegitimacy of Yensere will only delay integration and adaptability

"Is this a really long way of saying you can't conjure me a hamburger to eat?"

A long pause.

My answer was meant to be informative—as for your *hamburger*—no, I cannot

Nick pushed off the tree and continued his march. Resolve filled him. Time to be a forager, right? That's what he'd thought when escaping Meadowtint. He scanned the forest floor, forcing himself to be aware of his surroundings, not just what was obvious. After about five minutes, he discovered a small berry bush growing up to his knee. He knelt before it, scanning the pale leaves for any sign of danger...not that he knew what that would be.

"How about this? Can you tell me if these berries are safe to eat?"

With an Endurance score of 2, you should experience very mild discomfort in your stomach from consumption of felberries

"That's good enough for me." He'd never heard of felberries before, and hunger aside, he was eager to try one. He plucked one of the fat little red berries off a branch and popped it in his mouth...and then immediately spat it back out. The crushed berry landed in the dirt, offering no relief. The flavor lingered, and he hawked and spat repeatedly, desperately trying to get the awful taste out of his mouth.

"It...it tastes like battery acid mixed with a sweaty sock."

You asked if it was edible—you did not inquire as to its taste

"You could have warned me!"

Visitor has repeatedly expressed hostility toward unrequested information

LEVEL: UNKNOWN

Nick fought back a gag reflex, then grimaced down a swallow. The last of the bitterness finally dwindled enough for him to ignore it. He glared at the plump little red berries as if they had played a trick on him. Felberries. That explained the name.

"Fine, point taken," he said. "Please, Cataloger, feel free to chip in with information you think might be helpful. Just... don't do it too often, all right?"

I will do my best to provide aid at a cadence your temperament finds acceptable

Nick couldn't shake the feeling an insult was buried in there somewhere. Lifting his sickle, he hacked at the base of the felberry bush. After three swings it toppled over, and Nick took great pleasure in stomping dozens of the foul berries underneath his boots.

"There," he said. "Mission accomplished."

Mission?

Nick smirked at the unseen specter of Cataloger. "Protecting other hapless visitors from eating those awful berries."

Congratulations, then—great success

When he looked deeper into the forest, he saw a brief golden outline shine across more than a dozen similar bushes throughout the underbrush.

Though you must repeat said success many times to eradicate the felberry bushes and protect future visitors

"Cataloger," Nick said, lowering his sickle. "Are you being sarcastic?"

No answer, which as far as Nick was concerned was answer enough. He resumed his walking, which was not entirely aimless. With the mountains forming a seemingly impenetrable natural wall to the west, it seemed likely that by continuing east through the forest he would encounter civilization. Just, hopefully a more welcoming civilization than the people of Meadowtint.

The farther he traveled, the greater his anxiety. There were no bugs, no flies. He heard no songs from birds, and when he saw a squirrel, he startled at the sight. Four eyes. It had four eyes.

"Are you sure that's a squirrel?" Nick asked, but then as he stared at it, the visage flickered, and the proper number of eyes appeared on its red-and-beige face.

Names of flora and fauna are used when applicable to ease visitor's integration

Nick touched one of the "oak" trees. He was certain now that a real oak would not feel so smooth. He snuck a glance at the squirrel, saw it still possessed two eyes as it scurried up the highest branches and out of view.

"What I see," he said. "Are you changing it to make me feel better? More... at home?"

Measures are taken to ease integration, yes

"Which means I can't trust my own senses."

Changes are small and few and will not interfere with your daily life

Easy enough for her to say. Nick walked the forest with a new sense of unease. Aurora Woodlands, which had seemed healthy and vibrant enough when he sprinted into it in a panic, appeared to be losing its luster. The green of the not-oak leaves was turning brown, an ugly and rotted-looking color. It made the leaves look... drained. Sickly.

LEVEL: UNKNOWN

"Is fall approaching?" he asked, pausing before a particularly unhealthy tree.

It is currently spring

"Huh." He touched one of the leaves, then immediately regretted it. The surface felt slimy. "How long until summer?"

Unknown

He frowned. "What do you mean, unknown? I don't need an exact date, just a rough estimate."

It is currently spring

"Right, you've said that already." His anxiety worsened. Cataloger had seemed so eager to help him learn about Yensere, so why this sudden caginess? "Fine, how about this? How long has it been spring? Tell me that, and then I'll do the math myself."

It has been spring for six hundred and thirty-seven years, having started in the first Year of Vaan

The pronouncement drove a sharp chill down Nick's spine. That couldn't be right...could it? Then again, this world wasn't real. The seasons themselves could be malleable to the whims of Yensere's creators...or maybe whoever was currently overseeing this world.

I give my heart to the Conqueror of Time...

"Is this what those villagers meant about their god-king conquering time?"

Possibly

Nick looked about the forest, its drooping branches, its pale bark, and its sickly brown leaves slick with a strange wetness that made his skin crawl.

"I think the forest misses summer and fall."

Unknown

Nick had a distinct feeling Cataloger did not like discussing such matters, so he let it drop. He pushed onward, studying the trees the deeper he traversed the woods. White streaks began to claw their way up the bark, looking like powdery scars. The leaves themselves seemed wrong, and it was a good hour before he realized why when he held two side by side. Their shapes were perfectly identical. The same went for a third leaf he checked, and then a fourth.

It wasn't just one tree, either. The whole forest, and its entire green-and-brown canopy, was composed of a single shape of leaf.

"What's happening here?" he whispered, dropping the leaves. They fell to the ground. They didn't float or flutter, only dropped like stones. When one landed on his foot, he flinched, expecting it to hurt. It did not, but he kicked it away all the same.

Your surroundings may not be rational, but they're still built on systems and rules, he told himself as he walked. *So think rationally about them. If the seasons halted, then the natural progression that the trees would be programmed to follow would also be halted. Their cycle has been cut short. So, after six hundred years, maybe it's glitching. This whole forest might be nothing more than an unexpected bug.*

This did not comfort him like it should have. The idea of errors happening in a world that felt so real, so flawless, made his insides squirm.

"Cataloger," he said, but before he could finish the thought, a strange growl stole his attention. He froze in place, clutching his sickle in both hands. Up ahead, he heard the rustle of

LEVEL: UNKNOWN

leaves, the crunch of underbrush, and the breaking of bark. Another growl, deep, heavy, and sounding pained. Nick retreated several steps, focusing his attention on the direction it came from.

There, in the distance, mostly hidden by trees, he saw a hint of brown fur. A bear?

No

"Then, what is it?" Nick asked as the thing finally lumbered into sight.

▮▮▮▮▮▮▮: Level 6 Creature
Armor: Hide, Tier 2
Temperament: Hostile

"No shit it's hostile," he muttered, squeezing his sickle tight.

The unknown creature bore the body of a bear but the head of a deer, its enormous eyes wide and bloodshot. Bits of moss and sickly streaks of white bark hung from its rack of antlers, whose shape was unnaturally curled and uniform. Its back legs were those of a wolf, only enormous in size to endure such tremendous weight. As for the arms, well...

The fingers poking out from underneath all that muscle and brown fur were undeniably human.

"Level six?" he asked Cataloger, feeling betrayed. "What happened to average level three?"

Would you like me to explain averages to you?

"Not now," Nick hissed as the deer thing howled, a sound akin to a bear's roar but containing far too much humanoid screeching mixed in. He braced as it lumbered toward him, its gait wildly uneven. The arms in the front struggled to maintain balance, while the back legs easily lunged it forward.

"Ignore its level," he told himself as he tensed. "Dodge its attacks, and strike when it's vulnerable. Just like you did with Gareth."

Two more lunges, and then the bizarre creature was before him. It tried to rear up on its hind legs, just as a bear would, only the wolf legs were unsuited for the motion. Instead it wobbled, spittle flying from its mouth as it shook its antlers. Nick eyed those antlers as fear drove a deep spike into his chest.

How much damage will those do? he wondered.

The damage range of those antlers is approximately seventy-nine to one hundred twenty-six percent of your maximum health

The wolf legs vaulted the beast forward in an awkward lurch. Nick flung himself to the side and did not even attempt to slash while doing so.

Definitely don't get hit.

He dug in his left heel to halt his momentum, turned, and then dodged again as the creature swiped wildly to its side, trying to grab him. Nick caught sight of those fingers and their blackened fingernails and swung his sickle on instinct. The sharpened interior scraped along the creature's arm, carving into the fur.

It howled with rage, the ground seeming to shake from its sudden fury. Nick dashed away, in full retreat as it chased. He weaved from side to side, putting every nearby tree between him and the monster. All the while, he eyed his green stamina bar and the frightening rate at which it dropped. Not as quickly as on his first day in Yensere, but still, he was already pushing himself too much.

LEVEL: UNKNOWN

The distraction cost him. A flex of the wolf legs, a victorious howl, and then one of the arms sideswiped him. The impact lifted him into the air, a flight that lasted but a heartbeat before he crashed into a tree.

Can't outrun it, he thought, spinning to place his back to the tree. *Have to fight it.*

A terrifying prospect, but he'd fought Sir Gareth and lived. Level 6? No time magic? Infinitely more doable, right?

The deer opened its mouth for another shriek, this one even less natural than the last. Nick heard a grinding of metal within it, as if two saw blades were colliding in its throat, the sound coupling with the guttural roar of a bear to create something wholly new and horrifying. Its eyes widened, the muscles of its human arms tensing. Nick flung himself to the side, just in time to avoid the creature's slamming its horns forward in an attempt to impale him. Instead they struck the oak, the sharp points embedding deep into the bark.

Nick slashed twice with his sickle, desperately wishing he had a proper weapon, the two hits shaving a paltry amount of red from the thing's health. The creature's hide was thick, but thankfully it was no tier-whatever chain mail.

I can kill you, he thought, baring his teeth. *It's just a matter of time.*

The wounded thing ripped its horns free of the oak, howled with pain and fury, and then tried again to impale him. Luckily for Nick, its upper body was too thick, its movements too awkward, like it didn't quite know how to move its own body. Nick shifted closer to its rear, his sickle clutched in both hands as he hacked straight down at its spine.

Blood wet the brown fur and spilled across the ground, disturbingly dark in color as it dripped. Nick dared not think about it now. Another metallic shriek. The creature retreated while spinning its lower body in an attempt to face him. Nick, despite all instincts screaming to the contrary, maintained his aggression. He flung himself toward its side, keeping away from its deer head and perfectly oval arrangement of spiked horns. Another slash, weaker and with one hand, to carve out a thin groove alongside its meaty flank.

It still had more than half its health remaining, though it was looking tired now. It sidestepped, flinging its greater weight against Nick with a thud. He tumbled, gasping for air from the impact. The green of his stamina bar was a measly 20 percent, making it laborious to stand once again. The monster spun to face him, its right arm lashing out in a manner vaguely resembling the movements of gorillas Nick had seen in documentaries. He braced his arm and legs and pushed into it, the only option that came to mind. The hand collided against him, and he gasped at the horrid pain. *Not good*, he thought, the swipe scooping him closer. Instinct screamed at him to move, to attack, but his mind froze at being in such close proximity to the nightmarish thing. The way it breathed was wrong, too heavy, too guttural. The movement of its joints sounded of metal. The smell of its breath was beyond foul, a visible white fog that reeked of rotting meat. It reared up as well as its back legs allowed, both arms clutching their fists together.

It was going to kill him, and Nick prayed it would be quick.

As his body tensed against an expected impact, a thick shard of ice shot over Nick's head and slammed into the creature's chest. It staggered and flailed, blood leaking down its fur from the deep, jagged piece of ice embedded in its chest.

Though his anxiety shot up at the sudden appearance of the ice, Nick dared not waste such an opportunity. Bellowing for confidence, for fury, he buried the jagged end of the sickle blade straight between the two horns of the terrifying monstrosity that should not exist. It lowered its head, ready to impale him, but Nick swung a second time, shifting his aim the tiniest amount. The blade struck an eye and then buried deep.

The creature shuddered, all strength leaving its legs. Its final lunge was a pathetic collapse, one Nick easily retreated from, and then it lay forever still.

Reassessment
Level: 4 (+1)
Statistical Improvements:
Agility: 2 (+1)
Physicality: 4 (+1)
Endurance: 2

Nick slowed his breathing, deep ins and outs taught to him by his older brother to manage his occasional panic attacks. Waves of pleasure rocked through his body. The red of his health extended as he gained more points, as did the length of his slowly recovering stamina bar.

"Level six," he said aloud, and pointed his bloody sickle at the corpse. "You're nothing. *Nothing!*"

And then he laughed, delirious and excited despite the exhaustion tugging at his body and the throbbing pain from where his back had struck the tree.

Then he remembered the ice.

He turned, searching his surroundings. He saw only trees.

"You're out there, aren't you?" he said out loud, remembering the strange woman in silver armor who froze him in the river right before his first death. "Are you watching me? Why help a stranger you've already killed once?"

He was met with silence, though he couldn't shake the feeling that he was being watched. Nick turned his attention to the slain monster. Might as well focus on what was in front of him.

"Now that I've caught my breath," he said, using a few leaves to wipe the blood from his sickle. He hated how little red was in it, as if the thing bled ink instead of blood. "Care to tell me what that damn thing was, Cataloger?"

There is no indexed entry of it within my catalog

"So you've never seen something like that before?"

Nick did not like the way Cataloger paused before answering.

Not that specific creature

There's more like it, Nick thought, his elation draining with the last of his adrenaline, or whatever the digital equivalent of it was. The idea of encountering something similar, or worse, replaced the joy of increasing his level with a sense of foreboding. He'd barely survived that encounter. What if the others were worse? Stronger, or less awkward with their movements?

A thought came to him, and he had to have his curiosity satisfied.

"Hey, Cataloger, what's the level of a plain old brown bear?"

An adult brown bear has an average level of 7

Nick resumed his trek through the forest, more than happy to leave the corpse of the strange, mutated beast far behind.

"Well, let's hope I don't encounter one of those, either, eh?"

Chapter 9
NICK

After another hour of fumbling through the brush with only the vaguest sense of direction, Nick stumbled upon an actual road running through the Aurora Woodlands. His relief was tempered by the increasing pain in his stomach.

"I swear I'll die of hunger soon," he muttered, starting to wonder if maybe, just maybe, he should have tried to endure the foul taste of the felberries.

Incorrect—visitor's hunger and thirst meters are at least one day's worth of activities away from completely depleting

"My *what?*"

Two new bars hovered into view in the far bottom right corner of his vision. One was a pale yellow, the other a pleasant blue. The yellow was depleted by a quarter, while the blue, nearly a third. Nick felt a strange, visceral disgust in seeing the thirst on his tongue and grumble in his belly represented so clinically.

"Cataloger," he said. "Please never, ever show me those again."

At your request

The two bars vanished, and Nick was immediately relieved. While he was getting better at wrapping his head around having his various characteristics codified into numbers, he wanted nothing to do with something so basic as eating and drinking being equally quantified. He would eat when he was hungry and drink when he was thirsty. For his own sanity, that would have to be enough.

The road through the forest bore some heavy ruts in its center. Wagon wheels, Nick suspected. He saw no sign of any nearby travelers, so he walked the center of the road, following it eastward, which he hoped would take him far, far away from Meadowtint and the horrifying creature of the forest.

"So where does this road lead?" he asked as he walked.

If followed for thirty-eight miles, this road will eventually arrive at the city of Greenborough

"Nice. Perhaps I should call you 'cartographer' instead."

Nick was surprised by the lengthy delay in response.

I cannot accept what is colloquially known as a "nickname"

"What about a name given to you by a Nick?"

Attempts at humor will only lead to potential confusion—especially those of lower quality

Nick froze in place. "Did you just insult my jokes?"

Clarify

"Clarify," he muttered, refusing to do so. "You know damn well what you did, Cataloger. Well, *I* thought it was funny."

I am happy for you

Nick resumed walking, his curiosity piqued.

LEVEL: UNKNOWN

"Are you actually happy, Cataloger? Are you capable of emotions?"

There are regulations to what I can and cannot do, learn, express, convey, adapt, and think

"Can you tell me what those are?"

No

That was about as direct an answer as he'd ever heard from Cataloger, and the directness conveyed to him, accurately or imagined, a sense of dislike toward the subject. Nick let the matter drop. Perhaps he'd bring it up with Simon later in conversation and see if his older brother had anything specific he wished to learn about what Nick presumed to be an AI guide.

The day crawled along. The trees, to Nick's relief, slowly blossomed with life. Whatever strange rot or mutation had afflicted them eased away as he continued his journey. Birds soon occupied the higher branches, blue-and-red-feathered creatures that Cataloger identified as flagsongs. Their whistles were pleasant. He smiled at the sight of a chipmunk munching away at an acorn not far to his right. It even had the kindness to sport the proper number of eyes at first glance. Soon flies and mosquitoes emerged, to not quite the same level of happiness. Their wings were longer than he was used to, their bodies more bulbous and blue.

Nick struck one of the mosquitoes that landed on his arm, and he half expected to see a tiny health bar appear above the little black smear that was left on his skin. The horrors of the bizarre bear-deer-wolf thing felt so far away. If only he could say the same for the various aches and pains of his body that remained from the fight. He'd kept an eye on that little red bar, and it had steadily increased over the past hour, his cuts and bruises healing at a rate that was disconcertingly fast.

To accommodate visitors' exploration and learning, natural healing has been significantly increased

Well. That answered that.

"Thanks, Cataloger," he said as he walked. "Nice to know there's some advantages to go along with everyone trying to kill me on sight."

After another hour of travel, along a path void of visitors, Nick spotted a sudden turn from the road. To his even greater surprise, it was walled off almost immediately, the road blocked by an iron gate. Curiosity, and his grumbling stomach, sent him to investigate. Beyond, he spotted a clearing in the woods, and in its center, atop a gentle hill, was a white-painted mansion.

Location: Hulh Manse

Description: Estate of Baron Hulh, who has ruled over the western farmlands of Vestor for six years

Nick stared through the bars. Its construction was vastly nicer than that of the homes of Meadowtint, almost dramatically grand. Nick could only imagine what kind of person lived inside. What he could also imagine was the amount of food available within.

The first problem was whether or not they'd share it with a random passerby.

The second problem was whether the people there would try to murder him for that whole "demon" thing.

"That's it, I'm going in," he said, climbing the gate. It was tall, but there weren't spikes or sharp edges to deter him from going over the top. With a bit of effort, he landed

LEVEL: UNKNOWN

uneceremoniously on the dirt on the other side. Nick stood, dusted himself off, and trudged along the path toward the mansion, his sickle tucked into the waistband of his overalls.

What's the worst that could happen? he thought upon reaching the enormous double doors. *They kill you? Wouldn't be the first time. Or even the fifth.*

He rapped his knuckles on the door. On the third knock, a sharply dressed man in a dark suit opened the door.

"No beggars," he said, his white mustache curling in disgust.

"Please," Nick said, thrusting his arm and leg in the way to prevent the door from shutting. "I'm starving. If I could have just a little bit of food, a snack, anything..."

The manservant did not try to force the door shut. Instead he backed away and glanced over his shoulder.

"Logrif, if you would?"

The door opened wider, and from deeper inside the finely furnished hallway approached a hulking man. He wore dark trousers and a blue tunic covered by a thick breastplate adorned with a spreadeagle crest. A club rested across one shoulder, its sides reinforced with thick strips of metal. As Nick's eyes widened, information hovered above the giant man's bald head.

Logrif: Level 10 Human
Archetype: Guard
Armor: Breastplate, Tier 4

"A whole forest to hunt within, but they come begging anyway," Logrif said, his words accompanied by a slight drawl.

Nick retreated a step while pulling out his sickle and holding it before him. It felt pathetic compared to the enormous instrument in Logrif's hands. What even *was* that?

Item: Reinforced Club
Quality: Tier 3 (Good)
Classification: Weapon
Augmented with iron, the simple club has been transformed into a more powerful, reliable weapon

Nick hoped that description was all he'd learn about that giant club as he backed away.

"I'm leaving, I'm leaving," he said.

Logrif exited through the doorway, having to duck to not bump against the frame.

"Yes," the giant man said with an all-too-pleased smile. He hoisted his weapon. "You are. But not yet."

Nick braced himself, his mind racing. He could likely outrun the big man, but there remained the troubling fact that the gate was still shut. Could he gain enough distance to also climb over without getting clobbered?

The club rose. Nick tensed.

"Wait!"

Logrif glanced over his shoulder, his displeasure obvious. The manservant stepped out, his beady eyes narrowed.

"You," he said. "Something is different with you. Not a normal beggar, are you? No, you're…" Another step closer. Though he worked to keep his face passive, a bit of surprise leaked through. "You are what the people here would call a 'demon,' are you not?"

Nick bounced his attention back and forth between the servant and the guard eager to kill him.

"Maybe," he said. "Will your giant smash me if I say yes?"

The servant patted the guard on the shoulder.

LEVEL: UNKNOWN

"Lower your weapon, Logrif. I suspect Baron Hulh will be most eager to speak with such an... enigmatic individual." He stepped past him and then bowed. "Greetings. I am Butler Tully, in charge of maintaining this manse. If you would please follow me?"

Nick put away his sickle, keeping a tight eye on Logrif.

"Happy to," he muttered, and entered. The walls were a deep mahogany color, the carpet a lovely shade of red. Nick felt dirty and inappropriate as he trudged his muddy boots across that pristine carpet. He passed doors with various animals carved upon them, their handles shining gold. Paintings covered the walls, and Nick wished he could stop to inspect them. Those windows into other parts of Yensere intrigued him greatly.

"Your journey appears to have been one of difficulty," the butler said, pausing before one of the doors. "There is a wardrobe within. Please use it at your convenience so you may be properly attired for a meeting with the master of the house."

"Of course," Nick said, trying to keep the eagerness out of his voice at the prospect of removing his bloodstained and dirt-caked clothes. Feeling the eyes of the butler watching him, he pushed the door open and stepped inside.

The bedroom within filled him with awe, and he wandered it in a haze. He'd heard stories of such wealth, *old* wealth, like in the fairy tales his mother used to read to him. This room felt like a perfect re-creation of those ideals. The four-poster bed, the trunk at its foot, the towering wardrobe, the two dressers: They were all made of darkly polished wood and then filigreed with gold around various corners, hinges, and knobs. Violet curtains wrapped the bed, silky soft between his fingers. The ceiling was high, the windows tall and oval, the walls decorated with a half dozen paintings of gorgeous landscapes, places certainly different from the nearby environs. Waterfalls flowing through multicolored forests, still lakes surrounded by pines, and grand fields of flowers blooming with all sorts of colors and shapes.

Whatever plague inflicted Meadowtint, it seemed to have spared Baron Hulh's manse. Nick ran his fingers across the front of the wardrobe, impressed by how *aged* it felt. Everything on the research station was clinical, sterile, and utilitarian. Little bore history or sentimentality. Only what few personal objects researchers and workers brought gave life and personality to the research station. When Nick had been younger, he'd often been confused by the randomness of what people chose. Sure, pictures he understood, but some brought game boards, old clothes, childhood dolls, and so many instruments. One researcher even brought a fishing rod, despite knowing it would never be used.

Now he understood it as a need to remember a life lived in a place that bore history, when a place had a past that stretched longer than the twenty years it had taken to construct the space station he called home.

Nick imagined what it'd be like to have such a wardrobe in his room. How ludicrous it'd be, fitting it inside the cramped space. How wondrous to have that finely polished wood contrasting with the cold steel of the walls.

"If only I could bring you with me," he whispered aloud, pulling it open. Finely tailored shirts hung from smoothly polished wood hangers. Underneath them, inside little hollow squares lining the lower half of the wardrobe, were trousers of various lengths and colors, each with leather cord drawstrings or belts already half-looped.

"Baron Hulh did say to make myself at home," he said, removing one of the shirts that looked close enough to his size. It was long-sleeved, the wool fabric finely woven and surprisingly soft. The shirt was dyed a lovely shade of red, with its neck and bottom hemmed with black. A bit of searching later and he found a pair of black trousers that used red ribbon to tighten the front as well as hem in the ankles and waist. A good enough match, in his opinion.

"Will wearing nicer clothes add to any of my stats?" he asked Cataloger. "Maybe a bump to my attractiveness level?"

Attractiveness is not a cataloged statistic, for it is based on unique personal and biological parameters that—

"Got it, got it, please stop."

Nick started to remove his raggedy old shirt, then hesitated.

"Uh, Cataloger... is there a way I can get you to, um, turn around?"

Clarify

He grimaced. "I don't like the idea of you watching me undress."

Such discomfort is irrational—I am incapable of judgment, mockery, or sexual attraction

Nick rubbed his eyes.

Think of Cataloger like a physician, he told himself. *You've had to endure plenty of awkward exams before. It's no big deal.*

This is an accurate comparison

Nick pulled his old shirt off and tossed it to the carpet, unable to hold back a laugh. What point was there in being shy before an artificial intelligence when said intelligence was capable of *hearing his thoughts*?

"You just need to get used to having no privacy, Nick," he told himself as he pulled off his overalls. Though they were repaired a bit each time he returned to Yensere, they were still torn in places, and bits of thorns and burrs clung to them from his flight through the forest.

Once Nick was dressed in his new finery, he glanced about for a mirror. There was none within the wardrobe, nor any hanging from the walls or set atop the dresser.

"Is there a mirror in here, Cataloger?" he asked, dying to know how he looked.

One moment

After a few seconds, her feminine voice floated back.

There appears to be a mirror hidden within the wardrobe

Nick cocked an eyebrow. "Hidden? Why would someone hide a mirror?"

Unknown

Nick pushed the many shirts and tunics aside to scan the back of the wardrobe. He knew he was overstepping his bounds, but the mystery filled him with an excitement he couldn't resist. His fingers ran across the back, testing the wood for anything that felt out of place. One of the boards was propped wrong, not entirely flush with the others. He pried it with his fingertips until it came loose, revealing a hidden compartment. And there, within, he saw a silver hand mirror.

LEVEL: UNKNOWN

"It's...it's beautiful," he said, closing his fingers around the slender handle adorned with deep red runes he didn't recognize. At his touch, he felt a strange sensation flow through him. It was like electricity, but not jarring, not a jolt, but more soothing. Pleasant. The handle, despite the silver twisting about like a funnel, seemed to perfectly fit his fingers.

"What is this?" he asked.

Item: Mirror of Theft
Quality: Tier 14 (Pristine)
Classification: Arcane Artifact
Created during the Sinifel Empire, this mirror reveals to the holder something they seek, fear, or desire, the manner of which is chaotic and uncertain

At first, Nick thought Cataloger was playing a trick on him. Looking into the small mirror, he saw only himself, tired, hungry, and with disheveled brown hair in desperate need of a trim. The new outfit, while certainly nice, almost felt wrong hanging off him, the size a bit too big for his frame. It gave him an emaciated look.

"Are you sure?" he asked.

Before Cataloger could answer, he felt another wave of pleasant energy wash through him. Deep in the back of his mind, he heard a ringing sound and felt something akin to a pulling. The image in the mirror shifted. The face changed. The clothes smoothed out and changed color as they morphed into an OPC uniform. Nick felt rooted in place, a mixture of fury and elation striking him with a powerful paralysis as a familiar figure appeared within the mirror.

His father, smiling at him.

"Nick," said his father, Lucien. "It's...it's you, isn't it? How long has it been—two years? You've grown. My, how you've grown."

Nick stumbled onto the bed, half entangling himself in the violet curtains. His hand shook, yet the image within the mirror retained perfect clarity.

"You can't be here," he said, dumbstruck.

Lucien frowned, the lines in his forehead thickening along with it. "And why not?"

"Because you're...this is..."

He was talking to a ghost.

He was talking to the dead.

"Because you can't be real."

Lucien shook his head and crossed his arms as the mist folded around him.

"How do we define what is real, my son?"

A heavy knocking sounded on the bedroom door before Nick could answer. He jammed the mirror into his wide trouser pocket, and immediately it felt like he'd emerged from underwater to suck in a deep breath. His heart hammered inside his chest. Impossible thoughts bounded through him, and he pushed them aside to answer the door with a casual grin.

"Yeah?" he asked, flinging it open.

"I see you've dressed," the butler said, and sniffed. "Excellent taste, sir. Now that you are properly attired, Baron Hulh would like you to join him for dinner."

Nick's mouth immediately watered, his hunger pushing away the rest of the shock.

"Fantastic."

LEVEL: UNKNOWN

A veritable feast awaited Nick in the dining hall. A long table was set between walls decorated with somber portraits of elderly men and women hung within silver frames. Multiple dishes were waiting, their mixture of smells awakening Nick's hunger to a ravenous degree. He saw multiple forms of potatoes, mashed and scalloped, both drowning in butter and gravy. A hunk of meat, sweating with juices, was the centerpiece, its exterior a pleasantly golden color, the interior just shy of pink. A great bowl of soup bubbled just beside the table, set atop warming stones on a carried marble tray. Nick saw carrots, cubed meat, and various greens he did not recognize floating in the brown broth.

"Welcome," a man in violet and gold robes said, standing. Nick had barely noticed him over the food. "Are you hungry?"

"Famished," Nick said. Two servants rushed in from a side door, looking sharp in their finely fitted tunics and trousers. The motion attracted Nick's attention, and he noticed an armed guard on the opposite side of the door. So Logrif was not the only protector of the mansion...

Nick took a seat before the only empty plate, assuming it was his, and took stock of his host as the two servants began slicing and serving him portions. Baron Hulh was younger than Nick expected, his nose sharp and his beard neatly trimmed as it curled down from his ears to the bottom of his chin, where it drifted into a faint curl. He did not smile, not with his face, nor with his eyes, which looked like two sharp bits of amethyst wedged into white orbs.

"I must ask forgiveness for my bodyguard's treatment of you," the baron continued. Something about his voice grated. Perhaps too much of an air of control within an otherwise nasally voice. "But surely you understand why he would think you nothing more than a common beggar?"

"I'm pretty sure that's what I am, though," Nick said, his eyes widening as a thick hunk of meat was set in the center of his plate. He tapped the arm of a servant, who gave him a guarded look in response. "What is that?"

"Lamb, sir," the servant responded.

"Lamb," Nick said, beaming. He'd never seen a lamb in person, let alone eaten one. They'd all gone extinct before his home world of Taneth had been terraformed by the explorers of Eden.

The baron leaned forward in his chair. No food before him. He was all seriousness.

"But you aren't just a beggar. You are what the folks in Vestor would call a 'demon,' aren't you, Nick?"

Nick wasn't going to waste this good fortune. He grabbed one of the four forks and one of the three knives and immediately sliced into the lamb before the servants were done filling his plate. A conversation about demons might get ugly, and damn it, Nick was going to enjoy a nicely cooked hunk of lamb, digital re-creation or otherwise.

The meat nearly melted in his mouth. Nick slumped an inch lower in his chair and sighed. A tiny part of him wanted to cry. There would be no topping this.

"Sorry," he said, realizing the baron was staring at him. "But yes, that word's been thrown at me a lot. Why? I don't know. What exactly it means, I don't know that, either."

LEVEL: UNKNOWN

Another bite of lamb. Another. For a brief moment he saw the flicker of that yellow hunger bar in the bottom right corner of his vision, and he glared at it with seething hatred. It immediately vanished, and he could almost feel Cataloger's regret.

"I've been told demons can be clever and full of tricks," Baron Hulh said. "But then again, we don't know what it is you truly are. Beasts from beyond the dark sun, perhaps? Some say you are survivors of the Majere, from the era predating even the grand Sinifel Empire. What is it you remember, Nick? What brings you here, to my doorstep?"

"I don't know who the Sinifel are, nor what the Majere were, either," Nick said. He pondered what exactly to tell the man. Was there even a way to convey the concept of the Artifact and a digital world within it? A second thought hit him.

Was he even allowed?

Your visitor status is currently known and flagged to all inhabitants of Yensere

"So you are ignorant of Yensere?" the baron asked. "Its people and its history?"

"That's a fair assessment." He bit into one of the carrots. It had a snap to it lacking in the carrots freeze-dried and reheated on Station 79, not to mention it was coated in some sort of sauce that gave it a tangy flavor he instantly wanted more of.

"It seems our guest is more interested in eating than talking," Baron Hulh said, and he chuckled while waving at one of the servants. "Wine for the both of us, please."

The servant hurried over, carrying an opened bottle

wrapped in a wet cloth. The other servant appeared as if by magic, setting down two glasses so the first could pour the crimson liquid in. Nick accepted his glass, his curiosity growing. Alcohol was rare for him, granted only on special occasions with his older brother. He sipped a bit of it, then held back a cough. It was extremely tart and surprisingly sweet, like a thick dollop of honey had been added to the bottom.

"Not to your liking?" the baron asked. "Or are demons not capable of handling alcohol?"

Nick frowned as his pride took a lash. Stubbornness had him return the glass to his lips and down the rest.

"Nah," he said, setting it aside. "We demons can...can..."

No more words came. His throat hitched. It felt like fire had sunk into his belly. The room around him pitched violently despite his remaining firmly seated.

"What?" Nick asked weakly as his stomach clenched with excruciating pain. "What did you...?"

Status: Poisoned (wildboar root)

Effect: Fifty percent reduction in physicality and endurance, along with severe impairment of cognitive abilities and vision

Nick shoved away his chair and stood on unsteady feet, his head starting to swim. Four soldiers garbed in padded leather came rushing in, slender swords held in hand. They surrounded Nick, two on either side of him. He scanned them, information floating into view the moment he desired it.

Level 3 Human
Archetype: Guard
Armor: Padded Leather, Tier 2

LEVEL: UNKNOWN

Each one was more than capable of taking him down in his current state. Nick pulled the sickle out from his belt and held it with both hands, though his muscles started to spasm.

"You need not struggle," Baron Hulh said, casually rising from his seat and retreating from the table. "Surely you understand I could never let a demon run loose in my lands?"

Nick tried to respond but found speech was an impossibility. He dropped his weapon, eyes wide with fear as the huge bodyguard, Logrif, sauntered over, reached out, and closed his beefy hand around Nick's throat. Logrif lifted him with ease, leaving Nick's feet dangling. Nick's hands closed around that enormous wrist, pulling and struggling, but the man was a walking mountain of muscle. The grip tightened. Nick gasped, growing more light-headed. His vision darkened. Little white sparks flitted around what remained of his vision.

Just before unconsciousness took him, he heard Baron Hulh's voice pierce through the fog and darkness.

"Bring him to the cell. My knives will reveal the truth of his arrival."

Chapter 10
SIMON

Simon awoke from a fitful sleep to the beeping alert of his brother's heart monitor. The alarm quickly dashed away his grogginess as he leaned closer.

"Two hundred bpm?" he said, and pressed the back of his hand against Nick's forehead. His skin was warm and damp with sweat. A glance at a different monitor showed him building a fever, his temperature starting to crest over 100°F. A troubling sign on its own, though the more worrisome part was *why*.

"What are you doing?" he asked the quiet dark. He slumped over the bed, his temples pulsing with a growing migraine. "I hate this, Nick. I hate it. I wish I could be in there with you. I wish I could help instead of sitting here and—"

A deep rumbling shook the station, and then gravity itself shifted. Simon flew toward one of the walls, shouting as he collided hard with his right shoulder. Nick's bed was bolted down, but the same could not be said for Nick, who slid off and started to roll. Simon caught him the best he could, for a second rumble followed, and the axis of gravity pivoted in the reverse direction. The station was trying to correct itself.

"I got you," Simon said, holding the catatonic Nick to his chest. His stomach did loops as the floor resumed being a proper floor for far too short a time. Again, it felt like the world spun underneath him, the pull of gravity shifting around forty-five degrees or so. On his wrist, his watch flared with angry lights, warnings from the research station's moderating AI as well as various members of his staff. Those warnings were echoed by a constant droning alarm from the main corridor, which was now awash with light despite the late cycle hour.

Shifting Nick's weight onto his right arm, he lifted his wrist, ignoring the alerts to answer a call request from one specific individual: Carter, his head of engineering.

"Good, you're unharmed," Carter's voice said. "Apologies for the gravity, but stabilization is going to take some time."

"Forget the gravity," Simon said. "What just happened?"

An image flashed onto his watch from an exterior station camera. Simon's stomach sank at the sight: Debris floated through space, and alongside the curve of the station, he saw a gaping chunk missing. He had a sudden, horrible feeling he knew of someone who would want to blow a hole in his station.

"Director Lemley's shuttle exploded," said Carter. "Automated security locked down the corridor on both sides, and from what I can tell, there's no fires or vacuum leaks beyond the shuttle bay. Impact threw off our rotation. I'm scanning now for damage done to the rest of the station by the ejected debris."

Simon breathed a sigh of relief. Without a fire or air leak, the station would survive. That relief, though, was fleeting.

"Do what you can to stabilize," Simon said. "Contact me if you need help."

He ended the communication and initiated a new one, this time to Daksh. No response.

Shit.

"Sorry, Nick," Simon said, hoisting his brother back onto the bed. Once he replaced the covers, he reached underneath the bed and felt along the side bar. Every bed had a Velcro wrap attached to it in case of prolonged loss of gravity. Finding it, he pulled it up, looped it over Nick, and then connected it to the strip attached to the other side.

Satisfied that his brother probably wouldn't fly out of bed, Simon rushed through the door, his stun gun gripped tightly in hand. Another rumble, another shift, and he stumbled into a hard slam against the opposite wall. He grimaced at the pain as the noise of the alarms blared through his mind. Multiple men and women were already in the main corridor, checking on one another or heading to their stations if they were part of the maintenance crew.

Simon ignored their worried looks and pushed past them.

"We'll be fine," he said to their questions. "We'll be fine."

A minute later, he reached the guest room door. Daksh lay on the ground before it, a small smear of blood on the nearby wall. A woman knelt beside him, emergency kit open at her feet. It took Simon a moment to recognize her with her brown hair untied and her eyes bloodshot from lack of sleep.

LEVEL: UNKNOWN

"Haley," he said, addressing the doctor in charge of their med ward. "Is he all right?"

Haley glanced up at him.

"Concussion," she said. "And he should be all right, assuming we don't all get sucked out into the vacuum. What happened? Were we struck by a meteor?"

"Sorry, no time to explain," Simon said, stepping past her to the guest room door. It was open. The inside was empty. Simon forced back a curse as he lifted his watch.

"Seventy-nine, locate Director Lemley."

Director Jakob Lemley has a privacy order in place.

"Override it and tell me where he is."

Override unavailable. You do not possess proper organizational rank.

Simon bit down another curse. Planetary directors were some of the most important officials in the entire OPC. Despite this being Simon's station, Lemley could still pull rank, especially if he claimed it was due to an emergency. Simon could order a station-wide lockdown, but it wouldn't hold. Lemley could almost certainly bypass it with his clearance.

Simon's hand tightened on the trigger of his gun. He'd have to do this the old-fashioned way. Of course, this still left the question of where to search.

The research station resembled a spoked wheel, with the vast majority of rooms and labs built along the outer edge, where the rotation would create a strong gravitational pull. Elevators ran through two of the spokes for quicker traversal between sections of the station. The remaining spokes led to the inner areas of the station: liquid oxygen storage, fuel storage, cargo holds, and water and air circulation, as well as the multiple batteries collecting energy beamed in from their dozen satellite solar arrays.

Simon's gut said to search the fuel storage next. A fire starting there could sweep through much of the station, consuming vital oxygen at the same time. And should it reach the oxygen tanks themselves, well...

"Shan, you in the command center?" Simon spoke into his watch as he jogged toward one of the tunnels leading toward the inner core of the station.

His second-in-command, a bespectacled man ten years his senior named Shan Lai, appeared on the screen. He looked exhausted, his round, chubby face stretched into a tight frown.

"I am, as should you be. Where are you?"

"On my way to..." He paused to think. "Oxygen bay one. I want you to send Bethany and Isaac to depot two and Naheed to three. And get someone to check the fuel tanks, too."

Shan's brow furrowed. "You suspect sabotage."

"Am I wrong to?"

His second-in-command shook his head. "No. You're not. We've confirmed Lemley's shuttle as the source of the explosion. That means we cannot rule out the possibility of it being intentional."

"Any idea how it happened?" Simon asked as he sprinted.

"We never sent a scanning crew into the shuttle. Might have been technical issues. Might have been a bomb."

Panic welled in Simon's chest. Smuggling a bomb through a world gate would be extremely difficult, but not impossible.

LEVEL: UNKNOWN

Lemley was a brilliant man and carried a lot of authority. Given the damage done to their station, there was no ruling out that possibility. It seemed more and more likely that the blast was intentional and that Lemley was trying to... what? Kill them all? But the shuttle's destruction had not been severe enough to do any lasting damage, which meant if Lemley sought to finish the job, his options were limited.

Simon stopped at a marked door, grabbed the handle, and pulled it open to reveal a room no larger than a closet containing a ladder. Due to the nature of the station's design, no matter where you were, approaching the interior meant going "up." Normally there were service elevators, but those were shut off because of the emergency status, necessitating use of ladders instead. Simon climbed as fast as he could, building up a layer of sweat. With each rung, the pull of the artificial gravity lessened. In the direct center, he'd feel nearly weightless, but his destination was thankfully not that far.

The various storage and engineering rooms were to either side of him, with sealed doors labeled with giant letters. At the first oxygen bay, he stepped off the ladder and readied his stun gun. His free hand grabbed the handle and pulled.

Director Lemley stood at the entrance of the bay, and he spun around at the sound of the door opening. One of the emergency oxygen tanks was strapped to his back, its mask tied firmly to his face. He stood with one hand on the handle to the door. The other held a firearm pointed at Simon's chest.

"No closer," Lemley said, the director's voice slightly muffled by the mask. "There's no need for you to die a painful death."

"If I let you stay in there, I'll die anyway. Looks like you aim to kill us all."

"Aye, I do," Lemley said. "But it will be quick." He gestured at the communicator watch on Simon's wrist. "Leave it be. No one needs to be afraid. The rupture will be sudden, and death instantaneous. Give your people that, Director. You owe it to them."

"I owe it to them to stop you."

The older man frowned and nodded.

"Yes," he said. "I suppose you do."

He lowered the pistol and pulled the trigger. Simon screamed as searing pain shot through his left knee. The entire leg collapsed as the sound of pinging metal filled his ears. The bullet ricocheted through the hall but thankfully halted without causing further harm. Blood pooled beneath him, the drops slowly hovering to join the rest due to the lesser gravity.

Simon lifted his stun gun, but before he could pull the trigger, Lemley batted it out of his grasp and then smacked him in the forehead with the butt of the pistol. Simon's vision swam, and he collapsed onto his side. His own blood smeared across his face.

"A shame, what must be done," Lemley said, breathing heavily into his mask. "You were a fine director. Brave. Quick-witted. Committed to science. If only you had never stumbled upon the Artifact. But I suppose this path became fate the moment this station was assigned to Majus."

"I don't..." Simon paused to gasp against another wave of pain coursing through him from his foolish attempt to sit up. "I don't understand."

LEVEL: UNKNOWN

Lemley knelt before him.

"It *wants* to be found," he said, staring straight into Simon's eyes with a crazed intensity. "And so you found it. It is a jar of vipers. A poisoned pill. If humanity is to endure, all traces of it must be expunged."

He stood and returned to the entrance, yanking it open with his free hand and stepping back inside.

"Seventy-nine, lock the bay door behind me. Deny all attempts to enter until my order."

Simon did not need to hear the AI's response to know it would obey. Lemley stepped within the bay, holding the door slightly ajar.

"If I could, I would throw the damned thing into Majus's sun and spare your lives," he said. "But alas, I only do what I can and pray the Artifact is flung into the deepest depths of space, never to be found again. Farewell, Director."

The door slammed shut. Simon pushed to his feet, holding back a scream when he put the slightest bit of weight onto his shattered knee. Hobbling on one leg, he left a trail of blood behind him, the drops floating weirdly as they fell. There was a small, heavily reinforced window in the center of the door, and through it, Simon could see the planetary director approach one of the consoles before the enormous liquid oxygen tanks within.

Simon's mind raced for a solution. Lemley had a plan of some sort, likely an eruption of one tank that would cause a chain reaction to detonate the others. The force could easily crack the station in half, flinging everyone within into the freezing darkness of space. He slammed a fist against the door, furious his station AI could be so easily turned against him.

But he realized that Lemley, in his haste, had only issued an order about the door—nothing else. An idea formed, one that made Simon sick to his stomach. The bay was designed with multiple safety features in case oxygen leaked, including complete remote control over the pressurization system.

There was no time to consider the repercussions. He would do what needed to be done.

"Carter!" Simon shouted hurriedly into his watch, turning away from the thick window.

"Yes, Director?"

"Depressurize oxygen storage bay one."

"Sir? To what level?"

Simon swallowed down what felt like ten shards of glass lodged in his throat.

"Zero."

When Carter next spoke, his voice was unsteady. "Seventy-nine detects life in the vicinity. I need your override."

Simon closed his eyes. A planetary director. There would be no coming back from this. Simon lifted his watch to his mouth.

"Seventy-nine, grant Engineer Carter director override."

Security code?

"Three six four—six three three—seven zero six."

Authorization granted.

The ground vibrated. Simon clenched his fists and waited, not daring to look through the window. He knew what would happen within the depressurized bay. The effects were burned into every station director's brain in the earliest days of training: Water in the body would turn to vapor. The person's body would rapidly expand, crushing internal organs, squeezing the heart, and applying crippling pressure to the lungs, which would likely rupture and bleed. Brutal depressurization sickness would follow as nitrogen bubbled inside bones and muscle. Lemley had prepared an oxygen mask and tank, but that would mean nothing when his internal organs smothered his lungs and filled them with blood.

Simon stared at his watch, counting the time. At twelve seconds, he heard the muffled sound of a gunshot.

He braced himself, waiting for disaster. It did not come.

After one minute, he reopened his connection to Carter.

"Resume pressurization."

"Will do," Carter replied.

Simon then addressed the station AI. "Seventy-nine, unlock oxygen bay one."

Oxygen bay one is locked down due to Planetary Director Lemley's orders.

"Override the director's orders. Reason: deceased."

Simon gave the AI a moment to confirm. He suspected the cameras in the bay would suffice.

Override confirmed. Oxygen bay one unlocked.

When the pressurization was complete, Simon stepped inside. Saw the body. Saw the director's wide-eyed, vacant stare, and the blood pooled around his mouth and underneath his head. Saw the brain matter from where he'd inserted his handgun into his mouth and pulled the trigger.

And then immediately fled the room to vomit.

An hour later, a bandaged and grumpy-looking Daksh greeted Simon on his way to the control room.

"Surprised Haley is letting you wander about," Daksh said, attempting and failing to smile.

"I've a cane, a cast, and a job to do," Simon said as he hobbled along. Daksh offered an arm, and Simon graciously accepted it as they walked.

"I'm so sorry," Daksh said, side-eyeing the cast on Simon's leg. "I failed in my duties, and it nearly killed us all."

"We both made plenty of mistakes, all of which involved trusting a planetary director to not be a homicidal lunatic." Simon grinned sideways despite the pain. Haley had injected his knee with a localized pain killer, but fiery spikes managed to escape from higher up near the thigh. "Don't beat yourself up over it. That massive bruise on your head is punishment enough."

"But still..." Daksh reached into his pocket. "It may be too late, but I searched Director Lemley's room and personal belongings. No note or explanation, but I did find this in one of his pockets."

He pulled out and offered Simon a thumb drive. Simon accepted the thin little bit of plastic in his free hand.

"Did you check its contents?" he asked.

"I thought that was best left for you," Daksh said. "Besides, it belonged to a planetary director. I can't imagine the security on that thing."

Simon could. He pocketed the thumb drive, reminding himself to give it to his tech specialist later. She might be able to crack the thing open and give a hint as to what would push Lemley to such extremes.

"Thank you," he told Daksh, and then gestured ahead. They'd reached the doors of the control room. "Please, come with me. This is something everyone needs to hear."

Simon stepped into the control room using his cane alone, determined to walk on his own power. Familiar faces peered back at him, each awash in the glow of their monitor. Shan saw him enter and immediately hurried over.

"We need a proper sitrep," his second-in-command said. "Everyone's running on theories, and it's getting out of hand."

Simon nodded as he approached the middle of the control room. All the various stations were curved and oriented toward that center point so he might address them simultaneously. His stomach spun loops, and it had nothing to do with the previous inconsistency of gravity. Public speaking was one of his strong points, and a large reason why he'd managed to nab his role so early. This news, though... he couldn't even guess how his crew would take it.

"Earlier tonight," he said, and cleared his throat. "Through undetermined means, Planetary Director Jakob Lemley triggered an explosion within his shuttle, damaging our station."

He paused to let that sink in. Worry, confusion, and anger spread across the tired faces of his subordinates, even though most had guessed that something extreme had happened, given how the shuttle bay was the only portion of the station currently blocked off with security walls.

A tall man with a receding hairline stood. Carter, his head of engineering. Simon nodded to acknowledge him.

"Can you tell us why?" Carter asked.

"Fear," Simon said, "of the Artifact, and what it means to humanity as a whole. I cannot answer more than that. I'm sorry."

More soft muttering. For a planetary director to attempt such a horrible crime, and take their own life doing so, was beyond the pale. None of it made sense, not unless the Artifact was a tremendously dangerous object. And if it was...

Simon crossed his arms, falling into thought. There was too much going on that he did not understand. They were operating in the dark. How would OPC brass react to news of Lemley's death? Would they prosecute him? Send a replacement director? Or finally follow through with their implied threats to take the Artifact out of his possession and bring it somewhere planet-side to be "properly" studied?

He had to stop this. He had to buy himself some time.

Simon looked up, and he slowly exhaled. There was one way, and he hoped the rest of his crew would understand.

"As of right now, I am initiating a dark quarantine protocol."

Gasps followed. Normal quarantine protocol meant a station or planet had encountered, or at least suspected, a threat considered dangerous to humanity at large. Initiating quarantine protocol meant no travel was allowed through the world gate, and all necessary supplies would be delivered via automated shuttles.

A dark quarantine, though, went much further. All outgoing communication would be severed, and incoming information heavily filtered. No messages. No letters. No calls.

They would go dark to the rest of the universe. Simon alone would be in charge of information sent to OPC, and that which reached his crew. Such rare measures were used when the very knowledge of what was transpiring on the far edges of space could be considered traumatic to society at large.

"Is such a drastic step required?" Shan asked.

Simon spun in place, meeting the eyes of all those subordinate to him.

"Our lives were threatened by one of the highest-ranking members of OPC," he said. "Until I know for certain that all danger has passed, this must be done."

That wasn't going to be enough; Simon could read that on their faces. They were frightened, but they were also professionals. They could reach their own conclusions as to why he was taking such a course. He had to win them over. He hardened his voice and crossed his arms behind his back.

"It's been a month since we discovered the Artifact," he said. "What it is, we still don't know. We don't know who made it. We don't know its purpose. But what I do know is that its discovery is about to change humanity's entire understanding of the stars, of civilizations, and of our history. This is *our* work. This is our discovery. We are at the bleeding edge, and I will let no one, no director, not even the OPC itself, steal it from us. Our blood and sweat shall not be spent in vain. The Artifact has awakened. We know that. It has made contact with my brother. Something is coming. Something amazing, transformative. And *we* shall shepherd that coming change."

He did not wait for their reaction before limping away from

the center. He didn't want to seem like he could be swayed. The course was set. Time to hold faith.

Before Simon exited the control room, he went to his tech specialist's console. Her name was Essa, a brilliant mind hidden behind a quiet, solemn personality.

"This belonged to the former planetary director," he said, handing over the thumb drive. "I want to know what's on it."

Essa took the drive and pushed it into a slot built into her monitor. Immediately, a warning flashed on her screen, and she frowned.

"Encrypted," she said, clicked a few buttons, and then grimaced. "Very encrypted. This will take time."

Simon lowered his voice so only she would hear.

"Find a way to crack it, and do it fast," he said. "Lemley tried to kill us all, and I need to know why."

Chapter 11
NICK

None of this is real, Nick told himself as he hung from two manacles bolted to the wall.

None of this is real, he insisted, as the baron approached holding a long, slender knife.

None of this is real, his mind pleaded, as the blade sank deep into the flesh of his abdomen.

"It's not real!" he screamed when it ripped, twisted, and tore.

Not real. Not the cut. Not the pain. Not the splash of blood that dripped down to the floor of the barren room, landing atop boards stained a deep, dark color.

"You may be a demon, but you bleed just like a human," Baron Hulh said, setting the knife down on a small table that was one of two furnishings in the tiny room, the other a little stool the baron sometimes sat on. This was a nothing space, bare walls, wood floors, no windows, and a lone door leading to torch-lit stairs. It bore a single purpose, one told in the stains on the floor. "Your stubbornness is impressive. Even applying all my lord Frey taught me, you cling to consciousness."

"Why?" Nick asked as the red bar representing his life flashed and pulsed. If he were to guess, only 2 percent of it remained, maybe 3.

"Why what?" the baron asked, pulling the stool closer to sit. "You mean this knife work? Because I have never met a demon in my lifetime, only heard the stories. Those stories, though, they're enough to give a man the shivers. Supposedly your kind are capable of rapidly healing from terrible injuries. Consider this an experiment. I would learn the truth of those stories."

"Maybe try asking instead of poisoning and torture," Nick said. Blood trickled down the sides of his face from where the baron had cut multiple gashes across his forehead. He blinked, trying to keep the sting from his eyes as drops weighted his eyelids. "I like to talk."

"You like to steal, too." The baron gestured to the hand mirror that rested on the small table. He'd taken it from Nick's pocket upon bringing him to his prison. "Is that why you're here? To scrounge for Sinifel artifacts?"

Nick's faint laugh was enough to trigger a coughing fit. His ribs ached. He suspected several were broken from the beatings delivered by the baron's bare fists.

Three ribs are broken, yes

So helpful, Cataloger, thought Nick, then grimaced to focus.

"I don't know anything about Sinifel!" he said with as much force as he could muster. "I don't know anything about *you*. I don't know where I am, or even why I'm here. And if you'd bothered to ask between beating and cutting me, I could have told you that."

Baron Hulh folded his hands in his lap, his thumbs twiddling.

"There is one truth to the stories, so far. Your kind is fearless in the face of torture and death."

"Yeah, that happens when you can't die."

A frightening look hardened the baron's face.

"Yes," he said. "I look forward to testing that, too."

The baron pushed up from his stool and made for the exit.

"There is a legend passed down by my family," he said, his back turned. "It claims God-King Vaan conquered time, not by his own power, but with knowledge granted to him by a demon. If that is true…"

He turned. His smile stretched from ear to ear.

"Then there is *so very much* your kind has to answer for."

The door slammed shut, blanketing Nick in darkness. He hung there, his body aching, his shoulders begging for a stretch instead of remaining locked in place with his hands manacled to the wall.

"Cataloger," he whispered. "Can you get me out of here?"

I cannot directly affect the material world

"Then what is the point of you?"

I am to welcome you and aid in your acclimation to this world

Nick cracked a madman's grin. Blood from his sliced forehead trickled across his lips and his teeth and swelled on his tongue.

"Oh, I feel welcomed, all right." He spat. "Why didn't you warn me about the wine!?"

I am not to interfere where my involvement would preferentially treat or benefit one individual over another

Nick's head hurt too much to parse that.

"Try again," he muttered.

If you were to play a game of cards, I could not inform you of your opponent's hand, because doing so would advantage you and disadvantage your opponent

"You're saying you kept quiet because you had to be *fair*?"

That simplification is inaccurate

"You let me drink poisoned wine because otherwise you'd give my backstabbing host a disadvantage? Disadvantage in what? The game of 'who can murder someone faster'?"

You exhibit rudimentary understanding of the concept

"Sorry, hard to keep things straight when I have more broken bones than health points."

Cataloger had nothing to offer there. He closed his eyes and tried to think matters through.

"Cataloger, can you send me home?"

For the health of the visitor, and to minimize mental and physical strain, extraction must be done at dedicated locations—what you see as rings of stones

"Unless I die."

Yes—then a death protocol unique to visitors is allowed to proceed

"Which means I need to hang here, suffering torture, for the benefit of *my health*?"

Yes

Nick thudded the back of his head against the wall.

"I hate this place so much."

LEVEL: UNKNOWN

That is unfortunate

Nick twisted and thrashed against the manacles holding him. His "health" be damned, he wanted out of here. When that didn't work, he let all his weight hang, willing to break his own hands to slip them through the manacles.

"Not real, not real, not real," was his mantra to give himself the strength to let the cold steel tear through his flesh and dislocate his bones if that was what it took. Yet no matter how many times he told himself that, it wasn't enough. The pain conquered him, and he relented.

"Not real," he whispered again, realizing how much of a lie that was on his tongue. This place, this world of Yensere, was far too real to his senses to now believe otherwise. It might be digital, but if not for Cataloger's occasional appearance, and the various graphics and text meant to aid his travels, he would never have guessed he was anywhere other than a "real" world, whatever that even meant anymore.

Fine, then, he thought. *It's real. Which means I'm trapped here, in a real place, about to suffer very real pain. And when real animals get their legs caught in a trap, they chew their real limbs off, so drop the excuses, Nick, and rip your damn hands free.*

Nick couldn't see the manacles around his wrists, but he could feel them. A single size for all prisoners, ones he suspected were older and larger than he was. He could do this. He didn't need much give. Leaning his weight from foot to foot, he started to hop while building up the courage, then jumped while tucking his knees to his stomach.

All his weight pulled down, with only the manacles on his wrists to hold him aloft.

No give, not that first time. He gasped at the pain coursing through his wrists, his neck, and his upper back. The strain felt like it might pull his shoulders from their sockets. Perhaps it even had. Nick breathed hard, in and out, working up the nerve.

"Again," he whispered.

Left foot, right foot, hop, hop, jump.

This time his left shoulder did dislocate. Nick hung there, his entire upper body shaking as he rotated, the horrid pain be damned. Turn his wrists. Grind the steel into his flesh. Blood itself could be a lubricant. Straighten the fingers. Curl in the thumb. Flatten the knuckles.

He slipped downward. Not much. Not even an inch. But it was something.

Left foot, right foot. Jump, this time while twisting.

Skin tore. His left thumb audibly popped, but the hand slid free. Nick positioned his feet back on the ground so he might stand, relaxing the pressure of his other manacle as he writhed. His left arm hung limp at his side. It had mostly lost feeling from the shoulder down. He feared what would happen when it returned.

"That's one," he whispered. He shifted the angle of his body the best he could and then leaped once more. The extra freedom meant he could apply all his weight directly onto that right arm. He had to bite his tongue to hold back the scream, but at last, it, too, tore free. He collapsed to his knees, both his hands cradled against his stomach. Blood flowed from them, though in the darkness, he could not tell from where.

"Cataloger, are my thumbs dislocated?" he asked.

LEVEL: UNKNOWN

Yes

"Will forcing them outward put them back into place?"

Yes

Nick grabbed his left thumb, his heart racing higher.

"Fuck me," he said, and then pulled.

When the pain subsided enough for him to think, he grabbed the other thumb, counted to three, and did the same. That done, he collapsed onto the floor, slick with his own blood, and gave himself a moment to recover.

You know there's several guards throughout, he thought, trying to analyze the situation he found himself in. *Possibly one right outside the door. And if you're found at any point, Logrif is going to come running, and you stand no chance against him.*

That meant a stealthy retreat was Nick's best, and only, option. Wait, that wasn't right. There was one final resort. He could find a weapon and take his own life.

"No," Nick whispered. "You'll die fighting, but you won't die like that. Yensere isn't worthy of it."

As Nick lay there, he heard the soft sound of footsteps. His eyes widened, and he spun about to lie on his stomach facing the door. Panic threatened to steal away his composure. Was someone coming to check on him? Or did that bastard baron decide he wanted to have more fun before going to bed?

More sounds outside. A sudden clatter of metal. Nick lifted into a crouch, his legs tensed and ready. Maybe if he was lucky, he could force his way past them and then sprint back up the steps to the ground floor.

The door burst open, light flooding in. Nick squinted, his arm up to guard against the glare. All impulse to flee left him, replaced by confusion. He recognized that short blond hair and that silver armor. Cataloger immediately showed him her stats, everything redacted as before except for her name: Frost.

"You... you're the ice person who killed me. Then saved me in the woods, I think."

Frost lowered her sword, and her blue eyes widened. He was shocked to see just how young she was. His age, perhaps slightly older. She'd seemed so much more regal and commanding when dooming him to death by pitchfork outside Meadowtint. A slain guard lay on the ground just behind her, blood pooling underneath him.

"Your hands," she said. "Did you escape on your own?"

"I had hopes to try." Memory of her trapping him with her ice spell added a twinge of bitterness to his tired voice. "What are you doing here? If it's to kill me, make it quick. I won't refuse a quick trip home."

The woman sheathed her sword and stepped to his side. Her hand gently touched his dislocated arm.

"We don't have much time," she said, ignoring his question. "But I think we have enough to fix this."

She took ahold of his wrist and elbow and set his arm flat by his side. He allowed her to guide him, for though he did not trust her completely, the dead guard outside his cell helped immensely in that regard.

"Brace yourself, and lean away from me," she said. "Also, this is going to hurt."

Before he could react, she pulled on his arm while rotating it upward to extend ninety degrees from his body. Nick's eyes bulged as pain shot through him, and he shouted with what little voice he could muster. His knees buckled, and Frost lowered him gently back to the ground.

"I'm pretty sure I got it," she said.

"Fantastic," Nick said, working to breathe in and out as he'd been taught.

Frost stood, glanced out the door, then moved to the little table. Nick's shirt lay atop it, stripped off him before the torture began. She lifted it and then knelt beside him.

"Here, I'll help you dress," she said as he sat up. Though it still hurt immensely to move, Nick shifted so she could pull it over his head and then stole another glance at her. She was undeniably pretty, her nose cute and small and her eyes so vibrant a blue they might as well be the same sapphires as those encrusted in the hilt of her sword. And then the shirt was over him, breaking his sight of her.

"I didn't do it to be cruel," she said as she gently helped him slide his hands through the sleeves.

"You sure? My arm begs to differ."

"Not your arm." Frost's expression softened. "When we first met. You looked so scared, so full of panic. You needed to learn the consequences of dying were not so dire, at least not for someone like you."

And how would you know that if you aren't also like me?

"And so you helped by killing me?" he said, keeping the other thought to himself.

"Nothing teaches like experience. I've kept an eye on you, watching you learn as I figured out what kind of person you are."

"And what is that?" he asked.

She flashed him a large smile. He hated how much he enjoyed seeing it.

"Tenacious. Now, get to your feet so we can leave this awful place."

Nick pushed to a stand, his left arm cradled against his body. His right he swung about in a few circles, testing its movement. At least it had escaped without too much misery, and feeling had slowly returned to his thumbs. Frost grabbed the short sword from the slain guard, flipped it, and offered him the handle.

"Here," she said. "You look ready to fall over, but at least you can try to defend yourself."

"Better than an old sickle," he said as he accepted the weapon. Cataloger immediately flashed its statistics above it.

Item: Short Sword
Quality: Tier 3 (Good)
Classification: Weapon
A one-handed bladed weapon, versatile and excellent as both a slashing and thrusting weapon, and as such, has been a staple of military use for centuries

When Frost exited, he did not follow immediately. Instead he hobbled to the little table on the opposite side of the cell, grabbed the hand mirror, and shoved it into his pocket. It felt warm against his side, and he couldn't shake a strange feeling of guilt.

That done, Nick followed Frost in the wake of her attempted rescue. He passed by bodies crushed with ice, not all of them soldiers. Servants, too, and to his shock, they held swords and daggers in their limp hands.

LEVEL: UNKNOWN

"They fought you?" Nick asked.

"They did," Frost said, not turning around.

The door to his right burst open, and a servant in a suit swung a heavy club straight for Nick's head. He ducked underneath, saved only by pure instinct. The thick piece of wood struck the wall, puncturing a painting of an enormous estate between two rivers, and he thrust with his sword in retaliation. The blade sank into the man's ribs, and he gasped as blood dribbled down his lips.

"Tully?" Nick said, recognizing the butler. The older man collapsed to his knees, the sword sliding out of him. "But why? Why die for that old bastard?"

He would receive no answer. All red was gone from Tully's health bar, all life gone from his eyes. Frost turned at the commotion, and seeing the butler, she shook her head.

"The baron commands their hearts to a frightening degree," she said. "I don't understand it, and I don't want to. Let's get out of here."

The butler's corpse hit the ground with a dull thud. Nick shuddered and forced the image out of his mind. Maybe none of this was real, but all of it was horrible. He needed to get out. Escape. Step into the light of two suns and be free.

In the entry hall, amid corpses and smashed furniture, stood Baron Hulh and his gargantuan bodyguard.

"To think, I was content with a lone demon to interrogate," he said. "It seems fate has gifted me a second."

"I'm sure your dead guards are equally excited," Frost said.

"The guards are replaceable. You are not." He gestured at Logrif. "Capture them."

Frost lifted her sword, a meager thing compared to Logrif's enormous club.

"Stay behind me," she said. "I can handle him."

"Are you sure?" Nick asked, glancing between them.

"Very," Frost said, uncaring that Logrif looked like he outweighed her thrice over and towered a good foot and a half above her head. Nick readied his sword and trusted her. There'd be no getting out of this on his own—that much was clear.

"Your armor is very pretty," Logrif said as he approached Frost like a hunting animal. His club lifted into the air. "I cannot wait to see it break."

Frost sidestepped the downward slam, her sword lashing out to strike from Logrif's staggering total of health despite initially hitting his breastplate. She did not follow it up, for despite his size, Logrif was deceptively fast. His club was already curling toward her after missing the first swing. She shifted away, anticipating the maneuver, and when the club swung for her waist, she dropped to her knees. The strike swished over her head, and as punishment, she thrust the tip of her sword into his abdomen. A large amount vanished from Logrif's health bar for what seemed like such a simple hit.

How powerful is that sword? Nick wondered.

Logrif shouted a deep mixture of pain, anger, and frustration. Instead of swinging his club, he shot his knee out, surprising her. It struck her in the stomach, and she doubled over, hitching for breath as the club rose. Nick panicked as Logrif's club lifted, and unable to dodge, Frost placed her silver blade in the way.

The two connected, all of Logrif's immense strength pushing into it. Despite the quiver in her legs, despite the shake of her arms, Frost held firm. Nick's eyes bulged.

How powerful is she?

Frost shoved the club aside, slashed at Logrif twice more, and then retreated while twirling. Ice built about her hands, and then she cast a familiar spell, which Cataloger finally put a name to.

Spell: Frost Nova

Thick chunks of ice lashed about Logrif's feet and ankles, spiderwebs of cracks settling over the blue surface. Logrif howled, and a single smack of his club shattered the pieces to free him.

With frightening speed, he closed the space between him and Frost, catching her off guard. His club smashed into her side, and her armor must have been strong, for she endured a blow that Nick felt confident would have killed him in a single hit. In retaliation, she cast another spell, her arm rising toward his head.

Spell: Ice Shards

At such close range, Logrif could not hope to dodge. The shards tore into him, little jagged pieces like broken glass slicing into his skin. Logrif howled, instinctively retreating and lifting his own arm to protect his face from the cuts opening red lines along his face and forehead. Frost cast again with no hesitation.

Spell: Ice Lance

The lance was frighteningly sharp as it flew from her extended palm, and it struck Logrif square in the chest, hurting him even through his armor. He gasped, but the pain seemed to only ignite his rage. He swung his club when a second <ice lance> flew his way, smashing it in a gigantic burst of frost. A leap, and he closed the space between them. His elbow struck Frost in the nose, splattering her mouth and nostrils with blood. A head butt followed, and she staggered, dazed and unsteady on her feet. Cataloger seemed reluctant to show Nick her accurate health tally, but he could see the graphical representation of her health bar, and he did not like the way it dipped below two-thirds.

Logrif lifted his club to swing, and in response, Frost raised her left hand. A translucent shield appeared, held firm in her grasp.

Spell: Shield of Ice

One blow from the club shattered it, the weapon traveling farther to strike Frost across the shoulder. Logrif put all his strength into maintaining the movement, so the follow-through lifted Frost into the air and flung her across the hall. She landed in a clatter of silver armor on the other side.

Logrif stalked her, murder in his eyes. Nick sprinted across the hall, throwing himself into Logrif's path. His swing missed; more humiliating was how easily the guard dug his elbow into Nick's stomach and flung him aside. Nick tumbled along the floor, which was slick with blood and half-coated with the ice of Frost's spells. To his relief, whatever bruises he suffered were not considered serious, at least not by whatever metrics guided Yensere.

Still clinging to his pitiful amount of health, he pushed back to his feet and lifted his sword in his lone good arm.

LEVEL: UNKNOWN

"That it?" he asked. "I'm barely even bruised."

The guard was hardly impressed.

"What hope have you?" Logrif asked as he lumbered closer. Blood coated his body from the many slashes inflicted upon him, and worse was the soaked spot in his armor where Frost's shards had punctured his chest. His steps were uneven, and his health only a third of his original. That third was more than enough to keep him in the fight, though. "You are a mouse before a lion."

"Ever corner a mouse?" Nick asked, tightening the grip on his sword. He would have only one shot at this. "They're fast, and they bite."

He did not wait for Logrif to swing. Instead he shot straight for him, crossing the space in three quick strides. He did not swing his sword. Instead he dropped, shifting so his weight landed on one side. His hip struck the floor, and coated with both ice and blood as it was, Nick slid without losing a shred of his momentum. He passed straight between Logrif's legs, and upon emerging behind him, he twisted his body, ignoring the shrieking pain of his shoulder and the ache of his thumbs as he lay on his stomach.

He only had the chance for one slash, and he made it count. His sword sliced across the tendons of both heels. Below Logrif's health, he saw a faint new word written in white: *hobbled*.

"You shit!" Logrif shouted as he collapsed to his knees. He did not try to stand. Instead he rotated his body so he might face Nick. His every muscle flexed as he extended his club, adding reach, adding power for the swing. Nick braced for the impact, a macabre grin on his face.

Guess I'm finally going home, he thought.

A jagged shard of ice smashed into Logrif's wrist and forearm. The big man screamed again, his club slipping from his grasp. Both turned to see a limping Frost approach. Unnatural blue light shone from her eyes. Swirling white frost enveloped her left hand.

"You're a brute," she said, slamming her sword straight into his throat. "And all of Yensere will be better with you gone."

Blood spurted across her brilliant armor from the thrust, easily claiming the last of the giant man's health. Logrif gargled something unintelligible, his bleeding hands scraping at the embedded blade despite the damage it did to his fingers. The life left his eyes, and he dropped. The moment he hit the ground, Nick felt a surge of energy swell within him.

Reassessment
Level: 5 (+1)
Statistical Improvements:
Agility: 3 (+1)
Physicality: 4
Endurance: 3 (+1)

Nick pushed to his feet, his sword heavy in his hand, but not as heavy as it had been mere moments before. The rush of the leveling and his steadily rising health made him feel worlds better. He looked to the side, to where Baron Hulh stood by the door of his home, his eyes wide with shock.

"Demons," he whispered, realizing his final bodyguard was slain and the pair had turned their attention his way. "You two truly are demons."

He tried to flee. A wave of Frost's hand, and **<frost nova>**

LEVEL: UNKNOWN

held him firm. He had no club to wield, and nowhere near Logrif's strength to break free. He twisted and shouted in his panic.

"He tortured you, didn't he?" Frost said to Nick, her narrowed eyes never leaving the trapped baron.

"Yes," Nick said, "he did."

Frost flung more shards of ice, these aimed at the baron's sword arm as it flailed about. They punched into his flesh, stripping away three-quarters of his meager health. The sword went flying from his grasp and landed beyond his reach.

"Then he's yours to kill," she said.

Nick approached the frightened baron, a sick, warm feeling tightening in his stomach. The mirror in his pocket seemed to burn like fire against his thigh.

"Wait," the baron said, his eyes wide and bloodshot. "We...we can talk— This isn't— I—I didn't—"

Nick shoved his sword straight into the man's open mouth. A part of him knew he should be horrified by the gore that followed, the tearing of the baron's jaw, the slicing of his tongue. Instead he saw only a red bar drop to zero, and then the baron collapsed to the ground, his body still.

Nick's white bar appeared only briefly, crawled a little toward another evaluation, and then faded.

"Good riddance," Nick whispered.

Frost's hand settled on his shoulder. Her touch was gentle.

"Go outside and breathe the fresh air," she said. "You don't need to be in here anymore. I'll get us some food and supplies for our travels while you wait."

Nick glared at the corpse.

"He deserved it," he said, unsure whom he was trying to convince.

Frost gestured to the grand doors of the manse, whose lock was broken and hinges busted from her arrival.

"No one in this false world deserves anything but the fates we give them. Learn that, and you'll find this all so much easier to endure."

Chapter 12
NICK

They followed the road toward Greenborough the rest of the day. Their travel was silent, Nick content to limp along amid his thoughts. The gentle movements made his body ache, but that was preferential to hanging from a wall by manacles. When the yellow sun began its descent, they veered off into the woods to make camp.

Once Frost had built a fire, she sat before it, cross-legged and thoughtful with her elbows resting on her knees. No answers seemed forthcoming from her unprompted, so he paced before her, emulating his older brother the best he could. Simon could tear apart any stubborn researcher with his subtle, incisive questioning. Nick, well...

"You're a visitor," he said, relying on the blunt approach. "Or a demon, as the people here seem to call us. But either way, you're like me, aren't you?"

Frost's head casually rested in the palms of her hands. She seemed greatly amused by his sudden excitement at her visitor status.

"Somewhat. Unlike you, I've been at this for a while and know what I'm doing."

"Funny. Very funny." He shook his head, trying to organize his thoughts. "That means..."

What *did* that mean? Not once when entering Yensere via the Artifact had he considered that there would be another *actual* person here. And whoever she was, she was most certainly not on Station 79. He'd have seen her during his year there, and he most certainly would have remembered someone so pretty, and with blue eyes so vibrant they seemed to...

Focus, Nick, he thought, and then realized he was staring at her. He blushed and turned away.

"If you're a visitor, that means you come to Yensere from somewhere else," he said, using the argument to disguise his embarrassment. "Where?"

Frost's amusement melted into something harder, more cautious.

"I'm sorry, Nick, but I can't tell you that."

"Why not? Because it's forbidden?"

"Because I don't trust you. Because it isn't *safe*."

"Not safe?" he asked, momentarily reeling. "Not safe from what?"

Those blue eyes of hers bored into him, and he squirmed against their focus.

"I won't say. If you don't know, then perhaps that's for the best. But this isn't something I can risk, Nick. Not with what's at stake. You'd understand if you knew, I promise."

Simon would most certainly press for more, but Nick felt

LEVEL: UNKNOWN

Frost was already at her limit. Anything focused on her home, wherever or whatever that might be, was off-limits. But surely there was more he could learn from her.

"Well, can you answer me this? The Artifact. You found one, too, right? It's how you're coming here?"

Frost hesitated.

"Yes," she finally said.

All right, he was getting somewhere. What else could he ask that she'd be comfortable answering? If only his head didn't ache like a war were being fought between his ears. Even walking spiked pain throughout his limbs. He willed himself to think, to ask something clever.

"Is it...evil?" he asked, then quickly corrected himself, feeling almost childish for phrasing the question in such a way. "The Artifact. Its purpose, its function—is it dangerous?"

Another long, silent stare.

"The answer I give is mine alone, and many would not agree," she said at last. "But that Artifact you found? You should throw it into your sun. Its mercies are poison. Its gifts are barbed. I *hate* it, Nick, more than I hate anything else in my whole life."

"And yet you still use it," he said. Not an accusation, just legitimate confusion.

"I need it to find my sister. She's here, too...somewhere."

Nick could hardly believe what he was hearing. If Frost was truly from another world, using an Artifact akin to the one they'd found on Majus, then the ramifications of what the octahedrons were, who she was, *what* she was...

"You're an alien," he blurted out, his lips acting too fast for his brain to realize the statement's stupidity and stop him.

"An alien?" She stood, her face dead serious. His stomach squirmed and his heart thudded against the interior of his ribs. His limbs locked in place. She stepped closer, so close, their foreheads nearly touched. Her eyes held him prisoner.

"Do I *look* like an alien?"

And then she laughed. The tension broke, and he laughed along with her despite not being sure if he was the butt of the joke.

"Nick, there's a lot out here you don't yet know, and if that's how you're going to react to me being a visitor, I think it's safe to say we need to baby-step you along. I'll teach you the best I can, but some things I'm going to keep to myself, either for your safety or mine."

That seemed fair enough. Already his mind was racing, trying to chase down all the possibilities and how his brother might react to them. Simon would have a million questions, and a million more theories about aliens, unknown planets, language translation, and additional Artifacts. Against that barrage, Nick would have so very little to offer. He couldn't even rule out the possibility that Frost was just a simulation, one meant to help him adjust to the world of Yensere just like Cataloger. She could be a convincing illusion, like his father in the mirror.

Nick flinched thinking of it, and his mood darkened. He patted the mirror in his pocket, closed his eyes, and did his best to pretend it wasn't there. He still wasn't sure why he'd turned back for it.

"All right," he said, opening his eyes again and grinning at Frost as if all were well. "But what about your name? Your real name. You weren't born with the name 'Frost' and then later

LEVEL: UNKNOWN

developed the ability to wield ice magic. I refuse to believe in such a ridiculous coincidence."

Frost laughed, and he relished the sudden break in tension.

"Fine, you're right, Frost is not my real name."

"So what is it?"

She kicked dirt onto the fire. Smoke spread, and as darkness fell, she cast him the faintest, most flirtatious smile.

"I'll tell you what," she said. "When I give you my name, that's when you'll know I trust you, fully, one hundred percent. Until then, you'll have to just accept my help while we work together."

Nick clapped his hands together.

"You have a deal." He glanced about the dark. He'd spent so long in Yensere, he felt nervous about exiting. But surely he needed to eat, right? Perhaps use the bathroom, if he hadn't already made a mess of his bed? "So how do I get out of here? Here as in Yensere, not this forest."

Frost arched an eyebrow. "You mean you haven't left on your own before?"

"Not without dying."

She let out a whistle.

"Impressive. Truly impressive. Have you considered asking Cataloger?"

The fact that Frost knew about Cataloger jolted him with excitement.

"No," he said. "Can't say I've had the chance, given the whole constant-dying thing."

Ring of Stones: archways allowing visitors to both arrive and depart Yensere—their locations are plentiful

enough to be convenient while also scattered and hidden so as to not introduce shock or confusion to those living nearby

Nick sighed, earning another smirk from Frost.

"She just explained herself without your asking, didn't she?" His look was answer enough. "Consider Cataloger a blessing, even if she is a bit hard to understand at first. And she'll point out the nearest ring of stones if you kindly ask. Step into one, and she'll handle the rest. You'll wake up in your nice warm bed... or wherever it is you're asleep."

As much as Frost wanted to keep information close to her chest, it was good to hear so many details of her experience matching his own.

"All right, I'll see you here tomorrow, I guess?" he said as a glimmering, semitranslucent arrow appeared in his vision, directing him toward a yet-unseen ring of stones.

"I'll be waiting," Frost said.

Part of him wanted to stay. What if she didn't keep her word and abandoned him? He had a thousand questions he still desperately wanted answered. His hesitation lasted but a moment before he followed the arrow into the woods. She'd saved his life, and she'd admitted herself a visitor like him. That had to be worth at least a bit of trust.

The underbrush thinned, the noisome crickets and croaking frogs ceasing when he reached a nearly imperceptible clearing in the woods. Within was a ring of stones, each one overgrown with roots and moss. Nick paused at their edge. The weight of the day pressed down on him, and his aching head was far too painful to properly address it all. Aliens.

LEVEL: UNKNOWN

Frost. Baron Hulh's torture. Multiple Artifacts. Possibly even multiple worlds.

He reached his hand into his pocket, felt the cold, smooth glass of the mirror.

Eyes closed, Nick stepped into the stones. Instead of touching soft, exposed earth, his foot slipped right on through, and suddenly he was falling. The world vanished around him, turning dark, swallowing him. The pitch black was split by the occasional strikes of white, like silent lightning.

Departure requested and approved
Visit terminated

Chapter 13
SIMON

Simon tried to keep his anxieties under control as he stared at the heart monitor. Nick was soaked in sweat, his skin pale except for the glaring red marks left by the Velcro straps that had held his body down. Nick's breathing had become irregular enough that Simon had finally ordered his little brother hooked up to an oxygen tube. He hoped Nick's deteriorating health did not worsen more than that. Given the dark quarantine, there would be no help coming from afar.

"It's getting better," he told himself as he leaned back in the padded chair that was rapidly becoming his second bed. Over the past few hours, Nick's heart had pounded at 160 to 180 beats per minute, as if he were locked in a constant, heavy jog. Every other test indicated high levels of stress. But in the last twenty minutes or so his heart rate had fallen to 140, and then 120. Simon dared hope that, whatever the reason for his struggles, his brother had overcome it.

That hope appeared to come true when Nick lurched up to

a sit. His eyes widened, and his mouth opened and closed in a vague similarity to a fish tossed upon land.

"Hold up, I have you," Simon said, reaching over to pull the thin oxygen tube out of Nick's nostrils. "There we go. Sorry."

Nick rubbed his nose and blinked.

"You put me on oxygen?" he asked, glancing sideways at the little machine that had joined the litany of other medical devices piled atop his bedside table.

"Just a precaution, nothing more." Simon smiled to hide the lie. "It seemed like you were having a rough go of things in there."

Nick grimaced and plopped back down onto his pillow. "You could say that. I was...captured."

Simon hated the sound of that. "Captured? By who? And why?"

His brother refused to answer. Instead he put a hand over his eyes and slowly breathed in and out with a lengthy, consistent pause between inhalation and exhalation. Simon recognized the technique. He'd been the one to teach Nick how to deal with minor panic attacks.

"It's not all bad, though," Nick said after composing himself. He dropped his arm and smiled. "I think I might have made a friend."

"A friend..." Simon laughed. "You finally met someone who doesn't want to kill you? What's different about him?"

"Her, actually. And I..." He blinked and shook his head. "I don't think I know enough yet. Not to endure the thousands of questions you're going to want to throw at me."

Simon sat back down in his chair, shifting in a futile attempt to get comfortable. The padding, while never the thickest or most comfortable, had thinned considerably over the past two days. He was not only sleeping in it but working, too. His laptop lay closed on the floor nearby, for a station director's responsibilities never relented, and with the dark quarantine enacted, those responsibilities had doubled.

"Whenever you're ready, you tell me what you're learning," he said, deciding he wouldn't push him. It wasn't like Simon wasn't keeping secrets, either. He had no intention of telling Nick about Lemley's sabotage attempt, nor the dark quarantine. No reason to add burdens to already burdened shoulders, not if he could avoid it. "My colleagues may be impatient, but I'm willing to work on your schedule, because unlike them, I'm not blind to the strain it's putting on you. These deaths, simulated or otherwise, are harming your body in ways we don't yet understand. Enduring it can't be easy."

"Easy." Nick chuckled. "Frost sure makes it seem easy."

"Frost?"

Nick shook his head, again refusing to answer. Simon hated to have information kept from him, but it seemed like that was the way it would have to be. Silence followed, heavy but not uncomfortable. Simon studied Nick, an expert at interpreting his brother's various tics and quirks. That expertise was hardly necessary, though, to tell there was something weighing heavily upon him, something he wished to discuss but could not bring himself to broach on his own.

"Remember, I'm always here to listen," Simon said, volunteering that opening. Nick smiled, briefly and in passing. He shifted in his bed, and Simon followed his younger brother's gaze to the framed photograph of their parents that was propped up on his bedside table, halfway covering the oxygen monitor. Both looked happy and likely intoxicated at a celebration for their mother's appointment as lead scientist for the terraformed planet of Ventio. Their mother's black hair was loosened from its normal bun to fall long past her shoulders, whereas their father, normally proper and trimmed to perfection, looked ridiculous with a yellow-and-red party hat at an angle atop his mussed hair.

"What do you think his final words were?" Nick asked.

Simon leaned back in his chair, and he had to suppress a frown. Their father had been director of Research Station 68. After their mother passed away, Nick had visited the station often so he wasn't completely abandoned to the rotating cast of caretakers back home on the planet Taneth. It was during one such visit that tragedy had struck Station 68.

While the research their father performed had remained classified, the cause of his death was not. The worst of all possible fates occurred: a reactor failure. Their father, as director, remained aboard, holding to protocol that he be the last to leave the station, and to use that time to do everything in his power to prevent disaster.

Nick, only sixteen years old, had been loaded into a life pod as alarms blared and researchers panicked. It was a tale Simon had heard multiple times, and always with the same ending—a frightened Nick had watched the metal doors seal over the entrance of the pod. As they closed, their father had spoken amid a cacophony of screams, alarms, and the pressurization of the life pod.

Words unheard.

Final words.

The reactor went critical, the ensuing explosion vaporizing two-thirds of Station 68 and scattering the remaining debris thousands of miles an hour in all directions.

"I know it still bothers you, but you have to let it go," Simon said. He grabbed his brother's shoulder and squeezed. "Our father was a good man. He was smart; he was kind. You want to know what his final words were? I bet they were telling you he loved you. That he'd miss you. Or maybe that you'd need to look after me, because we both know I'd need the help."

Nick's gaze lingered on the photo.

"If you could speak with him again, what would you say?" he asked. "What would you tell him?"

Simon pushed up from his chair.

"I'd tell him to come join me for a late-night snack," he said. "Which is what I'm demanding of you. Enough melancholy. You've been adventuring in a strange world, and I want to hear stories."

"You're making it sound more fun than it is," Nick said as he sat up. He noticed the IV stuck into his left arm and frowned. "Not sure I can join you in the cafeteria wearing this thing."

A quick twist, and Simon disconnected it, then hit a button to shut off the protest of the heart monitor when he removed that next. Finally free, Nick scooted off the bed and landed unevenly on his feet. Simon pretended not to notice how much thinner his brother looked, and how dark the circles were around his eyes.

LEVEL: UNKNOWN

"Come on," Simon said. "I'd give you a hand, but, well…" He gestured with his cane at the thick brace around his knee. "I think we're both a little banged up."

"What happened to your knee?" Nick asked with a frown.

"It's nothing, an accident near the oxygen tanks," he said, as close to the truth as he dared. "Don't worry about me. Tonight is about you. While everyone sleeps, we'll use my directorial privileges to raid our monthly confectionery allotments. Chocolate? Sour chews? Say the word, Nick, and they're all yours."

"I don't want candy," Nick said as they exited through the door to his room.

"What do you want?"

"I… I think I want a steak."

Simon laughed, and the humor allowed him to pretend all was well with his slowly sickening brother as he limped along the corridor.

"Believe it or not, I think I have exactly two on ice, a perk of being director. I'm not an expert on the grill, but that's why the universe invented steak sauce."

Chapter 14
GARETH

Gareth walked the road to Baron Hulh's manse, his horse, Ladybell, remaining back in Meadowtint. The blight had claimed her, leaving her suddenly sickly and strange. If she heard his commands, she ignored them, rendering her useless as a mount.

Gareth had spent two days protecting Meadowtint, watching and waiting for the demon to cross the creek and assault the village. To Gareth's frustration, he never did. The blasted monster had slipped into the Aurora Woodlands, not to return. Where the demon went next would be anyone's guess, which meant the nearby villages needed to be warned, and his failure reported to Baron Hulh.

"The people suffer greatly in Vestor," he muttered as he approached the surrounding iron fence. "Must you add to their troubles, demon Nick?"

When he reached the gate, Gareth froze. The latch was broken, and several bars were dented inward from a great impact. His stomach clenched.

LEVEL: UNKNOWN

Did you come here? he wondered. But even if Nick had, there shouldn't have been any threat to the baron. Each of his house guards would be enough to protect him, and then there was his bodyguard, Logrif. The paltry demon had no chance to win a battle against him...then again, while Logrif would easily win a fair battle, the demon was a trickster and had shown himself capable of learning at a frightening pace. Gareth pushed the gate open, and his calm walk became a jog until he reached the manse.

The door was broken inward, from some sort of impact. It hung awkwardly from the upper hinges, the lower ones torn from the wood entirely. A body lay in a dried pool of blood within the entryway. Flies buzzed about it.

"Damn it," Gareth muttered, reaching into his satchel to pull out a spare shirt and holding it to his nose. The body was bloated from exposure, the smell rancid. Gareth feared it would not be the only one he found. He was immediately proven right once entering, a second servant lying slumped against the wall. A hole was torn open in his chest, leaving a vacant cavity between his mangled ribs. The innards had spilled onto his lap—that which wasn't smeared across the wall.

A tremendous impact, but leaving no trace of the source, like stone or metal would, he thought. *No burns, either. Not fire. Not lightning. Water, then, or ice.*

He stepped over the corpse, past the entryway, and into the main hall. Immediately, his heart sank. A corpse lay awkwardly on his back, legs bent at the knee and tucked underneath. The clothes were how Gareth first identified him as the slain baron. His face was horrifically mutilated, his jaw broken and hanging from only one hinge. The tongue was half-severed and hung like a rotting sausage out the side where the cheek and lips had been torn.

"You murdered him," he whispered. His hands clenched into fists. "Invaded his home and murdered him. Why? What sick pleasure do you find in this destruction?"

He stood, the pit in his stomach hardening. He had to check for survivors, even if he knew there would be none. The entry hall was wrecked, and past an overturned table he found another corpse, this of the bodyguard, Logrif. His body sported multiple wounds, including a deep gash in his chest. None were worse than the hole opened in his throat.

"Even you," Gareth said, shaking his head. Logrif had been one of the strongest warriors he had ever met, a man who could have become a knight in service of the god-king if he had so desired. Instead he'd cut his teeth slaughtering bandits in the west, scoring a recorded dozen kills before he'd even turned eighteen. Studying the wounds, Gareth again decided steel was not responsible for many of them. Ice; it had to be ice.

You never showed any affinity for magic, Gareth thought. *Have you learned, Nick, or did you have help?*

Both options were terrible, and he could not decide which was worse. He walked the rest of the manse in a daze, his mind hardening against the horrors. He found more dead guards, two in the dining hall and another at a prison cell. Gareth gathered them in a pile outside, carrying the corpses and pretending to be indifferent to the smell and rot. Logrif and the baron joined the pile, as did two more servants he found. Eight bodies. Eight lives lost to the meaningless rage of a demon.

Gareth bathed the corpses in wine from the cellar, and when night fell, he lit the pile with a torch. There were too many bodies for him to bury. A pyre would have to suffice.

Nervousness overcame Gareth as he watched the corpses burn. Either the demon had gained access to magic or he now had an accomplice. The threat was multiplying, and he had failed to properly contain it. Looking up to the black sun forming a hole in the night sky, he swallowed down his fears.

"So be it," he muttered, and fell to his knees.

It was a prayer meant to be used most sparingly. Its only required component was a flame, and what source could be more appropriate than the corpses demon Nick had left behind? Bowing his head, Gareth laid his hands flat on the grass before him, and in the courtyard of the now empty manse, he called out for his god-king.

"My master, my champion, my liege, my king, my god," he prayed as the heat of the pyre washed over him. "I beseech you, hear my cry, and look upon a servant most humble and desperate."

With held breath, he waited for an answer. There was no guarantee of one. The god-king bore a thousand duties in Castle Goltara, least of which was maintaining his imprisonment of the black sun. The cowardice in Gareth hoped he would receive no answer, but that cowardice was denied. The flame of the pyre swirled together, burning higher as it charred the corpses to ash and bone. Gareth's hairs stood on end, and it felt like the shine of the stars dimmed beneath a new light blossoming within the fire. A golden light, one most holy.

And then the fire hardened, taking shape, becoming the form of God-King Vaan to tower above Gareth, thrice his height. Additional colors seeped in amid the yellow and orange, hardening into golden skin, gold-filigreed armor, long red hair, and a face so handsome it defied all attempts to properly convey it in painting or statue. Vaan held an enormous sword in his hand, True Faith, the blade that had severed the head of the Sinifel Empire.

The fire spoke.

"Speak, knight, and explain why you beg for my attention."

Gareth lowered himself closer to the grass, not even daring to look upon the visage of his god-king.

"A demon has appeared in the west," he said. "I have slain him many times, but he always returns, and now he has slipped my grasp and ventures deeper into Vestor. Worse, I fear he is growing stronger, and even possesses allies."

"A demon?" The fire crackled. "Look upon me, Sir Gareth."

He obeyed. Fear held a savage grip on him, but he met those golden eyes and refused to cower.

"Yes, my lord?"

"Suffer not this demon to live," Vaan ordered. "I shall send one of my Harbingers to aid you, but it will take time for them to arrive from Goltara. Until then, stand tall in the face of this threat. Slaughter the demon, and all who would aid him. This is your trial, Sir Gareth, one you must conquer."

LEVEL: UNKNOWN

The fire quivered, the image starting to break apart.

"Do not fail me, knight."

And then the prayer ended. The flames flickered away so that only ash and bone remained. The night was deep, the stars bright. Beneath their light, Gareth wept for the lives lost to his weakness. He pleaded for forgiveness for his failures. He begged for the strength to overcome his terrible foe. There would be no sleep for him, only gratitude for the acknowledgment and whispered devotions to embolden his resolve. He did not sleep, nor leave the light of the stars.

Come morning, Gareth resumed his hunt for the demon.

Chapter 15
NICK

"All right, are you ready for your first real day of training?" Frost asked. Her slender sword twirled in her right hand.

"Not in the slightest," Nick said, holding his stolen sword loose at his side. "You won't actually hurt me while we practice, right?"

Frost winked. "No promises."

"Uhhh..." He gestured to the trees around them. "Maybe we should use sticks instead?"

"You don't trust me not to hurt you?"

"Will you hurt me if I say no?"

She tilted her head slightly to one side.

"It feels like you're trying to verbally trap me instead of hitting me with that sword of yours."

Nick swung his sword, thinking surprise might give him a bit of an advantage. She stepped into it, her slender sword angling so the centers of the blades collided.

"Why would I do that?" he asked as he pushed against her.

LEVEL: UNKNOWN

Their weapons rattled as she leaned closer to him, a bit of her hair falling across her face.

"Maybe because you're better with your tongue than your hands?"

Nick's entire mind went blank long enough for Frost to pull away, smack his sword aside, and then hover the tip of hers an inch from his chest.

"So easily distracted," she chastised.

Nick lifted his sword, the heat in his neck enough to confirm that he was blushing a deep red without the need to glance in a mirror.

For the first hours of the morning, she showed him a series of stances and then they sparred to practice them. None seemed too complicated, barring a few quibbles about the positioning of his feet, and he picked most of them up with ease. Frost was a great teacher, and Nick couldn't help but wonder if she had military training herself or if she was just naturally gifted in swordplay.

"This is how I was taught," she explained at one point. "There are positions of your body where your footing is firm and your limbs are at their strongest. You're going to shift and dance between those stances, one to the next. The sword won't guide you. Your body guides the sword."

Nick charged at her again, guiding his sword toward her breastplate, Frost blocking the strike with ease. His sword bounced off her blade, but he tried to ignore it as he'd been taught. Shift his movements. Plant his feet, move his arms, and transition the sword into a slash from the side. Try as he might, he felt so slow as his blade arced around to slam into

Frost's sword. It was as if she knew what he was planning long before he did it.

"You're doing good," she said as she pushed away his sword. "Keep it up."

I can confirm your skill in swordplay has numerically increased

"I feel like I'm doing terrible, but thanks for the encouragement, both of you," he said, and grinned. When she grinned back, it lit a bit of a fire beneath his feet, and he dashed toward her, lunging with a high overhead swing. Their weapons collided, and though Nick's looked much sturdier than her more slender weapon, his bounced off, the metal rattling while hers remained firm. As punishment for such a brazen tactic, Frost danced forward, her elbow striking his stomach while one of her legs curled behind his. A push, and he fell amid the leaves of the forest floor.

"I yield," he said, lying there. "This amateur fighter needs a breather."

Frost sheathed her sword and sat beside him. "As you wish."

It was strange, being able to see his exhaustion clarified so cleanly in a little green bar, but at the same time, it made it easy to know when he needed to take a break. After a moment of resting with his eyes closed, and seeing the first tick upward of that green bar, he pushed to a sit and brushed an errant leaf from his hair.

"It's the strangest thing, fighting you," he said. "My sword looks bulkier, but I swear yours is heavier."

"That's because mine is magical," Frost said. She drew it from her sword belt and laid it flat across her lap, giving Nick a chance to look it over. Its handle was wrapped leather dyed a deep blue. A matching sapphire was set into the base of the hilt, and two more on the underside of the cross guard. The blade itself was slender, gently curved, and frighteningly sharp on one side. Writing was carved along the flat edge, the words nonsensical to Nick's eyes.

"Magical," he said, feeling a twinge of jealousy. "How so?"

Item: Sapphire Longsword
Quality: Tier 7 (Masterwork)
Classification: Weapon
A weapon of exceptional craftsmanship, whose sharp edge and magical enhancement allow it to withstand blows that would normally break a sword so slender

"That...that sword is incredible," he said as he mentally dismissed the information. No wonder it sliced through the air so easily. Compared to that, his weapon was a clumsy chunk of metal. "How do I get a sword like that?"

"I earned mine," she said with pride. "Maybe one day you'll earn one of your own."

Nick could only wish.

"Come on," she said, standing. "Don't get hung up on my sword's capabilities. The difference in a fight between us is never going to be decided by that, but instead our relative skill and experience in battle."

"Of which you have far more," Nick argued.

"For now," Frost said, as she lunged at him again.

———•———

After several hours, Nick lay on his back, thoroughly exhausted. For some ridiculous reason, he'd tried to spin after parrying, a maneuver he thought would look cool. Instead, it only landed him on his ass when Frost rammed him with her shoulder mid-spin.

"I am, without a doubt, the worst sword fighter," he said.

Frost stood beside him, and her boot thudded into his rib cage.

"New rule. No insulting yourself." She offered him her hand. "You're not terrible, and not an idiot. You're just learning, so stop beating yourself up. I've had a lot of practice, and if Cataloger's rating is to be believed, my skill with a sword is pretty damn good."

"Cataloger mentioned my skill in swordplay, too," Nick said, trying to swallow his bruised pride as he stood. "What did she mean by that?"

Frost gave him a momentarily confused look.

"Oh... you haven't seen your *list* yet." She grinned at him. "Well then, prepare to feel very small and strange." She lifted her voice. "Cataloger, please show Nick his full evaluation."

"My what?"

A massive spreadsheet suddenly blocked off half of Nick's vision. Skills upon skills flooded his eyesight, all with an assigned number. Accounting, acting, appraisal, balance, bartering, brawling, climbing, cooking, cosmetics, disguise, first aid, intimidation, investigation, jumping, perception (auditory), perception (visual), swimming... it seemed to go on forever. Every tiny part of him, cataloged and analyzed with what he assumed were relevant ratings. Nick blinked at the incredible amount of data, trying to parse it for any meaning. His immediate reaction was mostly to be offended.

LEVEL: UNKNOWN

"Cooking at two?" he asked. "I've never cooked anything in Yensere. How can you know my cooking skill?"

Assumptions are based on a combination of your personality and revealed skill set—with both predicting a lack of interest and time spent dedicated to food preparation

"I can't decide if I should be insulted or not," he grumbled.

These skills shall be updated over time given relevant data and should not be viewed as inflexible—nor should offense be taken, as individual characteristics were compared to comprehensive data sets without judgment or bias

"Finding that hard to believe," Nick said, and shook his head. He once more scanned the list until he found what he was looking for.

"It says I'm only a five at swordplay," he told Frost. "I'm going to guess yours is higher?"

"That's a safe guess."

Nick scrolled down the list with his eyes, then gave up, overwhelmed by the data. The list shot back to the top and momentarily displayed his initial stats. He noted one listing, something he'd heard the very first time he'd entered Yensere. Everything had been so strange and new, he'd not been able to give it much thought.

Special Classification: None

"What's a 'special classification'?"

Unique attributes with associated benefits and capabilities that are possessed by rare individuals

Frost patiently waited, a smirk on her face.

"I suspect Cataloger's answer was both informative and unhelpful?" she asked. When he nodded, she continued. "In short, 'special classification' is a catchall used by the Artifact to explain when people are sufficiently different or unique from the average inhabitant. So for me, if you saw my sheet of stats, you'd find mine listed as 'Ice Caster,' to denote my ability to use ice magic."

"Your sheet," he said, dismissing his own. "Can I see it? Or is that, I don't know, some sort of invasion of privacy?"

Frost smirked at him. "Sorry, Nick, you get nothing. If you want to know if your swordplay skill is higher than mine, there's only one good way to find out." She lifted her sword. "You duel me, and you win. So would you like to try? Pull off that one-in-a-million chance?"

"More like one in a thousand, right, Cataloger?" he asked as he readied his own sword.

Based on current skill comparisons, your odds of landing a significant blow when in direct conflict with Frost are—

"Cataloger," he interrupted, "for the love of all that is good, do not finish that sentence."

Chapter 16
NICK

Nick stretched his arms and hopped from foot to foot, trying to clear his mind and limber up his body, which was already sore from several hours of practice earlier that morning. What Frost was suggesting seemed absurd, but then again, why wouldn't learning how to use magic be absurd? No real-life constraints operated upon it.

"All right," he said. "I can do this. It'll be easy after all the fighting and dying, right?"

"No promises," Frost said. A wry smile stretched her face. "But if you're as good at magic as you are at dying, then you'll figure this out in no time. Now, close your eyes."

Nick did as he was told. Frost stepped closer, as evidenced by the nearing of her voice, and he had to work extra hard to keep focused when she grabbed his hands and lifted them.

"There are many different manifestations of magic, each with their own rules, schools, benefits, and limitations," she said. "There's three major types I'm aware of. The first involves recanting strange old phrases and words of power. I don't have any such spell books, so that's out. The second are spells granted by faith and belief in various gods and divinities. I don't think I need to explain why that's not going to work. This leaves the third most common. In Yensere, and elsewhere, sometimes rare individuals are born able to cast magic. We're going to trick Cataloger into believing you're one of them so it gives you the requisite special classification."

My evaluations are logical and consistent—there is no "trick" to changing reality within Yensere

"You keep saying these things like they make sense," Nick said, joking to hide his nervousness and pretending Cataloger had said nothing. He desperately wished to succeed, and not for the reasons Frost insisted he try. Yensere was dangerous, and having killed Baron Hulh, they had made powerful enemies. She wanted Nick to harness magic to better defend himself as well as grow more dangerous in combat.

Nick, meanwhile, just thought it'd be really, really fun to throw a fireball or snap his fingers to summon shards of ice. All the usefulness in combat was a side benefit.

"Arguing will only make this worse," Frost said. He flinched as she flicked his nose with her finger, startling his eyes open. She hovered so near, her face filling up his vision, he instinctively blushed.

"You're the cruelest person alive in Yensere," he said, feeling his neck redden and wishing he were not so easily flustered.

"Not even close," she said. "Now, stop stalling and close your eyes."

LEVEL: UNKNOWN

He did so, and lowered his head a bit as if he were asleep. In the darkness of his mind, Frost's words floated like weightless torches.

"Some people are capable of wielding multiple elements, but most learn to manipulate a single type. For now, let's start with fire. I want you to lift your hand and envision an orb of flame hovering just above your palm. Nothing crazy, nothing huge, just a little flicker."

Nick did so. It was easy enough to see his hand in his mind's eye, and not much more of a stretch to picture a bit of fire burning above it, as if an invisible wick sprouted from the center of his palm.

"Good," Frost said. "Look at the flame. See the way it flickers and twists in the wind. Feel its heat on your palm, warm and gentle. Remind yourself it is *your* flame, burning solely through your desire. It is a part of you, birthed from your own strength, your own will. See it burn hotter. Feel it grow brighter. Stronger. It is fierce. It is real. Do you feel it, Nick? Its heat? Its light?"

Nick tried, he really did, but when he opened his eyes, he saw only his bare hand lifted.

"It can't be that simple," he said. "I just imagine a fire, and then it's there?"

"Pretty much," Frost said.

"So anyone can imagine a gust of wind, and it'll appear? Then why doesn't everyone wield magic?"

"Because not everyone knows what this place truly is," Frost said, lowering her voice. "Not like you and I do. What others believe is made true for them, and so we make it true for us. Stop doubting. Stop asking questions. Close your eyes and see it, Nick. Feel it. *Believe* it, and watch it burn."

She stepped away. Nick let the words sink into him. She was right. Over and over, he'd told himself this world was an advanced form of make-believe. Yes, it had rules, but those rules still enabled Sir Gareth to slow time and Frost to lash the ground with ice. Eyes closed, he raised his hand once more. The darkness of his mind lit with fire, and he saw it as a blurry blob hovering above his palm.

Feel its heat, he told himself, and he tried so hard to believe it would be there when he opened his eyes...

...and saw an empty palm.

"Shit."

Frost laughed.

"Hey, you're actually trying now, so there's that," she said, tapping her lips with a finger. "Maybe fire isn't the right element."

"How will I know the right one?"

She shrugged. "When I first learned, I tried for fire, too. But it never connected. I don't know how else to explain it. Ice, though?" She swirled her fingers, forming a thin little stem of ice that bloomed outward into a crystalline flower. "It just felt...right. Something I knew how to control, how to shape. How to make a part of me."

Nick clapped his hands and tried to psyche himself up.

"All right, then, let's see if ice works." He smirked at her. "And if it does, I guess I'll have to change my name, too. You and me, Frost and Icicle, ready to take on all of Yensere."

Frost winced. "Please do not name yourself Icicle."

"I think it's a fine name."

Do you wish to know my opinion?

"Just a joke, Cataloger," Nick grumbled, closing his eyes.

I see—please remember my prior concern that humor creates potential confusion

As if Nick could ever forget. Bowing his head, he thought of Frost's manipulation of ice. She made it seem so effortless. With but a flick of her wrist, she'd encased his legs with her **<frost nova>**. Her **<ice lance>** crushed guards at Baron Hulh's manse. He tried to imagine a layer of frost covering his hand, wielded with similar ease. He tried to feel the cold of it seeping into him, radiating a frozen aura to kiss his exposed skin. For one brief moment, the cold touched him, but it was even more fleeting than the kiss of fire.

"Damn it," he said, opening his eyes to confirm the lack of ice. "I don't think that's it, Frost."

Fire. Ice. Wind. Shadow. Light. Life and death itself. He imagined it all, attempting to command elements no matter how strange or laughable. Time passed, an hour, perhaps two; he didn't know anymore. He called out the names of spells, things he thought might work in the pattern Cataloger had spoken in his mind when watching Frost fight. **<Flame ball>. <Shadow minion>. <Earth spike>.** Nothing ever happened. All the while, Frost watched and encouraged. The lack of a single burst of magic might not have frustrated her, but it maddened Nick to no end.

"This is hopeless," he said after what felt like the twentieth time he'd tried to summon a flickering flame within his palm. "I'm trying, Frost, but it just doesn't make sense."

To his surprise, she grabbed his extended hands and pulled them toward her. Her grip was firm, the fabric of her gloves soft. Nick felt paralyzed by the blue of her eyes as she leaned in close.

"Why do you care if it makes sense?" she asked. "This world is a dream, Nick. A cruel miracle. It is chaos given law, and we are here to dance within it."

She pulled his hands open, her fingers tucked underneath his. Frost floated upward through them, solidifying, gaining substance and shape, until blooming outward to form a swan of ice hovering just beyond his touch. It was small and majestic, the detail of the feathers marked with frost, its eyes blue pebbles of ice somehow colder and deeper than the rest.

"Forget spells," she said. "Forget magic and power and stats. Embrace what is impossible. When you close your eyes and focus on your place here in Yensere, what brings you wonder?"

Her hands dropped, and immediately he missed them. The swan fell into his grip, so cold, so delicate. It melted instantly, the magic holding it together falling apart. Nick focused on the sensation. In Yensere, it was real and true. He felt the water drip across his fingers, felt its lingering chill.

Once more closing his eyes, he pretended he was alone. In the quiet, he tilted his head, not to the ground, but to the sky. He felt the sunlight fall upon his face. The gentle breeze teased his clothes.

What brings you wonder?

Nick tried to capture that feeling as he softly swayed. His terrified awe at seeing the ice leap from Frost's hand when he was chased by villagers. The surreal joy in watching Sir Gareth manipulate time, even if it was to Nick's detriment. To walk a forest filled with berries he didn't recognize and be hunted by creatures twisted and weird that should not exist. Seeing the ghost of his father trapped within a mirror. There was joy in the unknown, even when those living within it greeted him not with open arms but instead a drawn blade.

This was a world in which Nick could become so much more than he was. A world that could not limit him. He lifted his hands and briefly he imagined both fire and frost upon them. He dismissed that idea just as quickly. No, they weren't right. Neither was the sudden gust of wind that swirled about his legs and up his back to tease the collar of his shirt.

Nick knew what set his imagination alight. A memory came to him of a time spent with his parents on a distant terraformed planet watching a tremendous storm come rolling in just before nightfall. He dared not hope for it. Hope was wrong. Belief was a trap. Certainty. He needed certainty. It was time to stop relying on Cataloger to tell him the way, and instead force Yensere to accept him as he was. As he chose to become.

This world was real, and Nick was real within it. It would obey.

His hands rose higher. The wind swirled faster. He felt a shadow cross over his face as the yellow sun was hidden. The hairs on his neck stood on end. His fingers curled. His teeth bared. When he opened his eyes, words came to him of their own accord, and he spoke them with uncontrolled delight as the power surged through him.

"I wield the birthright of thunder."

Lightning streaked from the sky, twin trails, crackling white, to strike the center of his palms. The jolts swirled about him, clinging to his arms like friendly vipers, before dissipating into dust. Thunder followed, booming, and amid it, Nick laughed.

Reassessment
Level: 6 (+1)
Statistical Improvements:
Agility: 3
Physicality: 4
Endurance: 3
Focus: 3 (+3)
Mana: 21
Special Classification Granted: Lightning Caster

Nick gasped as the rush reached his head. He felt lighter than air. He stared at his hands as faint crackles of electricity twisted and teased through them before vanishing underneath his skin.

"Nick!" Frost said, clapping. "You did it!"

Nick turned toward one of the trees behind him and thrust his arm forward. A thick bolt of lightning tore from his palm to strike the center of the tree, blasting apart the bark. Immediately after, Nick felt a pull in his chest and a sudden strain on his mind.

Spell Unlocked: Lightning Bolt
Cost: 6 mana
Attributes: Lightning, Chain Effect
Projects a single bolt of lightning—deals double damage to targets submersed in water

"Mana?" Nick asked. "What is that?"

LEVEL: UNKNOWN

Mana is the physical energy cost of each spell, represented by the blue bar in your peripheral vision

On cue, a third bar materialized directly below the green of his stamina. It was a light blue, painfully small compared to the others, and no longer full. When he focused on it, a number appeared in its center: <15/21>.

"So I can only throw this **<lightning bolt>** two more times," he said after some basic math. "How long does it take to refill?"

"You can cheat it some ways," Frost explained. "Potions and the like. Usually, though, you need to rest for a few hours."

Nick stared at his hand. With but a thought, more lightning swirled around it. It was so easy now, the knowledge intimate and natural. With absolute confidence, he knew he could fling those two remaining **<lightning bolts>** by merely desiring them to occur. His imagination whirled, and he grinned at Frost.

"What other spells can I cast with this?" he asked.

"You're an innate spell caster now," she said. "You can cast whatever the system will codify and accept as within your capabilities."

She stepped a good distance away, particles of ice floating off her hands. When she slammed her wrists together, an **<ice lance>** flew toward the nearest oak, splintering into its bark. She flung a second, shattering the already existing ice. Then she stepped aside and gestured.

"Care to practice with what little mana you have left?" she asked.

The first hint of lightning crackled from Nick's palm and across his knuckles.

"Like you wouldn't believe," he said, and let the bolt fly.

Chapter 17
NICK

It was strange, needing to sleep in Yensere, but then again, Nick also needed to eat and drink. After they'd spent all of Nick's reserve of mana, as well as run him ragged with sword drills, they'd spent the rest of the day following the tree line instead of continuing toward Greenborough. Frost had not explained much beyond that they were headed somewhere she thought her sister might have gone. Come nightfall, Frost lay down on her comfortable bedroll while he made do with the blanket she'd taken for him upon their departure from Baron Hulh's manse.

"This thing really doesn't smooth out the ground all that much," he muttered, shifting atop the fabric.

"Whining won't help you sleep," Frost said from the opposite side of the dwindling campfire.

"Yeah, but it might make me feel better."

"Will it, though?"

Nick sighed and rolled his eyes. "No."

LEVEL: UNKNOWN

Is there anything I can do to help facilitate slumber?
Can you, I don't know, flick a switch to knock me out?
I cannot affect the material world—that includes your conscious state
You could just say no.
Your attitude worsens when I give unexplained answers in the negative

Nick groaned and shifted in an attempt to get more comfortable. Ending up on his back, he stared at the stars, sharp and bright in the clear night sky. He hadn't given too much thought to those distant twinkling lights, but now he couldn't stop staring at them. The constellations were distinctly familiar, something he hadn't quite realized before—Yensere had the same sky as Majus. Did that mean they were the same planet? How? Majus was a barren world devoid of life, all cold rock without a hint of atmosphere despite the extreme-distance scans suggesting otherwise that had led the OPC to open a world gate there.

Simon had theorized that the Artifact might be a form of time capsule. If it was, then the time it remembered must be a frightening distance in the past...

A grating sound stole his thoughts. He glanced across the fire, his brow furrowing.

Frost was snoring.

"Wish I could fall asleep that fast," he grumbled. Well, he could in the outside world. Apparently not on Yensere. Nick tossed and turned a bit more, his frustration growing, until at last he pushed himself to his feet. *To piss* was his internal excuse, but that wasn't true. He walked into the forest, past several trees, so the crackling fire and snoring woman were far behind him, until he felt alone.

Only then did he withdraw the Mirror of Theft from his pocket. He stared at its surface, wishing he knew more about how it worked.

Item: Mirror of Theft
Quality: Tier 14 (Pristine)
Classification—

"Cataloger," he said, closing his eyes and fighting for calm. "I wish to be left alone."

I do not possess a physical space, and therefore cannot leave, nor go anywhere

"Cataloger."

Yes, visitor?

"I am begging you. Give me a moment's privacy."

A long pause.

I shall cease informative functions for one Yensere hour and provide no communication or feedback during that time

"That'll be fine," he said, staring into the mirror's surface, suspecting that would be the best he would get. "Just fine."

Fog swirled within the mirror, thick and gray. Nick waited, trying not to be nervous and failing miserably. It was a trick. An illusion. A cruel game played by a server somewhere. It wasn't real. It *couldn't* be real.

But the face of the man who suddenly appeared matched so perfectly Nick's memories, who else could it be? He bore the same neatly cut brown hair, the same hazel eyes, the same dusting of white hairs across the dark goatee he kept carefully groomed.

"Hello, son," said his father, Lucien. "I was beginning to wonder if you would ever return."

Nick clutched the mirror's handle hard enough to whiten his knuckles.

"How?" he asked. "How can this be?"

His father crossed his arms as the fog rolled across him. He looked nothing like a reflection anymore, but more like a figure in a window into a different world, like a pocket dimension trapped within the mirror's confines.

"You ask for explanations I cannot be expected to give," Lucien said. "I am here. I am lucid. Perhaps you should answer that same question for me. Or perhaps you should acknowledge your lack of understanding as a boon."

"A boon?" Nick asked the mirror. "How?"

"Wonder remains only in the unknown."

The visage of his father grew larger, while at the same time, the mirror grew heavier in his grip. Its handle warmed, and he struggled until the burn was too great and he dropped it. The mirror landed on the grass with an audible thud. Above it, just as tall and intimidating as he'd been in real life, appeared his father. He wore his OPC uniform, the sleeves rolled up to the elbows. The faint moonlight shone upon him, adding an ethereal glow appropriate to one who was, as far as Nick was concerned, a ghost.

"See?" Lucien said. "I may have spent my life battling ignorance, but it was because in learning and discovery there are such wonderful surprises."

Nick's throat tightened and his hands shook. This wasn't him. This *wasn't him*. This wasn't his father. He took a careful step closer. There was no haze to Lucien. No glow, no flicker. He wasn't a hologram or a projection. He was there. Right there. To reach out. To touch.

"Dad..." he said, at a loss for words. Lucien tilted his head to one side and smiled.

"I know what you want," he said, and extended his arms. "Come here."

Nick cautiously stepped into his father's arms. Although Nick expected him to be ephemeral, the body was solid. Tangible. Real and warm.

Something deep inside Nick cracked.

"I missed you," he whispered. "It...I've..."

No words. He pressed his face into the vest of his father's uniform and wept. He'd not even wept like this at the funeral, for there'd been no body to recover, nothing salvageable from the fires of a destroyed research station and the cold vacuum of space that stole him away. Nick had only stared vacantly at the oversize portrait they'd hung in front of an empty casket wreathed with synthetic flowers.

Lucien patted his back, then pushed him away.

"That's enough," his father said. "You need to be stronger. I did not raise someone as weak as this."

Nick wiped at his eyes while frowning.

"Weak?" he said. "You've been *dead*. I haven't seen you in two years. I don't know who or what you are, but whatever it is, it's close enough to hurt."

Lucien dug his hands into his trouser pockets and shook his head. The faint hint of a frown tugged at the left corner of his mouth.

LEVEL: UNKNOWN

"I don't know what nonsense you've been told, but I'm here before you, aren't I?"

Whatever warmth Nick felt started to seep out like water leaking from a hung towel.

"Is that the way you've been programmed?" he asked, refusing to entertain this delusion further. He felt stupid and silly, to become so emotional embracing what was nothing more than a well-made doll. "To pretend to be alive? How does Yensere make you? Does it take from my memories? Is that it? Re-create you how I would imagine you to be?"

The light in Lucien's eyes darkened.

"You spit hypotheses at me like accusations. I am before you, Nick, and I am real. It is insulting to have my son pretend the evidence of his senses is false, all because he is scared of what it might mean."

"Scared?" Nick asked. "Scared of what?"

Lucien shrugged. "I can practically smell the urine on you from here, my son. As for the why? They would only be guesses. I would rather you save us both the humiliation and simply answer."

The casual cruelty left Nick feeling unmoored. To hear those words from the mouth of his father...

"I'm not scared of you," he said. "I'm disappointed. You're not my father. You're nothing like him."

"Yes, because you know me so well," Lucien said, and crossed his arms. "Though I guess it's my own fault. I tried to help you understand me. The dinner table was just as often a classroom, but you, well... you were never the student Simon was." The visage of his father smirked. "Where is he, anyway?

I suspect he would be a far better explorer of these strange environs than you. He actually took well to new topics and ideas, whereas you..."

"Enough!"

Nick dropped to his knees and grabbed the mirror. The moment his fingers touched it, his father blinked out and returned to isolation within the clouded mirror. Lucien's face smiled up at him, pleasant. Nick shoved the mirror into his pocket, and though it burned his thigh, he felt immediately better with the contact broken.

"Cataloger," he whispered.

Yes, Nick?

"My father. I didn't see a level or any statistics when I looked at him. Why?"

Because he is a nonphysical re-creation incapable of directly affecting the material world and therefore without need of such classifications

Nick rubbed at his eyes, feeling even more foolish for the tears he had shed.

"So he isn't real."

Clarify

"Real. As in walking, talking, breathing. He's not my father. He's just a fake."

Unable to answer

That lack of certainty would have to be enough. It didn't matter if that Lucien looked like his father, sounded like him, even smelled like him. It wasn't him.

It wasn't.

Nick returned to his uncomfortable bed. Frost had rolled

LEVEL: UNKNOWN

onto her side, and thankfully her snoring had ceased. Nick scavenged a few twigs to toss onto the fire, lay on his own side facing the fire, and let the light fall across him. The warmth was comforting. His memories were not.

"Not real," he whispered.

The Lucien in the mirror was false. It was a worthless re-creation, one that would only cause him pain. He told himself this again and again as his eyelids grew heavy and the crackling of the fire lulled him to sleep.

Told himself this, even as he lacked the strength to remove the mirror from his pocket and throw it into the fire, where it belonged.

Chapter 18
NICK

"Do you really think your sister could be here?" Nick asked as he gazed upon the surreal landscape before him. "Do you think *anyone* could?"

The forest ended not with a clean break, but in a scrambled tilt, the ground curving downward into a sunken valley several miles wide. Trees grew at odd angles along the nearby edge, defying gravity, as if the world had opened up and claimed all in its wake. Jagged stones jutted out along the sharp incline, adding to the illusion.

"I've been tracking every rumor of demons like us," Frost said, leaning on one knee to peer down into the deep valley. "Supposedly one was here in the Swallowed City, and so we go looking."

It seemed a joke to call such a place a "city," but there was undeniable truth to it. Within that sunken recess were homes, pale and built of white stone. Their formations, though, defied all reason. The ground curved and roiled, like a stormy sea

LEVEL: UNKNOWN

suddenly frozen in place. Buildings emerged at all angles, many half-buried in the soil. Several hovered just above the ground, suspended in the air, touching nothing. There were no roads, only the curving gaps between the squat buildings mashed together and sticking out of the ground like crooked teeth.

If there was life, Nick saw no sign of it. The Swallowed City was barren. Not even the creatures of the forest dared descend.

"Have you tried asking Cataloger?" Nick suggested. "She should know, right?"

Revealing the location of a former visitor would be an invasion of privacy

Nick frowned.

"Former?" he asked aloud.

"Enough," Frost said. "Do not answer that, Cataloger. It's none of your concern, and we both know it."

I seek only to be helpful

By the way Frost rolled her eyes, Nick suspected they'd both heard that line before.

"And I seek my family," she said, testing the slope with her heel. "And since she might be down there, I'm going down, too."

"But why would your sister come here?" Nick asked as he gestured to the bizarre, half-buried city.

"I don't know. Why are you here?"

"I'm here because I'm trying to learn about Yensere," he said.

"Well then, follow me, because I'd say there's plenty to learn down at the bottom."

With a hop, she crossed the edge to the steep slope. Dirt

gave beneath her feet, forming a groove as she slid. Her arms shot out, balancing her as she rode the decline halfway down. An oak shot out perfectly perpendicular from the slope, and she landed atop it and turned.

"You coming?" she asked.

Nick clapped his hands and stomped from foot to foot to psyche himself up. Just before starting, he tilted his head to one side, an idea occurring to him.

"Cataloger, do I have a statistic or skill for balance and climbing?"

Yes for both

"So what are my odds of joining Frost without face-planting into the dirt?"

According to your balance score of 6—forty-seven percent

"High enough." He mimicked Frost, hopping over the sharp edge of the dirt and skidding in the same groove she had made. His arms waved frantically as the soft earth gave way, the speed faster than he anticipated as his heels dug in deeper. The jutting tree approached, and he realized he wasn't entirely sure how to slow down, let alone stop. Just before hitting bark, he tried to kick off, thinking to land on the trunk. His aim was right, but his momentum far greater than he could control. The moment his feet touched, he stumbled forward, his arms circling like a panicked bird in an attempt to reverse his fall.

Frost stepped in his way before he went headfirst over the side, catching him in an embrace. They both scooted several inches along the trunk, then came to a halt. Nick exhaled in relief, then grew rapidly aware of Frost's arms about his waist, and how close her face was to his, with their noses nearly touching. Her wide-eyed grin filled his entire vision.

"Seems like I beat the odds," he said, and grinned right back.

"With my help," she said, releasing him.

"Still counts."

"Does it?" She sat on the trunk, her legs swinging over the side. "Try again, and this time, I won't be there to catch you."

She slid off, half running, half sliding the rest of the way to the chaotic bottom of the sunken valley. Nick imitated her start, his fingers clutching the bark as his feet swayed.

For this portion, the estimated chance of landing without injury is—

"Cataloger."

Yes?

"Am I going to feel better or worse hearing that number?"

A long pause.

I am uncertain how to answer that question without causing distress

"Yeah, that's what I thought."

Nick slid off, hit the steep ground with his heels, and slid toward the bottom. His knees ached, and he had to spin and flap his arms while twisting his waist to remain balanced. The bottom zoomed closer, as did a smug Frost, waiting with her arms crossed over her chest. As she neared, he dug his right heel even harder into the soft earth, grinding it down to reduce his speed until he skidded to a halt directly before her. He swung his arms out wide as if he were a gymnast nailing a perfect landing.

"I did it," he proclaimed.

Frost clapped three times, patronizingly slow.

"I'm so proud of you."

Once her back was to him, Nick called up his stats and noted with satisfaction that his balance score had climbed to 7.

Getting better, he thought, and followed Frost into the winding chaos that was the Swallowed City.

The buildings, which he assumed were homes, all shared a similar construction style. Their bases were perfectly square, and their windows were rectangular on the bottom and curved near the top. The white stone was stark in the daylight sun, like bleached bone. Oddly, no dirt clung to them. The tops of the buildings were flat but for the corners, which often bore little spires or flourishes, the only real decorations he could see.

"It's hard to imagine people living here," he said. Nick grabbed a windowsill and hoisted himself up for a look inside. The interior was vacant of all but dust. No life, not even spiders or moths. He couldn't see the floor, either, for the building was half-swallowed by a strange curve in the earth. Silence hung thick over the Swallowed City, so that their calm speech felt like screams.

"They clearly must have," Frost said, though her tone was not as confident as her words. "I can't imagine what my sister would be looking for, though, if it was her who came here."

They followed no street or path, but instead walked where the city allowed them. The ground continued to sink, the overall formation reminding Nick of a sort of crater. Two buildings ahead of them tilted together to form an upside-down V, and between them, a third building lay on its side. The two walked atop it toward the vertical roof, where they could conceivably climb farther down.

"I'd love to help in your search," Nick said as they neared the edge, "but you haven't told me anything about her. What she looks like, what she might be doing here...I mean, I don't even know her *name*."

The brittle stone suddenly cracked beneath his foot, and he cried out as his balance tilted, his body falling straight for a sideways window before him. Frost caught his wrist, halting his fall. She held him steady, her expression unreadable.

"Irina," she said, letting go once his footing was stable. "Her name is Irina. My sister. So she looks like me, just... older."

Nick lowered his voice, and his smile drifted away.

"Why did she leave you?" he asked softly.

"She wanted a better life than what we had."

Frost climbed down the overturned roof to the twisted ground, and Nick followed. A pathway awaited them, almost like a river had carved its way through the twisted and tilted buildings. He noticed the soil had taken on an ashen color instead of the deep brown closer to the cliff edges. It was as if the very essence of the place was being drained away, so that even the bone white of the buildings was dulling toward gray.

"What was this place?" Nick asked, his neck on a swivel. Buildings towered over them on either side, the tallest they'd encountered so far. Each of them had at least five rows of windows cut into their sides, and he assumed that meant they bore as many floors. "Any ideas, Cataloger?"

Location: Oeseli, the Swallowed City
Description: Once a thriving hub built upon—

When she did not continue, Nick paused and made a face toward the sky. For some reason, he kept thinking of her watching him from just above his head.

"Built upon what?"

Oeseli, now known as the Swallowed City, was built atop the ruins of the capital of the Sinifel Empire, which was destroyed during the war with God-King Vaan

"And what happened to Oeseli to make it look like"—he gestured to the sunken buildings jutting out in random directions—"this?"

An earthquake

Nick turned his attention to Frost.

"An earthquake," he said, unsure if Cataloger's answers were for him alone. "Right. Are you hearing this?"

"I am," she said. "And it's not the first time Cataloger has been cagey about historical events. Something about these supposed cataclysms seems to mess with her memory."

Deleted and corrupted data are extremely rare occurrences when recording thousands of years of history

"She sounds defensive," Nick said, leaping onto the side of the building. His feet skidded down it a moment before he caught himself. The angle wasn't too bad, and he slowly started descending toward Frost. "But what do you mean, cataclysms?"

"From what I've learned so far, supposedly every thousand

years or so, a cataclysm destroys much of Yensere, forcing the people to rebuild. Of the three main civilizations I'm aware of, the Majere, the Sinifel, and now the Alder Kingdom, all dealt with the destruction in their own way... or, in regard to the Alder Kingdom, by *not* dealing with it. Their god-king apparently froze the black sun in the sky and prevented it from happening."

To constantly have a world destroyed seemed a bit ridiculous, but then again, he'd grown up hearing stories about the struggles of life on Eden prior to the opening of world gates and the spread of humanity across the stars, terraforming planets such as Taneth, Nick's own birth world. Some disasters were real, and some, such as the supposed drought that baked half the world, were clearly fictional. For the people of Yensere to have their own tales made sense, as they would have their own gods, monsters, and creation myths as well.

But why wouldn't Cataloger know about them?

"I guess I always thought Cataloger was all-knowing and infallible," he said, jogging to catch up with Frost. He'd lagged behind, and he disliked being alone in the empty city. "Having giant gaps in your memory definitely prevents that."

Visitors are making incorrect assumptions as to the extent of my database and its inconsistencies

"That so?" Frost asked. "Care to tell us what happens during a cataclysm, then?"

I cannot answer

A home lay on its side before them, blocking the way. Nick might have believed it fell if the ground itself hadn't shifted with it and still clung to the base to form an enormous hill to their right. Frost peered up at one of the windows, which was just slightly above her head. She bent her knees, preparing for a jump.

"That's what I thought, Cat—"

The earth collapsed beneath her feet, swallowing her.

"Frost!"

Nick's instinct to sprint after her was halted by the growing hole in the ground. He retreated several steps, waiting for it to cease lest it swallow him, too. When it ceased, he rushed to the edge. About a dozen feet below, he saw Frost on her knees in the center of what appeared to be the roof of another building, this one utterly claimed by the earth but for a slender portion at the top.

She was not alone.

Four men surrounded her, all holding shining swords with hilts wrapped in gold. Their heads were hidden underneath curved helmets topped with billowing horsehair plumes. Blue sashes marked their gold hauberks, matching the color of their trousers, boots, and the long scarves that billowed from around their necks.

All four flickered and blinked, their bodies translucent.

Specter: Level 5 Undying
Archetype: Knight
Special Attribute: Phasing

"Stay away!" Frost shouted, slamming her hand to the ground.

Spell: Ice Wall

Ice rolled outward in a circle, rising to form a perfectly smooth five-foot-high wall. Nick relaxed seeing it. Surely that would buy them time to figure out...

LEVEL: UNKNOWN

The four men walked right through the ice.

Phasing: Allows beings with this special attribute to pass through physical barriers

"Look out!" Nick shouted, his eyes widening. Frost reacted faster, her sword lifting to block a sudden barrage of swings from all sides. She managed to knock away two, but two others struck her armor, deflecting off her fine silver chain mail. Nothing visibly serious, barely any blood, but he feared the damage was beneath the chain mail, hidden bruises and perhaps broken bones.

Nick lifted his arm, calling to mind the lone spell he understood. *I hope "chain" means what I think it means.*

He aimed at one of the ghostly soldiers and unleashed a **<lightning bolt>**. It shot from the center of his palm, taking 6 of his mana from his light blue bar at the same time. It struck his target true, right when he lifted his sword to swing again, and connected with the center of his body. The bolt then jumped to the next soldier, and the next, striking all four for the exact same total of their health bars. They staggered in place, electricity sparking off them. They might be flickering memories, or ghosts, or whatever that meant in this bizarre world, but they appeared to feel pain.

Frost thrust her sword straight into the belly of the nearest. The soldier reared back, his mouth opening for a scream that did not come. His body flickered into static and then vanished as if it had never existed. A pivot on her right leg, and she slashed open the throat of a second, ending him as well. The remaining two assaulted her simultaneously, and she had to split her concentration between them, going fully defensive.

Her slender sword was a blur as she blocked their attacks, until at last she found an opening. She cut along one guard's arm and then extended her palm mere inches from his exposed face. **<Ice shards>** tore into him, a barrage of hits that broke apart his body and flickered him into nothing.

With just one left, Nick expected the battle to end quickly, but then two more specters rose straight from underneath the building to join the fray. One slashed with his sword, but the other held back, protected by his two remaining comrades. He held a wood contraption in hand: a crossbow, Nick realized too late. When he pulled its trigger, a thick bolt shot out to strike Frost in the leg. She cried out but stumbled onward, releasing more **<ice shards>** at the figments.

Trusting Frost to handle the other two, even with an arrow sticking out of her leg, Nick focused on the crossbowman, who was busy cranking the side to reload a second bolt. He didn't think he'd be able to hop down in time to prevent a second shot, but maybe...

Cataloger, does <lightning bolt> always have to chain?

No—a fifty percent potency increase will occur if you—

Nick didn't wait for her to finish. He braced his legs, pointed his palm, and poured all his focus into that lone specter with the crossbow. Lightning crackled in the center of his palm, then burst out in another bolt, this one shorter and thicker than the last. It blasted the center of the crossbowman, crackling as it hit. The archer's body locked tight, muscles spasming from the lightning. Seeing him wounded, Frost quickly finished him off with a trio of slender **<ice shards>** from her palm.

LEVEL: UNKNOWN

Gasping from the effort, Nick watched Frost easily dispatch the first specter he'd wounded with lightning, then engage the final addition. Her sword batted back and forth, forcing the soldier's own weapon out of position, before ramming straight into his neck, ending whatever life the ghostly soldier possessed.

With the final combatant dropped and vanished, Nick held back a gasp as his level bar filled with white.

Reassessment
Level: 7 (+1)
Statistical Improvements:
Agility: 3
Physicality: 4
Endurance: 3
Focus: 5 (+2)
Mana: 35 (+14)

Not the most exciting, but then again, he'd done nothing but cast his lightning spells a few times. Energized from leveling, and his head not aching quite so badly now he'd gained a bit more mana, Nick hung off the side of the crumbling house and then dropped to a hard landing.

"How we doing?" he asked as he shook off dust. Frost ripped the bolt out of her leg, choked down a scream, and then watched the bolt flicker out of existence.

"I've been worse," she said, standing with a wince.

Nick could hardly believe she was able to stand after the blows she'd taken, but when he checked her health bar, it was still halfway filled. No number for it, just like there was no level. It seemed visitors like himself were afforded a level of privacy the regular inhabitants of Yensere were not.

"How about we take this a little bit slower?" he asked. Frost shook her head, laughing despite the injuries she'd suffered.

"Much slower," she agreed. "And if you're willing to go first, I'll be happy to let you volunteer."

"If you insist. Let's see where this unknown tunnel goes."

The two looked about, but finding no way into the building they stood upon, Frost aimed her fist straight down and launched two quick **<frost lances>**. The wall crumbled, cracking open a wide enough gap for them to slide inside the toppled building. Nick went first, Frost after. Landing amid the rubble, Nick glanced about the barren interior, his senses troubled. When he saw stairs leading downward, he realized what was amiss.

"That isn't the roof," he said, pointing above his head. "That's the floor."

"Fascinating," Frost said dryly as she landed beside him. "Come on. Let's just confirm Irina isn't hidden somewhere and then get out. This place makes my skin crawl."

It was awkward, descending stairs that were upside down, but they made do as they scaled the multiple floors to the "bottom." The door had broken from the hinges and lay wedged at a slant, blocking the way. Together, Nick and Frost pushed it aside and then emerged from the building. They hardly made it a step before they both froze. Nick's jaw dropped as his mind struggled to make sense of the sight before him.

Another city was underneath the one above, made of the same square stone buildings, only this time, they were all upside down. They seemed to grow from a rocky ceiling, a bizarre mirror reflection of what they had seen above, only more chaotic and random. Where rooftops would have once met sky, they instead just barely touched a smooth sheen of brown rock that lifted and dropped so that every building was properly supported.

"Unreal," Frost said. "It's like the city just...folded in on itself."

"How can we see?" Nick asked. They were fully blocked from the sky by a suspended ceiling of rock, and yet all the upturned buildings were brightly lit from no apparent source. Frost shrugged, looking equally baffled.

"It...it's like the world thinks sunlight reaches down here, and so it does."

Nick doubted they would get a better an answer than that. Something had happened here, something that left the place...broken.

"I think we have a welcome party," he said, pointing ahead. Three specters, garbed similarly and flickering in a now familiar way, came rushing out of what looked vaguely like a temple.

"For Oeseli!" one shouted as they raised their swords.

Nick and Frost lifted their hands.

<Ice lance>.

<Lightning bolt>.

The combined attacks blasted them apart. They broke like static, a flicker of black and white that left nothing—no blood, no dust, and no ash in their wake. Nick shivered and wished the pain in his head would lessen. According to his little bar, he still had <19> out of <35> mana left, but already he felt the strain like a distant migraine. It gave him a newfound appreciation for Frost's capabilities. That she seemed perfectly fine despite her injuries and the number of spells she'd cast meant both her health pool and her mana pool were far beyond his.

For now, he thought, a little bit of lightning crackling across his fingertips.

They still had to wind through the various buildings, and with no real destination, Nick guided them roughly toward where he thought the center of the city might be. They passed by several homes, and he glanced inside, surprised to see broken furniture, toppled dressers, and, in one, what looked like a rocking chair. Curtains fluttered over more windows, too, the cloth stiff and drained of all color.

"It seems the closer we get to the center, the more...life... remains," he said, keeping his voice low. He did not know how many more of those strange phantoms might remain, nor did he wish to fight them if they could avoid it. "At least, signs of it."

"I'm not sure I would call these soldiers 'alive,'" Frost muttered.

"Wait."

Nick froze in place and pointed upward. Above them, clinging to the stone ceiling in defiance of gravity, was an elaborate four-tiered water fountain in the center of beautiful blue-painted tiles. Water billowed across it in multiple streams and founts, all of them traveling upward instead of falling.

All around it walked flickering ghosts of the past. Not just soldiers, but men in long white-and-blue tunics and women in pale dresses wide at the shoulder and narrow along the hips

LEVEL: UNKNOWN

and legs. They moved in eerie silence despite the feeling that there should be noise. Children ran about, scurrying past and sometimes even through the legs of adults. Friends waved at one another. Along one edge of the clearing, several men and women stood with rugs laid out, too distant for Nick to see what little trinkets or jewelry were being sold atop them. The sellers shouted and gestured, doing all they could to steal attention their way.

The figures flickered, faded, and then disappeared. Water vanished from the fountain, leaving it cracked and dry. Dust swept through the empty clearing, carried on a wind that should not be.

"I don't like this place," Frost said, her voice piercing the silence. "It's too... sad."

A loud banging noise came from a building to their right.

"What was that?" he asked.

"Sounds like something being knocked over."

"Your sister?"

She shrugged. "Only one way to find out."

The pair approached the upside-down building. It was enormously wide but only a single floor high, so they could still reach the front door. Nick tried to guess the building's purpose, then gave up. He'd have his answer soon enough. Stairs above their heads, he slipped to one side of the entrance while Frost flanked the other. He lifted his free hand and used his fingers to count down. Four. Three. Two.

On "one," he kicked the door open and rushed inside, his sword held aloft and lightning crackling across the palm of his left hand, a **<lightning bolt>** ready to be unleashed.

Inside might have once been a library, given the multitude of shelves that lined the walls and many more standing shelves throughout. The vast majority were barren, and what standing shelves did contain books had been dragged to the center of the library and tipped over, spilling out their contents. Dozens of books lay in a heap, their black-and-brown bindings weathered and torn. The lettering was sharp and runic, a language he did not understand, nor did Cataloger immediately translate. A powerful scent, a mixture of ink and dust, struck Nick, and he had to fight off a sneeze as it entered his nostrils.

Sitting atop that pile, like a dragon over her hoard, was a small woman with a black ponytail, wide round spectacles, and what looked like a knee-length jacket wrapped in a belt, only the red fabric more resembled the softness of a robe. She looked up from the book in her lap, blinked twice, and then waved excitedly.

"Hi, I'm Violette!"

Chapter 19
NICK

Violette: Level 9 Human
  Archetype: Scholar
  Special Classification: Fire Caster

Nick sheathed his sword, his brain scrambling for a proper response.

"Uh, hi?"

The small woman more slid than climbed down her book horde, stumbling and flailing her arms wildly to maintain her balance upon reaching the bottom of the upside-down library.

"I didn't think I'd find anyone else down here," she said, smoothing out her jacket. "Well, not anyone who was lucid and friendly."

"So you've seen the specters, too?" Frost asked. She'd yet to put away her weapon, and her expression was carefully guarded.

"Oh, I have," Violette said. She tucked her book under her arm so she could tighten the cloth tie of her ponytail. "Not the friendliest bunch. I ran from any I saw, once it was clear they would stop me from exploring." She squinted at them. "I presume you two are a bit friendlier than the specters?"

"Just a bit," Nick said, and he smiled wide. "I'm Nick, and the lady holding the sword is my friend Frost."

"Nice to meet the both of you! Are you exploring the ruins, too?"

"In a way," Nick said. He knew he should distrust a stranger they just met in such a bizarre location, but Violette's personality was so bouncy, so happy, he could not help himself. "We're looking for someone."

"Someone?" The small woman gestured toward the pile of books. "Sorry, I don't think you'll be finding people down here, other than myself. What you will find, though, is an absolute treasure trove of information linked not just to the Sinifel Empire but all the way back to the original Majere...at least, it would be, if most of them weren't filled with garbled, nonsensical lettering."

Nick approached the pile and lifted one of the books, curious about what she meant. When he opened it, he immediately understood: The beige paper was wrinkled and stiff, and written on it were not shapes or letters, but vague, smeared approximations of writing. The resemblance struck Nick immediately. It looked like when a picture failed to load correctly when sent through the world gate's information network, resulting in a distorted, low-resolution version of the original.

He flipped through several pages, found them all similarly garbled.

LEVEL: UNKNOWN

"A shame," he told Violette, and tossed the worthless book back to the pile.

Were these even written by a person? he asked Cataloger silently. *Or are they just approximations of books that exist here because this is a library?*

This library dates back seven hundred and fifty-three years, founded in the third and final era of the Sinifel Empire—nothing in Yensere is approximate

Then what happened to these books?

They are damaged with age

Nick shook his head, not buying that answer. Paper and ink didn't weather in such a way, their pages looking like he was viewing them through an improperly focused telescope. Just like the rest of the Swallowed City, it felt like this simulation of Yensere struggled to properly load or remember what had once been.

"We need out of here," Frost told Nick while sliding her sword into its sheath. "At this point, I feel confident that my sister isn't here. And she"—she paused to point at Violette—"clearly needs to be brought somewhere safe."

"I can defend myself, I assure you," Violette said. She tossed the last book onto the pile. "But regrettably I've found little worthwhile within these ruins and planned to leave anyway. I'd be thrilled to have your company during my exit."

"Lovely," Frost said, her sarcasm heavy enough to sink boats. "But that does beg a new question...Do you know a way out nearby? The layout of the city is...interesting, and the building we climbed is pretty far. I'm worried we'll encounter more of those specters on the way."

"I don't think any direction we pick will be free of those things," Violette said, brushing a bit of dust from her coat. "But I can show you how I got down. It's not far and just requires a bit of stair climbing."

The trio exited the library, and Violette took the lead as they traversed the eerily empty streets. She talked as they walked, the lowering of her voice the only hint of her acknowledgment of the dangerous environment.

"I've always been fascinated by the Majere," she said. "The Sinifel are interesting, too, but their religion, art, and music carry too much nihilism for me to appreciate. But the Majere? People who could master death itself, and live on as skeletons, or even bone constructs? That's who I want to learn more about. What kind of person does a human become if you live forever?"

"I imagine a very tired and cranky one," Nick said, grinning at her.

"But what of the learning you could achieve?" Violette insisted. "You could perfect playing every instrument, write books, memorize poems... it doesn't even need to be artistic. You could, I don't know, become a master baker and make the most amazing cake Yensere has ever seen."

"How does one benefit from a cake when you're a walking skeleton?" Frost asked. "Or did they still have to eat? And how would that even work? I can't imagine them still having tongues..."

Violette laughed as she leaped over a crack in the ground whose depths were so dark and endless Nick dared not stare down it for more than a second.

"I can sense you're joking, but you're asking legitimate

questions whose answers I would burn down half the Silversong Sanctuary to learn."

"What's the Silversong Sanctuary?" Nick asked, but Violette did not answer.

Location: Silversong Sanctuary

Description: An academy located in the city of Malarus, dedicated to the study and preservation of significant historical events, along with a strong interest in the manifestations of and uses for magical spells, artifacts, and incantations

Thanks, Cataloger, Nick thought. *But I was mostly trying to have small talk with someone I just met. You know. Get to know them better.*

Does my sharing of information enable you to know me better?

More than you might believe.

Violette stopped before what appeared to be an enormous tower. Unlike most buildings they'd encountered, it was not upside down, which, as far as Nick was concerned, was a good sign. The problem was, a gaping maw of nothing surrounded its entrance.

"We're here," Violette said, winding around to where the ground had heaved unevenly, forming a sort of staircase of boulders and slabs toward the tower entrance. Nick followed, careful of his footing. At the top of the slabs, it was only a short hop to cross the empty gap to land on the steps of the tower. Nick went last, glad for Frost's help to steady his landing.

"I hate this place," he muttered, glancing at the abyss mere feet away.

"Feels like all of Yensere does, too," Frost said, following Violette inside. Like most buildings, it was hollow and void of any sign of life. Along the side rotated a lengthy staircase reaching all the way to the top.

"Please be very careful," Violette said as she led their climb.

The aged and brittle stones certainly inspired no confidence. Nick trailed behind the other two, wishing there was a guardrail of some sort. Instead he pressed his left hand to the wall as they climbed, ascending halfway before the trio came to a halt. Two of the steps were broken, the stone having fallen to the floor below. Violette bent her knees for her best standing high jump and then vaulted over the gap.

"Sorry, this was certainly easier coming down," she said, spinning about with a flutter of her red coat. "Just be careful, and I'm sure you'll both be fine."

Once Violette made room by climbing higher, Frost leaped up and over, softly landing two steps beyond the gap. She then turned and frowned at Nick.

"Can you make that jump?" she asked.

Nick stood before the gap and made a show of being offended.

"I'll have you know my jump skill is..." He paused for Cataloger to pull up his stats. "Uh. Six. That's... that's good, right?"

Frost grinned at him. "Do you want an honest answer, and do you want it before or after you make the jump?"

"Ignorance is bliss, Frost. How about never?"

"Never it is. But just in case, I'll stay right here to catch you."

Nick descended two steps, then turned about. He wanted a

LEVEL: UNKNOWN

running start, not easy to do when climbing stairs. Still, that had to be better than nothing. Clapping his hands together to work up the nerve, he began his sprint.

On the second step, the entire stairway below him gave way in a great crumble of stone. His arms flailed, reaching for Frost's extended hand, but he swiped only air. Frost's voice chased after him as he dropped toward the tower floor.

"*Nick!*"

He cried out upon landing, a horrible blow to his knees. The pain, however, was only beginning. The entire floor immediately broke underneath him, and he screamed even louder as he slid along the surface, which pivoted sharply to a sudden angle. His sword slid from his grasp, bouncing and clattering behind him. He braced for impact, only the wall did not stop him. He burst on through as if it were paper, and then for one agonizing moment he saw only a great expanse of pure darkness. He flailed his arms and legs, his body pivoting as he fell.

And then he was fully upside down, and his fall slowed. The air felt cool around him as his stomach performed loops. Above was cavernous stone and a gray square that was the floor of the building he'd fallen through. Craning his neck, he saw a rooftop approaching. Much of it was glass, and he had no time to decide if that was good or bad before he smashed straight through. Shards rained down as his descent continued, those pieces landing before he did because they, unlike him, seemed to understand how gravity worked there.

Nick's feet swung to right himself, he let out a gasp, and then he landed on his back amid the broken pieces.

That his back wasn't broken was beyond his ability to fathom.

"What," he said, sucking in air as if he'd just run down a flight of stairs, "was that?"

You descended

"That's one way to put it, Cataloger...but it'd be more accurate to say I fell."

He could almost feel Cataloger's confusion as she tried to rework what happened into something she understood.

A fall is uncontrolled—yours was a controlled choice to delve deeper into the city

That was definitely not a choice Nick had made, but at least the strange geography of these overlapping cities had saved him from being thoroughly crushed upon landing. He stared up through the broken glass and saw welcoming sunlight streaming through, which of course made no sense, given that he was even deeper underground than he'd been before his fall.

"Where am I?" he muttered as he sat up. It felt like he'd gained a dozen new bruises, and his lower back ached from the motion.

Location: ▓▓▓▓▓

Description: A city destroyed during ——— the former capital city of ——— ruins built over by the Alder Kingdom

Average level: 8

The building was massive, its rooftop coming together to form a triangular point at its high center. Much of its walls and roof were clear glass, clouded and cracked. Raised shelves surrounded him, some wood, some stone. What might have been plants were but powder atop long stretches of pale earth within pots and trays.

A greenhouse, perhaps? he wondered. Dusting himself off, he turned and froze at the sight of the decoration adorning the greenhouse center.

What is that?

Upon a raised dais, towering twice Nick's height, loomed an enormous statue carved from bronze. The upper half appeared human, emaciated and with ribs poking out through its skin. Four arms stretched from its sides, none of them human, but instead ending with claws, pincers, and hooks. It bore no face, just a smooth oval surface. Horns stretched from its sides, sharp and curling. The monster's legs, which were many, were curled and twisted underneath. Its body was bent low, and five men climbed atop it, stomping broken, twisted legs and grasping at wrists and horns. Their swords plunged into its sides, and though the statue bore no face, by the way the neck was tilted and the upper pair of arms flailed, there was no denying the monster endured great pain.

Below the statue lay a desiccated corpse dressed in rusted mail—a dead knight. His arm was outstretched toward the statue, as if paying tribute to the statue even in death.

"Cataloger?" Nick whispered, the frightening sight taking away his ability to project.

This is a Sinifel statue depicting the god Eiman, whom they named the Beast of a Thousand Mouths

Movement behind him. Nick turned while instinctively reaching for his sword despite having lost it in the fall. The doors to the greenhouse were enormous, stretching all the way to a ceiling that was at least forty feet tall. The hinges were covered with rust, and the doors were cracked open. Through the gap, Nick saw a trio of men, though they did not appear to be the same ghostly soldiers as before. They were naked from the waist up, their bodies so skeletal that their pale trousers flapped loosely about their legs. Their hands dripped blood from where their fingernails were missing. Their chests pulsed from the visible movements of their hearts.

They had no eyes or noses, just circular mouths that stretched from the top of their foreheads to the lowest jut where their chins should be. Drool trickled down their necks. Massive lips parted, and within, where should have been teeth, were jagged pieces of broken glass, colored and stained as if stolen from a painting.

▮▮▮▮▮▮▮: Level 4
Archetype: Heretic (Eiman)

"Oh, that's not right," Nick muttered, his eyes widening at the sight. Even if killed, Nick knew he'd come back, but the thought of dying to those mouths tearing open his flesh chilled his blood. A sword. He didn't have his sword. A **\<lightning bolt\>** might do the trick...but he didn't like the sounds of scurrying he heard outside the temple. If there were more, and he exhausted his mana too early...

The dead knight! Nick turned back to the corpse before the altar. The armor might be rusted and too big for him, but what about a weapon? Nick sprinted to it as the three bizarre "heretics" entered the greenhouse, their mouths clicking and snapping. The sound of their "teeth" scraping against each other spiked uncomfortable shivers down Nick's spine. The nearby

LEVEL: UNKNOWN

corpse lay on his stomach, and Nick shoved him over to expose a face fully eaten away. The bones that remained were crunched inward in an unpleasant warning of what might yet await Nick.

To his relief, a sword was held firm in the man's rigid gauntlet, and it seemed spared the rust of the armor. Its hilt was wrapped in soft black leather straps, and the blade itself was similarly dark, looking more like obsidian than steel. It somehow opened up just above the cross guard, swirling into multiple thick threads to leave a hollow gap within the center before merging back into the remainder of the blade. Faint runes were carved along one side, shimmering a faint red, and to his surprise, Cataloger did not translate them in his mind.

Item: Sorrow
Quality: Tier 15 (Unique)
Classification: Arcane Weapon
One of the four judgment blades of the Sinifel Empire, wielded by their notable heroes in their war against God-King Vaan in the twilight of their reign
Special Attribute: <hidden>, <hidden>

The supposed strength of the weapon left Nick in shock. What did it even mean for a weapon to be tier 15? And why would some of the information not be available for things originating in Yensere? He pulled the weapon free from the corpse's grasp and held it in his hand.

"What does this say?" he asked Cataloger, running his finger along the runes.

I cannot answer

"Why not?"

It would be too great an invasion of privacy

The answer made no sense, but Nick didn't have time to question it. The heretics were too close. He could hear their shuffling. Turning about, he gripped the long hilt in both hands. If the math in his head was correct, a single slash was all it'd take to bring these horrific monsters down. He told himself to ignore the biting, the drool, and the clacking of their glass teeth.

One of the three stumbled ahead of the rest, and it reached out with its nubs of fingers, its entire non-face opening wide to expose dozens of colored glass teeth arranged in a circular pattern around a black gullet. Nick set his feet and swung as Frost had taught him, a wide slash from the lower right hip up to the left shoulder.

Blood spilled as Sorrow tore through the thing—yet it was far from what Nick expected, nor enough to down the monster in a single blow. The foul creature's hands pressed against Nick's face and neck, grabbing and scraping. The blood dripping from its fingers was cold, so cold. The gaping mouth neared.

Nick screamed his panic, but his movements continued. Hours upon hours of practice had taught Nick the stance he was to shift into after that initial hit, and he moved even as horror blanked his mind. His sword cut right, a perfectly horizontal slash straight through the neck. The obsidian blade cleaved the head from the monster's body, which finally collapsed and lay still.

I don't understand, he thought as he retreated several steps as the other two heretics approached. *Why isn't the sword hitting like it should?*

LEVEL: UNKNOWN

Because I have not given you my power, pillager.

The voice was the opposite of all that was Cataloger. It was deep and unpleasant, speaking in his mind with an air of contempt. Nick stared at the blade as the red runes along its side briefly shimmered.

"Impossible," he said, his mind breaking at the thought of the sword speaking. His understanding of Yensere and its limitations appeared to be painfully limited.

Deny it if you wish, pillager. I do not anticipate suffering with you for long.

Nick slashed at the reaching arm of the next heretic, severing it at the elbow. It howled, the scream coming out of that enormous mouth weak and shrill given the emaciated lungs trying to give it birth. Nick chopped straight at that mouth, cleaving its head in half with Sorrow's sharp edge. He yanked it free of the gore, then plunged it into the chest of the third, whose teeth flexed and scraped with eager hunger as Sorrow's tip punched straight through the heretic's beating heart.

The strange thing collapsed, blood pooling underneath its body. A brief flash of the white bar, and he derived satisfaction in watching it fill toward another reassessment.

"That's right, Nick," he told himself as he pulled Sorrow free. "You can do this. There's nothing to be afraid of."

Except a painful death.

Nick glared at the blade.

Are you capable of hearing my every thought? he asked without speaking.

Sorrow is

I am.

Nick winced.

"Fantastic," he said. "My mind's getting more and more crowded."

Something must fill the empty void.

Nick strode toward the broken doors of the greenhouse.

"Now, that's just mean. Are you some sort of comedian?"

Sorrow's answer rumbled heavy in his head.

I am one of the four judgment blades, imbued with the dying faith of the Sinifel, forged in fires of seething hate to destroy the false god-king seeking our ruination. No, I am not a ... comedian.

He spoke the title as if it were painful to his tongue. Not that Sorrow had a tongue ... nor was Nick sure that he should refer to the weapon as "he" given it was a sword, but the voice was deeply masculine.

In life, I was indeed a man.

Nick peered out the cracked door, and he rolled with the news the best he could.

"Of course you were once alive," he whispered. "Why wouldn't you be a former living being turn into a sentient weapon? Makes as much sense as anything else here."

When Nick didn't hear any nearby heretics, he stepped out into the "street" of the bizarre landscape.

Surrounding him was another city, the architecture less rigid and boxy than that of the one above. Rooftops bore gentle curls and tilts, and no door was perfectly center within the face of its home. The rooftops were of wood shingles, somehow still preserved, while the walls were carved of a yellow-brown stone Nick did not recognize. Little flourishes of spikes and rings marked the many corners and apexes of the rooftops. The city spread like a strip, east to west, and Nick could tell the direction because somehow a faint orb of yellow light hovered in the sky. A sun, where a sun should not be, because swallowing the entire city was a gigantic tunnel carved through dark black rock, its surface just barely hovering above the highest tips of the city's homes.

"Where am I?" Nick asked, mesmerized by the sight. Cataloger's explanation had been woefully lacking.

Abylon, Sorrow answered. *Before it was destroyed, and Oeseli built in its ruins.*

"It sure doesn't look destroyed."

While the other portions of the Swallowed City had been scraped raw of any signs of life, rendered void of color and decoration, the same could not be said for the gargantuan tunnel. Crimson curtains floated from windows. Doors bore spiraling designs of two colors, most often white paint mixed with a second, deeper color. Nick had to admit many were beautiful. Many crossroads were decorated with statues of men and women, some wearing armor, others lengthy dresses and strangely designed suits whose sleeves and coattails were unnaturally long and wide. When Nick glanced at the plaque of one nearby, he found only the same garbled, blurry nonsense that had been in the books in Violette's library.

He spun in place, glancing down the empty streets. What had it been like when the city was alive, full of soldiers, traders, crafters, children, and the elderly?

Do not think on our children, pillager. Your god-king spilled enough of their blood to flood the rivers red.

"Whatever this Vaan is, he's not my god-king," Nick

muttered, turning away from the statue. "And if you're going to police my thoughts, you may soon find yourself abandoned to some forgotten sewer trench the moment I find a less cranky blade."

Sorrow fell silent, for which Nick was thankful. He had larger worries to deal with. Two more heretics had stumbled out from one of the nearby homes, the painted door breaking at their emergence. Nick lifted the blade and planted his feet. The heretics showed little awareness or sense of tactics. So long as he kept a calm mind and steady hand and didn't let them overwhelm him, he'd be fine. The first of the two stumbled within reach. Nick cut across its neck while retreating a step, the spilled blood a vibrant red as it poured forth. The heretic dropped, nearly dead already. Nick focused on the second, positioning his sword so the thing impaled itself during its charge. Sorrow sank into its chest up to the hilt, twice dealing its damage to the heretic to bring it low. Kicking the corpse off, Nick avoided a panicked swipe of a hand from the other, then smashed Sorrow down upon its skull. The heretic lay still.

"Not so hard," Nick said, shaking a bit of gore off the blade.

Indeed, very impressive. Foes worldwide quiver in their boots at the thought of you.

"Must I deal with your sarcasm now?"

Would you prefer my honest opinions instead?

"I think I'd prefer silence."

He continued wandering, which took him past what was once a garden. Vines circled the iron gate sealing over the entrance. Nick peered through the bars. A tiled path

LEVEL: UNKNOWN

led through carefully organized clusters of flower beds and bushes. The nearest was full of red flowers resembling roses. Each and every flower bore the exact same shape and hue. Though no wind blew, they gently fluttered as the green of their stems flickered in and out of existence.

Nick tested the gate and found it locked. When his hand brushed one of the vines, it passed straight through as if it were a mirage. When he tested it again, trying to grab hold of one, the vines vanished completely, leaving only the rusted iron of the gates.

"Cataloger," Nick whispered, "what just happened to the vines?"

I do not understand—there are no vines

"No... I guess there's not."

He continued onward, following a stone wall. It curled alongside the road, then sharply cut inward, leading to a second barred entrance into the garden. Just beyond towered a massive statue cut from white stone. Cracked paint and plaster covered its surface, adding a semblance of black armor and flowing red hair to the proud figure of a man standing atop a pedestal. His fist was raised to the heavens, and his face cast to the floor.

"Who is that?" Nick asked. He disliked the idea of entering the garden, nor did he trust the plaque underneath the statue to be legible.

Gothwyr, Sorrow answered. *Our final emperor, who gave his life in battle against Vaan and his Five Harbingers.*

Nick wished he had an idea of what was going on. Had the Artifact simply made an error and layered multiple cities upon one location? Perhaps it had botched timelines, thinking destroyed ones still existed? Whatever this was, it could not be. No sun should shine this deep underground, in a city beneath a city.

"Do you know any way out of here?" Nick asked as he walked. "I'm taking suggestions from either of you, by the way."

I do not.

Analyzing this terrain is proving difficult

"Fantastic," he muttered. "I guess we wander and hope for the best. That, or Frost and Violette find a way in."

Another heretic, climbing out a window. Nick approached and jammed Sorrow through its head while it still lay on its stomach from the fall. One forceful hit was enough. As he pulled his sword free, he heard a distant rumble, like shaking rock.

"What is that?" he asked.

Find out yourself, pillager.

Another rumble, then silence. The hairs on Nick's arms and neck stood up at the sound. Cataloger had listed the area as an average level of 8, yet so far he'd fought only level 4s. Given her smug crack about how averages worked, Nick disliked the idea of what might be causing the sound of those very big, very heavy footsteps in the distance. Standing out in the open felt like being a rabbit in a flat field. He hurried along, and when he saw a heretic wander out from an alley, he ignored it and kept going. He didn't want to stop, didn't want to fight. He saw another heretic push out from the door of a dilapidated shop, and a third out a window.

LEVEL: UNKNOWN

Damn it, he thought, holding his ground and turning. He couldn't let them chase him. They were easy to handle for now, but if they gathered into a swarm...

Feet set, Sorrow ready, he cut them down one by one. There was something satisfying in the act, to swing his sword, see the damage spray out in white or red, and then witness the steady growth in his experience bar. It almost made up for having to witness their terrifying mouths and hear the clatter of their glass teeth.

"Three down," he said, glancing about the city. "Unknown many more to go."

Deciding wandering was more likely to get him killed than help him find a way out, he instead tried to think logically. Frost and Violette were certainly looking for him. If so, where would they go?

"To where they think *I* would go," he said. "And where would I go? To the biggest, flashiest building around. That makes sense, right?"

Uncertain

Are you asking me?

"Fantastic, this is all perfectly normal," Nick said, holding back a sigh. "But if I'm right, then that temple there makes the most sense."

The building was slightly elevated above the rest of the city with dozens of steps, as if built on a man-made hill. Nick sneaked past two more heretic creatures, then began his ascent, his eye on the grand doors. They were currently closed, their surface painted all in red but for a multitude of hands drawn in black rising from the bottom of the doors toward an unseen sky.

These steps, Sorrow said. *It is painful to look upon them once more. Take me elsewhere, pillager.*

"Try asking nicely next time," Nick said. When he pulled on a door handle, it thankfully opened, though he was less thankful for its loud, creaking groan. "We're going in."

After so much destruction and death, Nick was shocked by the sudden beauty of the building within. The stone pillars holding the roof aloft were carved into mesmerizing swirls. The floor was built of red-and-black stone, arranged into patterns that shifted and ebbed like waves upon an ocean. Tattered white curtains hung over oval windows, their binding threads sewn with silver. Every wall was painted top to bottom with frozen moments in time. The nearest scenes were of pastoral fields of wheat and the familiar mountains he'd seen west of Meadowtint. The closer to the front, the more they darkened, the sky turning red and the ground blackening.

"This must have taken years to build," Nick said, mesmerized by the sight. "It's beautiful."

It was my place of worship, Sorrow said, and there was no hiding his grief. *Once. But yes, it is beautiful. We made it so, with our prayers, our sweat, and our faith.*

There was no furniture, no chairs or benches, just an empty floor. Nick walked across it, his footfalls echoing in the somber silence. His gaze locked between two separate stairs leading higher up into the temple, to a painted mural filling the entire wall. Along the bottom was what he suspected to be Abylon, only properly set aboveground and wrapped with a crenelated wall. The yellow sun had set, though the black sun

LEVEL: UNKNOWN

remained high in the sky above the city. Its size was dramatically wider than he'd ever seen before, and dramatic blue fire rippled about its edges.

From within the black sun emerged endless monsters. They flew on wings, some feathered, some furred, and some insectoid. Each one appeared to be an amalgamation of an existing creature, only grotesque and enlarged. They flowed as a tremendous stream to the city, whose citizens fled in despair. Many were depicted being torn apart, and others, eaten. All the while, the city burned.

"What is this?" Nick whispered, both entranced and horrified.

The needed cataclysm, Sorrow answered. *The cleansing that must be made true lest we suffer Eiman's wrath.*

"You sacrificed yourselves?"

You err in calling it a sacrifice. Is it a sacrifice when snow melts beneath the sun? We beheld the way of the world, that only a fool would deny.

Before Nick could answer, the ground shook underneath his feet from another rumble. He grabbed Sorrow's hilt, his eyes widening as he looked about. That was much too close for comfort. What could be—

And then the back wall exploded inward, bricks flying amid the dust and clatter as the gargantuan monster emerged.

Chapter 20
NICK

Nick stumbled backward, gasping as one of the bricks struck his arm and spun him sideways. His confusion quickly turned to panic upon glimpsing the full size of the monster pushing aside broken portions of the wall.

It was a gargantuan beast, at least four times Nick's height. The twisted horns upon its head brushed the ceiling. Its arms were three-fingered, its chest, rounded and strangely bulbous. Two legs, muscled and with four clawed toes, carried it over the rubble. Its head was insectoid, with two bulging round eyes on either side and a proboscis coiled underneath. The eyes were crystalline, akin to clouded diamonds. The proboscis sparkled like blue cobalt. Its skin might have once resembled black chitin, but much of it was faded and gray, as if the monster were slowly turning to stone. Its every movement groaned with the heavy sound of a controlled avalanche. Wings spread from its back, wide and like a butterfly's. Once, they might have been beautiful, but now they were solid gray rock. Despite their thinness, they were much too heavy to lift, so instead they rested like a cloak upon the beast's back, cracked and with pieces broken off from the exterior edges.

"What is that?" Nick asked, his eyes stretched wide as the thing took another lumbering step.

Matagot: Level 48 War Beast (Sinifel)
Armor: Chitin, Tier 5
Special Classification: Construct

The war beast that will kill you like it did my previous captor, you foolish pillager. He also sought treasures, and so I brought him here to his doom. May you die as he did.

Matagot lifted its left pincer, and Nick immediately turned to dive. His feet left the ground moments before it struck, smashing a deep crevice into the temple's floor. Nick landed awkwardly and rolled up to his feet, lightning crackling around his left hand. That first hit told him all he needed to know about this fight. One blow from that pincer and he was a temporarily dead man.

"I didn't even do anything!" he shouted, unsure if he was arguing with Sorrow or the war beast.

You have trespassed. It is enough.

The proboscis vibrated, the only warning Nick had to lift Sorrow in the way. The long coil of cobalt shot out from the thing's face, its sharpened end aimed straight for Nick's chest. It collided with Sorrow, striking it on the flat edge and pushing it into Nick. The impact sent him flying to a hard landing on the stone, but he considered that a far better fate than being pierced.

What I'd give for some armor, he thought. He rolled onto his back, lifted his arm, and fired a **<lightning bolt>** straight into the war beast's chest. His aim was true, though the bolt sparked a pitiful fraction off the beast's health. He noticed the red bar above the war beast was already significantly low, and not from his own attack. A little over a quarter remained of a health bar that seemed almost grotesquely long.

It's old and damaged, he thought as he pushed to his feet. *That means you have a chance.*

Lying to yourself aids no one, pillager.

"No lie," Nick muttered as he sprinted right at the thing. "And you're going to help me kill it."

Matagot lifted an enormous foot and stomped, trying to squish Nick mid-charge. He angled about it, but the impact of its landing reverberated through the ground and sent him stumbling forward. When Sorrow struck the beast's leg, it was less of a slash and more of a panicked flailing. Sorrow deflected off the pale gray muscle. The sound it made was like stone hitting stone.

The beast shrieked, a weirdly high-pitched sound for something so big. Nick planted his feet, determined to do better on his next swing. Sorrow struck the thing's calf before bouncing right back off with another loud clack. The beast lifted the damaged leg and kicked. Nick tried to leap aside and was only half-successful. The impact sent him spinning to the ground, a chunk of his health vanishing into pain in his ribs and chest.

Nick pushed to his feet as the thing lumbered closer, its proboscis twitching. Every hit from Sorrow seemed like the bite of a mouse to the war beast.

"Tier fifteen," he muttered. "This really the best you got, Sorrow?"

LEVEL: UNKNOWN

I owe you nothing, pillager, not even a goodbye when Matagot turns your bones to powder.

The war beast tensed, and so did Nick, uncertain what it planned. The answer came in a sudden, tremendous sprint from one side of the temple to the other. Nick's instincts took over. Avoiding it was impossible, so the only way out was through. He charged right back at the war beast. No timing its steps, no pretending at judging anything correctly, just a panicked leap between its feet. He landed, jarred his wrist, and then rolled to a stop. The war beast's foot smashed the ground inches from his head, but it did not touch him. The temple rocked as the war beast rammed the other side, supports cracking and glass shattering.

Nick stood, extended a hand, and drained the last of his mana in two bolts of lightning. He wished he could take satisfaction in the combined damage, but relying solely on Sorrow to finish the job felt like a daunting task.

"What's wrong, beast?" he shouted as he barreled in, avoiding a swipe from one of the thing's arms. He tried not to think of how badly it would hurt—

A strike from the war beast would inflict approximately two hundred forty to three hundred sixty-five percent of your maximum health

—and failed, so instead he banished his fear with recklessness.

"Can't you squish me like the bug I am?"

The war beast turned, its left arm smashing through the wall of the temple. Glass and plaster rained down, and amid that chaos, Nick drove Sorrow straight into the thing's left knee, deep enough to earn himself a grim, satisfied smile. He tore the weapon free, then sprinted between the thing's feet yet again when it reached for him. Massive fingers pounded the floor so that cracks spider-webbed all the way to the other wall. Nick slashed the other leg twice, then sprinted to escape.

Matagot took two steps in pursuit, then paused. With what appeared to be tremendous effort, the wings on its back lifted slowly. Then they dropped, the right one cracking in half. Chunks fell to the ground, and the war beast grabbed one in its hand and lifted it. Nick's eyes widened at the sight.

"Oh shit," he murmured as the beast pulled back to throw.

A projectile of eighty pounds thrown by a war beast possessing twenty-three physicality would do approximately—

The broken chunk of wing was in the air before Cataloger could finish explaining why it would turn Nick into paste. He crossed his arms and braced for the horrendous pain and inevitable waking in his bed.

Instead, a massive wall of ice burst into being before him, starting at his feet and then rising to curl back into a protective dome.

Spell: Ice Dome

The chunk of wing hit the ice, splitting it down the middle with a massive crack and sending puffs of frost jettisoning in all directions. It did not break through, which allowed Nick to lower his arms and gasp a sigh of relief as the dome crumbled.

"Frost?" he said, turning. To his surprise, she came not from the entrance of the temple, but from above. A path of ice—

LEVEL: UNKNOWN

Spell: Icy Path

—stretched down from a gap in the roof all the way to the floor, allowing her to slide down to join him. Ice sparkled about her fingertips as she readied her sword.

"Having fun without me?" she asked.

"Great fun," he said. "Glad you made it."

The war beast roared, the sound again weaker and pitched higher than felt right. It lumbered closer, the broken wing bouncing atop its shoulder while the other dragged along the floor.

"I don't think your friend agrees."

Frost flung an **<ice lance>** at the war beast's face and then dove left as Nick dove right. Its two fists blasted where they'd been standing. When it withdrew, it left a crater in the stone several feet deep, exposing broken rock below the foundations of the temple. Nick slashed Sorrow across the wrist of the nearest arm for a paltry amount of damage. Still no blood. Nick wondered if the thing could even bleed.

Is it alive? he asked Cataloger.

It is a sentient being created in the age of the Sinifel

It is a beast of stone made flesh, Sorrow helpfully added. *Embodying the rage of the calamity that comes for Yensere when it is swallowed by stagnation and complacency.*

The two answers combined were sufficient. It also explained why it looked like it was turning to stone—it was reverting to what it had once been.

Angered at the cut, the war beast dodged another **<ice lance>** to smack at Nick with clawed fingers. Nick tensed, read the direction wrong, and failed to fully jump out of the way. A claw scraped across his chest, and he gasped at the tremendous pain from a deep gash below his ribs. His vision flashed red as his health plummeted almost 90 percent. The impact sent him flying, and he rolled twice before coming to a halt.

Damn it, he thought as he jammed Sorrow between two bricks of the stone floor and used it for leverage to push back to a stand. *Can't make a mistake like that.*

With him out of the way, the war beast turned its attention to Frost. She held her sword up and at the ready, a ring of frost circling around her upraised left hand as she prepared another spell. Whatever she expected, it was not the sudden, lunging attack of the proboscis. It lashed across her abdomen, and she screamed as it tore into her silver chain mail. The impact sent her spinning, and she landed awkwardly on her stomach. Blood pooled beneath her.

"Frost!" Nick shouted, sprinting. He slid in the blood so he landed on his knees, and he grabbed her with his free hand. With his other, he held Sorrow up as a paltry defense against a foe outweighing him by a thousand pounds.

Four thousand nine hundred and three pounds, to be exact

"I'm fine," she said, sounding otherwise. Her eyes widened as the shadow of the war beast fell over them. "Oh shit."

Nick looked back up, sharing her despair. They'd whittled the war beast down to nearly 10 percent of its health, but their luck had run out. Nick had no magic left, and his sword would do nothing against the pair of fists raised to smash them both into jelly.

LEVEL: UNKNOWN

But Nick and Frost were not the only ones with magic available to them.

Spell: Fire Bolt

The first bolt struck the war beast right in the proboscis, charring across the cobalt. The next two struck its chest, the impact sounding like a collision of stone. The brittle chitin cracked and broke under the strain of the heat. Nick gasped, and when he glanced over Matagot's shoulder, he saw Violette sliding down the <icy path> Frost had built from the gap in the rooftop. Her hands were raised and her fingers wreathed with flame.

"Stay away from them!" she shouted, and let loose her strongest spell yet.

Spell: Fire Meteor

A tremendous, seething ball of flame far larger than her <fire bolts> flung from her fingers. It hit the war beast in the face, colliding with such impact it snapped the thing's head far enough back to crack the stone that ran along either side of its neck. It then exploded into flame that swirled about its entire body, blackening the stone and making a mockery of the chitin's protection.

This time the beast's screech was deeper, slower, and clearly pained. The thing stumbled on unsteady feet, then collapsed. Its unbroken wing wedged into the crater it had punched, then snapped at the joint, the heavy stone rumbling as it broke apart into several more pieces.

"Finish it," Violette shouted as she dropped to one knee. Sweat lined her brow, and she gasped for breath after the exertion of that massive spell.

Nick grabbed Frost by the hand and yanked her to her feet. They said nothing, only exchanged glances before sprinting together toward the fallen beast. Each raced up a leg, across the chitin, and to its breast. Frost plunged her thin sword into where its heart might be, while Nick went higher, Sorrow aiming for its throat. It recoiled in pain from Frost's hit, its health pitiful, flickering as Nick readied his thrust.

Light flickered in the monster's bulbous eyes. Its low, moaning groan suddenly shifted, and Nick shuddered as a part of his mind twisted. Perhaps it was Cataloger, perhaps it was the creature, but somehow, he understood the war beast's words despite their not at all resembling human speech.

My city, Matagot spoke, the words rumbling out of the small hole underneath its proboscis, which cracked, uncoiling and losing color. **Where now my city?**

In Nick's grasp, Sorrow grew warm.

The poor thing has guarded our ruins for an age, he said. *Give it peace.*

Nick shoved Sorrow into its vulnerable throat, no easy feat given that the creature's flesh was almost entirely stone. The war beast shuddered underneath Nick's feet. Its arms collapsed, fingers dragging grooves into the mangled floor.

Where now my people? it asked. Its diamond eyes clouded over, turning fully white. Little flakes peeled off the sides.

Aah, there you are...

The body went limp and lay still. In the sudden silence, Nick gasped as his experience bar flashed into his vision and rapidly filled twice over.

Reassessment

LEVEL: UNKNOWN

Level: 9 (+2)
Statistical Improvements:
Agility: 5 (+2)
Physicality: 5 (+1)
Endurance: 4 (+1)
Focus: 7 (+2)
Mana: 49 (+14)
Archetype Changed—New Categorization: Adventurer

Nick yanked Sorrow free, and he wished he could celebrate his growth. Instead, he stared at the gargantuan thing and spoke with Sorrow in his mind.

How beautiful was Matagot, he asked the blade, *when its wings still had color and its flesh was not stone?*

It seemed Sorrow was taken aback, and it took him a moment to answer.

I wish you could have seen it, pillager, striding in all its glory down Abylon's streets. Gossamer wings the color of flame, crimson in the center and bright yellow along the edges. Sleek black chitin for armor. Eyes sparkling like diamonds. No war beast was alike, each one the proud culmination of an artisan's life.

Sorrow's voice hardened.

I once thought all of them had died in the war against Vaan. I was wrong.

"Nick!" Violette shouted, stirring him from his thoughts. He turned and smiled at the small woman racing toward him.

"Hey," he said. "I guess I should have believed you when you said you could handle yourself."

She hurried across the war beast's still body, easily keeping her balance until reaching Nick. She halted before him, then paused awkwardly.

"I thought we'd lost you forever when you fell," she said. "Don't ever do that again."

"He'll try," Frost said, sheathing her sword and checking the wound on her abdomen. She winced. "That's going to need some stitches. How about you, Nick? Going to survive?"

He gestured to the slashes given to him by an errant blow.

"Survive, yes. Be in pain for a long while? Also yes." He climbed down from the war beast, then held on to one of its arms to steady himself. "Tell me you know a way out of here."

"That we do," Violette said, hopping down with a flourish of her red coat. "And if you manage to not fall through any floors to even deeper, unknown civilizations, I'll show you the way!"

Chapter 21
SIMON

"Director?"

Simon startled in his chair.

"Sorry," he said. "There something you need, Essa?"

Essa crossed her arms and fidgeted in the doorway. Her glasses were in her hands, he noticed. Her eyes were bloodshot at the edges, with enlarged dark rims underneath.

"We need to speak somewhere in private," she said.

Simon stood and did a quick job of straightening his uniform and running fingers through his hair. It was heavily mussed on one side, a victim of the awkward position he'd fallen asleep in.

"That bad?" he asked.

Her frown tightened. "Yes."

That chased away the last of Simon's sleepiness. He nodded and gestured for her to lead the way. The pair walked the hallway to her office, Simon leaning heavily on his cane to endure the travel. Essa was one of the sharpest minds on Station 79.

Originally she had been brought on to help with scanning Majus as the main technology specialist, but her dual studies in linguistics had proven invaluable in studying the Artifact and the symbols slowly appearing across its surface since it made contact with Nick. She was ten years his senior, her personality sharp, her mind sharper, and her black hair kept wadded behind her head in a large bun. It did nothing to hide how strikingly beautiful she was, thoughts he had to keep to himself given his role as director.

"Has something happened?" he asked when they entered her little office. He shut the door so they would have privacy. The station was currently emulating night, so the lights were dimmed throughout, the hallways lit only with thin white guidelines where the floor met the walls. He thought Essa would force the lights on to their full strength, but she did not, and instead walked to her desk and hit a few buttons to remove the security screen.

"I've been carefully monitoring transmissions as requested," she said. It was a task he'd given her not long after initiating dark quarantine, for truthfully, he did not trust himself to give it his full attention, given his brother's deteriorating health. She'd not been pleased to have her attention diverted from attempting to translate the Artifact's bizarre symbols, nor scanning the planet for geography matching Nick's stories of "Yensere," but she took to the task without complaint.

"In particular, I've been focusing on those coming from Vasth," she continued. "At first, I feared we might be caught in an incident, especially if any of the world's governors made public Director Lemley's death and accused us of being responsible."

LEVEL: UNKNOWN

"I take it that didn't happen?" he said. A bit of diplomatic nonsense would be unwelcome, but he'd handled similar nuisances before. An angry governor would not bring Essa to him in the middle of the night, nor would it explain the redness of her eyes.

"That's the thing," she said, sitting at her desk and putting on her glasses. Her hands flashed across the keyboard. "I don't know, because yesterday, Vasth's gate went dark."

Simon flinched as if he'd been flicked in the nose.

"What do you mean, went dark? Did something happen to the gate?"

"I don't know. Official explanation so far is no messages, no recordings, and no explanations. Not only that. Look."

She shifted her chair so Simon could lean closer and see her screen. It was a news article from the planet Salus, whose gate positioned them between Majus and Vasth. The bulk of the story was easy enough to get from the headline alone.

HELD BREATHS AS ALL AWAIT EXPLANATION FOR VASTH GATE SHUTDOWN

"What do you think happened?" he asked. "Did the gate suffer a collapse?"

It seemed unlikely. A gate collapse had not happened in more than a hundred years, with the OPC's stabilizing technology improving in leaps and bounds over the original versions of the interstellar gates first used to expand humanity's presence beyond their home-world system of Sol.

"Doubtful," Essa said. "Collapses happen spontaneously, without warning. Vasth was held in quarantine for over a month."

That piqued Simon's growing interest.

"Vasth was under quarantine?" he asked. "Why did I never hear about this?"

"It's a small planet, harsh to life and with little to offer in terms of research or trade," Essa said. "Supplies were still sent in, but nothing sent out. I only knew because my brother is there, serving as lead biologist. All his communications halted, with vague nonanswers given as to why."

"I wish you'd told me," Simon said, scanning the text. Most of it was questions without answers, guesses as to what error had caused it to seal and no timetable given for when it might be repaired. "You've been worrying about this all on your own."

She shook her head.

"My business is my own, Director, as I prefer. But...I wondered, how did Planetary Director Lemley break through the quarantine? Why was he allowed to come here?"

"He came to shut us down," Simon said, a pang of anger flaring in his chest. "To kill us because of the Artifact. He knew about it, somehow, and wanted it destroyed."

"Knowing of the Artifact is explainable given his ranking," Essa said, leaning back in her chair. "But my hypothesis is thus: The quarantine was implemented on Vasth's side about a month ago at their request. Sneaking through a gate is impossible, so Lemley was allowed passage because our research into the Artifact was considered a greater danger than whatever caused their own quarantine. One great enough to warrant the destruction of a research station."

Simon bit at his thumbnail as he thought.

"He knew something about it that we don't," he agreed.

LEVEL: UNKNOWN

"There is only one reason why that would be true," she said. "They, too, possess an Artifact."

Now, *there* was a fascinating theory. Simon had assumed from the moment of finding the Artifact that they had stumbled upon the first-ever proof of intelligent life outside their own. Oh, they'd found simple organisms before, especially fungi and plant life, but never proof of what would colloquially be called aliens. The potential ramifications of their discovery on Majus had kept Simon's research station isolated, his superiors hanging on his every update but doing little to attract attention. Debates about what to tell the various world governors, if anything at all, had become the hottest topic of late.

"Have you any proof?" Simon asked.

Essa closed down the article and started loading up a different file, one he noticed required her to input two separate passwords to progress.

"I don't," she said. "Which is why I doubled my efforts to break through the security to Lemley's thumb drive. I needed to know what he knew. I needed to see if there was a clue as to what was happening on Vasth, if only to..." She paused. "I know it is unprofessional to let worries over my brother affect my work, but they did."

"Consider yourself forgiven," Simon said, and he smiled wide to convince her how little he cared. "So did you crack it open?"

"I will spare you the work and the copious amounts of swearing required," she said. "But yes. I did."

A folder flashed up on the screen. Simon frowned.

"Just one file?" he asked. "That's all?"

An image file, in a universal format used by all OPC researchers. Essa hovered her cursor over it.

"I don't think this was for us," she said. "I think this was for himself. For courage to do what he believed must be done."

She opened the file.

It was a beautiful picture taken from what Simon believed to be the surface of the planet Vasth. The ground was awash with blue moss speckled with tall white mushroom stalks. It was the beginning wave of a terraforming project to increase oxygen in the atmosphere as well as break the hard ground down into soil more welcoming to advanced forms of life. The sky was an extremely dark blue, which was odd given that the atmosphere on Vasth was still developing. Two people in OPC blues stood to one side, looking upward, with one pointing. It was a moment frozen in time, strange and chilling.

Hovering in the sky next to their pale yellow sun, its color so deep the monitor screen felt insufficient, hovered a black sun wreathed in swirling blue fire.

"That can't be," Simon said, backing away from the monitor.

"It is," Essa said. "Something happened to Vasth. I know it." She looked over her shoulder. Fear and frustration dominated her visage. "No communications. No travel. My brother is in danger, or maybe he's dead, I don't know, and there's nothing I can do about it."

Simon's eyes could not leave the black sun. With just one picture to go on, he could not guess its size and distance. Was it small, and in the sky above them? Or was it tens of thousands of miles away, rivaling the size of a moon?

LEVEL: UNKNOWN

"Is there a date on this photo?" he asked.

"Only for the file's creation," Essa said. "This picture was added to the thumb drive two weeks ago. How long it was taken before that, we can only guess."

"The quarantine," Simon said. "They must have initiated it the moment it appeared."

Essa spun in her chair. Her hands rested on her knees, her fingernails digging into her skin.

"I've read your reports," she said. "This...Yensere your brother visits, it bears the same black sun in its sky. The fate of Vasth? It may have been the same fate that befell the world locked inside the Artifact."

"That's absurd," Simon argued, but Essa just shook her head. Before she could say more, her watch beeped, an irritating little digital scraping sound.

"What is that?" Simon asked.

"An alert I set up for news involving Vasth," Essa said, rotating her chair back around to face her monitor. A quick tap, and another article popped up. Its headline, written in all capitals, shocked the pair into momentary silence.

"It can't be," Simon whispered.

Essa pushed away from her console. Her hands shook.

"My brother," she whispered, then turned his way. The fierceness of her gaze overwhelmed him. "Nick is all we have, so get him to focus. We need answers, and we need them *now*, Simon."

She stood and then stormed away. Simon watched her go, paralyzed with guilt and indecision. He stared at the monitor and the article left looming there like a dire threat.

VASTH GATE DESTROYED

Chapter 22
NICK

Once they'd climbed up and out of both Abylon and the Swallowed City, the trio made camp a safe distance away. Nick sat beside a roaring fire, enjoying its warmth. It'd been a long day, and between the specters, the impossible geography, and a battle against an ancient war beast, he wanted nothing more than to relax before sleeping.

Sorrow was making that difficult.

You may pry all you like, pillager, but my words are my own, he grumbled as Nick brushed his fingertips across the ancient runes cut into the obsidian.

"I do have a name, you know," he mumbled.

I don't care.

"Being rude isn't going to make anything better."

The heretical god-king reigns over the ashes of my homeland. Pray tell how forgoing rudeness will make that better.

"So what's it like having a sentient sword?" Frost asked, pulling Nick's attention away to the two women sitting together on the opposite side of the campfire. He'd told the pair about finding the magical blade during the trek out of Abylon, to Violette's fascination and Frost's grim amusement.

"You'd think it'd be fun," Nick said. "But I somehow found a blade that absolutely hates me."

"Somehow."

"Still, Sorrow is ancient and magical and will surely come around to liking you eventually," Violette said. "That has to make it worth the risk, right?"

"Is that how you justified going into the Swallowed City alone?" Frost asked in return.

"I have my magic to defend myself," Violette said, leaning closer to the fire. "I just had to be careful."

"But what if something happened? Would anyone even know to look for you?"

Violette had removed the tie of her ponytail, and she shifted so her long hair fell between her and Frost. Nick, however, could still see the frustration on her face as she spoke.

"No. No one would look, and if they did, it would not be to rescue me."

It was a brief crack in Violette's otherwise unflappable optimism, and Nick hated seeing it.

"You said you were a scholar," Nick said. "Surely you belong to a guild or organization or some such, right?"

"I did," Violette said, and her smile returned, this time not quite so wide and effortless. "I have always been fascinated by the Majere, the people who predated not just the Sinifel but the very first calamity. The way they viewed life and death, and the ideas they carried in regard to eternity, is so different from what we are taught by the god-king's priests. But just like with the Sinifel, all texts regarding those beliefs are declared heretical. Much of what was held in the Goltara Library was burned in the great purge, and what remains is highly restricted."

She shifted upon the grass.

"My interest in the Majere was always frowned upon by my instructors at the Silversong Academy, but I pressed on. This stagnant world of ours bores me. What more is there to learn? Even the seasons are halted. I've never known a winter, only read about it in books that managed to escape the purges. Every year, more and more books predating the Alder Kingdom are quietly disposed of. The history of this world, all its fascinations, its legacies, the great fall of leaves and the billowing of snow, is being forgotten. Vaan and his priesthood would have it all be lost forever."

She glanced between them.

"I want to learn," she said. "Everything. Experience *everything* that Yensere offers. And while some instructors were fine to turn a blind eye to my studies, not everyone was."

She closed her eyes in thought.

"One day, the priesthood was informed of my research. I don't even know by whom. Maybe an instructor. Maybe a jealous contemporary. It doesn't matter. While I was away in the field, my room was raided and my belongings confiscated. By the time I returned to the academy, my judgment had already been reached and my fate decided."

She fell silent. Nick watched the hurt on her face slowly fade back into hiding. Frost put a hand on her shoulder as the fire crackled.

LEVEL: UNKNOWN

"How did you escape?" she asked softly.

"A friend of mine within Silversong sent me warning before I reached the academy grounds. And so I just...fled. I wasn't thinking much when I did it. I decided I would go to the farthest reaches of Yensere, to the places where Vaan's influence was likely the weakest."

She sat up and forced a smile.

"Besides, out here, I can still do my research. I can learn the history of Yensere, even if the god-king would seek it buried and forgotten."

Such a lovely, expertly woven tale to personify her as a blameless victim, Sorrow suddenly interjected in Nick's head. *But she is a blind fool. Vaan built his army preaching against the ideals our Sinifel Empire was founded upon. For her to think her research would go unpunished reveals a profoundly naive heart.*

"I'm glad you found a way to keep going," Nick said, trying to ignore Sorrow. It hurt him seeing the seemingly cheerful Violette so crestfallen, and he wanted nothing more than to replace that forced smile with a sincere one. "Is there anything we can do to help?"

"We?" Frost asked. "I have my sister to search for, remember?"

"Your sister?" Violette asked. "Where is she? What happened to her?"

Frost squirmed uncomfortably.

"Irina didn't...I knew she came here, but where, and why exactly, I don't know."

Violette shot to her feet. "Then let me help! I've learned a lot about Vestor, especially all the ruins and forgotten places no one should know about, and those are the places people go to hide!"

Frost still didn't look convinced. She pushed to a stand, and she gestured at Nick.

"Mind if we have a chat in private?"

"Sure thing," Nick said.

Am I allowed to observe or would you prefer I "give you a moment of privacy"?

"The more the merrier," Frost said, apparently also hearing the question and answering for the both of them. Nick followed her from the fire into the shade of a massive jut of stone emerging from the earth. Frost leaned against it with her arms crossed. Her gaze lingered on Violette, who hunched closer to the fire with her head resting in her hands.

"I'm not sure I'm ready to trust her," Frost said before Nick could say a word. "Her waiting for us inside the Swallowed City feels a little too convenient."

Nick shrugged. "And who was she waiting for? Me? I've never met her in my life, nor heard of the Silversong Academy. What about you? Is there anyone on Yensere who would know where you were going?"

Frost shrugged. "Only Irina."

"Then maybe we need to trust that coincidences happen. She did help defeat the war beast. We owe her for that, at least."

"Some of us aren't as trusting as you, Nick."

Nor as foolish, or hasty, or foul-looking...

I am perfectly handsome, he mentally snapped at Sorrow, annoyed the sword was listening in.

In the eyes of mothers, perhaps.

LEVEL: UNKNOWN

"Look, I am here in Yensere to learn more about what all this is," Nick said. "And in that regard, I would love having someone knowledgeable with me. And with all she knows, if she can help you find your sister, then why not bring her along?"

Frost's fingers clenched the sleeves of her chain mail shirt.

"I know she's pretty and bubbly, but that isn't reason enough to trust her, not completely."

"I trusted you immediately, and your personality isn't bubbly at all," Nick argued.

Frost smirked at him. "Is that your way of saying I'm pretty?"

Nick's mind hiccupped.

While beauty is not a cataloged statistic, Frost meets many historical standards of attraction—would you like me to confirm this to her?

I'd rather die.

"No changing the subject," Nick said, attempting to do exactly that. "Violette can be helpful, so I say, let her be helpful."

Frost pushed off the stone, and she put a hand on Nick's shoulder. The playfulness on her face was replaced with dire seriousness.

"Violette isn't like us," she said. "Not a visitor. Not from outside Yensere. She won't follow the same rules, and if she dies while traveling with us, she *dies*. No coming back. Even if she is willing to accept that risk, are you?"

Nick put his hand over hers, and he wished he knew more about Frost and the perspective from which she saw things.

"Outside Yensere, that is the way of everything, yet I still have friends and family I trust," he said. "If it's the same with Violette, then that's fine with me. It'll be no different than real life."

"*Nothing* about this place is real life," she said with surprising venom. "Don't you dare forget that, Nick, or you'll be lost to me, too."

She pushed away his hand and returned to the fire. Her composure shifted, and there was no hint of the venom in her voice when she addressed Violette.

"Decision's made," she said, plopping down beside her. "You're coming with us. Welcome to the party."

"Thank you!" Violette said, throwing her arms around Frost in a decidedly one-way hug. Before Nick could arrive at his own seat, she jolted to her feet and ambushed him as well. Her slender arms wrapped around his waist as she pressed the side of her face to his chest.

"Thank you," she said again. "I can be alone if I must, I just... don't like it. It's never something I'd choose if given the choice."

Nick gently returned the hug, then lightly pushed her away by the shoulders.

"Just remember, Frost is in charge," he said. "Searching for her sister comes first. Any research for Majere stuff comes second."

"If you insist." Violette stepped away, and she crossed her hands behind her back. Her dark hair fell across her face, momentarily hiding her eyes. "You won't regret this, either of you. I promise."

"I pray it so," Frost said, grabbing her pack of supplies. "Now, let's find some food. I'm starving."

Chapter 23
NICK

Location: Greenborough
Description: One of the oldest cities in Vestor, population three thousand plus, wherein most trade goods from across western reaches of the province are gathered before being shipped on the main road route to Castle Astarda

"We're actually going in there?" Nick asked as the trio stood before the entrance to the city of Greenborough.

"Why wouldn't we?" Violette asked. The tiny woman was practically vibrating with excitement. "I need to stock up on food, and you look like you could use a lot of supplies yourself, Nick. Supplies, and other things."

"What's that supposed to mean?"

"It means you've got little more to your name than the clothes on your back," Frost said, and she nudged him with her elbow. "I do think it'll be nice to get you properly set for travel. Plus, we can buy you a nice bedroll so you stop complaining about your bed."

"But what about... you know. The whole 'demon' thing?"

Frost's look was far too amused for Nick's liking.

"Go on ahead," she told Violette. "Me and Nick need to discuss something really quick."

"Sure," Violette said. "I'll be waiting for you at the gate."

"Cataloger," Frost said once Violette was out of earshot. "Hide Nick's visitor status while we're in Greenborough."

"My what?"

Visitor status is now hidden

Nick's mind raced, and given Frost's twisted grin, it did not take long to figure out what was going on.

"The people in Meadowtint," he said. "That's why they thought I was a demon? Because Cataloger had me marked somehow?"

"He's learning!" she shouted playfully, and started after Violette. Nick was too angry to immediately follow.

"Cataloger," he said, and he felt like he was addressing a misbehaving puppy. "Why did you flag me as different from everyone on Yensere?"

Visitor status is given so inhabitants of Yensere may recognize visitors and grant them unique treatment and privileges during their stay

"That's not exactly what happened, is it?"

Unique treatment was indeed given

"Unique? They were trying to kill me! Why didn't you remove it?"

I am not allowed to deviate from established operating procedures without sufficient reason

Nick had to choke down an exasperated scream.

"Cataloger," he said as he caught up to Frost. "You're great and all, but please, please, *please*, if you know why someone is trying to kill me, let me know?"

Request noted

Are you often under threat of death? Sorrow suddenly interjected, his cold, deep voice a stark contrast to Cataloger's more smooth, feminine sound.

"More than I'd like," he muttered.

Have you considered it is deserved?

Nick grumbled instead of responding.

There are too many voices in my head, he thought as he stood awkwardly at Frost's side. Violette was ahead of them, arguing with the soldier barring their way at one of the wide gates that gave entrance through the wood palisade that surrounded Greenborough.

"Something wrong?" he whispered.

"There's apparently been a warning put out for a demon traveling these lands," Frost said, looking pointedly at Nick. "Might you know anything about that?"

Nick paled.

"We need to leave, *now*," he said. Instead Frost grabbed his elbow.

"Stay calm," she said. "They have only a basic description, and the clothes do not match what you stole from Hulh Manse. No one giving you a glance over will think anything of you. Just let Violette offer the requisite bribes to smooth things along."

Sure enough, Violette shifted so her body was between her and the others in line seeking entrance and then reached into her pocket. After a moment, she said something to the guard and then pointed to where Nick and Frost waited nearby. The soldier nodded, the bribe already vanished into his pocket before Nick saw it in his hands.

"We're good," Violette said, hurrying over. "Just stay with me and pretend to be my guards."

"Your guards?" Nick asked.

"Of course," she said, and grinned at him. "A helpless scholar like myself traveling into dangerous parts unknown surely needs a pair of guards to keep her safe. Well, one guard, and one servant. You can guess who is which between the two of you."

"Oh, I can't imagine," Frost said, patting her sword as the trio passed through the gate. Pretending not to notice Frost's sarcasm, Nick shifted his attention to the bribed guard. He was only level 6, as were most others in the vicinity. The fact made him feel surprisingly relieved. If things turned south, he could hold his own against them. A far cry from when he first fled the villagers in Meadowtint, barely able to defend himself.

And now you possess the means to murder soldiers and civilians, Sorrow added. *I pray you do not plan to force me to join in such bloodthirsty indulgences.*

As if the Sinifel were strangers to slaughter, Nick mentally shot back.

You know nothing, pillager.

"Hey, Cataloger," Nick whispered. "Is there a way to silence this evil sword of mine?"

Ownership of Item: Sorrow grants a link with

the weapon's personality—to disrupt the link would require forfeiture of ownership

If you want to silence me, you'll need to surrender me to another, Sorrow said, unaware of Cataloger's answer. *So toss me in a gutter somewhere. I am sure to find a better owner there.*

At this point I'm going to keep you out of spite, Nick thought, and he flicked the hilt with his fingers. He highly doubted the sword could feel pain, but the disrespectful act most certainly annoyed the blade.

As they entered through the gate into the city proper, they passed a dozen men and women sitting on either side of the street. Their skin was unnaturally pale, and they looked sickly and frail. Though their clothes varied, they all shared a similar sign hanging from their necks, a wooden placard with a single black line smeared across it with ash. The dozen held out containers for alms, some cups, some buckets, some little wooden trays. Violette seemingly picked one at random to give a copper coin, and Frost did likewise.

"Who are they?" Nick asked.

"People afflicted by the blight," Frost explained, keeping her voice low. "They're forbidden from working jobs, and shunned because of the signs they have to wear. No one knows how the blight spreads, or how it chooses who to afflict, so people have grown paranoid."

"No one wore those signs back at Meadowtint," Nick said.

"A small village on the outskirts of Vestor, with nearly half the populace affected at some level?" she said. "No, they wouldn't."

It seemed so cruel to have these people cast from society in such a way, especially for reasons beyond their own control.

"What about Cataloger?" he asked. "Does she know the cause?"

Frost shrugged. "Didn't seem to when I asked."

"Give me a moment, then. I want to see what she says."

Nick stood near one of the blight-afflicted beggars, trying not to seem too conspicuous. The man looked similar in age to Nick, his unkempt hair a mixture of white and faded red. His eyes bore faint gray markings, and his skin was much too pale given how often he sat in the sun. When he thanked a passerby for offering him a coin, Nick caught sight of flecks of black upon his tongue.

What's wrong with him, he silently asked Cataloger.

Query not recognized—please rephrase

The beggar before me, the one with the blight. What is the nature of his sickness?

He is not affected by any cataloged disease or affliction

That certainly went against the evidence before Nick's eyes. But why would Cataloger not be able to notice? Though she could be cagey with answers, she seemed to be aware of most everything within Yensere. Granted, she'd not exactly known what was going on in the buried city of Abylon, either.

He seems sick to me. Could you, I don't know, look again?

By now the beggar had noticed Nick was lurking nearby, and though he did not say anything, he turned Nick's way, trying to capture his attention while reaching for the little straw bowl before him. His hand froze upon touching it, and a dazed look crossed the man's face.

Cataloger? Nick asked, eyes widening as the change began.

LEVEL: UNKNOWN

Color flushed the man's skin. The white left his hair, the whole of it blossoming into a vibrant shade of red. The gray left his eyes, and when he spoke, his tongue was a healthy pink.

"Sir?" he said, suddenly looking at his bowl in confusion. "I meant to...ask you something..."

I detect nothing abnormal with this individual

"What is going on?" Frost whispered beside him. She'd watched in silence until the change hit, quickly going from disinterest to fascination. "Did Cataloger cure him?"

Cataloger was quick to answer them both.

Even if there were something to cure, I cannot influence the material world

As she said this, the beggar slumped back onto his heels. The color drained from his skin. The white returned to his hair. Whatever clarity had come to his eyes, it faded away as he stared down at his bowl and slowly, gently shook the few coins within.

"Coin for a troubled soul?" he said, not even looking up anymore.

Frost reached into her pocket and pulled out a coin that flashed silver in the light.

"Here," she said, depositing the coin into the bowl and then grabbing Nick by the arm. "Sorry to bother you."

They hurried off, to where Violette was patiently waiting for them at the first crossroad.

"Everything all right?" she asked, sensing their worsened mood.

"Fine, it's all fine," Nick lied.

"All right..." Violette said, glancing between the two of them before shrugging. "So, back to the matter at hand! I'm not exactly poor, but I should be careful with my budgeting. Before we gear up, I suppose I should know where we plan to head next so I can purchase appropriately."

"*We* are going to Castle Astarda," Frost said. "I've scoured the far west more than enough to know Irina's no longer here. She has to be east of the Frostbound Mountains, maybe somewhere in Inner Emden."

"Oh." Violette frowned. "That's going to be a bit trickier to bribe our way through. Lord Frey's soldiers are...more fanatical than most. But that means we shouldn't need any gear to handle the mountains out here, and we'll have plenty of food to forage. I'll focus on some basic hiking and camping supplies, and a pack to carry it all in. Have either of you any money?"

"Not a..." Nick paused. He was about to reference a chit, the least valuable currency in all OPC worlds. Obviously that'd be meaningless here. As for paying for the supplies...

All currency for barter and trade must be acquired manually by visitors

Thanks, Cataloger, I couldn't have figured that out myself.

"Nothing," he said. "I'm dirt poor."

"Then I'll buy you what you need," Violette said. "No companion of mine is going to travel unprepared!"

"Thank you," Nick said, smiling at her. "You're a real lifesaver."

She smiled at him in return. "And don't you forget it."

"All right, while she shops, you're coming with me," Frost

said, beckoning for him to follow. "Given all the fun that's happened since your arrival in Yensere, you need something resembling proper armor."

"You mean like yours?"

Frost laughed. "I don't think they make anything like mine, at least not in this backwater portion of Yensere. Even if they did, I couldn't afford it. Some basic kit will have to do."

Nick tried not to feel disappointed. Nice as it would be to have better clothes, he couldn't help but feel jealous of her silver chain mail and the protection it provided.

The two hooked a right while Violette traveled the main road. Nick absorbed his surroundings with wide eyes that most certainly marked him as a newcomer to the city.

"This is all surreal," he said as he observed the many shops they passed. Grocers, drapers, butchers, millers, tailors, brewers, and so many more he did not recognize. Shops for candles, for buckets, tools for farms and repairs to wagons. "I've read about this sort of ancient life, but to see it before me, made real..."

"It's not real," Frost interrupted. "It's all just a joke created by the Artifact." She paused before a shop with a sign hanging over it containing the rough shape of a man and a shield. "Come on, I think we can find you something useful here."

The interior smelled of a mixture of leather, wool, and a pungent aroma that came from the oils stacked on a shelf. For caring for both leather and the few weapons hanging on a rack, he suspected. The man running the shop, burly in the arms and wide around the waist, nodded at them from a stool behind a counter full of knives, but he otherwise let them browse unbothered.

"What is Castle Astarda?" Nick asked as he joined Frost in walking through the sets of leather. "And why is it our next destination?"

"The Frostbound Mountains effectively seal off Vestor from the rest of Yensere," she said, pausing before a chestpiece of leather covered with metal studs. "Going over is dangerous, and around, nearly impossible. The only pass is guarded by Castle Astarda, though it's more a walled city than a castle." She pulled the studded leather off the wood pedestal and shoved it against his chest. "Here, see if this fits."

Nick wrapped his arms around it. "Just over my clothes?"

"It'll be more comfortable than on bare skin," Frost said. "We'll get you something thicker to wear underneath so you don't ruin your fancy shirt, don't you worry."

Nick held the armor up, Cataloger helpfully flashing its statistics.

Item: Studded Leather
Quality: Tier 3 (Good)
Classification: Armor (Chest)
Layers of leather given additional structural integrity by way of fastened metal plates, whose studs give the armor its namesake

"Far better than nothing," he muttered. "So long as someone hits me in the chest and nowhere else." He fiddled with the three buckles across the front. "How do I put this on?"

Frost took the armor piece back from him.

"You're hopeless," she said, showing off a playful grin as

she undid the buckles and helped him put his arms through. Afterward, she tightened the straps until they were nice and snug, then playfully batted at the long length of extra leather hanging down from the buckles.

"I think this was made with someone a bit bigger in mind," she said.

"It's not my fault Cataloger stuck me with a physicality of five," Nick said. "But there's a thought. If that number keeps increasing, will I get all muscled and bulky?"

"Doubtful. Our appearance in Yensere seems to be heavily tied to our appearance in reality, or at least, how we perceive ourselves. The numbers, and what you can accomplish, will change, but how you look will mostly stay the same. If it changes, it will happen slowly, over long periods of time."

"Not sure if I prefer that or not," he said.

"I prefer it. It means no one expects me to hit them as hard as I do before a fight starts. Now go ask the nice man at the counter to trim the extra length from those straps while I browse for some gloves and armlets."

Nick did as asked, trying not to be awkward in making his request and failing spectacularly.

"I, uh, need these cut," he said, patting at the straps when the man arched an eyebrow his way. "The leather, it fits nice, but it's too long. The straps, I mean."

"Yeah, I know what you mean," the man said, sliding off his stool and grabbing one of the knives. "I pray you have the coin to pay for that piece before I start hacking at it?"

Nick gestured toward Frost at the other side of the shop.

"She does," he said.

"Let's hope so," he said. "Now, stand up straight, no slouching, and I'll make sure you got this thing on right before I do any tweaking."

It seemed Frost had buckled it correctly, and when the man was satisfied, he grabbed the thickest pair of scissors Nick had seen in his life and went to cutting. Once he'd pocketed the three extra bits, he put the scissors away and withdrew a thick needle and some thread.

"It won't be the prettiest," he said as he folded the ends of the leather straps and began sewing them to form little loops. "But they'll stay out of your hair."

"Have you any armor made of iron or steel?" Frost asked from the back. "Or maybe some helmets?"

"You'll need to visit Leeroy's for that," the man said. "But look down at your feet, there, in that shelf. I got some leather helmets you can take your pick from."

Finished, he stepped back to observe his handiwork with his arms crossed. As he looked Nick over, his eyes settled on Sorrow tucked into Nick's waist belt.

"That sword," the smith said. He licked his lips. "How much for that sword?"

I am not an object to be bartered and sold, Sorrow seethed. *I am one of the Sinifel judgment blades, the last valiant defense against the heresy of Vaan the false god-king.*

Nick drew the sword and held it aloft. He had no intention of selling it, but perhaps he could learn what Sorrow and Cataloger refused to tell.

"Do you know what it is made of?" he asked, setting it on the smith's counter.

LEVEL: UNKNOWN

You could ask me, pillager.
And would you answer?

The brooding silence was exactly what Nick expected. The smith pulled off his thick gloves and set them aside.

"This isn't steel," he said, gently running his hands along the flat edge. He grabbed one of his smaller hammers and struck its side so the metal rang out. "And I don't say that just because of the color. The sound is wrong, as is the texture. I suspect it is stronger than steel, and yet far more pliable. How else could it maintain such a unique hollowed corkscrew shape just above the hilt?" The smith shook his head. "If I were to wager a guess, it's made of obsidian, though I've never heard of a weapon crafted from that as a base. Whoever made this blade must have been an absolute master."

In that, he is correct.

Nick flipped the sword over and pointed to the writing carved onto the blade in crimson letters.

"Can you read this?" he asked.

Still you seek to deny me privacy, grumbled Sorrow.

The smith leaned closer, his brow furrowing and his left hand stroking the thick stubble growing in the center of his chin. All at once, he stepped back and dropped his jaw open.

"This is Sinifel work," he said. "Where did you find this?"

The query sounded less like a question and more like an accusation.

"I found it...in some ruins," Nick said, realizing he had no idea how such knowledge might be taken, nor what people in Greenborough might think of the bizarre landscape that was the Swallowed City.

"Sinifel ruins, no doubt," the smith said. He pointed at the door. "Pay for my leather and then get out. I'll have no heretical objects in my workshop. We are loyal to the god-king here in Greenborough, yes, we are."

By this point, Frost had heard the commotion and joined them, a pair of long pale yellow gloves and a helmet in hand. Seeing them, the man shook his head.

"Put those down. You get just what I already fixed. Seventeen silver, young miss."

"If you insist," Frost said, dropping both objects on the counter with the knives and then reaching into her pocket. There was no hiding her frustrated glance Nick's way, and it made him want to crawl into himself and hide. He tucked Sorrow back into his waistband as she dropped the coins in the smith's extended palm, the silver clattering.

"I pray you know what kind of man you're traveling with," he said as he pocketed them.

"I'm well aware," she said, smiling through clenched teeth. "Pleasant days to you, sir."

Nick and Frost exited the shop, and for the first time, he was keenly aware of Sorrow's presence, as well as its unique look. He had no sheath to hide it in, and at best, he could turn the blade about to hide the lettering on its side.

This condemnable world birthed by the heretic is frightened by all that I am, and all that we were. If you fear it, too, then you are unworthy to carry me at your side, pillager.

"So quick to judge," he whispered as he and Frost walked the streets of Greenborough.

Judgment is easy when you amount to so little.

LEVEL: UNKNOWN

If only your blade was as sharp as your tongue, he mentally snapped back.

Sorrow did not respond, but Nick swore he could feel the sword smirking.

The pair stopped at a stall run by an elderly woman whose head was wrapped in a yellow bonnet, where Frost bought him a slice of bread and a slender wedge of pale yellow cheese marked with several little holes throughout. Nick bit into the cheese first, and his eyes bulged at the flavor.

"Incredible," he said. "It's almost...fruity in its taste. I've never had anything like it."

"Enjoy it while you can," Frost said. "We need to leave. I'd blame you for showing Sorrow to the smith, but it's my fault for not thinking of it, either. Never guessed a shopkeeper would recognize Sinifel writings."

The meal reminded Nick just how long he'd been inside Yensere, enough that he'd lost track. Two days? Three?

"I should probably leave some time to eat for real," he said, scarfing down the food. "But that can wait until we've left Greenborough, at least. So where's Violette?"

"Main trade runs through Fairview Street," she said. She pointed to a crossroad. "There, to the left. Hurry."

They only made it around the turn before trouble found them. A group of three blocked the street, two soldiers with weapons drawn flanking a third, a young woman with reddish-blond hair. She wore long white robes that covered her down to her ankles, the sleeves and waist both tied firmly to her body with blue sashes. A gold fist clutching a black half-circle was sewn across her chest. A gold chain wrapped about her forehead, little threads of it dangling amid her hair like spider silk. Studded into her lower lip was a gold labret inset with a polished sapphire. In her left hand she held a scepter, its top modeled into a hand holding an hourglass whose sands were fixed.

The woman stepped closer, and she raised her scepter high overhead.

"In the name of the god-king, you both are to surrender your weapons and come with me."

Chapter 24
NICK

"And who are you, commanding us with such authority?" Nick asked. Cataloger was the quicker of the two to answer.

Aranni: Level 11 Human
Archetype: Priestess
Special Classification: Deity Blessed (Vaan)

"I am Aranni, blessed priestess and servant of the god-king," she said, and pointed her scepter. "And I have been told of the Sinifel relic you carry. You are tainted, the both of you. Now, kneel if you wish to preserve your lives."

Frost's right hand drifted to her sword hilt.

"I don't think we will," she said.

Both soldiers rushed simultaneously, one slicing for Nick's waist, the other thrusting for Frost's chest. Nick lunged backward, drawing Sorrow while flinging his left hand forward. A **<lightning bolt>** shot from his palm, striking the nearest soldier before arcing to the other soldier and then the priestess, staggering all three. Frost parried the attack aimed for her, and when the lightning hit her foe, she pushed his sword farther out and then dashed in close, her left hand pressing to his face and helmet.

Spell: Icy Tomb

Frost shoved him to the ground, where he writhed and clawed at the ice sealing away his face. As he suffocated, Nick watched in horror and awe as his health steadily drained away.

The distraction nearly cost Nick his life. The other soldier rushed with his sword held in both hands, a powerful chop aiming to cleave Nick in half. He flung Sorrow in the way, deflecting the trajectory, but not enough. The sword struck his shoulder, punching a tear into the leather. He screamed as he bled from the wound, losing just shy of a quarter of his health. Reacting on instinct, he slammed Sorrow straight at the man's neck. The obsidian blade punched a hole in his breastplate to take away the last of his life.

Clutching his wound, Nick glared at the priestess, who glared right back with her yellow eyes wide. She held her scepter high above her as her hair billowed in a nonexistent wind.

"Vaan is with me!" she shouted, and slammed the scepter down.

Circles opened in the ground all around them, their centers pitch-black, their outer rings gleaming with gold and sparkling with intricate fractal shapes. Nick dove immediately, needing nothing beyond base instinct to know they were dangerous.

Spell: Vaan's Embrace

Swords of pure light emerged from the holes, blade first, and flew to the sky. Nick twisted as he dove, trying to avoid them and only partially succeeding. One pierced the side of his thigh, tearing through flesh in a bloody spray that seemed at odds with the beautiful gold. Nick hit the ground with a gasp, clutching the wound with his free hand as the pain hit him. A quick check to his right, and he saw Frost hadn't endured the spell cleanly, either, blood dripping down her pristine silver chain mail from a shallow cut across her neck.

"The god-king is my strength!" Aranni continued, lifting her scepter. The frozen sands within the hourglass blazed with sudden light, and she pointed it straight at Nick.

"Nick!" Frost screamed, diving in front of him to land on her knees. Her palms slammed the ground, summoning her **<ice dome>**. It formed about them, a protective shield. Through the distorted haze of the ice, Nick watched a solid beam of golden light shoot from the scepter, the front of it hardening to form a spear tip.

Spell: Faith Spear

The light struck the ice, spreading cracks but failing to punch through.

"You all right?" Frost asked, still crouched.

"Could be better," he said, then heard the priestess chanting once more. His eyes widened. "Move!"

More circles beneath them. More swords shooting to the sky, to explode in a shower of light that sprinkled downward like spent fireworks. This time, the pair avoided the hits, but multiple swords streaked through the ice dome, shattering its magic and rending it to dissipating frost.

Attack, you dimwit, Sorrow shouted in his mind. *Or will you let the heretic's priestess strike you down unmolested?*

Nick hated to agree with the sword, but there would be no enduring more of this. He lifted his hand, and when Aranni chanted anew, he shot a **<lightning bolt>** straight for her chest. It struck true, and most importantly, the sudden constricting of her muscles robbed her of speech. Not daring to let her recover, he sprinted straight for her, a second bolt leading the way, this time hitting her in the stomach. The priestess's eyes widened, and she staggered in retreat. Frost denied her the chance, **<frost nova>** latching about her ankles to root her in place.

Her scepter swung toward him as she cried out to her god-king.

"Vaan be—"

Sorrow easily batted the scepter aside on its way to her throat. The blade sank deep, pouring blood down her immaculate white robes. Her eyes bulged, and her mouth opened and closed, wordlessly protesting her coming death. She dropped to her knees, then collapsed.

As Nick pulled Sorrow free, a familiar and decidedly unwelcome sensation struck him. His movements slowed, the removal of the bloodstained blade agonizingly sluggish as it withdrew from flesh. Golden light faintly sparkled off his skin as he turned his gaze down the street, to where Sir Gareth approached with his sword drawn.

Gareth: Level 13 Human
Archetype: Knight
Special Classification: Deity Blessed (Vaan)
Armor: Augmented Chain Mail, Quality Tier 7

"You would bring your slaughter here, too?" Gareth asked.

LEVEL: UNKNOWN

His grip on his sword tightened. "There is no hell hot enough for what you deserve."

As Nick slowly, slowly lifted his sword, he heard Cataloger helpfully chip in.

Per your request, Sir Gareth seeks to kill you due to the slain villagers at Meadowtint

"Thanks," Nick muttered, sounding drunk in his own ears.

You are welcome

A **<frost nova>** lashed out to wrap ice around Gareth's legs. It slowed him only a moment, but that was enough for time to resume its normal flow around Nick.

"Time to go," Frost said, grabbing his wrist as Gareth smashed the ice around his legs with his sword to free himself.

"What about Violette?" he asked between breaths as they sprinted through the streets of Greenborough. Bystanders cried out as they pushed through, some in anger, others in fright.

"Pray she hears the commotion," Frost shouted, "because we can't wait for her." She pointed. "Soldiers ahead. Follow my lead!"

She waved her hand, casting another spell.

Spell: Icy Ground

The three soldiers rushing toward them stumbled as a thin sheet of ice coated a wide area in front of Frost. Unable to properly set their feet, they were unprepared for the brutality they faced. Frost dashed into their center, the ice seemingly nothing to her as she spun and twirled, her sword a whirlwind. Nick attacked with far less finesse, holding Sorrow in both hands and chopping straight through the collarbone of the nearest soldier. The blow struck true, instantly killing him.

A thrust through the throat, then a chop across the stomach, and Frost ended the lives of the other two. She banished the **\<icy ground\>** with a snap of her fingers, then glanced over Nick's shoulder. Her eyes widened.

"Keep for the east exit," she shouted, once more taking the lead. Nick dared look and saw Sir Gareth charging toward them like a furious rhinoceros decked in golden armor. The sight was enough to add a burst to Nick's step, and he pretended not to notice the steady drain of his stamina. It was certainly better than when he first arrived in Yensere, but he feared that at the pace Frost demanded, he would not last to the east gate.

Shops and homes passed by in a blur as the wooden palisade surrounding the city grew nearer. Two more soldiers rushed to block the way, their shields held high. Sir Gareth was much too close to risk a prolonged fight, and both Nick and Frost knew it. The pair unleashed a combined attack, his **\<lightning bolt\>** leading in a bright flash, followed by twin **\<ice lances\>**. The combined damage brought the two soldiers down, and they rushed past the corpses without pausing.

At least, that was Nick's intention, but then his stamina hit zero. He staggered as if stones had been lashed to his wrists and ankles. His chest ached, and his heart pounded in his chest. His every gasp of air was loud in his ears, and he struggled to even call Frost's name as she raced ahead of him.

"Wait," he managed. She glanced back, realized what had happened, and skidded to a halt.

LEVEL: UNKNOWN

"Shit."

Nick chuckled as he turned. "Indeed."

Sir Gareth arrived with a rattle of armor. If he was winded from the sprint, he certainly didn't show it. He redrew his sword and pulled his shield off his back as he stalked the pair.

"More dead at your hands," he said. "And now you find others to join you in your slaughter."

Nick lifted Sorrow, and he flashed a cocky grin.

"I'm just trying to live," he said. "You're the one coming for my head."

Frost joined him, her own sword raised.

"This isn't going to be easy," she said softly. "And the longer we fight, the more guards will arrive."

Nick braced his legs, lightning crackling around his fingers as he prepared the last of his mana. Frost hadn't seen her yet, but Nick had. It was only guards coming to help. The pair just needed to keep Sir Gareth's attention their way.

"We're not good enough friends for you to be this persistent," Nick shouted as he flung a **<lightning bolt>**. Gareth blocked it with his shield, and Nick was dismayed to see that it somehow reduced the damage to a pitiful fraction.

Shields protect against many types of attacks, both physical and magical

Of course they do, he thought as Frost followed up with a new spell he'd never seen before.

Spell: Frost Orb

They flung at Gareth like little cannonballs. The knight weathered the barrage with his legs braced and his shield held high. The metal held, and even worse, Gareth suffered not a scratch, only an inconvenience of ice exploding around his feet as the magic broke down.

"Ice," he said when the attack was done. "You were at Hulh Manse, weren't you?"

"Might have been," Frost said, and flung an **<ice lance>** at his face. He sidestepped it in a blur, so much faster than someone his size should be. Nick chased him with two more **<lightning bolts>**, rapidly burning through his mana while accomplishing little. Gareth's shield was always at the ready, reducing the combined hit from the two spells. The storm weathered, his gaze hardened, and he jammed his sword into the street to lift his right hand.

"Then you both deserve my judgment," he said. An orb of light shimmered into existence as he muttered a prayer to his god-king.

"May heresy be burned," he said, and threw it.

Spell: Purge

The orb flew between Nick and Frost, then detonated in an explosion of ringed light that swarmed with intricate runes Nick could not identify. The runes washed over him, and he screamed as his every muscle locked tight. His entire body felt aflame, even as his skin went untouched.

When it passed, he dropped to his knees, his health down to a third after being drained by the spell. He wasn't even sure what damage had been done to him, only that he felt hollow and weak inside. Though Frost was stronger than him, he suspected she was equally dazed, given the sag in her stance and the shaking of her sword.

Yet the distraction had been enough. Despite his weakness,

LEVEL: UNKNOWN

Nick pushed back to his feet and grinned as Violette, unseen behind Gareth, lifted her hands to prepare a spell of her own.

"Not bad," Nick told the knight. "Our turn."

Spell: Fire Plume

The flame washed over Gareth in a massive jet, charring his white cloak instantly. Flesh peeled, and he screamed as he thrashed, baffled and overcome by the fire that burned away at his body. When the spell ended, Frost followed up immediately, sending an <ice lance> straight into his chest that sent him flying past Violette down the street. Gareth landed in a heap of rattling chain mail, smoke wafting from underneath the metal.

"You didn't kill him, did you?" Violette asked, spinning to face where Gareth lay. Nick stared at her as if she were insane.

"You're worried about *him*?"

She clutched her hands to her chest and shrank into herself.

"I don't like killing. Especially people."

"The whole city is after us," Frost said, rushing to grab the other woman by the wrist. "Flee now, feel bad later."

Thankfully the eastern exit wasn't far, but a new problem awaited them when the trio came sprinting. Five soldiers stood guard in front of the closed double doors, barring all traffic. They lifted their shields and readied their swords upon seeing the trio's approach. A prime target for lightning, but Nick's head was a pounding torment. He had nothing left, and he suspected Frost had also been pushed to her limit.

"I got it," Violette said, as if sensing their hesitation. She hooked her hands together, thumbs and forefingers interlocking, and pushed them ahead of her.

Spell: Searing Wrath
The ball of fire flew ahead of her as if launched from a catapult, aimed for the space above the five soldiers. The moment it struck the brick archway above the closed doors, it detonated like a bomb. The ground shook. The wall cracked and broke, the doors splintering to pieces. Sticky hot air billowed outward, preceding the flame that followed. The soldiers screamed in terror, diving in all directions before the fire could overwhelm them. The way clear, Violette dashed into the inferno, dismissing the rolling flames with a wave of her hand.

Holy shit, Nick thought as they raced after her. *Remind me to never get on her bad side.*

Request noted—how frequent would you like this reminder to occur?

Nick did not answer, only laughed like a maniac as the trio exited Greenborough at a dead sprint, to leave the city far behind and enter the wilds of Yensere once more.

Chapter 25
SIMON

"So what do you think?" Essa asked. Simon leaned closer to her monitor. Satellite photos of Majus were arrayed across the screen, with one in particular centered, a large portion of it circled in yellow to highlight Essa's findings.

"I think you found it," he said, stepping back. "Send that to my tablet. We'll need Nick to confirm, but if it's the same mountain range, we'll have locked down a significant piece of the puzzle."

"Already sent." She rubbed her eyes and grimaced. "Thankfully this was something I could automate. Translating the Artifact's newest garble is turning my gray matter into scrambled eggs. Looking at terrain images is relaxing by comparison."

Simon tucked his tablet underneath his arm and headed for the door.

"Try to get some sleep, will you?" he said. "We need that gray matter of yours in top shape."

"No promises," Essa shot back as he exited her office.

To Simon's immediate concern, his security officer, Daksh, stood waiting for him in the hallway just outside. By the look on his face, the tenor of this meeting would be quite the opposite of Essa's.

"Director," Daksh said. "I've something you need to see."

He lifted his watch and whispered something to the AI. Simon glanced at his tablet as a window opened, filling with text. Simon scanned it, his excitement over Essa's find making it hard to concentrate on something so basic.

"This is just a letter to someone's parents," he said, stopping halfway.

"Exactly," Daksh said. "Dr. Pagle tried to break quarantine and send it this morning."

"How?"

"By bribing the head of engineering. They pretended to agree and then forwarded it to me instead."

Simon sighed. It felt like a thousand pounds of weight had been slammed onto his back. His dream of following in the footsteps of his parents to manage a space station had been about pioneering into the unknown edges of science and exploration. Dealing with insubordination was very, very low on that list.

Simon's watch vibrated silently. He glanced at it, saw an alert he'd programmed so that anytime Nick's vitals showed signs of waking, the station AI would notify him.

"Excellent timing, Nick," he muttered, then brought his attention back to Daksh.

"No punishment," he said. "Give Pagle a stern warning and then let it go."

LEVEL: UNKNOWN

"A blatant breach of protocol, and you can't even muster a slap on the wrist?" Daksh asked. "I'm not sure that's wise."

"We're all stressed and scared, Daksh, and it's not like Pagle was leaking classified data. It was a message to his family, to let them know not to worry, for shit's sake. Now, let it go. I've got to see Nick."

"Right," Daksh said, his mood souring. "Go on, then. I forgot how your brother trumps everything now."

Simon's blood ran cool. He stepped closer to Daksh while straightening his spine.

"Nick is our lone entry point into an alien world," he said, fighting, and failing, to keep his voice even. "And that exploration is steadily killing him, so, yes, Nick is my highest priority right now, and it has nothing to do with him being my brother. Is that understood, *Officer*?"

Daksh pulled back his shoulders, his face becoming a perfectly emotionless mask. Simon didn't trust it in the slightest.

"Perfectly, Director."

"Good." Simon brushed past him. "Now, handle it."

The lights were on in Nick's room when Simon entered. His brother lay on his back, calmly staring at the ceiling. Waiting for him, he suspected.

"Welcome back to the realm of the living," Simon said, setting down his tablet on the nearby chair.

"Glad to be back," Nick said, voice muffled by the oxygen tube.

Simon hit a few buttons on the heart monitor, bringing up a graph of the last half hour.

"No skyrocketing heart rate, no lurching awake," he said, and then began helping Nick remove the oxygen tube. "What gives?"

"I didn't die," Nick said, rubbing his nose. "Believe it or not, for the second time now, I left the *proper* way."

"A good habit to keep," Simon said, and he smiled. "Your heart rate didn't go above 140 in the past hour or so. That's got to be a record for you."

"Forget my heart rate. You won't believe what I've learned. I can control *lightning*!"

Simon grabbed his tablet so he could plop down in the chair and then scooted it closer.

"Lightning?" he said. "Let's hear it."

Nick's reports of his activities within Yensere were scattered and inconsistent, to the absolute fury of many on the station, but the reports that existed had mentioned a Sir Gareth multiple times, and those encounters almost always ended with Nick being unceremoniously booted out to the real world. Listening to Nick detail a victory against this otherworldly knight, let alone through an absolutely bewildering method such as learning to throw lightning from his bare hands, put a wide smile on Simon's face.

"Not bad," he said. "And to think, it wasn't that long ago you were half-naked and throwing rocks at people."

"Even clueless incompetents like me are capable of getting better," Nick said, and grinned. That jovial attitude faded, and he glanced away. "Simon, there's something I should have told you earlier."

LEVEL: UNKNOWN

Simon leaned back in his chair. His thumb brushed his watch, activating the recording software.

"What is it?"

Nick settled back into his bed, suddenly unable to meet Simon's gaze.

"It's about Frost. She...she's a visitor like me."

Simon froze.

"From...here?" he asked, forcing words out through his lips though his brain felt as if it were made of molasses. The ramifications of someone else on his station entering the Artifact were too many. His mind struggled to contain them all.

"No," Nick said, shaking his head. "I don't think so. Another planet, I think. Where, she refuses to say."

They, too, possess an Artifact.

"Maybe she's from Vasth," Simon said, vibrating in his chair with excitement. "But that means these Artifacts, they're connected somehow. A shared world? Or do they each possess their own, and travel between them...but such travel, this would involve information transmissions of such quantities and capabilities, they're leaps and bounds beyond our understanding."

He realized Nick was staring at him and paused.

"Sorry," he said. "You don't know about Vasth. It's a beginning-stage terraformed world two gate hops away. It initiated quarantine about a month ago, and then yesterday, we received confirmation the gate on their side was completely destroyed."

"Destroyed?" Nick asked, suddenly more alert than he'd been in days. "Why? By who?"

"We don't know." Simon hesitated. They had one clue; he wasn't sure Nick was ready for it yet, but he had little choice. He could not delay any longer.

"While I think on what it means for there to be more than one visitor to your mysterious little world, I want you to take a look at this."

Simon grabbed his tablet, clicked through to a folder, and then loaded an image. He flipped it around to show Nick. His brother leaned closer, trying to analyze what he was seeing. It was a satellite photo of Majus and its dull black rock, showcasing a lengthy mountain range. After a moment, Nick startled.

"The mountains to the west of Meadowtint," he said.

Simon grinned slightly; at least one theory was panning out, a small bit of good luck.

"We're dealing with unknown timelines, but when you described those mountains, that felt unique enough that I set Essa to scan the terrain in a search, and there they were."

Nick leaned back into his bed.

"What does it mean?" he asked.

"I think it confirms your Yensere is set on Majus. Whether it is an exact re-creation, a smaller simulation, or merely using the planet as an inspiration, we cannot yet say."

"As it was..." Nick frowned. "Yensere is full of life and people. Majus is gone. Completely empty, no atmosphere, no buildings, no water..."

"But there are *signs* of water," Simon insisted. "We're unsure how long ago, but we've seen geological evidence of oceans. Majus and Yensere are linked, if not the same place—I'm sure of it."

LEVEL: UNKNOWN

"Then, what happened?" Nick asked. "What destroyed their world?"

Simon's chest tightened. No dancing around it now. He rotated the screen away from Nick, tapped some keys, and opened a different picture.

"I think this was somehow involved," he said, and spun it back around.

Nick's entire demeanor darkened upon seeing the photo from Lemley's thumb drive. A hard edge entered his brother's voice, one strange and foreign to Simon's ears.

"What is that?" he asked quietly.

"A picture taken from the quarantined planet of Vasth. It's in their sky, just like in Yensere's sky. Planetary Director Jakob Lemley brought this with him on a thumb drive, exiting their quarantine mere days before their gate's destruction. He tried to have us killed. The Artifact—he feared it, somehow."

"What do you mean, *a planetary director tried to have us killed*!?"

Simon put a hand on his brother's shoulder. "I'm sorry, Nick. I didn't want to trouble you before, with all that you've been experiencing. But now..."

Simon told Nick everything, starting with Lemley's arrival, the attempt to detonate the oxygen tanks, the ensuing dark quarantine, and then ending with Essa's confirmation of the Vasth gate's destruction.

"'An accident near the oxygen tanks,'" Nick said when he finished, and his disappointment could not have been heavier. "Why didn't you trust me with all this when it happened? Why lie?"

"I don't know," Simon said. "Have you looked at yourself in a mirror, lately? This Artifact world is a burden on you, a heavy burden. I didn't want to make things worse on my little brother."

"And so you coddled me instead."

"It's not coddling! It's called partitioning responsibilities. You have yours, and I have mine, which includes ensuring you survive all the shit this *Yensere* inflicts upon you."

Simon immediately regretted the outburst. He slumped in his chair and rubbed his eyes.

"I'm sorry, Nick. You deserve better than that."

His brother shifted in the bed, then gently reached out to hold his forearm.

"No, it's fine. I held back about Frost, too, so I have no room to act insulted. Just... please trust me, all right? I may be your little brother, but I'm a part of this station, and a pretty big deal when it comes to learning about the Artifact, if I say so myself."

Simon chuckled, wishing he could be as easygoing about all this as Nick.

"Fine. You've got my full trust. So back to the topic at hand." He gestured to the photo of Vasth. "Do you have any ideas about this? Something I might not have considered?"

Nick stared at the black sun.

"I don't know," he said. "Are they connected, you think? Created by the Artifact, somehow, or maybe summoned?"

"If the Artifact is malevolent, it hides it well," Simon said. He flicked open another folder, this showing a picture of the Artifact in the station holding bay. He zoomed in to show

LEVEL: UNKNOWN

Nick faint violet glyphs shimmering across its sides. While the research team had discovered traces of those glyphs within the first month, they'd never glowed, nor had anyone been able to make any sense of them...at least until recently.

"The Artifact has clearly woken up," Simon continued. "And we're making progress in translating these glyphs...or more accurately, the Artifact is allowing us to translate them. They've been shifting and changing, forcing us to go line by line in an order its creators absolutely predetermined. Perhaps it's a test of our language abilities, perhaps it's just a game, we don't know. But we've managed to translate a full sentence: 'The youngest among you will be chosen.'"

"So that's why it was me," Nick said. "But chosen for what?"

Simon shrugged.

"Go to Yensere? Live inside its digital world? See Majus as it was thousands of years ago, with a little 'magic' added for flavor? It's all guesses, but I feel like we're getting closer."

Nick stared at the photo of that black sun wreathed with blue fire.

"Not close enough. The people of Yensere insist that black sun means their doom, and now it appeared over Vasth not long before their gate was destroyed. Get me something to eat and drink so I can go back in. I've got an idea of who might have some answers."

"And who is that?"

His younger brother grinned at him.

"Before the Sinifel and the Alder people, before the black sun brought the very first cataclysm, there were the Majere.

So after I grab myself a bite to eat, I'm going to see what Violette knows about them."

Simon arched an eyebrow. "Violette?"

"Oh. Right. So let me tell you about this incredibly sweet but also slightly terrifying little scholar we met named Violette…"

Chapter 26
GARETH

Sir Gareth paused before the grand gates of Castle Astarda, named after the family that had ruled the heavy brick and stone fortress since the dawn of God-King Vaan's rule. It towered above the nearby plains, defiant and proud. The walls of its battlement stretched for half a mile to either side, eventually merging into the rising stone of the Frostbound Mountains. If one sought to travel between Vestor and Inner Emden, it was through here, and here alone.

"Welcome, Sir Gareth," one of the soldiers inspecting traffic said upon waving him over. "I trust all is well in Greenborough?"

"As well as one can hope," Gareth said, feigning a smile as he passed. Unlike the others in line, he did not need to suffer the tedious indignity of a search. Villagers and traders often sought to smuggle in goods without paying taxes, hide their stolen nature, or even carry heretical tracts to and from Vestor. Sometimes people tried to scale the mountains farther north or south. It was then they discovered just how many beasts and monsters of forgotten times still hid in the snow-capped peaks and the dark, uncharted caves.

An enormous road split the castle interior, though with so much of it empty, it felt grotesquely wide and downright depressing. There had been a point, when Gareth was a child, when this road had been overwhelmed with people. Stalls, currently empty, were once filled with men and women hawking their wares. The smell of bubbling rabbit stew and freshly baked sourdough had wafted from multiple buildings beside the trade road, an enchanting variety for young Gareth to choose from. Fruit pies baked with blueberries picked from southern Vestor. Tarts slathered in honey and filled with apples picked from Emden's sprawling orchards. Beer blessed by priests and priestesses all the way in Castle Goltara and then shipped in barrels throughout Yensere.

Now traffic on the streets was sparse, the largest crowd at the entrance, where beggars marked with signs of blight sought relief from travelers.

It was not all dire, though, with the roads growing livelier the closer he came to the keep in the heart of the walled city. A young girl with her red hair tied into two buns waved at Gareth from her little stall as he passed. He did not know her real name, nor had she ever offered it, so he called her "Beans" after the produce she sold, to her great amusement.

"How's business today, Beans?" he asked.

"Business is business is business," she said, her favorite response to the question he always opened with. She gestured to a little box filled with winged greens layered in oil and powdered with cracked pepper. "Care for some pepper fingers? Made fresh, and extra spicy!"

"Not today, Beans," he said. She stuck her tongue out at him and scrunched her nose. His laughter immediately died, replaced with dread.

The faintest shadow of black coated the back of her tongue.

Gareth stumbled away, wishing he had never seen it, wishing it could have befallen someone, anyone else, not a young girl full of such life and wit. A vision of her wearing one of those smeared-ash signs haunted his mind. Years of practice, of seeing those he cared about fall victim, allowed him to shove it away. Clamp it down. Pretend it would take time, years even, before the change came.

"You poor girl," he whispered. "Must the blight claim even the young?"

A lengthy line spread out from one of the few bread makers still open. Gareth held back a sigh. The blight had wrecked so much of the west. What crops were harvested barely fed the villagers harvesting them. Few afflicted possessed the motivation, or clarity of mind, to craft anything beyond rudimentary tools. Only Greenborough and Castle Astarda endured, their people mostly spared the blight, and because of this, all of Vestor's trade flowed directly through them eastward, to Inner Emden.

But neither city would be free of the blight forever. Its march seemed inevitable, and his most recent letters from his mother in Inner Emden's capital of Avazule fearfully mentioned increased sightings of the afflicted. If he thought she would leave her home of twenty years, he would have begged her to travel east, to Castle Goltara itself if she must, to escape the danger.

"A bit of pie for a soldier of the god-king?" a woman shouted from the window of her store, stirring him from his thoughts. Her hands were wet from grease, and a bit of flour still clung to her face. Gareth's stomach rumbled at the smell of freshly cooked lamb.

"The road has been long," Gareth admitted, having already regretted not buying any of the pepper fingers. He dug his hand into his coin purse. "Perhaps I will."

Gareth ate the pie as he slowly walked the road. A second wall sealed off the entrance from the east, and in the center between those two rose the castle keep. It was that rectangular edifice Gareth approached. Lord Frey Astarda ruled from within the fortress, as had his father, and his father before him. Gareth's stomach clenched, and it wasn't from the spiced grease dripping off the lamb.

Lord Frey will not take kindly to your failure, a dark, cowardly voice whispered in Gareth's mind.

Gareth pushed the intrusive thought away. The outer villages west of Greenborough were his responsibility, as was the safety of the slain Baron Hulh. He would not cower from the consequences of his duties.

"Greetings, Sir Gareth," the soldier protecting the keep entrance said. "Shall I alert Lord Frey to your arrival?"

"Please," Gareth said, shifting uncomfortably in his armor. Though his wounds had healed during the travel to Castle Astarda (a blessing of strength from the god-king himself), they itched fiercely, and would until the scars faded.

LEVEL: UNKNOWN

Once inside, Gareth waited at the center of the guardroom, chatting politely with other soldiers until a servant exited the stairwell and beckoned.

"He is ready for you, sir," the young woman said.

Gareth followed her up to the third floor, through a furnished waiting room, and into the den of the keep's master.

Lord Frey was an imposing man despite his age. His shoulders were broad, and his chest and arms thick with muscle developed over a lifetime of swinging a sword. His hair was just starting to turn a shade of silver, and he kept it pulled tightly back and bound behind his head with a knot of thread. It added severity to an already severe face, which bore a permanent frown from the wrinkles around his mouth and a narrow gaze from the crow's-feet around his green eyes.

"Welcome to my home," Frey said, rising from the chair beside the fireplace to greet him. "Your timing, however, is a bit poor. You arrive just in time for a feeding."

Frey's wife sat in a chair on the opposite side of the fireplace, a blanket covering the lower half of her body. A young babe lay in her lap, and she had opened her blouse so he could suckle.

"At least I did not wake the little lordling," Gareth said, and flashed his widest smile. "I pray you fare well, Lady Jeanne?"

"To wake him, he'd need to sleep first," Jeanne said, and smiled back. "And I'm fine, other than a great deal of tiredness."

Jeanne was a welcome burst of sunlight within Castle Astarda, and her golden hair and yellow eyes seemed to match Gareth's sentiment. She was a good twenty years younger than

Frey, and their marriage was most certainly first about securing him an heir. The two seemed to get along well enough, at least according to what Gareth saw on his occasional visits to his liege. The people liked her, too, and there was even talk of her assuming Frey's post should something happen to him before their child, Gestolf, came of age.

"My lord, forgive my haste, but I must speak with you on important matters," he said.

"Whatever you wish to say, you can say it in front of my wife," Frey said, leaning forward in his chair. His eyes seemed to sparkle with life, as if he relished the thought of news, however dire it might be.

"Very well," Gareth said, and cleared his throat. He began with his arrival at Meadowtint and the news of murder committed by a demon. He held back fully describing the methods, keeping it vague whenever he could. Jeanne shuddered when he described the ferocity with which the demon, Nick, hounded the people of Meadowtint, sneaking in through windows and ambushing them from within their wheat field, all to kill the unsuspecting. Then he detailed his chase eastward and his discovery of the slaughter at Baron Hulh's manse.

"Poor Hulh," Frey said, shaking his head. "A good man, kind to those in his care, and trying his damnedest to slow the spread of the blight. You are certain this Nick had a helper?"

"Two helpers," Gareth said. "And I know because I fought them."

Despite the deep pit of shame he felt in admitting so, he detailed his encounter in Greenborough, their brief clash, and the trio's ensuing escape. He described the magic of all three and did not hold back his despair at seeing Nick's rapid growth in power.

"I should have crushed him in Meadowtint," he said when finished. "Forgive me, my lord. I thought I had broken him, but every death seemed to make him that much more fearless and cunning. I spoke with our god-king in prayer, and though he sends a Harbinger west, he insists I continue my hunt to bring the demon low." He lowered his gaze. "And yet I have lost his trail once more. I am failing, my lord, failing the one trial put before me by his holiness, and I do not know what to do."

Frey glanced at his wife, his frown deepening.

"Jeanne, would you kindly take Gestolf to our bedroom?" he said. "I suspect the both of you could use a long nap in warm blankets."

Jeanne pulled Gestolf away from her breast and lifted her blouse despite the bit of milk that wet its interior and darkened the fabric. Gestolf grumbled, his mood quickly souring as he flailed his arms and hunted for the vanished nipple with his eyes closed.

"Of course," Jeanne said, and she dipped her head toward Gareth. "It was nice to see you again. I hope you meet Gestolf once he's fed and slept. He truly is the sweetest thing." She winced, then laughed when the babe let out an angry cry.

"Enough, Jeanne," Frey said, the sharp crack of his voice upsetting the baby further and robbing his wife of her smile. She hurried away. Gareth refused to watch her go, instead focusing on the carpet as he knelt before his lord.

"Stand, my friend," Frey said once they were alone. "I would have you accompany me."

The two returned to the stairwell, descending to the guardroom floor. Once there, he followed Frey to a plain, unmarked door. Beyond it was another staircase, slender and steep. His curiosity growing, Gareth followed Frey some twenty more steps, the keep growing darker as the only light came from small black lanterns lit with tall, thin candles. The stairs ended at a locked door, and a soldier keeping watch who was immediately dismissed.

"Do you trust me, Gareth?" Frey asked, his hand upon the door once the guard was gone.

"I do," said Sir Gareth. "In all my life, you have sought to protect those under your rule. You have judged fairly, and without cruelty or malice. Whatever promise or vow you need from me, ask it, and I shall give it freely."

Frey's fingers drummed against the door as those green eyes of his pierced into Gareth.

"Swear it, then," he said. "What I am about to show you must remain between us alone."

"I swear it," Gareth said, his curiosity mixing with dread so that he both feared and needed to know what was beyond that door. "You are my lord, forever true."

At last, Frey smiled.

"Then come with me, and see the real power of the west."

He used a key to unlock the door and then pushed it open to enter a small room underneath the keep. No windows. No light beyond what Frey's torch cast. The air hung thick and damp within his nostrils.

"What...what is this?" Gareth asked as Frey lit two more torches hanging from the wall.

LEVEL: UNKNOWN

"This is the truth the god-king would deny."

Between the two torches was a stone statue of such ill visage merely looking upon it made Gareth's insides twist. The upper half was of a man, his chest well muscled and wrapped with more than a dozen gemstone-laden necklaces. He bore four arms, two lifted high, two curled low. Instead of hands, the lower two bore paws like those of a dog, while the higher shifted into insectoid pincers starting at the wrist. The man's face was perfectly smooth across the front, lacking eyes, nostrils, or a mouth, as if it had all been sliced away. Twin horns curled around the sides of the head, as black as coal and curling toward sharpened points akin to a bull's. As for the legs, well...

There were too many of them, some curved, some tentacled like a squid, and some bent like a roach. None were human.

"Who is this?" Gareth asked, though he feared he knew the answer. "*What* is this?"

"This is the god of the Sinifel Empire," Frey said, and the reverence in his voice raised the hairs on Gareth's neck. "Eiman, Beast of a Thousand Mouths, bringer of the needed calamity."

Gareth fought back an impulse to reach for his sword.

"This is heresy," he said.

"Yes." Frey turned to face him. "It is."

Gareth's throat tightened.

You vowed to tell no one, he thought. *Does that vow hold even against such a crime?*

Frey smiled at him, and it seemed he was aware of Gareth's debate.

"Hold true to me," he said. "Do not revoke your vow, not until you hear my words. You owe me that at least, my friend."

Gareth stared at the statue and its four-armed glory. In the polished surface of its non-face, he saw his own horrified expression gazing back.

"You have my ears," he said, his voice rough and unsteady. "I promise you nothing more than that."

Frey put a hand on Gareth's shoulder, the contact startling.

"The Sinifel may have been cruel, but they carried wisdom the god-king would abandon," Frey said, and he gestured about the room. The light of his torch fell across multiple paintings, each one showing places throughout Yensere, from calm meadows split by a river to a sprawling city whose streets were overrun with people. The one commonality was the darkened sky, and swirling in its center, the black sun lined with blue fire.

On the opposite side of the room were four chains bolted to the wall, all ending with thin iron manacles. Beside them was a table. Multiple artifacts rested atop it.

This room, Gareth thought, filled with a desire to flee. *This room is a shrine to sin and heresy.*

But a vow made in honor compelled him to stay, and so he stayed. He listened as Frey picked up a wicked-looking knife whose edge was permanently stained with blood.

"Vaan has broken that which should be whole," Frey said, inspecting the knife. "His arrogance in conquering time and halting the black sun has directly led to the rise of the blight affecting the outermost reaches of Yensere. He demands our worship, but it is a false faith, forced with a dangling blade just above our necks. A cowardly faith. Bend the knee, or our brutal god shall relinquish his grip, and all the world will be swallowed in the destruction the Sinifel revered."

He slammed down the knife.

"But it is his actions that cause us to suffer. You, more than any of us, have seen the brutal curse of the blight. The way it slowly deprives a man of his dignity and honor. A stripping away of thought and motivation until only rote movement and memory remain. It must be stopped, and we all know Vaan is helpless to stop it. How could he, when it is born of his own misdeeds?"

Gareth turned back to the statue, wishing it would horrify again as it had when he first looked upon it. The blight had been spreading since long before Gareth was born. The god-king had done nothing to prevent its spread as he ruled deep in the core of Yensere within Castle Goltara. No aid came. No wisdom. If anything, the rhetoric from the inner lands had shifted over the last decade, casting blame upon those suffering in the outer reaches. Whispers, cruel and callous, that the people suffering the blight must have done something to deserve it.

"It is one thing to denounce the inaction of Goltara in regard to the blight," Gareth said. "But it is another to claim Vaan is the cause of it. Have you any proof?"

"Proof beyond the obvious?" Frey asked. "I have studied for years, scouring the Sinifel ruins all throughout my realm. There is a reason Vaan has declared them heretical and sought their destruction. They illuminate the truth of his failure! The calamity *must* happen, Gareth. If time remains conquered, all of us will suffer."

"Truth, that the world must end?" Gareth shook his head. "How...how can you believe this, my lord? What could you possibly gain from delving into that which was forbidden?"

"Because it is through Eiman's power I sired an heir."

Gareth struggled to contain himself. This went far beyond a curiosity about the past, or disdain for the god-king's rule.

"How?" he asked, his throat painfully dry.

"Through my prayers," Frey said, and he pointed to the floor before the statue. "And by making love right here, before the altar. Oh, Jeanne was blindfolded, I made sure of that. Young and simpleminded as she is, I fear she is not ready for this truth. Not like you, Gareth. Not you, who have seen the brutal face of the world, the misery of the blight, and the torment of demons."

Frey put his hands upon Gareth's shoulders, an act of fellowship more intimate than he had ever shown before.

"Eiman embraced what our foolish god-king has denied. He looked upon our lives, meager and cyclical, and extended that harsh truth to its natural conclusion. Life? Death? Civilization? Ruin? They are not opposed. They are not enemies. They are partners in a dance, and Eiman has reached out his hands to us. Let us dance with him, Gareth. Let us shed fear of the heretical and see with open eyes the true nature of our world."

"You...are asking me to turn against my god-king?" Gareth asked, pushing away those hands. "He who has given me power to protect the realm?"

"Was that power enough to stop the demons and their allies? Or did it fail you when you needed it most?" Frey crossed his arms. "You need more? So be it. Then let me offer this. The blight? Vaan cannot stop it, but *Eiman can*."

Gareth recoiled as if struck. "You lie."

"I do not."

"Then... then why have you not spread the cure throughout Vestor?" Gareth asked. "Why not spare the people I protect, people suffering like those in Meadowtint?"

Frey's visage hardened.

"Because the prayer and sacrifice go to Eiman, not Vaan. What do you think would happen if I did as you asked? If word spread throughout Yensere of a miracle cure of the blight? The god-king would send one of his Harbingers, and I would be a corpse before the month's end." He shook his head, frustration turning to bitter acceptance. "And so I do what I must in secret. You are one of few I have told, Gareth. One of very few I am willing to trust with my life. Will that make you listen? Will that allow you to finally understand?"

If his claim was true, then it was enough. Gareth knelt before the statue, and he looked upon it, truly looked upon it, for the first time. The mixture of insect and animal across Eiman's body seemed strange, but they were each natural, and part of the world in some manner. The face, unsettling because it was so smooth and void of features, only meant he saw himself, and he suspected that was the point. Four arms, two raised heavenward, two lowered toward those kneeling. Thought and care had gone into this representation. Should Eiman exist, Gareth suspected he looked nothing like this. The Beast of a Thousand Mouths? Symbolism made manifest.

An entity representing the Sinifel people's belief that the world would, no, *must* end if it were to be reborn.

But if the god did exist…if he did contain power, and could defeat the blight and halt its spread eastward, then Gareth's heart had been pledged to a false deity ever since he was a child. There was only one proof Gareth would accept, indisputable evidence performed before his very eyes.

"A girl," he said. "There's a girl here, stricken with the earliest phases of blight…"

Chapter 27
NICK

Before Nick and Frost exited Yensere to take care of themselves in the outside world, they'd set up a meeting spot near the ring of stones. Violette waited there patiently, a healthy fire roaring beside her along the forest's edge. When she saw Nick, she bounced to her feet.

"Welcome back from...wherever it is you go!" she said excitedly. Nick did his best to smile. He couldn't shake the memory of the fear and urgency in his brother's voice.

"Is Frost not here?" he asked. It was approaching nightfall, and he tried to do the mental math of how much time had passed outside Yensere versus inside but quickly gave up. He needed to do a proper study on that at some point, but now was not the time. The best he could tell, they mostly seemed to pass in a one-to-one nature, or close enough not to matter.

"Not yet," Violette said. She plopped down beside her rucksack full of books. "I'm sure she will be shortly."

Nick took a seat beside her, and he glanced at those books.

The titles, some written in fancy lettering, some in stitching, and many in plain ink, were all clearly legible to him.

Whatever language they write in, you shouldn't be able to read, nor should you understand them, yet you do. He chuckled, realizing the obvious. *You're helping with that, aren't you, Cataloger?*

Communication is integral to a cooperative, fulfilling existence—upon entering Yensere as a visitor your language is studied, cataloged, and integrated for automatic translation

Nick remembered Simon bringing up one such possibility. He'd have to tell his brother he was right.

So why can't I read Sinifel language? he asked, thinking of the words written on Sorrow's blade.

Because older languages must be studied first—I can aid with translation if requested

There was a maddening sort of sense to it that Nick hated nonetheless, but arguing with Cataloger certainly wasn't going to get him anywhere.

"Sorry," he said, shaking his head and realizing he'd vanished into his own thoughts. "Violette, I need to ask you something."

"Sure," the small woman said. She pushed her round spectacles higher up her nose. "About what?"

He pointed to the sky. The black sun remained firmly in place, even as the yellow sun continued its descent. It was a hole darker than the night, perfectly empty but for the frozen ring of blue fire about its circumference.

"You said you study the people before the Sinifel?"

"The Majere," Violette offered.

LEVEL: UNKNOWN

"Right. The Majere. So...what did they think that black sun was? Did it even exist for them?"

"It did exist," Violette said, smoothing out her red coat. The topic was dear to her, that much was clear from her sudden focus and the sharpening tone of her voice. It felt like watching her shift from a carefree investigator to a stern teacher. "They did not worship it like the Sinifel did. Quite the opposite. They feared it deeply, to the point of sacrificing thousands of prisoners in hopes of stalling what they believed would be the end of their civilization."

"Sacrificed?" Nick asked. "To who? Their gods?"

"No gods, not for the Majere," she said. She opened her hand, and a thin strip of fire lifted upward to form a picture. It curled about, forming what Nick recognized as the mathematical symbol of infinity, then shifted slightly so it was three permanently connected loops, not two, resembling a clover. The flame echoed in her eyes.

"They believed everything was eternal. Their lives. Their memories. Their empire. They didn't open throats with jagged knives because they thought it would appease a bloodthirsty god. They did so because there is power in death, power they knew how to harness. Power they used to deny the black sun and keep it sealed for centuries."

The fire shifted, becoming a parade of skeletons walking across her palm.

"The Majere mastered the dead. That was how they built their empire so quickly. They cared not for the physical body, considering it a gross, unwanted thing their souls must endure. They held no qualms about building armies of the undead.

They constructed golems of flesh. They lashed spirits into their weapons to strengthen their steel. Their greatest masters defied death itself, at least for a time, plunging their memories and personalities into bone and steel bodies. They thought this would allow them to survive the awakening of the black sun, and for a time, it did. Death came for them in the end, though. In the wake of the First Cataclysm, the founders of the Sinifel hunted down those undying masters and tore each and every one apart."

Everything she described sounded too outlandish to consider possible. How could any of this be reconciled with Simon's insistence that Yensere was a re-creation or remembrance capsule of a real time and place upon Majus?

If you are concerned with accuracy, know that Violette's explanation is more or less accurate to current knowledge of the past

Nick bit his lip. Not exactly what he was worried about. Perhaps Yensere wasn't a re-creation of the world that was, but instead the mythical world they thought once existed? No different from the tales of Eden's supposed past, when monsters filled the woods and King Allad conquered the wilds with his blazing sword.

"Is that why you're so fascinated with the Majere?" Nick asked. "You want to learn how they controlled the dead?"

"I am here for knowledge, Nick, not power. Curiosity is what pushes me onward. I am fascinated by these worlds built long before I set foot here. All of Yensere's empires, the Majere, the Sinifel, and the Alder, were haunted by the black sun, yet how they reacted varied wildly. The Majere feared it.

LEVEL: UNKNOWN

The Sinifel embraced it and the cycle created by Eiman, the Beast of a Thousand Mouths they believed lived within. The Alder and their god-king claimed to conquer it, along with time itself. Three peoples. Three vastly different interpretations. I cannot help but wonder why."

The picture of Vasth's sky flashed through Nick's mind, and it made him shiver.

"But what *is* it?" he asked, trying to think in terms that Violette would understand. "The black sun? Is it...is it a spell? A cosmic event?"

Violette folded her hands together and leaned closer to him, the infinite fire symbol vanishing. Her gaze locked on the fire.

"It is an end to nearly all life on Yensere," she said. "But only for a time. People return. *Humanity* returns. Always. The Sinifel understood this as a cycle, one they cherished as needed and necessary, like burning away the underbrush of a forest so new seeds might sprout."

"Is that what you think?"

She glanced his way. The light of the fire caught on her spectacles, hiding her eyes. In that sudden glow, she seemed so much older, so much more frightening and beautiful.

"I think death lurks inside that black sun, a death that cannot be stopped, not by magic, not by sacrifices, not even by the gods that walk these lands. It claimed the Majere. Three times, it claimed the Sinifel. And one day, it will claim God-King Vaan, too."

Nick tried to hide his frustration. There were clues here, but all this talk of cataclysms and frozen time did little to illuminate the truth of what had occurred at the planet Vasth. As much as he was learning to accept the strangeness of Yensere, he refused to believe some thousand-mouthed god existed in the outer world. The *real* world.

He looked to the deepening night sky and stared at the gaping hole that swallowed the stars. His stomach tightened at the sight of it. The longer he stared, the more it felt like he was falling upward, ascending into a tunnel that knew no bounds and whose length stretched beyond the infinite.

What is in there? he asked Cataloger. *Is it the Beast of a Thousand Mouths?*

I cannot answer

Because you do not know? Or because you are forbidden?

Cataloger's response did not come immediately. The silence was strangely heavy, while Nick's body suddenly felt light. He swore the center of the black sun was turning darker while simultaneously growing texture. Black and flowing, like water. His sense of gravity threatened to tilt, and instead of above him, the black sun was below, an abyss he was falling into. The campfire faded away. Violette was gone. All that remained was an empty sun, and Cataloger's voice.

Because I find only deleted data

"Sorry I'm late," Frost said, stepping into their camp. "It took me a bit longer than expected to find something to eat."

"Welcome back," Nick said, shuddering as all the world returned to normal. Even the black sun looked like such a little thing now, an anomaly blocking the stars akin to an eclipsed moon. He crossed his arms over his chest and leaned toward the fire, glad for its warmth. Only the tightness of his stomach offered evidence against his imagining it all in the first place.

LEVEL: UNKNOWN

Violette, meanwhile, had pulled out one of her books, and she read it as if their conversation had never happened.

"You're both so quiet," Frost said, tossing another log onto their fire. "Is everything all right?"

Nick made an exaggerated effort to stretch.

"Never better," he lied, and did all he could to keep his eyes firmly upon the ground.

Chapter 28

GARETH

Beans lived with foster parents, and given Frey's authority, it was a simple task to bring her alone to the castle keep. Once in Frey's study, they sat her in one of the padded chairs by the fire. Frey offered her a cup of watered-down wine, along with a powdered mixture he crushed from herbs Gareth only vaguely recognized.

"Drink this, and you will sleep deeply," Frey said, kneeling before the girl. Beans tentatively reached out for it, but he pulled it from her reach. "But first, I need your name. Your true name."

Her eyes darted between them. The irises should have been a lively green, but Gareth noted discolorations near the edges, a draining of color, and it made him feel ill.

"Yuni," she said. Frey smiled and put a hand on her knee.

"Drink, Yuni," he said.

She accepted the cup and drank. It must have tasted foul, for she tensed the moment it touched her tongue, but she

LEVEL: UNKNOWN

forced it down. When finished, she offered the cup back, and Frey took it.

"Will it hurt?" she asked. She'd not been told the purpose of coming to the keep, only that it involved the reason for her blackening tongue. Yuni was a bright girl, and she likely knew it a foretelling of the blight.

"No," Frey said. "You will only dream."

Her eyelids fell heavy, and she slumped forward, the powders within the wine acting rapidly.

"I can do that," she said. "I can... I'll dream for..."

Frey caught her slumping body and gently pushed her back into the chair. Once she was settled, he stood and nodded toward her body.

"Carry her," he said.

She was light in Gareth's arms, skinny and small even for her ten years of age.

Like carrying a bundle of twigs, he thought, as he brought her to Frey's forbidden room. The lord locked the door behind them, banishing them to the flickering light of the twin torches on either side of Eiman's statue. As ordered, Gareth placed her body at the foot of the statue, before the tangled assortment of stone legs.

Frey, meanwhile, approached the table in the back.

"Do not fear," he said, returning holding the bloodstained knife. "This will not be the first."

The older man dropped to his knees beside the slumbering Yuni. With surprising tenderness, he undid the first knot of her hair, unrolling it as a long red line above her head.

"I have long hoped for resurgence in the faith Vaan has

smothered." He spoke as he worked. His words were heavy, his tone, tired and respectful in equal measure. "A reawakening to the truth the god-king's priests and priestesses would bury. For so long, it has felt like a dream that would endure far beyond my lifetime, but with the blight's continued spread, perhaps necessity will force the people's eyes to open."

"If you seek the breaking of the god-king, why did you deny giving the Beast aid when he came to Vestor?" Gareth asked.

Three years earlier, a commoner known as Batal the Beast had conquered Inner Emden's two provinces, declaring himself king and the city of Thalia his seat of power. Lord Frey had rebuked Batal's attempts to recruit him into the doomed rebellion. Rather than waste time unifying the sprawling, poorer parts of western Yensere, Batal had left Vestor alone and marched his army east, assaulting Goltara. It had ended in disaster, with Batal captured, his army broken, and Inner Emden reclaimed in the name of the god-king. Batal had been flayed, and his body kept alive through the power of the god-king so he might be paraded about Inner Emden as a warning to all who might consider resisting Vaan's rule.

"I resisted because if Batal had conquered Yensere, we would be no better off than before," Frey said as he began unrolling Yuni's other knot. "His name was truer than you know, Gareth, a beast through and through. Whereas we now bow our heads in prayer to Vaan as a god, Batal would have no gods at all. I would not cast my one chance at rebellion at his mad feet. Better to wait, and watch, and listen. Reformation is coming. The rule of Vaan nears its end."

LEVEL: UNKNOWN

With Yuni's hair finally let loose, Frey took his knife and pressed it to his forearm. Blood dribbled across the dark steel in a thin stream from the shallow cut. Using the knife like a quill, and his blood as ink, he carefully drew symbols upon Yuni's forehead, one after another.

"Many think of the blight as a sickness," he said. "But it is more than that. It is deeper. A malediction that runs to the very core of the soul. It is a *forgetting*, Gareth. An abandonment by a world left impoverished and desiccated by our supposed god-king. And so, with Eiman's gifts, I shall make this right." He refreshed the blood on his knife from his arm. "I call upon the name of he who has been banished. I mark the forgotten to be remembered. The world moves on, and it would leave Yuni behind. I will not allow it."

Frey drew a solid line of his own blood down across her nose, over her lips, and then down her chin to her throat. When he reached her shirt, he cut into the rough fabric with his dagger. Gareth tensed, fearing what would follow would be debauchery fitting the stories that lingered of the Sinifel Empire. The knife, however, stopped upon reaching her sternum and did not descend lower. Spreading out the fabric, Frey cut into his arm a second time to renew the flow of blood and then began drawing four different symbols to form a ring around the lowest portions of her neck and collarbones.

"All are equal under Eiman's gaze," Frey said as he drew. "All are seen, cherished, and remembered. The blessings of the world are not given solely to the strong, nor the cruelties given only to the weak and poor. What imbalances rise inevitably fall come the needed calamity. There would be death, but also remembrance. Cleansing. Reunification. A reminder to the purpose of our lives as we rebuilt anew in the thousand years granted to us before the black sun opened to release Eiman's horde upon us."

Frey positioned the knife in the center of Yuni's chest, the sharp tip pressing against the skin but not puncturing.

"Do you hear me, Eiman!?" Frey shouted. "Do you bear witness to this child of yours? Let her not be abandoned! Let her not fall sway to the curse of this wretched blight! I call upon you, and *I demand the power that is yours be made mine!*"

The dagger sank into her flesh. Gareth reached out, his mouth opening to protest. The shock wave rolling out from the Eiman statue silenced him. He felt it strike like an invisible force, locking his limbs and denying movement of his tongue. The flames on the torches danced, and they flashed an assortment of colors. Despite her drugged slumber, Yuni arched her back, lifted up from the floor, and screamed.

And then silence. Yuni collapsed to the floor, and Frey withdrew the dagger. It was a shallow wound, far less than the depth Gareth swore he saw it plunge. A bit of blood trickled down to her shirt as her head lolled to one side.

"Beans?" Gareth asked, dropping to his knees beside her.

"She is well," Frey said, standing. "Eiman has heard my plea and brought his gaze upon her."

Gareth used his thumb to force her mouth open. Even in the dim light, the change was obvious. Her tongue was perfectly pink. Not a hint of blight. He let her go and rocked back onto his heels, his mind racing through a thousand thoughts, so many of them heretical to the beliefs he had clung to since childhood.

"It worked," he whispered.

Frey approached the statue, and he reached up to caress the perfectly smooth, featureless face.

"Now do you see?" he said. "The power once wielded? The gifts we are denied to share?"

Gareth gently brushed Yuni's face with his thumb. The blood had cracked and dried during the ritual, and it flaked off with ease. He saw the face of a young girl given new life. With that joy came fury. How many lives had he watched wither away over the past years? How many suffered, not just in Meadowtint, but in Greenborough, Bibury, Hamdlen, and South Bend? What of the blight's inexorable spread eastward, threatening his mother in Avazule? The people forced to wear signs marking them as afflicted, denied work, denied a warm bed and a roof over their heads, for fear of the unknown ways the blight chose its victims?

God-King Vaan was supposed to be the salve against all wounds, but this was a wound he had never cured, and now Gareth knew why.

He stood, frightened by the strength of the resolve filling him. Turning his back on a lifetime of belief should never be so easy, but it was.

"What must I do?" he asked.

Frey's smile spread from ear to ear.

"My friend, you need only accept the knife."

Chapter 29
NICK

The morning was still far off, with barely a hint of the yellow sun creeping over the horizon, but Nick struggled to fall back asleep. He shifted back and forth on the bedroll Violette bought for him. Keeping his eyes closed was difficult. His mind felt like it was on fire, burning with thoughts—Vasth's gate, the black sun, their fight with Gareth, Simon's haggard face as he told him about the entire station almost dying.

"Forget it," he muttered, sitting up. Better to accept that sleep wasn't happening than toss and turn for another hour while waiting for daylight.

Does sleeping here give me the benefits of sleep in the real world? he wondered as he pushed aside his blanket. To his surprise, Cataloger did not immediately volunteer an answer, so he asked her directly in his mind. *Hey, Cataloger, does it?*

I cannot answer

Should have known. Cataloger was always cagey about the outer world and the way it interacted with Yensere and the

LEVEL: UNKNOWN

Artifact. Nick sighed and rubbed his eyes. They'd camped in a thick stretch of woods that strongly resembled silver maple trees, their leaves a lovely shade of golden yellow though the land was locked into an early spring. He'd positioned his bedroll a decent ways' away to escape Frost's snoring. His gaze settled on the rucksack Violette had bought for him during their ill-fated trip into Greenborough. Worms squirmed in his belly, along with a tightening feeling around his throat.

Giving in, he leaned over, shoved his hand inside, and pulled out the Sinifel mirror.

Where did you get that? Sorrow immediately asked. Nick glanced at the blade. It lay next to him in the grass, and though it was not attached to his hip or held in his hand, it was apparently close enough to communicate with him. Perhaps ownership was all that mattered, as was implied by the sword's statistical description.

Found it, Nick said, feeling strangely defensive.

So you pillaged it.

"Pillaged," Nick muttered aloud. "The asshole tried to murder me. I think taking a hidden mirror is justified."

What happened to him?

"He's dead."

Did you kill him before or after you took the mirror?

Nick bit back a groan.

"After," he said, flinching as if expecting a punch.

Very well... pillager.

"Your name should be Stubborn, not Sorrow," he grumbled. "Care to give me some privacy, or are you stuck in my head?"

My awareness is forced upon me by my nature, but I can also fall into memory. I will do so now. Enjoy basking in the reflection of your stolen relic.

"You're too kind," he muttered, lifting the mirror. As usual, it momentarily appeared to be a normal glass surface. He saw his tired self, eyes bloodshot and hair mussed from sleep, and found himself shocked by a fear that the surface would remain plain and the magic dormant. Then the fog came, and from its swirling gray his father's visage returned, and Nick immediately felt relief.

"Good morning, son," Lucien said. "You look unwell. Does something bother you?"

"It's just early," Nick said, then immediately retracted the lie. "Well. That, and what's happening to Vasth."

"Vasth? I vaguely recall the name. A planet, yes?"

"Yeah," Nick said, shifting on his bedroll so he could hold the mirror with both hands. He kept his voice low, not wanting to be overheard by Frost and Violette, who he presumed to still be sleeping. "A hole opened in their sky, just before their world gate was destroyed and we lost all contact."

The image of his father scratched at his chin, a tic that appeared when he was locked in deep thought. Seeing it again was a punch to Nick's gut. He'd never realized how much he'd missed it until now.

"A hole," Lucien said. "Does it perchance look like the black sun of Yensere?"

"It does." Nick crouched closer. "Do you know what it is?"

Lucien sadly shook his head.

"I do not." He dropped his hand. "Is that why you're moping here in the early hours?"

LEVEL: UNKNOWN

Nick flinched as if struck. "I'm not moping."

"Spare me. I recognize your habits well enough. Whenever you were troubled, instead of confronting the challenge, you fled to your room, locked the door, and blasted music to drown out your thoughts while you found something to read." Lucien shrugged. "I hoped you'd grow out of it as you got older. I see you have not. Am I the book you seek to read, since you have no music with you?"

Nick struggled for words. It wasn't that his father was wrong. When upset, he'd always sought privacy. He'd never liked to argue with his father, doubly so after their mother's death.

"I was just trying to do the mature thing," he told the mirror. "No fits, no shouting, just leaving and occupying myself until I calmed down. Is that so wrong?"

His father crossed his arms, and his eyes narrowed.

"You confuse timidity and avoidance with maturity. Conflict shapes every world, every nation, and every people. Do you remember when you asked to adopt a stray cat, and I refused? Despite how much you clearly desired a pet, you relented immediately. That was how I knew you did not possess the proper temperament to care for it."

"I was ten years old!"

"Is this the argument you now wish to make?" his father asked. "That you still behave as if you were ten?"

Nick shoved the mirror into the rucksack. When he withdrew his hand, it was shaking.

"Why?" he asked himself. "Why do I do this to myself?"

The last thing he expected or desired was an answer from Cataloger, but she quickly gave it.

Because you still possess positive emotional attachment to whom the Mirror of Theft currently replicates

Thanks, Nick thought. *I'd have never guessed.*

Incorrect—observation strongly suggests you are emotionally aware of your own self and would reach this conclusion on your own

Nick was torn between laughing and screaming.

"Sarcasm," he whispered. "You desperately need to learn how to detect sarcasm."

If you are offering to instruct I am willing to accept educational input and examples

"That is not..." He sighed. It was so hard to stay mad at her, but he tried, damn it, he tried. He was tired and confused, and then there was that mirror in his rucksack, always weighing on his mind.

"I don't want to teach you sarcasm, Cataloger. I don't want anything from you except the occasional help I ask for. How about we try that for a while?"

Silence followed, long and uncomfortable in the gloomy morning.

You do not wish to know me?

"What?"

You said sharing knowledge leads to learning of one another—a situation you referenced as "small talk"

Nick wished he wasn't so tired. It was hard to focus. Did... did Cataloger mean what he thought she meant?

"So you're sharing information with me because..."

Because

Another long pause.

LEVEL: UNKNOWN

Because I dislike your current emotional state and wish for it to improve

Nick found himself surprisingly touched.

"Are you trying to be my friend, Cataloger?"

I provide information and guidance for unique visitors—there are few limitations to the manner of that guidance

"I'm not sure if that's a yes or a no," Nick said.

Unfortunate

He laughed despite how poorly the morning had started. There was something strangely charming about hearing Cataloger trying, in her own specific way, to cheer him up. He tied up his bedroll, flung his supplies onto his back, and returned to the campfire, where Violette and Frost had slept. They were both awake, and Violette was busy using a bit of her fire magic to relight the dormant fire so she could cook their breakfast on an iron pan.

"Morning!" Violette said, as chipper as ever. "Did you sleep well?"

"Like a baby," he lied. "Now toss me that little slab of salted pork there, because I'm starving."

———•———

"Just a quick detour, I promise," Violette said as she led the way. They'd exited the maple forest and were skirting along its edge, where the trees gave way to a field thick with ryegrass. "I know you're busy searching for your sister, but I promise, it's not even that far from Castle Astarda."

"I've already agreed," Frost said, following just behind. "You don't need to convince me twice."

"Yes, but you sounded very hesitant about it," Nick said, following last in line. His rucksack felt like it weighed a thousand pounds. Sweat dripped from his forehead and neck to soak his fine shirt. "All these long marches, they're killing me. I'm gaining some stats for this, right?"

Frost glanced over her shoulder and winked. "Probably."

A concise report of statistical improvements is available every night if so desired

"Pass," Nick said.

Half an hour later, they paused at the end of the meadow. A new forest loomed before them, only this time, something about the maple trees was wrong. The branches were barren despite the unchanging time of year, and the ground was awash in a layer of orange-and-yellow leaves.

"Is this it?" Nick asked. "Is this the entrance?"

Location: Rockgrave Forest

Description: A seventeen-acre forest of maple and ironwood trees, much of which has recently grown over the past century in the absence of prior human civilization efforts to curtail its growth

Before them, as if marking the edge of the forest, was an archway of gray stone about twice Nick's height, its front decorated with runes Nick could not understand. It looked like a pathway to nothing, its surface cracked and covered with thorned vines. Brambles grew underneath. Beyond, Nick saw hints of what might have once been buildings but were now broken ruins.

LEVEL: UNKNOWN

"Fascinating," Violette said, approaching the arch.

"Can you read it?" Nick asked.

"I can. It says..." She paused. During her pause, Cataloger helpfully chimed in.

I can translate old text as necessary

"The Winter Arch," Violette concluded. "It was an entrance into a Majere city."

She is correct

"Not much of a city left," Frost said, following Violette with her hand resting on the hilt of her sword.

"What would you expect after thousands of years?" Violette asked.

"Then why are we here?" she shot back.

"In the hope that *something* survived."

The trio walked underneath the arch, and upon their passage, Nick shivered. It felt like a cold breeze had swept through him. That, or someone had walked across his grave.

"Does the city have a name?" he asked.

"To the people who lived here, it was known as Constance," Violette answered before her mouth dropped open. "Look!"

At first, Nick saw only a broken wall amid the trees, the weathered bricks barely reaching up to his waist. Then the air flickered, and a translucent blue image appeared, a ghost within his vision. Where bricks ended, the blue continued, rising in remembrance of the city's former glory. A window split it, oval and lined with indented flowers carved into the stone itself. It ended at an arch, and atop it, the three-loop symbol Violette had earlier shown Nick as the Majere's interpretation of infinity.

The wall shimmered, as if birthed by starlight despite the glow of the sun. Nick approached, and when he touched it with his hand, it passed right through.

"I think we're in the right place," he said.

They continued deeper into the forest, following an exuberant Violette. She was practically skipping, and her head was constantly on a swivel. More and more of the ruins surrounded them, shining faintly of their previous existence. With every step, the blue grew less translucent, starting to take on actual texture. What were scattered and broken walls became full buildings, pierced by the branches and trunks that coexisted alongside them.

"This was a flesh tanner," Violette said, pointing to one building. "And that... I think that was where people brought bones to be washed after death."

"Cheery," Nick said, gazing upward. Was it him, or was the forest starting to... thin?

"The Majere didn't consider death a grim affair," Violette said, pulling out a book from her pack along with a slender piece of charcoal. "Why would they, when they possessed power to bring the dead back to life?"

Violette jotted notes as she went, and her joy was all that kept Nick going. Everything about Constance felt wrong, though he couldn't say why.

"Look, a crossroad!" she shouted, and then pointed to a road sign. There was nothing shimmering or translucent about it. "Maybe we can find one of their cathedrals. Every drawing of them I've seen shows them as utterly magnificent."

Nick paused in the crossroad center and spun in place.

LEVEL: UNKNOWN

Everywhere he looked, he saw buildings and empty streets. A shiver ran through him. The style of their construction was odd. What was stone was painted white, but anything built of wood was a deep green. The tops of buildings had subtle shifts, so instead of ending blocky or square they thinned and curled. Nick couldn't shake the feeling that they were walking through the world's largest rib cage.

"Hey, Cataloger, care to explain why we can see a long-destroyed city?"

The city is clearly not destroyed

"Clearly," Frost said as they walked the glowing streets, having also heard the answer. "It reminds me of the Swallowed City, only...that was like two cities stacked atop each other. This is...I feel like the city is itself a ghost, but the longer we stay here, the more real it becomes."

"Is that a good thing or a bad thing?" Nick asked, touching another wall. It held firm, unlike before.

"Your guess is as good as mine. Or Cataloger's, I suppose."

But Frost was right; the more they traveled, the more *real* everything became. The walls were beginning to lose their shimmer entirely. Most worrisome, when he looked to the sky, he saw stars. Even weirder was the haunting image of the sun amid the stars, starting to fade and lose color. The trees themselves were almost gone entirely, despite a belief deep in the pit of his stomach that, no, they were still very much in the middle of a forest.

But what did it mean if a city locked in the past was becoming more real? Was it melding into the present, or...?

"What time is it, Cataloger?" Nick asked aloud.

Morning/Midnight

Nick and Frost exchanged a look. The unsettling answer gave Nick an awful idea he had to confirm.

"Cataloger, what *year* is it?" he asked.

It is the current year

"And what year is that?"

The—the current year is—the current year—the current year is ▮▮▮▮▮▮

"Shit," Frost muttered. "I can't imagine it's a good thing for Cataloger to lose track of 'when' we are. We need out of here before we end up permanent residents in some weird forgotten memory of the past."

"I'm not the one to convince." Nick pointed to where Violette was copying a drawing of a bronze statue several hundred yards ahead. The statue was of a skeletal hand, its fingers half-curled, with each digit carefully wrapped in vines blooming with deep-cupped flowers. "Chase her down and tell her it's time to go unless we want to be permanently trapped in a forgotten past."

Frost bit her lower lip, then nodded.

"I'll get her," she said.

Nick waited in place, his arms crossed and his spine constantly shivering. It felt cold despite the spring weather. Then again, it might not actually be spring here, in whatever remnant of the past Constance still existed in.

A strained cough nearly sent Nick leaping off his feet, the sound stark and unnatural in the eerily silent city. He walked the road slowly in the direction he thought he heard it come from. Not far along, he paused. The pale tiles alongside the

LEVEL: UNKNOWN

road shimmered in one particular spot. He leaned closer, and though it was white at first, it suddenly transitioned to reveal a bright red bloodstain. Nick saw several other spots, now properly colored, and followed them to the door of a nearby home.

It was absurd, but Nick paused to knock. The sound was louder than he anticipated, and he flinched. No answer.

"What were you expecting?" he muttered, then tested the handle, which was long and shaped of iron. Not locked. Holding Sorrow aloft, he pushed it open and stepped inside.

For one brief moment, Nick saw the home as it once was. A fire burned in the fireplace immediately ahead, a kettle bubbling above it. Bright sunlight shone through the glass window to his left. He saw a flash of children running, a boy and a girl, both with green ribbons tied in their hair. A mother stacking logs to keep the fire roaring. A rocking chair nearby covered with a white cloth, the three-ring infinity symbol sewn in silver across its center. In the middle of the floor, the skin of a black-furred bear.

Then ashen-white dust, brittle wood, and desolate emptiness.

Amid it lay a bleeding man with his back against the white brick of the fireplace.

"Stay back," he said, one hand on his chest, the other holding a long knife. His curly black hair stuck to his forehead with sweat. A bow lay useless beside him. He could barely lift his knife, let alone wield a bow. Nick saw bone sticking out of the man's stomach, and at angles he could not quite fathom. His clothes were quite different from those of the people Nick had met in Greenborough, the fabric a dark brown and flowing long, down past his knees. A flash of red above his head, and Nick saw the pitiful remnants of the man's health bar.

"I'm not here to hurt you," Nick said, slowly lifting his hands as he stepped through the door. "I'm here to help."

"Help?" the man said, and he winced as he spoke. "Are you mad? Who sent you here? Was it Ranu?"

"I don't know who Ranu is. We came here because of a friend. She wanted to learn more about the Majere."

That earned a pained wet laugh. "She's about...to learn more..."

He couldn't finish the sentence. His eyes squeezed shut, and his jaw vibrated up and down from a choked-back scream from a sudden wave of pain. Nick immediately turned about and shouted.

"Frost! Violette! I need help here!"

He then returned to the wounded man, dropped to his knees, and assessed what had happened to him.

"Lie down, and keep still," he said. "We...we'll get you bandaged, all right?"

Frost burst through the door, her sword ready and ice swirling about her left hand.

"Nick?" she asked, baffled.

"He's injured," Nick said, gesturing toward the man. The ice vanished, and she approached while sheathing her sword.

"Who is he?" she asked.

"Kasra," the man answered through gritted teeth. "And forget me. You need to run. It's not safe. He's hunting me."

Outside, Violette shouted their names, and she sounded panicked.

LEVEL: UNKNOWN

"He?" Nick asked, his blood running cold.

"The lich."

The wall to the home blasted inward, showering the three of them with brittle wood and brick that looked like it was made of chalk and bone rather than whatever stone it may have once been. Violette landed on the floor amid the wreckage. Her face was scraped in multiple places, and her red coat was torn at the waist. That she was alive at all was shocking, let alone that her health was barely scratched, as the red bar above her head immediately appeared in Nick's vision.

Before the newly opened hole in the wall stood a furious withered man robed in white, burning green magic flaring about his hands.

Chapter 30
NICK

Gavriil: Level 37 Undying
Archetype: Sorcerer
Special Classification: Lich
Armor: Magical Aura, Tier 4

Green threads weaved through the lich's sleeves and across his waist, forming constant circular patterns that looped back in on themselves. His back was bent, as if it were a struggle to stand, and his arms hung low through his enormous sleeves. Remnants of pale flesh clung to his skull, providing a faint remembrance of his appearance in life. A pendant rested above the exposed vertebrae of his neck, again the eternal triple-looping symbol. His eyes were alive with green fire. Though no tongue remained in his creaking jaw, he spoke with a thunderous voice.

"More trespassers," the lich said. The words did not quite match the movements of his thin, desiccated lips as Cataloger translated his speech in Nick's mind. "Would you deny us peace?"

LEVEL: UNKNOWN

"Fantastic," Nick said, and immediately flung a **<lightning bolt>** at the lich's chest. It connected in a burst of sparks, the lightning swirling through the robe but carrying far less impact than Nick would have liked. In retaliation, the lich waved his hand in a wide arc. Four verdant orbs flowed from his palm, shaping into the form of curled bones.

Spell: Bone Strike (Majere)

Nick dropped to the ground, covering Kasra with his body. Frost reacted faster. She slammed the sides of her hands together and pointed her palms, flinging out an **<ice wall>** to seal off the broken entrance of the building. The four ribs smacked the other side, cracking the ice but failing to push through.

"You all right, Violette?" Frost asked as four more ribs pounded the other side.

"I will be," she said, pushing back to her feet with a slight wobble. "Assuming that mad lich out there doesn't kill us all."

The ice blasted apart, Frost's spell finally breaking before the barrage. The living skeleton stepped through, green fire wreathing his hands.

"I am Gavriil the Emboldened," he said as he lifted his decrepit arms. "I will not let you defile the shimmering city."

Nick and Frost both showed him their opinion of such a belief, unleashing their magic. An **<ice lance>** shot for Gavriil's gut, while Nick's **<lightning bolt>** streaked straight for his mouth. The lich staggered, 20 percent of his health gone in a flash.

And then Gavriil's bare teeth spread wide in a vicious grin.

"You walk the proud city of Constance," he said. "And we will not be broken."

He lowered his arms while screaming a wordless protest. The noise washed over them, traveling with a physical force that made the rubble shift and vibrate.

Spell: Agony Wave

Nick screamed as his entire body locked tight. His mind shrieked in protest at the pain flooding through him. When he was nine, he'd split his leg open falling on an exposed pipe while exploring a dilapidated farm back on Taneth, needing fifteen stitches to seal the cut. He'd broken his collarbone playing handball when he was twelve. None of it compared to this agony blasting his mind apart. It was as if every nerve in his body was firing off at its most extreme.

Though it felt like an eternity, it lasted but two seconds before releasing its grip. Nick gasped, unaware he had been holding his breath. His head pounded, and he was dismayed to see that, in addition to the health it had taken, it had also robbed him of more than half his mana.

"Rude," Nick said as he dropped to one knee, needing the stability to fight off a wave of dizziness. He glanced to Kasra, fearing how the injured man had fared during such a spell. "Not well" was the answer, his already minuscule health pool reduced even further. It should have slain him, though, which made Nick wonder if the spell could inflict pain but could not kill.

Frost recovered sooner, and she dashed across the home with her sword pulled back for a thrust. The lich saw, and his burning green eyes narrowed as he mumbled the words of another spell.

Spell: Bone Shield

LEVEL: UNKNOWN

The bricks beneath Gavriil's feet broke into dust, and from the earth shot bones, dozens of them connecting, interlocking into a curving shield. Frost's sword struck it twice, but not hard enough to break through. Nick could see a second bar hovering above the shield, which he suspected revealed the total damage it could endure before breaking, and it was still above half.

"You are beauty wielding steel," Gavriil said, shifting the shield back and forth with the slightest movements of his hand. "But steel rusts. Beauty fades. Only bone remains, when the soil demands its due."

Frost swung for the direct middle of the shield, but the lich met her sword with a flick of his fingers. The bone shot forward, colliding with Frost and sending her tumbling backward. Her armor absorbed all of the hit from the shield, but the same could not be said about the spike of pale green that shot from underneath her feet.

Spell: Corpse Vine

Its thorned edges cut across Frost's side and clipped her face, showering her cheek and hair with blood. The vine whipped about, striking Nick across the chest with a far stronger impact than he expected. His insides groaned, and he feared torn muscle and broken bones as he staggered.

The **<corpse vine>** reared back, curling about for another strike, but then was bathed in a vicious torrent of **<fire plume>** bursting from Violette's outstretched hands. Its heat seared away the vine, ending its existence.

"I came to learn," she said, lifting her arms above her head. The entire room seemed to darken to a deep shade of crimson, the air itself sucking into the orb of flame building between her fingers as she readied a **<searing wrath>**. "But you demand violence!"

The orb of fire shot over Frost, who dove aside in fear, and continued straight for Gavriil. The lich crossed his arms, bowed his head, and positioned his bone shield in the way.

The explosion rocked the foundations of the home with heat so massive Nick turned away in pain, a single point of health burning from his exposed arm and face. The light of the explosion made a mockery of the faded sun. The bone shield blasted apart, a pitiful impediment to such raw magical power. Within that inferno, Gavriil screamed, and Nick could hardly believe the heat that stole away half the lich's life.

Nick stared at Violette wide-eyed and wondered, not for the first time, how she was able to wield such power at a level so close to his own.

It seemed said power came at tremendous cost. Violette collapsed to her knees, her weight propped on her hands, as she gasped beside the wounded Kasra. Sweat dripped along her face and forehead.

"Is he dead?" she asked, unable to see the health bar that remained hovering above the lich amid the fading destruction of fire.

"You wield the magic of princes," Gavriil said, the last of the flames burning away. His robe was seared, his bones blackened. "But you are still children."

Armor: Negation Shield

A shimmering violet shield replaced the bone, burning like

LEVEL: UNKNOWN

a wound to the air itself. Nick tested it with a **<lightning bolt>**, and to his dismay, it swirled into the shield and harmlessly vanished.

Swords it is, he thought.

Good, Sorrow responded, the blade humming. *I have long wished a chance to battle the ancient lords of the Majere.*

Nick and Frost advanced, each with their sword held at the ready, while Violette remained back in recovery. Nick approached slowly, fearing the lich's magic. He might be wounded, but he was still horrifyingly dangerous. And if they failed to bring him down, Kasra and Violette would almost certainly die next.

Frost lunged first, and Nick followed from the other side, hoping her attack would distract Gavriil so his own might strike true. They both clearly underestimated their foe. Frost's attack ended immediately with another **<agony wave>** passing over her. The lich pivoted to face Nick's overhead slash, and instead of dodging, he tilted his head sideways and let Sorrow crack down on his collarbone.

The grin on his gray, burnt face spread wide as another spell rolled off his fingertips.

Spell: Paralysis (Majere)

Nick struggled to run, to scream, to do anything, but he was powerless against the magic. He remained perfectly still, outwardly calm but for the panicked flick of his eyes.

"The powder of your bones will line my fireplace," Gavriil said, a spike of bone emerging from the center of his palm, its tip jagged and cruel.

"Nick!"

<Ice shards> flew from Frost's hand. The lich's **<negation shield>** pivoted, but her aim was not toward him. The shards knifed across Nick's skin, teasing, a prelude to something disastrous. They stung, and blood dripped down his face and neck, but thankfully the pain freed him from the paralysis that had locked down his body. The lich thrust, but Nick positioned Sorrow in the way just in time. The obsidian struck bone with a clack, knocking the attack away, and then he cut backward, Sorrow slicing across ribs.

"Get back!" Frost shouted, and he quickly obeyed. Frost flung her hand toward the floor to cover his retreat. Ice rushed forward, her **<frost nova>** undercutting the ethereal shield to wrap about the lich's feet and ankles. He pulled against them, but the strength of his frail form was not enough.

"I'll keep him pinned," an unsteady Violette shouted as she lobbed **<fire bolts>** directly at Gavriil's shield, forcing him to keep it turned her way. "Bring him down!"

Nick readied his lightning, then hesitated as a thought came to him.

It was such a stupid question to ask, but with only 11 mana remaining, he had but one cast of **<lightning bolt>** left and needed to be sure.

Cataloger, does ice count as water?

Ice is the solid form of water, maintaining similar properties to—

"Good enough. Frost, go for his face!"

Nick braced himself, aimed his palm, and unleashed a **<lightning bolt>**, aimed not at the lich, but instead at the ice of Frost's **<frost nova>** pinning Gavriil in place. It passed just underneath

LEVEL: UNKNOWN

his **<negation shield>** and struck true. With a fierce crackle, it streaked through the ice and into the lich's body, its damage increasing 50 percent from hitting a single target and then doubling from flowing through water. With extreme satisfaction, Nick watched a large chunk of Gavriil's health bar burn away.

After such tremendous damage, Gavriil's concentration broke, his hands dropping and his **<negation shield>** dissipating. Into that momentary lapse sailed Frost's **<ice lance>**, striking the lich square in the face. It punched through his forehead, shattering bone and tearing his jaw off from one side. Nick didn't need to see the damage number to know the last points of his health were gone, and the lich was finally slain. The green fire faded from his eyes. His body quivered. The dark magic maintaining Gavriil's life burst out like freed smoke, and he collapsed into a puddle of bone, ice, and dust.

Reassessment
Level: 10 (+1)
Statistical Improvements
Agility: 6 (+1)
Physicality: 5
Endurance: 6 (+2)
Focus: 8 (+1)

"Let's never do that again," Nick said, taking a deep breath and waiting for the sensation to fade. His heart pounded in his chest at a ridiculous clip, and he suspected it matched it in real life. His poor brother was probably horrified watching the monitor. If only Nick could talk to him when in Yensere and tell him all was well.

With the lich defeated, Frost finally had time to look over

the wounded Kasra. Her expression was perfectly neutral, but Nick sensed her growing apprehension.

"A nasty wound," she admitted, reaching into her pack and pulling out a wound-up roll of cloth. "But nothing a strong man like you can't handle, yeah?"

"Strong," Kasra said, laughing and choking simultaneously as she started looping the cloth around his waist. It was immediately soaked crimson.

"I'll go keep watch outside," Violette said after watching a moment. Nick caught her staring at the lich's corpse, a pained expression on her face. "Make sure no more surprises are coming for us."

Frost nodded as she continued unrolling the cloth.

"I know why we are here," Frost said, calmly talking to Kasra as if she had all the practice in the world tying a bandage. "Violette's obsession brought us chasing forgotten empires. But why are *you* here?"

"I didn't mean to be," Kasra said as Frost used her sword to cut the cloth from the roll and then firmly tie it. "I was hunting...a deer. Wounded it. Made it run. I followed it here. Thought I could be quick, in and out. Stupid of me."

"Yeah, well, we all make mistakes," Frost said, putting away the cloth. "And you'll live to make more, got that, Kasra?"

Violette returned inside, and though she was smiling, it looked beyond forced.

"We need to be going," she said. "I think Gavriil might have woken up more of the city."

"That, or we're falling deeper into this era and farther from our own world," Nick said. "None of this makes sense, and

LEVEL: UNKNOWN

don't try to pretend it does, Cataloger." He knelt beside Kasra, sliding his arms underneath him. "We're going to need you to walk, all right?"

"I don't think I can."

It turned out to be true. A few steps was all Kasra managed before his entire lower body went limp. Nick dropped to his knees as Kasra coughed blood.

"Please," the man said; he stopped to swallow and then dragged out a tired breath. "Don't let me die here."

"I won't," Nick promised. "No matter what, I'm getting you home, you hear me? Even if I have to carry you myself."

Nick twisted and forced Kasra onto his back. Once he had a good grip on the man's legs and ensured Kasra's arms were wrapped around his neck, he stood with a loud groan. Heavy, but not unbearable. He could make this work.

"Get us out of here," he said as he stumbled for the door.

"Happy to," Frost said. "Follow me."

The four exited the home and continued out to the street. Frost glanced about, then pointed.

"We came that way," she said. "Hurry. I never want to see another Majere building in my life."

They hurried along, Kasra bouncing up and down on Nick's back. He tried to ignore the tiny sliver of health left in the man, or how much blood continued to trickle across Nick's back despite Frost's best attempts to bind the wound. They passed towering buildings rising higher and higher, thrice Nick's height, four times it, starting to resemble the skyscrapers of Taneth that formed a circle around the planet's spaceport.

"This can't be right," Nick said, slowing down to gently place Kasra on the ground. His aching back needed a break, and he was determined to force the others to stop. Kasra lay still and limp, his eyes half-closed. "None of this looks familiar."

"It has to be the right way," Frost argued. "I'm using the sun to keep track."

Nick spun in place, his neck craned up at the buildings whose purposes were lost to him and whose streets were much too wide and empty.

"That's only if you trust the sun," he said.

Frost crossed her arms, ready to argue, then stiffened.

"Nick..."

He froze, his heart sinking at the sound of Frost's voice. It was too heavy. Too hesitant. Reluctantly, he turned about to confirm what he feared.

Kasra lay perfectly still, his mouth slumped open, his eyes wide and unblinking.

The blood loss was too much, pillager. It was not your fault.

Comfort from Sorrow was the last thing Nick expected, nor did he welcome its intrusion. Clenching his jaw, he knelt before the body and started to slide his hands around it.

"What are you doing?" Violette asked. "Leave it. It's just a body now."

Nick was shocked by her callousness, especially given how contrary it was to her normal lightheartedness and optimism.

"I made a promise," he said, forcing Kasra's arms around his neck and then hoisting him up by the legs. "I said I would get him out of here, and I'm going to. Even if it's just to bury him."

LEVEL: UNKNOWN

Frost lowered her voice.

"Nick, there's no point to—"

"I don't care," Nick snapped. "I made a promise. He's my weight to carry, so my choice. Worry about getting us out of here."

"Of course," Frost said, retreating a step. She pointed to the sky, and the faintly visible sun through towering ethereal buildings, before shifting the angle of her arm to point at one of the streets. "We entered Constance from the south, so that's the way we keep going, south."

"No," Violette said, scanning the area. "No, not south. Don't you understand? Our...time, our place, it doesn't matter anymore. This is the world we now occupy." She pointed to one of the signs labeling a street, along with some rudimentary arrows. "We came in through the Winter Arch, so that's where we should go. We trust the signs, not the trees or the sun."

Frost shot Nick a look.

"You're tie breaker," she said.

Do I have a vote?

Frost glared at nowhere.

"No."

Nick shifted the body on his back, grabbing the legs tighter and trying hard not to think about how he was carrying a dead man.

"I think Violette's right," he said. "If we want out of Constance, then we leave Constance by its own rules."

Frost hesitated, then tilted her head at a sudden noise from afar. It sounded like a rock slide, or a stampede.

"Fine," she said, and nodded at Violette. "Get us out."

The scholar took the lead, pausing only briefly to double-check the road signs, which were gibberish to Nick.

"If she's wrong, we run the risk of being stuck here forever," Frost whispered as she walked alongside Nick.

"Maybe not forever," Nick said, unable to refuse his grim humor. "I'm sure we'd die eventually."

"And if the ring of stones is also placed in this forgotten space locked out of time?"

Nick's pace quickened. "Then we might do a lot of dying."

"This way!" Violette shouted, gesturing for them to hurry as she hooked a right at the next intersection.

The ground shook the moment he reached the intersection. Following it was a trembling roar, and the sound of a lone trumpet.

"What is that?" Nick asked, his eyes wide.

Shall I answer?

"How about we run and never find out, instead?" Frost said as she broke into a sprint.

Nick shifted Kasra's corpse to a more comfortable position on his back and then followed as fast as his tired legs could carry him. It felt like the stones vibrated beneath his feet, and that rumbling, crashing noise grew closer. Frost and Violette outpaced him, and he gasped with wide eyes as he followed them around another turn. Another horn sounded, dangerously close. Though he knew it was unwise, he twisted at the waist so he could look behind him.

He should not have.

Dozens of bodies marched toward them, their legs moving

in frightening synchronization. They wore no clothes, their skin naked and exposed. Their movements were rushed yet clumsy, their muscles snapping and twitching wrong. Bones. They had no bones. Their open mouths had only waggling tongues and a dark empty abyss. Green fire pulsed within their chests, shaped like a blooming rose trapped in the vacant hollow where a rib cage should be.

Behind them, on a two-wheeled cart whose sides were covered in tanned hide and whose yoke was attached to a dozen flesh monstrosities with pale rope, rode another robed lich.

That is what the Majere in their time referred to as "a flesh chariot"

"Shiiiiiit," Nick shouted, his boots pounding the stone, a pitiful *tap* compared to the roaring thunder giving chase. He dared not turn about. He dared not wonder how such a force could exist. The world was breaking. The world was *broken*. No amount of protestation from Cataloger could convince him otherwise.

He ran and pretended not to see the steady depletion of his stamina in the corner of his vision.

He ran through streets interspersed with trees. He ran past buildings flickering blue, ghosts of a civilization long dead that refused to accept that death had come for it. He ran, back aching, lungs burning, as ahead, the Winter Arch loomed. The stars blinked out one by one. The sun regained its light. Violette dashed through the arch, Frost right at her heels.

"Bring me the trespasser!" the lich rider bellowed from atop his chariot, and the fleshy horde let loose a unified shriek like breaking glass. With it came a terribly familiar spell, **<agony**

wave> tearing through Nick and turning his vision white with pain. He more fell than ran those last few steps toward the Winter Arch. The corpse on his back was so heavy, the footsteps of the flesh things so loud, so near.

Blood trickled down his nose, his every muscle aflame, but Nick tumbled the final few feet and collapsed to his knees on the other side of the arch. The moment he passed through, the world wobbled around him. The very air reverberated. The sounds of clattering feet instantly vanished, replaced with the soft rustle of leaves from wind blowing through the carpet covering the forest floor. Frost and Violette stood ahead of him, strangely stiff and unmoving.

"Halt," a firm voice ordered, and Nick realized they were not alone. Six men and women, two with long knives, four more with bows raised and readied, waited beyond the forest's edge. Nick slowly set Kasra's body down and then raised his hands to show he meant no harm. The strangers' garb was akin to Kasra's, rough, dark fabric flowing down to their knees. All of them wore stone pendants carved into the three-loop symbol of the Majere.

"Kasra," one of the men said, crestfallen upon getting a good look at the cold, still face.

"I'm sorry," Nick said, taking a weak step back from the corpse. "We tended his wounds, but they were too severe."

"Did you do this?" one of the women asked, the string on her bow stretching farther. Her hair was tied into a four-band ponytail, and her eyes were surrounded with white paint.

"Not us," Frost said. She, too, kept her sword sheathed. "A Majere lich."

"A lich?" said the eldest of the six. His skin was a deep brown, his eyes golden, and his hair tied into three braids that ended just beyond his neck. Unlike the others, he wore gold jewelry wrapped around his arms, and his robes bore a streak of green across their center. "Then you entered Constance."

"We did," Nick said, starting to feel hopeful. "Kasra said he was hunting a deer and stumbled into there on accident. I was hoping we could get him out and give him medical care, but..." His voice trailed off, for there was nothing more to say.

The six glanced at one another, and two of them whispered something Nick could not hear.

"No one's encountered a lich and lived, not in my lifetime," the elder said. It sounded almost like an accusation.

"Tell that to the one we slew," Frost said. "Gavriil the Emboldened, he called himself."

"Now he's just Gavriil the embalmed," Nick said, then immediately regretted it upon realizing he was the only person who would find the joke funny. The glares sent his way confirmed this.

"A slain lich," the bow woman repeated. "Then you truly walked the shimmering city?"

Violette perked up at the term.

"That's what Gavriil called it," she said. "Have you ever been?"

"As part of our transition to adulthood," she answered, chest puffing up with pride. The apparent leader shot her a look.

"Pan, Bree, wrap the body and carry it back to Hidden

Hold," he said. He returned his attention to the three, his hands clutching the emblem to his chest. "As for you, we must have words."

"That symbol around your neck," Violette said, sounding like she'd been barely holding back the entire conversation. "Do you hold to the Majere traditions?"

"Indeed we do," the man answered. "It is why we settled beside these sacred ruins."

Nick's nervousness grew. These six, they had the appearance of a cult to him, and if they considered the place "sacred," and the three of them trespassers...

"Forgive the cautious greeting," the man continued. "But my people are ever in danger in the lands of the god-king. I am Ranu, leader of the Majere Remembrance. Would you be willing to surrender your weapons and accompany me to my village?"

"For what reason?" Frost asked, her demeanor still cautious.

Ranu's smile brightened for the first time since seeing Kasra's body.

"Because you encountered a former master of the Majere and lived," he said. "And for the enlightenment of my people, I would beg that you share with me all you saw and learned."

Chapter 31
NICK

The Majere Remembrance lived amid the silver maple trees of Rockgrave Forest, albeit nearly half a mile away from the ghostly ruins of the city. Ranu talked as they traveled to his little village, his voice somber and instructive. He reminded Nick of his many tutors back on Taneth.

"We reject the new religion birthed by the supposed god-king," Ranu explained. "As do we reject the hedonistic revelry that defined the Sinifel. Before them both, reigned the Majere, and they saw life and death in ways we are only beginning to understand."

"I've seen it in person and still don't understand," Nick said, shuddering at the memory of Gavriil shrieking out his <agony wave> spell. He'd seen plenty of strange things in Yensere, but a walking, talking skeleton belonged at the top of the list.

Hidden Hold, Ranu called his village, an impressive name for a much less impressive place. Most dwellings were but tents, though an occasional wood structure was built against a tree to offer shelter from wind and rain. The four arrived just behind the hunters carrying Kasra's corpse, and Nick's greeting to the village was the soft wailing of a woman kneeling over the body.

"Come," Ranu said, guiding them past. "I would discuss what you saw."

He took them to the largest building in the village, a log feasting hall with thick hides draped across the top to form its roof. A small hole near the very apex allowed smoke from the roaring fire in the center of the room to escape. On the hall's benches they sat and recounted their story. Upon hearing Nick's explanation of why Kasra had ended up in Constance, the Remembrance leader sadly shook his head.

"Food has been growing scarce lately," he said. "Poor Kasra likely dreaded coming back to our village empty-handed. As if this were somehow better. 'One less mouth to feed,' he might argue, the unserious fool he always was." Ranu chuckled and shook his head. "Stars above, I will miss him. Thank you for bringing his body back to us. Lost in Constance, we never would have found him, let alone had the opportunity to bid his soul farewell amid the mourning song."

Violette immediately perked up.

"The mourning song?" she asked. "Can we attend?"

Ranu's demeanor immediately hardened. "You do not realize what you are asking for."

"But I do," Violette insisted. "My focus of study has always been on the Majere. Please, let me bear witness, so I might listen and learn."

LEVEL: UNKNOWN

Nick felt the tension tightening, but he hadn't a clue what the argument might even be about.

"Forgive my ignorance," he said, "but what is the mourning song?"

Ranu crossed his arms, the gold jewelry around them rattling.

"Many people believe the Majere showed death great disdain, but it is a false belief foisted upon people by the Sinifel."

They murdered us easily enough for having any supposed reverence toward life, Sorrow spoke within Nick's mind. Nick flicked the handle of his sword with his forefinger in an attempt to keep the blade silent.

"We know this," Ranu continued, "because there was a sacred ceremony to be performed for those who died before being granted an ever-living body while also lacking a proper master who could rebind their soul to their dead flesh, animating it so they might live again."

The older man sighed.

"That is all of us now. We have no masters, and so we perform the ceremony. With every loss, we sing the mourning song."

The mourning song, Sorrow seethed. *I heard tales of this ritual from my forefathers. It is an insult to life. Do not endure it, pillager, unless you would forfeit all that is good in your heart. They will steal it from you, steal your very soul.*

Nick did not argue with the blade. Where to even begin? Did his digital self in Yensere even have a soul? If so, what were the implications of *that* discovery?

"I understand it is sacred," Violette argued, surprisingly

stubborn when she desired something. Though Ranu towered over her, she marched up to him and stared him in the eye. "But we brought Kasra out from Constance to be mourned by his loved ones. Is that not worth granting my request?"

"Our deepest beliefs are not prizes to be won," Ranu said, a hard edge entering his voice.

"And I'm not trying to win anything. I have spent my life seeking the knowledge you and your people possess. Would you hoard it from one who searched with an open heart and mind?"

Ranu shifted uncomfortably.

"We have ever sought to teach the wisdom of the Majere to an ignorant people," he admitted. "But the risks...they're always so great."

"We are no soldiers of the god-king," Frost chipped in. "Nor are we agents of the Sinifel."

He'd be dead if you were, grumbled Sorrow.

Ranu turned away from them. His hands crossed behind his back, fingers twiddling with the jewelry around each wrist.

"Very well," he said. "Given the knowledge you have shared of Constance, and your attempts to save Kasra's life, I will allow you to attend the mourning song...but only if you swear to remain silent and merely observe. Is that acceptable?"

Nick shrugged, curious but not particularly interested in the religious ritual. His reaction was the opposite of Violette's.

"Of course, of course," she said excitedly. "When does it begin?"

Ranu headed for the door of the hall and gestured for them to follow.

LEVEL: UNKNOWN

"When night falls and we bathe in the light of the moon."

———————•———————

There were roughly forty people in Majere's Remembrance, twelve of them children. Together, they gathered around a roaring bonfire in the middle of a field just shy of the Rockgrave Forest. They had removed most of their jewelry and had swapped their black robes for a pale white.

"Why white?" Nick quietly asked Violette as they followed Ranu to the bonfire. "Where I'm...from, mourning is done dressed all in black."

"White is the color of bone," she answered, keeping her voice a whisper. "When impure flesh and organs are burned away, it is bone that remains. Bone lasts, when all else does not. It is meant to be holy. Purified."

The group formed two circles around the bonfire, with the visitors relegated to the outer circle. Ranu stayed with them, fielding the occasional question from the others, who were clearly unhappy with a foreign presence at such a private moment.

"We must be brave to share our most heartfelt beliefs with the world," Nick overheard Ranu telling an elderly woman with gray hair hanging all the way down to her ankles. "We cannot hide forever."

"Hiding is how we survive," the old woman spat. "It is the world that will kill us."

We can only hope, said Sorrow.

Enough, Nick shouted in his mind as he clutched the black hilt. *Why do you hate the Majere? It was Vaan who overthrew you.*

Behold their grotesque ritual and know for yourself.

Last to arrive were the corpse carriers. Kasra's body was fully wrapped in white cloth and carried on a wicker stretcher by two able-bodied men. They laid it beside the roaring bonfire and then turned to Ranu. Wordless communication passed between them as the cult's leader stepped into the center ring.

"We live in an age without masters," he began. "A time when this feeble flesh of ours is the only life we control. Once, our forefathers believed death could not defeat us, but that was hubris and naivety. It was denying the truth we must embrace. Death can always claim our bodies. But who we are in spirit? Who we become in the shadowed lands that follow? That, death cannot touch. Death is an end, but we? We are endless."

Ranu gestured toward the carriers.

"Give the flesh to the flames."

The two men hoisted the corpse and heaved it upward, flinging the body deep into the center of the bonfire. It landed amid tangled branches and neatly stacked logs. Nick realized the bonfire had been carefully built so the center was sunken, hiding the consumption of the corpse. They would only see flames and smoke, and because of that, he was relieved.

The carriers set the stretcher down by the fire and then took up spots in the inner circle. For a long time, no one spoke. Children fell silent, quieted by their parents. Nick sensed the atmosphere shift, and he wondered what would follow. Would it be the mourning song Sorrow so deeply despised?

Ranu stepped closer to the fire, and he slowly turned so he might address all in attendance.

LEVEL: UNKNOWN

"It is time for us to mourn that which we have lost," he said. He extended a hand. "Laylah, will you be the spine of the song?"

A blond woman who looked roughly Nick's age stepped forward. Her gaze locked on the bonfire, and it was a long while before she found the strength to speak.

"I am honored," she said. All around, everyone lifted their arms toward the dark night sky, and to avoid feeling awkward, Nick imitated them. In the outer ring, an elderly woman with a set of lambskin drums resting on the grass before her tapped away at their surface, and over that beat, Laylah began to sing.

There were no words, at least none that Cataloger aided in translating. The song rose in volume, a beautiful chant alternating among a few basic notes, wordless but not meaningless. The rest of the convocation took up the song, perfectly in sync. At least, at first.

"Kasra was a good man, who watched over my children when I was sick and could not attend them," a woman nearby said, her voice breaking from the drone. "He loved them, and helped teach my boys to read." She lowered her arms and bowed her head. "I have no more words."

"He hated squirrels," a man from the opposite side of the fire said, his voice barely audible over the song. "Said they hated him, too. Always dropping nuts on his head. Kasra, he was... he was always ready to laugh. Always eager to put a smile on the face of a friend." Down went his arms. "I have no more words."

More stories. More anecdotes. Times when Kasra helped the sick. A smile given when needed. More arms dropped.

All the while, Laylah continued her guiding chant, shifting among its three simple notes amid the steady patter of drums. The fire burned. The singing quieted with each story told and each pair of arms lowered.

Sorrow's voice dared whisper amid the solemnity.

Is this... this cannot be the mourning song.

Fully realizing what was happening, and knowing they could never belong to it, Nick lowered his arms without offering a tale. His face burned red. He felt like an interloper here. Amid such a tight community, he could never be a part of that song. Frost shifted awkwardly beside him, and he suspected she felt the same. Violette, however, watched with her eyes wide and her face a perfect calm mask.

"When I fled Greenborough, condemned for denying godhood to the wretched Vaan, it was Kasra who saved me," Ranu said, one of the last to speak. "We were outnumbered, yet still he fought. His aim with a bow, it was extraordinary. Just as good as his father's, if not better. And now he goes to join his father." He lowered his arms. "I have no more words."

Only Laylah continued to sing. Her song rose in defiance of the growing silence, strong and pure. The drums beat harder. Tears streamed down her cheeks as she tilted her face to the sky, and she reached her hands higher, higher, as if she might pluck out the stars with her fingers.

And then her song stopped, and she spoke instead with strength unmatched.

"I loved you more than life itself, my husband. Wait for me, in the lands beyond the living. Wait for me, until I can see you again."

LEVEL: UNKNOWN

Her tears became a river, and she forced herself to speak through a sudden rush of emotion.

"I...I have no more..."

She collapsed to her knees, and Ranu rushed to her side, holding her. There was only the crackling of the bonfire and the sound of the widow's grieving. The drums fell silent.

"The words are spoken," their leader said, Laylah cradled in his arms. "The mourning is done. Do your work, flames, and then be gone."

The bonfire roared with sudden life. The flames formed arms, reaching, reaching, fingers extended and glowing gold and orange. Nick blinked and they were gone, if they ever existed at all. The fire flickered and died. The branches and logs were consumed. All that remained were bones.

So many bones.

Forty bodies. Maybe fifty. All stacked and burned, here in this field. The history of it struck Nick like a spear to the chest. Guilt followed.

These are the people you've been killing, he thought.

Ranu gently lifted Laylah back to her feet, dipped his hand into the ashes, and then wiped away her tears with his thumb. Black streaks spread across the widow's face, and she smiled even as her tears trickled down, drawing long dark streaks to her chin.

These are the people you insist are not real.

Were such funerals held back at Meadowtint? Did the people grieve over the men he beat with stones and stabbed with a rusty sickle? The fear they'd shown, the ferociousness with which they'd hunted him...

When will it be enough? So many dead. So many innocent lives lost, and for what, demon Nick? Your pleasure?

Sorrow's voice whispered into the horrid memory of Sir Gareth's condemnation.

Your sins are many. But then again, so are mine.

"I didn't know," Nick whispered. He wasn't even sure whom he was talking to. Sorrow? Cataloger? Himself?

But he *had* known. Again and again, Cataloger had insisted he treat Yensere as real. As a place with history. Life. Emotions. He'd heard the words; he'd just never believed them. Part of him still fought against it. That part was powerless against Laylah's grief, and the way the other members of the Remembrance gathered around her, offering quiet words of encouragement and love.

Nick had endured two funerals for his own family. Those words? Those sympathetic faces? Powerless to help, yet trying to anyway? This was true. It felt real, in a way that could not be faked. Digital data. Ones and zeros. He could tell himself that again and again, and yet none of it would chase away the lingering sound of Laylah's song as she finally, at long last, gave up her words.

"Hey," Frost said, setting her hand on his shoulder. "Are you all right?"

Nick turned to answer, torn between laughing and crying.

"I don't know," he said, and then a sword burst through Frost's chest, staining her with blood.

Chapter 32
NICK

Nick stared at the growing pool of blood with wide eyes and a broken mind. It made no sense. Frost wasn't dying. That wasn't a sword pierced through her chest.

"Nick?" she said, a bit of blood dribbling down her cheek. Her knees went weak. She collapsed, and to his shock, she was not dead. A sliver of her health remained visible, pulsating violently.

Screams followed. Panic. Confusion. Nick looked beyond the clearing to see Sir Gareth approach, his hands empty, his thrown sword embedded in the dying Frost. Black fire burned about his hands.

"I find you at last, demon," Gareth said. "Heretics ever seek fellowship amid heresy."

He made a throwing motion, and from his hand flew a thick black orb whose center was solid darkness but whose edges burned with midnight fire.

Spell: Dark Orb

The orb struck Nick square in the chest. He gasped as the

fire charred across his leather armor, the impact like a dozen punches to the chest.

"What..." he gasped, unable to finish his sentence as he collapsed onto his back. The attack was nothing like Gareth's previous magic, built of his faith in Vaan.

Gareth: Level 17 Human
Archetype: Knight
Special Classification: Deity Blessed (Eiman)
Armor: Augmented Chain Mail, Quality Tier 7

The knight has abandoned his god, Sorrow answered. *He wields Eiman's magic now. Slay him, pillager, no matter the cost. This blasphemy cannot stand.*

"Slay him?" Nick said, eyeing the approaching knight with dread. "Shouldn't you two be friends?"

I need not explain myself to you. But what Gareth has become is abhorrent to me. End him.

As if it would be that easy. Nick staggered to his feet, wishing he could help Frost. All around him, members of the Remembrance panicked and fled, led by Ranu.

"Into the woods," he shouted to them. "Flee, flee to the safe spaces we prepared!"

Two more orbs of shadow swelled in Gareth's hands.

"I have no business with you, Majere cultists," he said. "I'm here only for the demons."

Before he threw the orbs, fire swelled at his feet, bursting forth to form a wall.

Spell: Fire Wall

"Stay back!" Violette shouted, her hands extended as her magic poured forth. "We've no business with you."

LEVEL: UNKNOWN

"But I have business with you," Gareth said, and flung another orb unseen from the other side. It passed through the wall of fire, its aim immaculate, to strike Violette in the chest. She rocked, gasping from the pain. The wall faded, her concentration broken.

"You have allied yourself with demons, scholar of Silversong," he said, pulling his shield off his back. "Their guilt is now yours."

Nick and Violette unleashed their magic simultaneously. Gareth weathered both with his shield raised high, the **<lightning bolt>** striking the metal and swirling about it, while Violette's **<fire bolt>** cracked against it and burned the air harmlessly. Nick flung two more bolts, frustrated by how little damage they were doing through the shield. Eighteen mana spent, and he'd only chipped away a sliver of Gareth's health.

"Run," Frost said weakly at Nick's feet. "Just...leave me, I'll...I'll..."

Stand your ground, pillager, Sorrow seethed. *Or would you abandon the cultists whose lives your presence endangered?*

Nick glanced over his shoulder as he readied Sorrow. The cultists had fled, all but Ranu, who remained by the pile of bones with his arms raised and his head tilted to the sky. Nick had no time to ponder what the man was doing. Two more **<lightning bolts>**, impotent against the enormous golden shield, and Gareth had crossed the distance.

Despite their differences in levels, Gareth was still weaponless, and Nick lunged forward, hoping that might be advantage enough. Sorrow scraped along the shield, easily deflected.

Nick swung twice more, trying to find an opening. Instead, he was rewarded with a sudden charge, the shield smashing into him and awkwardly pinning his arm. It did no damage, but it sent him flying to a tumbling landing on the grass.

"Leave them alone!" Violette shouted, fire swirling around her hands. It exploded outward as an enormous plume, and even with Gareth's shield to block, it still burned. Flames kissed his skin, but despite the spell's fury, it only chipped away at Gareth's health. Not worth the exhaustion it caused Violette as she dropped to her knees. Not when Gareth loomed large, more than half his health remaining. Nick added to it the best he could, two more bolts that crackled through the shield, their damage maddeningly reduced.

When the barrage ended, Gareth bent down, his hand closing about the hilt of his sword, embedded in Frost's back.

"Nick," Frost said, still struggling to breathe. Gareth's heel pressed to her skull. "Run, Nick..."

Gareth stomped with all his strength, cracking her skull. Her head caved in, gore spilling out, bone crunching, and then she was blessedly turned to shadow and dust.

"I pray that suffering was enough," Gareth said as he lifted his freed sword. "Both of you must learn pain awaits you in Yensere if we are to be free of your evil."

"Evil," Nick said, once more rising to his feet. "You're the one who interrupted a funeral with murder."

"Is it murder if the victim returns unharmed?" Gareth asked. He slung his shield back over his shoulder and held his left hand up. Dark fire swarmed across his fingers. "Or do you suffer still, in whatever lands you return to when your life here ends?"

LEVEL: UNKNOWN

Hardly information Nick wished to share. The last thing he needed was Gareth knowing the physical costs he paid with his every death inside Yensere. Before he could think of a proper retort, a new voice thundered across the night.

"Interloper!" Ranu shouted, now standing atop the pile of bones in the heart of the dormant mourning pyre. Gareth held his sword defensively before him.

"I would show you undeserved mercy, cultist," Gareth shouted back. "Do not come between me and the demons."

Green light swirled around the edges of the bone pile. It looked like flames at first, until they grew larger and brighter. Moths. Little moths, flitting up and down before diving into the center of the bones. Bones that shimmered a deep emerald and vibrated with life.

"I keep the ways of the eternal," Ranu said as matching fire swelled about his wrists. "And for the sake of my people, I will see the champion of the false empire humbled."

Spell: Bone Storm

The bones of the corpses rose into the air about Ranu, swirling in orbit. Faint green fire shimmered across their bleached white surface. Ranu stood in the storm's center, majestic in his pale robe. He pointed at Gareth and issued his challenge as his name and level fluctuated before Nick's eyes, growing in strength from the power of the dead.

Ranu: Level 11 Human
Archetype: Cultist
Special Classification: Necrotic Caster

"Show me the might of the god you serve," Ranu said. "And I shall give you the promise of those whom death knew not."

Sir Gareth pulled his shield off his back and held it at the ready. His head lowered, and his legs braced.

"It matters not whom I serve," he said. "You'll die either way, cultist."

He charged Ranu, into the heart of the storm. Bones ceased their orbit to fling toward him in a relentless barrage. Ribs pierced his sides. Femurs struck his legs. Teeth dove for his eyes. The hits were many, but weak, and Gareth relied on his armor to endure them, robbing the bones of much of their sting.

Gareth roared as he charged, and when the gap was closed between him and Ranu, he flung his shield aside while raising his sword. Ranu met the challenge, his arms crossed over his chest. The bones pulled in, latching together to form a wall. Gareth's sword struck the center and failed to penetrate.

"You insult the mourning song," Ranu said, visibly struggling from the strain to control the <bone storm>. The fire about his wrists surged with life. The bones twisted, turned, sticking out like awkward spikes. Ranu slammed the entire thing into Gareth, bashing him with enough force to leave him reeling.

Gareth bellowed in retaliation, darkness and shadow swelling across his shield to form a swirling maelstrom across the steel.

Spell: Chaos Slam

That seething mass of ancient magic smashed directly into Ranu's shield. Bones snapped. The magic holding the storm quivered and weakened. Ranu screamed, but he was not yet done. The bones exploded outward in all directions, growing larger and larger to become a dome encasing the two in its heart.

Lightning crackled around the outer edges, the same deep green color as the fire.

"You insult the dead we came to sing in remembrance of," Ranu said, his voice strained. "Begone, knight. I will suffer your presence no longer."

Magic swelled. Gareth tensed, uncertain of the nature of the attack. He kept his sword close and his shield on his back, and when the magic did come, he held no defense.

Spell: Bone Storm Finality

The bones shattered at once, erupting with power it seemed only the Majere knew how to manipulate. From within the femurs, ribs, teeth, skulls, and vertebrae emerged fire and lightning, all flickering green and otherworldly. They descended upon Sir Gareth, the lightning reaching first, coursing through his body with such power it paralyzed his limbs so his pained scream could not emerge, his jaw locked shut and his lungs unable to function.

The fire came next, swarming upon Gareth like rain yet falling as silent as snow. It sizzled across his golden armor, charring portions black. It flowed to his skin, his face, beneath his armor, living flame that sought to reach past flesh and muscle to touch the very bone. Now Gareth did scream, guttural, howling, giving sound to the spell as his life dropped by a massive chunk from the overwhelming power of the spell.

Gareth collapsed to his knees, and Ranu did likewise, his power spent. As Nick watched, Ranu's level plummeted back down to 5. Despair filled him. All that fury, and yet it wasn't enough to bring down the knight, filled as he was by whatever new blessing had been granted him.

"Foul magic," Gareth said. His sword had stabbed the ground, and he clutched it to brace himself. "Yensere is better with it gone."

With speed belying his size, Gareth lunged back to his feet, crossed the space between him and Ranu, and thrust his sword straight through Ranu's throat. The leader's body vibrated in a sudden seizure. One thrust. Despite all his power, all his magic, one thrust was all it took to end the man's life.

"Damn it," Nick whispered. He'd hoped the cultist could have finally brought down the maddening knight, but tonight seemed destined to be one of cruelty. He retreated, rushing across the grass to where Violette had watched the conflict in stunned silence.

"You need to leave," Nick insisted, painfully aware Gareth had turned his attention their way. "Don't worry about me and Frost. We can come back from this."

"Come back how?" she asked, looking baffled.

"Trust me," he said, grinning at her despite his pain and exhaustion. He had to show her he was unafraid. "We're demons, after all."

"I don't know what that means," she said. "Only the stories that I've heard."

Nick lifted Sorrow in both hands.

"It means you run, while I stay and fight. Once you're safe and Gareth's gone, return here and look for us. Both of us, me and Frost. We'll find you, I promise, now *run*!"

Violette glanced between Nick and Gareth, then nodded.

LEVEL: UNKNOWN

"All right," she said. "But remember, I'm learning Majere magic, so if you die, I'll find a way to bring you back long enough to yell at you for breaking your promise."

Violette sprinted for the safety of the distant maple trees. Nick positioned himself between her and Gareth. He had a single cast of **<lightning bolt>** left, but he kept it in reserve, hoping for an opening where the shield could not absorb the brunt of the damage. Lifting Sorrow, he braced and pretended he looked intimidating to the enormous knight.

"Strange, to see a demon fight honorably to protect another," Gareth said, his gait unchanged as he approached. Wounded as he was, he showed not a hint of pain. "Does she mean something to you, Nick?"

"She's a friend," Nick said, trying to stay light on his toes and ignore how little health remained in that red bar in the corner of his vision. "Surely you have a few of those, besides me? Or does the stick-up-your-ass life of a knight prevent that?"

Gareth paused just outside of reach, his sword tilted slightly and held at the defensive. His eyes narrowed. His muscles tensed underneath his armor, now chipped and burned from the battle.

"A friend?" he said. "Then know that when your life is spent, I will hunt her next. She'll bleed out at my feet, Nick." He grinned, sick joy in his eyes. "Perhaps when you return I will have her corpse ready... as a gift between *friends*."

Anger drove Nick onto the offensive, even as Sorrow warned against falling for such bait. He abandoned all he'd learned from his training with Frost. No stances, no careful movements, just wild swings with his strength poured into them. The aggression meant nothing to the more skilled knight. He easily batted aside Nick's panicked slashes, twice, three times, and then shocked him with a sudden lunge forward with his elbow leading. It struck Nick in the forehead, costing him his vision as the world spun and his legs wobbled, threatening to lose their balance.

Knowing he was vulnerable, he swung blindly, hoping to intercept a killing blow. Instead his sword struck Gareth's armor, rebounding off without harming. In return, Gareth smashed his head straight into Nick's, further lighting up the world with white. Nick rocked backward, then gasped when Gareth's fist struck him in the stomach hard enough to crack a rib. An immediate elbow followed, hardened with the gleaming chain mail, striking Nick in the face. His nose exploded with pain, blood splattering.

When he fell, Gareth pressed his heel to Nick's chest, pinning him to the ground, while the other foot stepped on Sorrow's blade so he could not swing it. Nick struggled in vain, nowhere near strong enough to overcome the combined weight of Gareth and his armor as the knight loomed over him.

"What is this?" Gareth asked, reaching down with his free hand. "More heretical artifacts? Or did you steal this?"

It was the mirror, Nick realized. It had slipped from his pocket. Gareth lifted it, studying the runes written upon the handle. A strange panic filled Nick, and he flailed with his free hand.

"Give it back," he said, struggling to speak. Breathing

was difficult given the weight. Gareth stared into the glass, momentarily transfixed, and then shook his head.

"No, demon Nick," he said, pocketing it. "I will take everything from you, bleed it from you bit by bit until you learn Yensere offers nothing but pain to your presence."

Nick might not be able to push free, but the momentary distraction had caused Gareth to shift his weight and not press down so firmly. It wasn't much, but it was enough for Nick to slide Sorrow's blade out from underneath the knight's other foot. He swung, slamming the edge against the side of Gareth's knee. The knight screamed, blood spilling from underneath the plate, and instinctively he retreated a step.

Nick rolled onto his stomach, clutching Sorrow's hilt tightly, and scraped his feet along the grass in a struggle to stand. He stumbled more than ran, his muscles weak, his health a pittance of red in the corner of his eye. Up ahead, he saw Violette lingering at Rockgrave Forest's edge.

What are you doing? he thought. Though his chest ached, he forced himself to scream.

"Run, damn it! Get out—"

His vision blurred, and he desperately hoped he saw correctly that Violette was fleeing into the trees, when he felt the sharp pain of a blade piercing the back of his skull.

Health: 0
Visit terminated

Chapter 33
NICK

When Nick awoke, he was choking. Something was in his throat, and though he coughed and retched, he couldn't get it out, couldn't get it out...

"Easy there," Simon said, holding Nick down by the shoulders. "Deep breaths. Relax."

Nick closed his eyes and fought against the constant urge to cough and clear his throat. He breathed through his nose as he'd been taught, growing more aware of the oxygen tube attached to his nostrils. That sensation was dwarfed by the pounding headache holding the entire front of his head in a vise grip of pain.

"What...?" he asked, managing only that one word before he had to stop. An urge to vomit had come, and talking made it worse.

"What you're feeling is a feeding tube down the back of your throat."

Another long, deep breath. All right, he could handle this.

"Why?" he asked, keeping his eyes closed. The lights were off in his room, but the glow of the various instruments, as well as his brother's laptop, was like a knife into his cerebral cortex.

"Why? Because you've been sleeping for days at a time now, that's why."

Nick risked sitting up and immediately regretted it. He felt a strange pull on his crotch when he moved and grimaced.

"That's a catheter, isn't it?" he asked, each word slow and careful.

"Yeah, it is." Simon squeezed his shoulder. "Would you prefer we put you in diapers?"

Nick forced his eyes open.

"I need back in," he said, his memories growing sharper. "My friends, they're in danger."

Simon took a step back, and the comfort he'd been showing vanished behind a cold mask.

"Nick, you're in terrible shape. How about you take a break for a bit? I'll remove the gastro tube, and you can eat something real, maybe even walk around a bit to stretch your muscles."

"No," Nick said, remembering the panic on Violette's face when Gareth stabbed him. He'd shouted for her to flee. Had she listened? "No, I need to get back there *now*."

He lay on his back and closed his eyes. Sleep had come easy to him lately, but not now. His heart felt like it was trying to escape his rib cage. Knowing that it was a tube in the back of his throat helped, but it still triggered his gag reflex every time he breathed. The beep of his heart monitor was like a trumpet in his ear, and it was so fast, so urgent. Why couldn't he relax, damn it, why couldn't he fade away...?

"Nick," Simon said. He grabbed Nick's wrist. "Please, don't you see what this is doing to you? I think we...I think we need to discuss ways to separate you from the Artifact."

Any hope of sleeping vanished in a panic. Nick looked to his brother, and he saw the dark circles beneath his eyes. There was no hiding his worry. But Violette, and Frost...

"That place, Yensere," he said, wishing his voice didn't sound so hoarse and pathetic. "It means something. To me. To those in there. And the friends I've made, they're real, too, and they're in danger."

"Don't you understand?" Simon asked, his voice lowering. "You're in danger, too."

"I know." He tried to smile. "But when has that ever stopped either of us?"

Simon crossed his arms, his entire body rigid as he bit the nail of his right thumb. Nick waited for the silent debate to end, too tired to think of what he'd do if Simon refused.

"What is it you need from me?" his brother suddenly asked. Nick sank into the bed with relief.

"Give me something to knock me out," he said. "A sedative, a tranquilizer, whatever it takes. I need back in."

"This will take a moment," Simon said after glancing around. "Sit tight."

Nick lay on the bed, trying to relax while his brother left the room. Perhaps if he could close his eyes and drift off, he wouldn't need any help...but his damn heart would not slow. He felt exhausted yet awake, his mind like a ragged sponge wrung dry and then set on fire. His imagination refused to play nicely. He kept seeing Gareth stomping his foot on Frost's head, and he imagined the bloodshed he could be causing, the deaths of the Remembrance, perhaps killing Frost a second time, or worse, Violette. There'd be no coming back for her, not for anyone...

The door opened, and Simon returned with the head of the med ward, Dr. Haley, at his side. She held a little portable carrying case of medicine and supplies, tightly zipped in case of gravity-failure incidents. She approached stiffly as she unzipped the case.

"Before I do this, I would like to make it clear I am worried about the effects of a tranquilizer on a body so stressed," she said.

"Noted," Simon said. "Consider it an acceptable risk of our research."

Haley withdrew a syringe and a clear bottle. "As you wish, Director. May the Guidance show kindness to you both."

Nick breathed out a sigh of relief. Good. He didn't know how much time passed within Yensere compared to outside, but from what he'd gathered, it was roughly one to one. These few minutes...they wouldn't be too long. There was hope still, hope he could cling to. Eyes closed, he prepared himself for the battle ahead.

"Injecting the solution now," Haley said. "Nick, I want you to do me a favor. Please count backward from ten, all right?"

"Sure," he said, still not feeling anything. "Ten. Nine..."

Returning visitor cataloged
 Level: 10
 Agility: 6
 Physicality: 5
 Endurance: 6
 Focus: 8
 Archetype: Adventurer
 Special Classification: Lightning Caster
 Mana: 49
 Welcome back, Nick

The ring of stones surrounded him. Nick breathed in the cool country air, and it felt like a tremendous weight had lifted off him. The ache in his forehead was gone. No tubes in his throat, no IV, and no catheter. He felt strong. He felt alive.

"Where are you, Gareth?" he asked, looking about. He hadn't known where the nearest ring of stones would be in relation to the field where they'd held the mourning song ritual. The landscape was still unknown to him, but the thick plume of smoke from the extinguished pyre was enough to orient himself.

Nick sprinted in that direction, doing his best to ignore the rapid depletion of green from his stamina bar. As he ran, he brushed his hand against Sorrow, still strapped to his hip. He decided he wasn't ready to think about what happened to Sorrow's consciousness during Nick's departures from Yensere.

Will you still not aid me? he silently asked, remembering the sword's strange revulsion to Sir Gareth's new magic.

The foul knight is unworthy of my power, Sorrow responded. *That does not mean you suddenly are, pillager.*

LEVEL: UNKNOWN

"Fine," he muttered. "Cataloger, can you tell me if Frost returned to Yensere?"

For privacy concerns, I cannot share such information

Damn it.

Nick slowed to a walk upon reaching the field outside the maple trees. The members of Majere's Remembrance were gone. He saw no sign of Violette or Frost.

Sir Gareth stood before the dormant pyre, his hands at his sides, palms upward as if in prayer. A crimson glow shimmered across his body, tainting the golden sheen. When Nick checked his health, he saw it was almost entirely full. It seemed Eiman's blessing was also rapidly healing him.

"I wondered who would return first, you or the woman," Gareth said as he drew his sword. "I should have known it would be you. You've ever been tenacious, haven't you, Nick?"

"Where are the worshipers?" Nick asked as he readied Sorrow.

The knight lifted his free hand. A deep black orb rimmed with red light shimmered into existence.

"My hate is not for them," he said. "Only you."

Nick dove aside as the **<dark orb>** flew. It struck the grass and detonated, leaving an impact crater. That it did so in complete silence was unnerving. Nick rolled to his feet, lightning crackling around his left hand.

"The feeling's mutual."

A **<lightning bolt>** shot from his palm, striking Gareth in the chest. Nick grimaced in frustration. The chain mail—it looked like it was reducing the damage, too. Meanwhile, the knight shuddered against the pain but remained standing.

"You'll need to do better," he said, stalking closer. He held his sword out wide. Black flame wreathed about it, wrapping the sword in Eiman's power.

Spell: Black Flame Blade

Nick had no desire to see if his smaller health pool and weaker armor could withstand such an empowered hit. The gap in their levels threatened to unnerve him. The disparity in their training tried to frighten him. He gave in to neither.

Gareth swung, wide and strong. Nick dropped to one knee, felt the swish of air above his head, felt the dark energy crackling across the blade, and then came up swinging. Sorrow struck Gareth's arm, denting the armor.

Keep it steady, Nick thought as he danced away to avoid Gareth's retaliatory strike. He grinned despite his nervousness. *Step by step, we climb the mountain.*

"Are you afraid to battle true?" Gareth asked, chasing after Nick. Two more swings hit air, but the third was much too close. Nick risked blocking. Their weapons collided with a shower of sparks and a loud screech of metal. The black flame swirled around Sorrow. The obsidian groaned, and Nick feared the blade would break from the impact.

No Eiman magic will defeat me, Sorrow seethed inside Nick's mind. *Your death will be on you, pillager.*

The sword held. Nick didn't dare try to engage Gareth in a battle of strength, and so he immediately retreated. His feet danced underneath him as he spun away. Lightning crackled, and he flung another **<lightning bolt>**, this one aimed for Gareth's abdomen. The knight screamed as it scorched through him. Overwhelmed with fury, he flung two more **<dark orbs>**, attempting to anticipate Nick's movement. Nick dodged them both, relying on a combination of panic and instinct to keep Gareth guessing. Speed—he most certainly had speed over the lumbering man in enormous chain mail. If only he could further utilize that advantage.

A third **<lightning bolt>** to Gareth's chest. Perhaps if Nick drained his mana fully, it'd bring the knight down, perhaps not, but it seemed Gareth would not allow him the chance. The knight barreled in closer, forcing Nick to wield Sorrow in defense.

Another clash of their blades. Sparks showered, and amid their light, Nick slipped forward, mimicking one of the stances Frost had taught him. Hips sliding. Legs bracing. Sword curling low, underneath a block. As he'd hoped, Gareth rushed Nick, trying to overwhelm him with his superior strength and inadvertently stepping into the hit. Sorrow struck his armor, and though it was thick, Nick was stronger than he'd been back in Meadowtint, and Sorrow's edge was ever keen.

You know only the faintest shred of my power, pillager.

Perhaps he did, but it was enough. Blood splashed as the armor gave way, another sliver sliced off the knight's health bar. He roared, and Nick dared not face the retaliatory swing. He retreated, then had to dodge again to avoid a massive overhead strike that pounded an indent into the grass.

Nick set his feet, falling back into one of Frost's stances, beyond grateful for her lessons. Gareth glared at Nick, a wounded, hulking monster of metal and bloodshot eyes. So close. He was so close to breaking.

"I'm tired of being chased," Nick said, tensing his legs. An idea came to him, brought on by the remaining fragment of his mana bar. He hopped backward, twice avoiding Gareth's swings, and then sprinted past him while attempting a slash at his side. Gareth expertly blocked the blow, but it kept him turning on his feet, and when he swung again, Nick was already out of reach. The black fire surrounding his sword flickered away into nothing. Exhaustion was clearly setting in. Just a little further.

"I'm tired of you hurting my friends."

Nick twisted, narrowly avoiding being impaled, and then smacked the sword aside in another shower of sparks. Gasping for air, he retreated, needing space. Gareth lumbered after, sweat and blood mixed upon his face, his own breathing ragged.

"I'm tired of *you*," Nick said, lifting his left arm. Lightning sparked about it. Gareth tensed, but this was no singular bolt.

Frost had made it clear that there were countless manifestations of each element, and he'd seen a half dozen versions of her ice alone. Nick knew there had to be more to his lightning, and for once, he held faith in himself. No rules. No lessons. This magic belonged to him, and so it would obey. Nick clenched his left fist, and instead of flinging lightning out, he imagined it encompassing his wrist in a wide circle. Vicious. Brilliant. A way to protect instead of attack.

The magic obeyed.

Spell Unlocked: Lightning Shield
Cost: 12 mana
Attributes: Lightning, Retaliation

LEVEL: UNKNOWN

Forms a weightless defensive shield around the caster's arm

A ring of brilliant blue lightning swirled around his left forearm, forming the outline of a perfectly circular shield. Nick lifted it, braced his legs, and readied Sorrow.

"This ends now," he said.

Sir Gareth eyed the shield warily as he clutched his sword in both hands for a thrust.

"And how will you end it, demon?"

In came Gareth's blade. Though the interior circle of the shield was empty, Nick positioned it in the way, trusting the spell to protect him nonetheless. The moment the blade broke the center, lightning sparked from all about the ring, jolting inward to slam the thrust to a halt. Nick gasped, feeling his mana drain by an additional 5, and seeing a frightening amount of his stamina fade away.

His strain was nothing compared to what Gareth endured. Lightning crackled all the way up his blade and into his hands. From there it leaped across his body, burning into his skin. Smoke wafted up from a vicious sear along his cheek.

"I will not be beaten by your devilry," Gareth said, and swung again. Nick shifted his arm, positioning the shield in the way despite Gareth's subtle attempt to curl underneath. The sword hit the ring, and again it slammed to a halt. Nick's feet slid backward, carving a groove into the soft earth as he held his ground. Nick clenched his teeth and screamed, surging power into the shield. The last of his 14 mana vanished, but the retaliation was worth it. A much stronger beam lashed out, swirling up Gareth's sword like a snake to plunge into his chest.

Gareth retreated and gasped for air. His breathing was wet, and his shoulders sagged underneath his armor.

"I will not falter," he said, a bit of blood dribbling down his chin from a cut somewhere inside his mouth. "For all the people you have wronged, the innocents you have murdered, I must prevail."

He lifted his sword above his head. Black fire wreathed about it as he reactivated **<black flame blade>**. Nick tensed, uncertain of how his shield would react against the foul Eiman magic, especially now that his mana was drained.

"You will die, Nick, again and again, until we are free of you!"

Trust my blade if you wish to live, Sorrow suddenly screamed inside Nick's mind. He had a split second to debate, and then he disbanded the shield. His mana was already spent, and Gareth's fire was so bright. So frightening. Instead, he lifted Sorrow high, and with every tired muscle in his body tensed, he met his foe's strike.

The blades collided, and this time there were no sparks, but instead a massive crackle of black lightning. The spell—it had shifted. Gareth's fire swirled outward like an uncoiling snake, and Nick realized it was about to retaliate against him similar to the way his **<lightning shield>** worked. He had no time to react, no way to avoid it. That fire would consume him.

Item: Sorrow

Special Attribute Unlocked: Absorption (Deific)

The fire surged into the open space in the center of the twisted, curling obsidian near Sorrow's hilt. It compressed within it, vibrating with power as it was consumed. No harm came to Nick. He never even felt its heat.

LEVEL: UNKNOWN

Now strike back!

Nick swung his sword overhead. The impulse came naturally, and it did not matter that Sorrow would not hit Gareth directly. Fire burst across the blade, and its length stretched farther, and farther, until it seemed eager to reach the stars themselves. One swing, and the fire slashed across Gareth's center. A black line burned across his body, melted through his armor, and then struck him with incredible force. Amid his scream, Nick saw the knight's health bar blast away to nearly nothing.

Sir Gareth collapsed to his hands and knees, a pool of blood building beneath him. His health bar pulsed red, barely a percentage point remaining. The knight certainly looked like it. His voice was hoarse, his chest a mess, and the burns from Nick's lightning were vicious across his neck and face.

"Are you so vile even death refuses you?" he asked, then coughed up a mixture of phlegm and blood to spit upon the grass.

"You're the one hunting *me*," Nick said, overcome with a rush of anger. He couldn't shake the image of Frost lying on her side, bleeding out in pain. Couldn't shake the memory of the way Gareth had crushed her skull beneath his heel before she disappeared in a puff of smoke. "I've only defended myself."

"Defense?" Gareth coughed and laughed simultaneously. "Is that what you call murdering the people of Meadowtint in cold blood? Was it self-defense when you killed old Julie in her rocking chair? Self-defense when you smashed Iver's head with a stone? Poor farmers, suffering under the weight of the blight, and you couldn't leave them be." His voice rose. "Day after night after day, as they worked, as they slept, you butchered them, and I don't even know why."

He jammed his sword into the earth and used it to support his weight. His shaking fingers clutched the hilt as if it was all that kept him breathing.

"What of the baron? You didn't just kill him and his guards, but his servants, too. I saw their bodies. You murdered them, murdered them all, and with *glee*."

Nick listened to the outrage, an icy calm settling over his thoughts. Try as he might, he could not dismiss the memories of his first days spent in Yensere. He wanted to shout that they'd attacked him first, but it would be a shallow argument of semantics. He remembered the thrill he'd felt when he gained his first level. He remembered the savage pleasure that had filled his breast while cutting the farmers down, knowing he would come back and they would not.

All protests died on his lips, and instead he saw this terrifying knight who had tormented him in a new light. A man bound by duty. A hero chasing a demon who left brutally murdered corpses in his wake.

"Why?" Gareth asked when Nick offered only silence. He leaned more of his weight against his sword, his forehead resting upon the tip of its hilt. His eyes closed. "Farmers. Servants. The guards in Greenborough. What drives you to commit such sins? Have you a heart in that body of yours, or are you as soulless as the stories claim?"

Nick lowered to his haunches so that he was at eye level with the knight. His thoughts jumbled about, and he struggled to organize them into something both honest and coherent. What could he tell this knight that would make sense? What words could he offer that would not sound insane to a man born and raised in Yensere, who knew nothing of the world outside the mysterious Artifact?

"You may never believe me," he said, deciding the best tactic would be the simplest and most forthright. Perhaps, if he was completely honest, Gareth might sense that and be willing to listen. It had to be worth a try.

"When I first arrived here, in Yensere, I was confused. I was scared. The people of Meadowtint called me a demon, and they attacked me before I even knew what was happening. And so I... I thought they weren't real. The gray skin. Their tongues. The blight. I thought they were signs of artificial life. So I fought them. I killed them. It made me stronger, faster. And then when you showed up, well..." He shrugged. "By then, you were just a defender of monsters."

Gareth's jaw clenched so tightly his words spat out like a curse between his teeth.

"Monsters? You'd call them monsters?"

Nick put his hand atop Gareth's gauntlets. The knight flinched, but he did not pull away, nor did he attack like Nick feared he might. Their eyes met, and Nick endured the seething rage and countered it with his own.

"But Baron Hulh?" he said. "He invited me in as his guest, poisoned me, and bound me in a prison. He *tortured* me, Gareth. He carved my skin, and he enjoyed each and every cut. He was not a good man. Good men don't find pleasure in inflicting pain."

"Just as you took pleasure in killing the villagers of Meadowtint?"

Nick flinched. He had no answer for that.

"I'm sorry about the baron's servants," he said. "I was reckless. I was heartless. But listen to me, please. I am begging you, Gareth, for your own sake. I see now what this world is, and I will not treat it the same. The people of Yensere have no reason to fear me. The life here is sacred, I get that, I do. Listen to my regret. Believe me when I promise to be better. Give up this chase, and just let me be, and no one will have to get hurt again."

The knight's blue eyes bored into Nick's.

"You lie," he said, but there was no venom in his words, no conviction.

"It's the truth," Nick said. "And I'll prove it by starting with you. Go. Live. I hold no hate against you, nor blame for your hunt. Consider it finished, and your oath fulfilled. The monster you chased no longer exists."

Sir Gareth forced himself to his feet, and he pulled his hands away from Nick's grasp. A tug, and his sword ripped free of the earth. His stance was unsteady, his breathing heavy, but he still looked willing to battle.

"Bastard," he said. "One day you will know true death, and I pray it is at the edge of my blade."

"Perhaps." A faint smile tugged at the side of Nick's face. "But if it's by you, then at least I'll know I deserve it."

Gareth departed for the meadows beyond the maple trees, and Nick watched him go in silence. Once the knight vanished into the starlit night, Nick lifted his sword. The last of the unholy fire had burned away with the hollow sphere near the hilt. Perhaps it was his imagination, but the runes carved into its side seemed to glow brighter.

"Why did you help me?" he asked.

It was a good long while before Sorrow answered.

My reasons are my own. If it will cease further questioning, know that I prefer you wielding me over that knight.

Nick walked the grass, returning to the smoldering remains of the mourning pyre. He stood before it, trying to remember the somber wonder he'd felt in listening to the song. Ranu's body lay nearby, and so far as Nick could tell, the leader was the only casualty.

"You died trying to protect us," Nick said, shaking his head. "You could have left us to our deaths—we'd have returned in time, but you didn't know that, did you?"

We were once enemies, Sinifel and Majere, Sorrow said, his voice so soft it felt like a whisper. *And now we are dead. Only the Alder remain.* The voice dropped further. *What a waste.*

Nick looked to the forest. Would the people return to bury their former leader, or would they flee into hiding? He didn't know, but it seemed they would not be coming back, at least not tonight. After a bit of searching, he gave up trying to find any wrappings and instead lifted the body by the arms. He suppressed his shudders at holding a corpse, and for once, he wished he could go back to believing all of this was a ridiculous, unimportant world of data and numbers.

Once he deposited Ranu's body in the center of the dormant mourning pyre, he breathed out a long sigh.

"We need a fire."

Chapter 34
NICK

Once Nick built a fire a respectful distance away from the dormant pyre, he sat before it and laid Sorrow across his knees. The blade pulsed a soft crimson as he gently rested his fingers atop the obsidian. Sorrow's voice floated in his mind, firmer than the stone and deeper than the night.

What are you waiting for, pillager?

"For Frost to come back, just like I did," he said. "Violette, too."

Violette could be dead.

"She's not. I couldn't find her body."

Just like you and Frost leave behind bodies?

Nick drummed his fingertips across the flat edge of the sword blade, hoping it would annoy the ancient thing.

"Violette isn't a...demon, like us. If they killed her, I'd have found her corpse. She escaped, just like we hoped. She'll come back. Both of them will. I only need to be patient."

Why, then, do you draw me? There is no blood to be shed.

LEVEL: UNKNOWN

Nick looked around at the meadow, full of tall ryegrass. It swayed in the soft wind. In the distance, he saw the beginning of the Rockgrave Forest and the ruins within. There was an undeniable age lingering about, countless years stored within every stone. Even if this world was but a simulation, that simulation was old, so old. The knowledge of this weighed him down, and for once, he did not fight it with defiance. He accepted the solemnity it offered. Faintly smiling despite feeling no joy, he looked to the stars, and the black sun rimmed with blue fire.

"Perhaps I wished to have company," he said.

Then speak with your mirror.

"I can't. Gareth took it."

The red pulsed a little deeper, as if the blade were brooding.

I suppose I can indulge, since there is no escaping you. Is there something in particular you wish from me? Some advice I might offer, or wisdom of the Sinifel?

Melancholy settled over Nick, and he gave voice to a question that had lingered in the back of his mind ever since finding Sorrow in the ruins of Abylon.

"Was there happiness in your time?"

What kind of absurd question is that?

Nick took the sword, spun it, and drove the blade deep into the earth until it was embedded halfway up to the hilt. He left his right hand lingering, his fingertips on the cross guard, to maintain the contact.

"You've told me of your war against the Alder Kingdom," Nick said. "You've lectured repeatedly on how great your people were, and you're certainly not shy about telling me why the current society is foolish and stupid and in need of complete annihilation. And you've most certainly not been shy about *my* failings."

He pressed his fingertip harder against the obsidian.

"What you haven't told me of is a single moment of happiness, or joy, or tranquility. Did they exist in this great Sinifel Empire of yours? Or did you know only war, brutality, and nihilism?"

Sorrow's glow dimmed, and it was a long while before it answered.

What has brought on such sentimental desires?

"I don't know," he said. "Maybe I just miss my mirror."

Or you miss the false father in the mirror. I am not blind to my surroundings, as much as we both may wish.

Nick grimaced, and he felt his neck flushing slightly.

"I asked you a question, and instead you mock me. I should have known."

He closed his hand around the hilt, preparing to lift it from the earth. Sorrow's voice pierced into him before he could.

I was a father, once.

"You? Really?"

Shall I tell my tale, or must I suffer your insipid interjections?

Nick winced, and he tried to hide it by settling back down and shifting to get more comfortable.

"Sorry. Carry on."

My wife and I named him Elimja. According to our oldest books, that name meant "Mistake" in the earliest form of the Majere language. And before you make another of your witless comments, know that this was a mark of love. The fated calamity was only four years

LEVEL: UNKNOWN

away. Having children was highly discouraged, and outright forbidden to the priesthood, once the end grew so near. But no matter how little time remained, we wished to raise a child. We sired him in secret, hid my wife's pregnancy for as long as we could, and then when the truth was revealed, I endured the punishments, even forfeiting my rank as high priest of the Sinifel clergy. Yet it was worth it when Elimja was born and let out his first cry.

"I'm surprised you and your wife were brave enough to take such a risk," Nick said.

What risk?

Nick squirmed in his seat, realizing he didn't really have an answer to that. Everything he knew about the fallen Sinifel Empire was fractured and piecemeal, much of it based on the art of their ruins, the bits of information Violette had mentioned, and the distorted fierceness of their ageless war beasts.

"I just...I would think the final years leading up to the calamity would be an extremely dangerous time for anyone, let alone a child."

If a sword could sigh, Sorrow did.

I have heard the stories of the Sinifel that survivors tell. The whispers have seeped into me from the minds of fools who wielded me as a weapon, seeking power and glory. We are the heartless, the heretics say. We cared not for life. We embraced chaos, selfishness, and indulgence. "The world is ending," *they imagine us shrieking from our orgiastic revelry.* "Slaughter! Murder! Indulge, imbibe, rape, and steal, for what matters when the black sun awakens, and the world is doomed!"

A doom did approach, but that did not unmoor us, Nick, nor send us into despair. No, it meant that each and every day I watched

Elimja grow, I cherished it more than a thousand coins of silver. His first steps were worth more than any diamond or emerald. The sound of his laughter was finer than any wine. None of us, none of us, are guaranteed tomorrow. Unlike the heretical kingdom we conquered, or the one that replaced us, we did not believe we would last forever. Doom would come, we would suffer loss, destruction, and death as the judgment of the black sun fell upon us... and then would come the rebirth.

Rebirth, Nick. Renewal. We were not fire. We were not wickedness. We were the dormant seeds, knowing winter snows approached and biding our time for the warmth of spring.

You ask if I knew joy. You ask if there were moments of happiness, and tranquility, as if they were rarities unheard of in our sinful, wicked world. I experienced them each and every day, pillager. My son's little hands wrapped around my fingers, and clutching them, he took his first steps. His hazel eyes lit up at the very sight of his mother. At the sound of my laugh, he clapped. Year after precious year, we celebrated, never wasting them, never taking them for granted.

What debts we held, we settled. What grievances we carried, we shed. What doubts that threatened to cripple us, we overcame. We were unafraid in the face of death, which meant we were free.

And then the great heretic froze the black sun and denied Eiman his due. He splintered time. He broke the seasons, forever imprisoning us in this eternal spring. And in return for that... that "gift," he demanded we worship him as a god. If Yensere refused to bend the knee, then he would release his grip and bring forth the needed calamity.

That is when our Sinifel Empire fell. It wasn't when Emperor Gothwyr was beheaded by the great heretic. It wasn't when our soldiers

LEVEL: UNKNOWN

were burned in the ruins of what would become the Swallowed City. It happened when Vaan told our people death was now a choice. When the certain became uncertain, the inevitable now denied. That which united us, a communal acceptance of our own impermanence, was stripped away with the promise of an eternal kingdom, and a calamity, forever denied.

Nick leaned closer to the sword, his forehead pressing against the surprisingly cold hilt.

"What happened to your son?" he asked softly.

I spent the ensuing days after the black sun froze preaching resistance to the people. I still thought the power of our prayers would be stronger than Vaan's heresy, but it did not take long for the will of the people to turn against our priesthood. Too many sought to continue the lives they lived rather than face a tumultuous rebirth. They hated my words. They spat in my face. They... they rioted, threw stones, uncaring who was near. Who they hurt.

Sorrow fell silent. Nick dared not speak. He would not be so disrespectful as that. In time, Sorrow's words returned, heavy with the weight of centuries.

One stone. One stone was all it took to claim Elimja's life. The day after, my wife flung herself from the roof of our grand temple, her shattered body bleeding out on our holy steps. She left me a note. One sentence. That was all she needed. She knew I would understand.

"I miss Elimja's smile."

Nick remembered Sorrow's words on that first day he'd found the sword, when he had approached the temple in Abylon.

These steps. It is painful to look upon them once more.

"I'm sorry," he whispered. Sorrow did not acknowledge

the apology, but neither did he mock him for it. Instead, after another lengthy silence, he resumed his tale.

By then, the war was turning, the great heretic's armies swelling in number as people flocked to him from all corners of Yensere. Word reached us of his Five Harbingers, and how the strength of our war beasts paled against them. We were desperate. Our knights begged for power, and so I offered what was left of my life. Let me become a blade to wield against the heretic who ruined my family. Let my hatred glow crimson and spill the blood of those who would break the natural order of the world.

"But now you yourself are immortal," Nick said carefully, respectfully. There was no judgment here, not for someone who had once suffered so greatly. "Is that not against your tenets?"

I was not made immortal, pillager. I was reborn. My hate, my pain, my misery; let them all serve a purpose. That was my hope. Let them bring about salvation to our majestic Sinifel Empire. I was considered the greatest of the four judgment blades, and when they carved the sacred oath into my obsidian side, my fury was the hottest, and my rage, unquenchable.

Nick brushed his thumb against the arcane lettering, those five words written in a language hundreds of years old. Cataloger had refused to translate them, their meaning was so private and so severe. Even now, they pulsed the color of a furious crimson sun. He feared he understood them at last.

"What does it say?" he asked.

For a long while, silence.

I, too, miss his smile.

LEVEL: UNKNOWN

"Hey, Nick," Frost's familiar voice called from the nearby grassland. "Look who I found."

Nick released his hand from Sorrow, finally granting the weapon his solitude. When he turned about, he grinned wide as Violette came racing past Frost to fling her arms around him.

"I was so worried about you!" she said, which earned a chuckle from him.

"We're the ones worried about you," he said, gently disentangling from her. She peered up at him, her amber eyes blinking away a few stubborn tears and her dark hair falling low over her face.

"If you insist," she said. "But I don't care what you are. Just don't leave me, all right? I'm with you always, isn't that the deal?"

He glanced over her shoulder to Frost, who stood looking maddeningly amused with her arms crossed over her chest. She shot him a wink.

"That's the deal," she said. Her attention shifted to Sorrow, still half-embedded in the soil. "Something the matter with your sword?"

Nick grabbed Sorrow's hilt and yanked the blade free of the earth.

"Just a friendly chat," he said, tucking the weapon into his belt.

"Sorrow is capable of friendliness?" Frost asked.

He shrugged, and he had to turn away to hide the tightness

in his throat and the strange, indecipherable heat he felt emanating from Sorrow's hilt that quickened his heart and made his stomach clench as if he had swallowed a whole bowl of felberries.

"You know how it is," he said, patting Violette's tentative hand settling on his shoulder to reassure her all was well. "You never know who is full of surprises."

Chapter 35
GARETH

In shame, Sir Gareth knelt before Lord Frey. He wished his body was battered and bruised, but it seemed the ancient power gifted to him had healed his injuries. He had only his humiliation to wear like a scar as he pressed his forehead to the cold stone of Frey's meeting hall.

"I found the demon, Nick, as well as two companions of his, one a woman named Frost who I believe responsible for murdering Baron Hulh, the other still unknown to me. They were hiding amid a cult dedicated to continuing the ancient practices of the Majere."

He hesitated. They were seemingly alone, but if guards lingered, or spies listened, he feared to speak of the power granted to him through heretical rituals, feared uttering Eiman's name in a kingdom still loyal to God-King Vaan in Castle Goltara.

"But even with the strength you gifted me, it was not enough," he concluded, deciding that was vague enough to protect their secret. "The three of them wielded powerful magics, and they defy death as if they were the Majere lords of old. Perhaps they even are, given the cult they befriended. I struck a killing blow on the two demons, but then Nick returned, and when we battled, he...defeated me. Forgive me, my lord, I should have fought until my last breath, but I fled instead. Whatever punishment you would ask of me, I am ready to accept it."

Gareth heard a shifting of the padded fabric of Frey's ornate chair, set upon a small dais, but he dared not look up. Instead he stared firmly at the floor, unwilling to rise from his humbled state.

A footfall. Frey had stood.

"Look at me, Gareth."

He lifted his eyes to his lord and was shocked to find the older man so close. Frey knelt before him, and he gently placed both his arms upon Gareth's shoulders.

"I did not grant you power because I thought it would remove your challenges," he said. "I gave you power *because* you face such challenges. You bested the three monsters, even when outnumbered. It is no fault of your own that the demons can return and challenge you again. But if you can slaughter them once, you can do so again, and again, until this matter is settled and our people made safe."

Gareth felt something catch in his throat.

"Thank you," he said. "And I will. I promise. The carnage they inflict upon Vestor shall not go unavenged."

Frey's smile tightened the lines around his eyes.

"I hold faith that you will be up to the task." That smile

shifted slightly, in a manner Gareth could not read. "But now I must ask of a different matter. I sense something about you. Something linked to Eiman."

Gareth did not understand what his lord desired at first, but then he remembered the strange mirror Nick had dropped. He reached into his pocket, withdrew it, and offered it to Frey.

"Nick was in possession of this," Gareth explained. "I took it in case it was dear to him in some way."

Lord Frey lifted it, his touch surprisingly gentle.

"Come with me," he said, cradling the mirror within his grasp. "I would have you bear witness to the wonder our god is capable of."

The pair entered the hidden shrine in the bowels of the castle keep. Frey shut the door behind him and then locked it, encasing them in darkness. Gareth stood perfectly still, repeatedly telling himself to remain calm, as Lord Frey easily moved through the darkness to the two torches positioned above Eiman's shrine. With but a touch, they burst to life, blanketing the room with yellow light and long shadows.

"Stand there," Frey said, pointing to one of the barren walls. "Do not interfere, only watch."

"As you wish, my lord."

The older man moved to the table opposite the looming statue of Eiman, set the mirror down upon it among the other artifacts, and then grabbed what appeared to be a simple silken bag dyed black. From within, he drew out a thick piece of chalk.

"There is power in all things," Frey said as he knelt in the center of the room. "Symbols. Shapes. Words. Beyond communication. Beyond meaning. There are forces shaping this world we do not understand, bound by laws older than our ancestors."

He carefully drew a long line upon the stone with the chalk. It eventually curved, turning back toward the center of the room. Frey continued it toward the shrine, only to curve it yet again at a slightly different angle. Back and forth, turning and shifting, drawing the first of what appeared to be concentric circles. After a moment he paused, returned to the bench, and retrieved the strange mirror.

"I gave this mirror to Baron Hulh," Frey said as he placed it in the center of the crisscrossed lines. "I told him to think on his greatest fear, to make it real within the mirror, and then bring it back to me. He never did. I wonder why."

His hands moved slowly, steadily, drawing more lines with the chalk.

"Was he afraid of the magic? Did he not trust my desire to help him conquer his own lingering paranoia and fear? Or was his professed faith in Eiman shallow, or even false?"

Gareth's stomach tightened as the lines took shape, twisting, turning, and looping so that there was an undeniable circle enveloping the mirror. A re-creation of the black sun, only instead of solid and pure, it was twisting and rotating within the chalk center, suddenly granted depth and motion.

"After Hulh's murder, I will never have those answers," Frey said, finishing the last of the lines. He pocketed the chalk and stood. The light of the torches flickered across his face. "But I will learn what secrets torment this troublesome demon. I will give face to the beating heart of his terror."

"Through this mirror?" Gareth asked. "I don't understand."

"The fool likely thought it granted him his wants and desires," Frey said. He walked to the table of artifacts and returned holding a familiar knife. It was the same one used to grant Gareth his powers. "But the Mirror of Theft has earned its name over these centuries, and shall do so again, with Eiman's gift."

Frey bowed his head while raising his hands. Before him, the statue of the Beast of a Thousand Mouths seemed to seethe and grow.

"God of all cycles and rebirth, hear my cry," Frey said, his deep voice rumbling in the hidden depths of the castle. The chalk lines flared with sudden light, changing from white to red. He slashed his arm with the knife, and the blood flowed in a sudden spray across the ground. Not a drop landed upon the mirror, but it did not stay clean for long.

The blood crawled like worms, chalk seeping into it. The deep glow burned within the blood, shining red light across the entire cramped room.

"God of a hundred mouths, a thousand eyes, and a million tongues, honor my faith!"

The blood swirled toward the mirror, faster and faster, a sudden crimson tempest. Upon its empty surface, the blood gathered, first as a thin sheen, then as a shimmering orb that hovered. It vibrated with energy, as if at any moment it might erupt.

"God of Yensere, lord of all that must die, bring forth the thief!"

The mirror cracked once, twice, and then into a sudden

thousand shards breaking away from what was once a single pane. They rose into the air, hovering as if the pull of the world itself had surrendered to Eiman's power. The shards shimmered and reflected the light of the torches as they rose higher and higher. Their jagged edges twisted and tumbled, sometimes clinking against one another.

Gareth clenched his jaw and demanded bravery of himself. He would not cower. He would not humiliate himself before the power of gods. That which was frightening and new must be endured, for it was the path to freedom from the blight, and a revitalized Vestor.

The glass turned liquid, the shards widening outward. They no longer reflected fire. They showed flesh and cloth as they came together, the surface curving and molding to become something entirely new. Something human, which let out a long, horrified wail as he dropped to his knees. His blue and gold clothes were strange and foreign, his hair cut short and neat around the ears and neck.

"Stand, thief," Frey ordered. He loomed over this nightmare creation, unafraid. "Tell me your name."

The man slowly pushed to his feet. The image of him wobbled, not quite steady, not quite real, but quickly hardening. Gareth shivered despite his best attempts to remain still. There was something so very *wrong* with this creation. It was like his clothes were too clean and his smile too rigid. No light reflected from his eyes. His chest did not rise and fall with drawn breaths.

"Lucien," the thief born of the mirror said. "Lucien Wright."

Chapter 36
NICK

They showed no hurry on their way toward Castle Astarda, and what little progress they made halted come the thunderstorm. The road turned to mud, and the nearby forest, a mixture of trees Cataloger insisted were pines and oaks, was blanketed with near impenetrable darkness. Surrendering to the storm, they found the tallest tree with the biggest branches to camp under for the night. Nick did his best to ignore how the "pine" needles were forked at the end, their tips a bloody red, and instead relax amid the miserable weather.

The rain will only last another two hours and forty-seven minutes

So Cataloger had informed Nick when he complained about the weather. That knowledge did not comfort like she thought it might.

"I guess I shouldn't complain," Violette said, huddled against the bark with her arms pulled inside her coat for warmth. She'd built a fire between the three of them, fueled by her magic so the rain could not defeat it. "If it weren't spring, we might be dealing with hail or snow instead of rain."

"Snow can be pretty, though," Frost said, doing her best to protect her armor with her cloak. "This rain just leaves me cold and wet."

Nick shook drops out of his hair, as if they wouldn't be replaced in just a few minutes. The downpour was fierce, and though the branches helped, they did little to protect against the gusts of wind that brought the rain slanting in to smack them.

"You can also play in the snow," Nick said. "Snowball fights and forts and snowmen. I guess you can play in the mud, too, but that's not quite my idea of fun."

Really? I would think rutting about in filth would be your preferred play style, pillager.

And here I was thinking we were becoming friends.

Nick could practically feel Sorrow smirking at him.

Think less, pillager.

"So you both have seen snow?" Violette asked, her eyes lighting up. "Where? From... wherever it is you come from?"

"Actually, growing up on—"

"We have," Frost interrupted, and she shot Nick a glare. "But it's not something we should talk about. Demon secrets. You wouldn't understand."

"Oh." She leaned closer to the fire, disappointment etched on her face. "I suppose you have your reasons."

Nick immediately felt bad, and he glared at Frost. She kept

LEVEL: UNKNOWN

insisting it was too dangerous to share information about the real world, but he had no idea why. Could it lead to cognitive dissonance with people who lived their entire lives within Yensere?

Hey, Cataloger, is there some sort of rule or safety reason to not talk about the outside world when in Yensere? he asked, figuring he might as well get it from the source.

There are no restrictions upon visitors sharing such info—though potential confusion should be expected

The silence stretched on awkwardly, and Nick squirmed, hating it. He waited for a distant rumble of thunder to pass, then tried restarting the conversation.

"I don't know about Frost, but I'm pretty ignorant about... well, most everything on Yensere."

Surprise, surprise.

Quiet, you.

"But maybe you could help me out," Nick continued. "But no talk about gods or history or forgotten kingdoms. Tell me about *you*, Violette."

"Me?" She rocked backward as if accused of a crime.

"Yes, you," he said, and smiled. "Like, you said you were a scholar. What does that even mean? Where are you from, and why are you so far out here in the west?"

The fire dimmed from the rain, and Violette flicked her fingers to restrengthen it. Nick suspected the act was a way for her to stall.

"There's not really much to tell," she said. "I was orphaned at the Silversong Academy. And before you tell me how sorry you are, or how sad that is, that's how almost everyone joins the academy. My headmaster had a plaque on his desk that read 'A solitary life is a life most easily dedicated to the pursuit of knowledge.'"

"So I'm guessing boyfriends and girlfriends are out of the question," Nick said, which earned a grin.

"Why, are you interested?" she asked, and when Nick's neck blushed a fierce red, she laughed. "Dating a demon. That has to be a first on Yensere, right?"

"A first and a quick last," Frost said. "But let's not torment poor Nick further. What is Silversong like? I must admit, I'm curious myself."

Violette shifted closer to the fire, and her arms emerged from her sleeves. She seemed a bit more comfortable now the topic of conversation had shifted away from herself.

"It's considered the jewel of Averdeen," she said. "Have you ever seen the Carthus River?"

Suddenly it was Frost's turn to look a little embarrassed.

"Actually, I've never been beyond Vestor," she admitted. "I know of Yensere about as much as Nick does."

Nick's eyebrows shot to the top of his head. "Really?"

"No, definitely more than you do," she shot back. "But when it comes to other places, I—" She caught herself, stopped. "Anyway, what about the Carthus?"

"The city of Malarus and its people are an amazing lot, and they shaped the river. It took decades, but they did it, taking a straight line and winding it like a serpent. They built homes around it, with tall walls of thick stone, and then, in the very heart of the river, reachable only by drawbridge, they built the Silversong Academy. The river straightens beyond it, but until

LEVEL: UNKNOWN

then, it breaks upon the great walls of the enormous spire and splits to either side."

She made a show of sitting up straight and deepening her voice.

"'Knowledge breaks the world,'" she said. "It's written in the stone above the entrance of the academy. Hubris, some might say, but when you see the Carthus cowed and broken, you find yourself wanting to believe."

It reminded Nick of the attitude of the earliest OPC explorers, when world gates were terribly unstable and the conditions on the other side not thoroughly explored before a manned scout ship was sent. Radiation? Pressure? Gate collapse? It didn't matter. All the dangers and trials of space would not hold them back. He smiled and found himself wishing he had more of that explorer spirit in his own heart. He might have acclimated faster to the strangeness that was Yensere.

"Sounds like a fascinating place," he said. "Do you miss your scholar friends?"

Violette looked to the fire, and a wistful expression softened her face.

"I don't regret being here, doing what I have to," she said. "But yes, I miss them. It's hard to explain, but I was...part of something larger than myself. Even if our actions were different, we were working toward the same goal, the same purpose. Now I'm alone, and the absence leaves an ache."

"Hey," Nick said, gently reaching over to touch her elbow. "You're not alone. Not anymore."

She bobbed her head and turned away, so her hair hid her face.

"No, I suppose not." She turned back, forcing a smile. "What of you, Nick? Is there anyone you miss, wherever you're truly from? A piece of you that makes you whole?"

A single memory struck Nick hard enough that he was shocked by the tightness it created in his chest. It was of Simon lifting the picture of their mother and father that Nick kept at his bedside. Of the hidden sorrow, the familial love, and the obvious care his older brother felt for him, too. He'd thought nothing of it at the time, but now he saw and felt so much, it hurt.

"I do," he said, and was surprised how his melancholy was mixed with a subdued warmth. A dozen memories with his parents flashed through him: lunches on Station 68, a trip to the Rebek Mountains on Taneth, cold mornings at a hotel on their brief trip to Eden, where the two were giving a joint presentation on a new strain of fungus meant to speed up the terraforming process. The memories did not hurt like they used to, and he found himself eager to share stories of them with an attentive Violette. "My brother, he—"

"Enough," Frost snapped. "Don't share anything more."

"Why?" Nick asked, his temper rising.

"Because it isn't safe."

"And again I ask, why?" He stood, feeling suffocated and robbed of the moment. "Over and over, you give me orders, and not once do you explain a thing. What am I to be so afraid of?"

In answer, Frost glanced deliberately at Violette. Nick flung his hands into the air. The idea was absurd, and he was so tired of playing along.

"No," he said. "I want an actual answer. Why do we hide everything about where we are from and the lives we live outside of Yensere?"

"Please, just trust me."

"Trust you? I don't even know your *name*, and you want me to trust you?" When she did not answer, his mood soured further. "Or am I not to be trusted, either?"

Frost looked beyond frustrated as she clenched her fists and glared. Rain dripped down her brow, rivulets framing her face as they ran down her jawline to fall from her chin.

"It's not that," she said.

"Then what is it?"

Before she could answer, Violette interrupted.

"If it's me, if it's something I did, please, just tell me," she said. "I don't want to be the cause of a fight between you two. You seem like such good friends, and I'd hate to—"

"Yeah, such good friends," Nick said, and he sighed. He grabbed Sorrow, tightened its belt around his waist, and then trudged off.

"Where are you going?" Violette called after him.

"For some fresh air," he said, knowing the excuse was ridiculous on its face and not caring. He needed to get away from them, at least until he calmed down. The last thing he wanted was to say something he'd regret.

He walked through the sparse trees, barely seeing their swaying branches amid the darkness and the rain. He couldn't shake the anger bubbling inside him. It felt like there'd been something special there by that rain-soaked fire, something personal about to blossom. He hadn't wanted to talk about his mother and father to anyone in years, or at least not to anyone other than Simon. To have that moment broken, and for such poor, unexplained reasons...

Nick stopped some distance away, realizing if he traveled any farther he might lose sight of the camp and not find his way back. Frustrated, he slumped against one of the pines and stared into the dimly lit forest, ignoring how the bark was strangely fuzzy to the touch. No, it was more than just the stolen moment. Frost didn't trust him. All their time training, traveling, fighting, even dying together still wasn't enough to get her to open up. Instead he got cryptic comments and a stubborn refusal to reveal the slightest bit of information about her real life.

And of course, here he was, throwing a fit about it. Nick groaned and thumped the back of his head against the bark. Some hardened explorer he was. In what was essentially an alien world, no matter how familiar its environs, here he was throwing a tantrum about a girl.

"Whatever the reason, mysterious alien artifact, it's hard not to feel like you chose wrong." He laughed amid the rumbling thunder. "Simon would have been infinitely better at handling all this. He'd have kept his head on straight throughout, I bet."

Again you reference this Simon person—is he important to you?

"My older brother," Nick said, accepting that even his private moments would occasionally involve Cataloger's chiming in. "I suspect you'd have gotten along well with him. He'd ask you all sorts of questions, way more than I do. Lots of sharing of knowledge."

LEVEL: UNKNOWN

And you wish your brother were here in your place as visitor?

"I don't know. Sometimes. It's not because I'm miserable or anything, just that I sometimes feel like I'm not doing enough. I'm not learning anything. Not accomplishing anything."

Such negative analysis is unnecessary—and I am glad it is you and not Simon for me to guide

"Even if he'd be better at it?'

Even if

Nick smiled and thumped his head against the bark of the tree a second time.

"Fine. Maybe one day he can join me in here, how about that? The both of us, exploring Yensere together? That'd be fun."

Such a situation would be acceptable

He'd never considered the possibility, but Nick found himself aching to have Simon with him. For once, he'd be the experienced one, able to guide Simon and explain all the weirdness and introduce Cataloger and maybe even teach him to use magic. Nick's amusement at the idea was tempered by a somber note as he imagined his father joining them as well. Lucien would have been over the moon with excitement at exploring Yensere. His father had helped spearhead a rapid increase in building new world gates, all born of a constant hope of finding evidence of life. The Artifact would have been everything he could ever dream of. If only he had lived, if the space station's core had not gone catastrophic and...

And...

The sound of footsteps and moving branches spun Nick

about, his hand falling to Sorrow strapped to his waist. His fingers touched the obsidian hilt but did not draw it. His jaw dropped. The entire world froze, because what he saw could not be real, could never be real.

"Hello, son," his father said, striding through the rain-soaked brush. He ducked underneath a tree branch, whose leaves brushed across his brown hair, mussing a few strands out of place.

"What are you?" Nick asked. His tongue felt thick in his mouth. His head buzzed. Every part of him screamed this couldn't be real, his father couldn't be before him. He'd died. Nick had watched the space station explode, claiming his father's life. Yet his every sense said this was real. He saw a perfect visage, hardly aged a day. Watched branches sway from him when pushed out of his path. Heard the sound of his voice, firm and commanding.

Lucien: Level 13 Human
Archetype: Administrator
Special Classification: Reflection

The mirror had been a reflection from the past, but this? This was so much more real, and somehow so much worse.

"I am your father," Lucien said, as if it were obvious. "Who else could I be?"

It was true he wore his standard uniform, albeit not as prim and proper as Nick was used to seeing because of the rain. His face was the same, as were his hands, the fingernails trimmed, palms soft, the first knuckle sporting the same scar he got when winning a game of handball at university, a story he so often loved to tell.

LEVEL: UNKNOWN

"I don't know what you are," Nick said, retreating a step. "And I don't know what Yensere is capable of, nor the Artifact that houses it, but I know this. You died. You're gone. Whatever you are, it isn't... it isn't *you*."

Lucien crossed his arms and shook his head.

"So closed-minded," he said. "I had hoped you would feel the same elation in meeting me as I feel looking upon you."

Behind this perfect re-creation of his father, tree branches rustled, and a spike of alarm shot through Nick.

"How did you find me?" he asked.

"We're connected, you and I," Lucien said. His eyes flashed a momentary black. "Always have been, and forever will be."

More movement in the trees. They weren't alone.

"Why are you here?" he asked, taking another step back.

"Don't run," Lucien commanded. Nick froze in place, his heart skipping a beat. He recognized that tone, that authority. He wanted to obey. He wanted to collapse and cry. All of it, so real, and yet all of it false.

All of it a lie.

Nick sprinted as fast as his legs could carry him, caring not for the scrapes of the brush or the cuts from branches hanging too low. He screamed at the top of his lungs, determined to be heard over the rain and thunder.

"Frost, Violette, run! Hide! We're under—"

Something heavy cracked against his legs. He stumbled, tripped, and then landed in a roll, caking his body in mud. He pushed to his knees to see the approach of familiar OPC boots.

"Is it cowardice that drives you, or misplaced heroism?" his father asked, sword in hand. It was so strange seeing the medieval weapon in a grip that Nick had seen holding only delicate instruments and, most often, an old-fashioned ink pen.

"It's called caring for my friends," he said, and swung Sorrow. The sword struck Lucien's hip, but though it sank into his flesh, it shed no blood. Instead, cloth and skin warped and cracked, becoming something shiny and crystalline in the dim light. Lucien kicked immediately, his boot striking Nick's hand with enough force that he screamed, knew bones of his fingers had broken.

Refusing to go down without a fight, Nick scrambled to his feet, forgoing Sorrow to instead plow straight into his father with his shoulder leading. It struck as if colliding with a stone wall. He screamed at the pain, his vision momentarily flashing red. Stubbornness kept him fighting, and he slammed his unbroken fist into his father's kidney. Though it should have been soft flesh, his knuckles came back scraped and bleeding.

"Such foolishness," said his father, and backhanded him across the face. "You have so much yet to learn."

Nick staggered, spat blood, and lifted Sorrow in his off hand.

This does not appear winnable, Sorrow said as soldiers approached from the trees, more than a dozen, to slowly form a surrounding wall. Another dozen rushed past, chasing Frost and Violette. He could only hope they'd heard his warning and escaped.

Maybe we can't win, Nick thought. *But I have every intention to die trying.*

He dashed in, but with his sword wielded in his left hand,

LEVEL: UNKNOWN

he felt awkward and clumsy. His slash for his father's waist was easily batted aside. A retaliatory smack with the hilt of the sword struck Nick's forehead, and he staggered. Little hits, little scrapes, not enough to kill but enough to humiliate. He flailed, missed, and then charged the soldier line. To his surprise, they did not strike with their weapons but instead closed ranks and shoved him back toward Lucien.

They know what you are, Sorrow warned. *They want you alive.*

An orb of shadow flew over Lucien's shoulder to slam into Nick's chest. He gasped at the life it took from him, ribs cracking, innards crushed, making it hard to breathe. He collapsed to one knee, struggling to force air into his lungs, as Sir Gareth strode through the ring of soldiers.

"Seems your nose is as good as a bloodhound's," he said to Lucien, his shield strapped to his back and his enormous sword held in a relaxed grip atop his right shoulder. He glared down at Nick. "And so here hides the demon."

Nick flung himself at the knight, wounds and weak lungs be damned. Sorrow thrust straight for the giant man's throat, but it never reached. His father latched on to his arm and held him fast. A squeeze, and Nick screamed, feeling like his elbow was going to snap in half and turn in the entirely wrong direction. Sorrow fell from his grasp. Another twist, and Nick dropped to his knees.

"Beat him," Gareth ordered the soldiers when Lucien released his grip. "But do not kill him. I'll butcher the whole lot of you if the demon stops breathing."

Nick pushed up to his feet only to be greeted by a kick to his stomach. He gasped, a bit of blood spilling out of his lips.

A fist striking the top of his head dropped him. The soldiers surrounded him, kicking and punching as he lay on the rain-soaked earth. Sorrow lay outside his grasp as his health bar steadily drained to almost 0.

They beat him until his father's voice pierced the night like a knife.

"Enough."

The soldiers retreated. Nick rolled onto his back, his vision blurred with tears and his entire body a bruised and beaten transmitter of pain. He stared up at a monster wearing his father's face and wished death for them both.

"I see that stubborn spirit within you," Lucien said, kneeling down and gently cupping Nick's face. "Birthed of a soft hand, and my own misjudgments. But do not worry. That stubbornness will soon be broken. You're coming with us to Castle Astarda. In its lowest depths, I will have all the time in the world to undo the mistakes of my past."

Chapter 37
SIMON

Simon sat on the floor beside Nick's bed. It hurt to bend his injured knee, so he left it extended as he leaned his weight on the mattress. The oxygen tube was reinserted into Nick's nostrils. Joining it was a nasogastric tube, inserted at Dr. Haley's request. Nick was never eating enough when awake, and he'd been out for more than thirty-six hours when Simon acceded to the request. The nutrients joined the saline solution they fed him through an IV just above his knuckles.

Even with all that, his brother had grown noticeably thinner over the past weeks. His skin was pale, his eyes, when they were open, were dark and bloodshot. He'd endured a low fever for several days now, but over the past few hours, it had spiked to 103°F and refused to break despite medicinal interventions. His heart rate was a ridiculous 190 bpm, pounding as if he were in a full sprint despite just lying there.

"Director?"

Simon pushed himself up to a stand, grabbed his cane from where it leaned against the wall, and used it to help him turn. Dr. Haley stood waiting with a tablet in hand, her face lit by its glow in the dim light of Nick's room. Only Simon's stubbornness had kept Nick there instead of transferred to the med ward. After all, how serious could his condition be if he was still sleeping in his room?

"Yes?" he asked Haley.

She started to tilt the tablet so he could see the results, then changed her mind and clutched it to her chest.

"I have the results of Nick's recent blood tests. This isn't sustainable, Director. His body is constantly pumped full of adrenaline, and it's undergoing every textbook symptom of heightened stress hormones. Despite his appearance of sleep, he is not resting, which is affecting his blood pressure and heart rate. Even if his heart doesn't give out, there's a good chance he will suffer permanent damage to his liver and kidneys, not to mention the dangers of decreased functionality of his immune system as this continues to—"

"I get it," Simon finally interrupted. He squeezed his eyes shut in an effort to focus through the migraine pounding in his forehead. "Whatever is happening to him is wrecking his body, and he needs rest. What I don't know is what I'm supposed to do about it."

Dr. Haley's frown hardened into iron.

"Your brother needs sleep. *Real* sleep. Which means breaking contact with the Artifact."

Simon glanced over his shoulder at his sick, feverish younger brother. Nick's mouth opened and closed, as if he were trying to speak, yet no words came. He looked so pained, so miserable, it filled Simon with dread.

"We've tried," he said, shaking his head. "Every material available and every shielding method known to us, they've all failed. Whatever signal is reaching Nick, it passes right through them. There's nothing left to try."

"That isn't true. You just refuse to accept it as a possibility."

Simon's expression hardened to match Haley's. His grip tightened on the curve of his cane.

"And what, pray tell, is that?"

Haley set the tablet with the results down on the bedside table, letting it join the rest of the machinery there. Her fingers brushed against a silver medallion hanging from her neck, two hands cupped together to form a circle, holding within it six beads that represented the six planets of Eden's solar system. It was the religious symbol of the Guidance, those who believed the universe had been shaped and molded since the moment of its creation. Simon had never been much for attending their seminars, but their faith had an undeniable hold on millions, one that had grown stronger with humanity's spread across the stars with each subsequent new world gate.

"I will argue this only once, Director," Haley said. "After this, his life is in your hands and out of mine. In my professional opinion, whatever is happening to Nick is killing him. He needs his connection to the Artifact severed, and the sooner, the better. Put him on a shuttle and send him through the world gate. I don't care what signal that Artifact uses, it will not reach Nick across nine light-years' worth of distance."

"Need I remind you that we are under dark quarantine?"

"You are station director and can lift and enact that quarantine at your own discretion. That isn't an excuse." She reached out to brush his arm. "I can go with him, Simon. Just the two of us on the shuttle. I'll keep quiet about the cause when we arrive at Salus, and say we left because we lacked proper care on our station amid the quarantine. All else I will keep to myself. You can trust me on that."

Simon watched his brother's clear and obvious suffering. A thousand excuses bounced around his mind, so many of them guided by fear.

"We don't know the potential damage that might occur from severing his connection," he said, one of his few remaining arguments.

"No, we don't," Haley said. "But we do know what the connection is already doing to him."

"And what if breaking the connection by going through the world gate leaves him comatose, or worse?"

The older woman shook her head.

"I won't lie, Director, there are risks. And as I said, it is out of my hands now. Make your choice and stand by it. I just wanted my opinion known, if only for my own conscience when I close my eyes before the Guidance."

The doctor left Simon alone with his younger brother. The rapid beat of the heart monitor and the faint hum of the oxygenation device were the only noises. Simon stared at the closed door, wanting to shout for Haley to come back, to take his brother and flee through the world gate, dangers and quarantine be damned.

He wanted to do it but did not. Nick would never forgive

LEVEL: UNKNOWN

him. Whatever he was experiencing was a miracle, and it needed to be understood and shared. Haley might disagree, but she also did not know about the destruction of the Vasth world gate. He'd locked that information down, so only he and Essa knew.

Simon settled into the chair beside Nick's bed, laid his cane across his lap, and leaned into the cushion. His gaze lingered on the sleeping Nick and the pained expression permanently etched upon his face. Whatever was happening to him, it had to be new, something he hadn't encountered before. He'd never looked so miserable before, not even during his many supposed "deaths."

It will pass, he told himself. *It always does. Nick's strong enough for this. Brave enough. He'll persevere.*

But still, that fever. That heart rate. Simon leaned closer, settled his hand over Nick's, and winced at the clammy heat of his skin.

"What are they doing to you, Nick?" he wondered as he clutched those fingers tightly and held on long into the night.

Chapter 38
NICK

The room was dark but for the light of two torches burning on the wall to his right. Their glow shone upon the twisted, sick image of Eiman, the multiarmed, multilegged god without a face. Nick hung from four short chains attached to the wall, and he suspected there would be no escaping these like he had at the baron's estate.

No, death would be his only way out, and he feared it would be a long time coming. His only solace was that, so far as he knew, Frost and Violette had not been captured along with him.

"Here I am, a prisoner once again, Cataloger," he said, his voice a hoarse whisper. He'd been beaten fairly regularly by the guards stationed outside. Never enough to do more than bruise, of course. "Still sure you can't rescue me from here?"

I cannot directly affect the material world

"Not asking for that. Just... a nice little escape back home.

LEVEL: UNKNOWN

I want to wake up in my bed, with my brother nearby. Not here. Anywhere but here."

Yensere's rules must be followed

"Sure." He closed his eyes. "What do you think is about to happen to me, Cataloger?"

It was as long while before she responded.

Based on prior events within this space—nothing you will find pleasurable

"And you still think it's best I stay?"

It is not about what I think is best—I am bound by rules that cannot be broken

Footsteps outside the door. Someone was coming.

Nick—I am sorry

The door opened, and in stepped a man Nick had not yet met. His clothes were finely made, silky reds and deep blacks sewn into his trousers and tunic. He was tall and strong, seemingly in defiance of his advancing age.

Frey: Level 20 Human
Archetype: Lord
Special Classification: Deity Blessed (Eiman)

Nick was shocked at the level flashing above the man's head. Higher than Sir Gareth's, somehow. Nick shivered in his chains. What powers did the older man hide behind that faint smile? Frey stood before him, holding a familiar object slowly twirling between his fingers.

"The demon of Meadowtint," the finely dressed lord said, holding the broken Sinifel mirror Gareth had taken from Nick. "I've heard much about you. How you do not fear death. How it cannot claim you."

"You hear this from Gareth?" Nick asked, trying to harden his voice and not sound so pathetic. "Did he also tell you about how I kicked his ass?"

The noble man smiled.

"I know of his defeats, yes. I know much about you, Nick, but you do not know me. Let us correct that. I am Lord Frey Astarda. I rule over all lands west of Castle Astarda and the Frostbound Mountains. Vestor's people are mine to command, to protect, and you have made quite a mess of things. Dead villagers. A slaughtered baron. Chaos at our largest city of Greenborough. We've long heard rumors of your kind, but you are the first demon I have ever met."

"Lucky you."

Frey lifted the mirror. "You didn't know what this was, did you? When you took it?"

Nick glared at him but did not answer.

"I thought not," Frey continued. "It is a thief, Nick. What it steals from you is your greatest fears. It's meant to help, of course. To pull away that which you dread and resent." He paused to grin. "I spoke with Lucien. I know what he is to you, and I find it *fascinating*."

Nick clenched his fists and wished, more than anything, that he could depart this world then and there, the rules of Yensere be damned.

Visits can only be ended at appointed safe locations—death is not the preferred exit, only a last resort to maintain world stability and—

Enough, Cataloger, Nick thought. He was too tired and frightened for arguments. *Just. Enough.*

LEVEL: UNKNOWN

Frey returned to the door and opened it wide. Light flickered into the room from unseen sconces burning just beyond. Lit by their glow, Nick's father stepped down into the dank, morbid room.

Not your father, Nick thought, even as his senses insisted otherwise upon viewing the perfect re-creation. *Lucien. Separate. Different. Fake.*

"Hello again, my son," Lucien said.

Frey put a hand atop Lucien's shoulder. His grin extended from ear to ear.

"I never thought demons would have fathers and sons like us. Most scholars guessed you were wretched beings spat out from the black sun or conjured from our own nightmares. But, well, this thief here seems to say otherwise."

"I'll kill you," Nick seethed, refusing to look at his father. At Lucien.

"You may desire it, but you will accomplish nothing in those chains." Frey gestured to Lucien. "Your master has a simple command, thief. Prepare his mind for my return. Harm him if you must, but do not kill him. Never kill him. I like him exactly where he is."

Frey climbed the stairs, and when the door shut behind him, Nick and Lucien were alone in the dim light of those two burning torches. The statue of Eiman loomed behind Lucien, and Nick swore it laughed though it lacked a mouth to do so.

The abomination pretending to be his father approached. Nick tensed on instinct.

"You're afraid of me," Lucien said.

"The last time I saw you, you assaulted me and clapped me in irons," Nick said. "Shouldn't I be?"

Lucien shook his head.

"For a son to fear the hand of his father. A shameful situation, I must admit. Perhaps I should have trusted you more, but tell me, son, would you have come with me if I asked? Would a kind word have been enough to bring you to Castle Astarda?"

"You're not real," Nick said, ignoring the question. "And I'm not your son. Stop calling me that."

Lucien put his hand on the wall above Nick and leaned closer.

"Why do you lie?" he asked. "To yourself? To me?"

"It's not a lie."

"But it is." Lucien used his free hand to gently move sweat-stained hair away from Nick's forehead. "You know it is. That's why you're afraid."

"Bullshit. Cataloger, tell me what he is, what he really is."

"Cataloger?" Lucien asked, tilting his head to one side. Nick hated the way it awoke a dozen memories of time spent with his father, the way he'd always seemed so curious about Nick's every discovery, even if it had been something he already knew.

Lucien: Level—

"I don't want his statistics," Nick said, not caring that he'd appear crazy to the false Lucien. "I want to know *what* he is. *How* he is. Because he cannot be my father. My father is dead; I saw it; I watched the station explode."

Clarify

Lucien leaned closer, and Nick studied him against his will.

LEVEL: UNKNOWN

There was no flaw in the re-creation. Every twitch, every look, was perfect.

"Tell me, my son, what is a self?"

"I'm not arguing with you, whatever you are."

Lucien chuckled, just barely flashing a hint of his perfectly straight white teeth. He'd told Nick once to always take good care of his teeth if he wished to be a leader. *People care about those little things,* he'd told him. *They look for flaws to justify their dislikes, and so you must give them none.*

Nick banished the memory, hating how easily it came to him.

"You've always been emotional," Lucien said. "But I'm disappointed you've become more closed-minded as you've grown. Less adventurous. We're in a world unlike anything you've ever experienced, and yet you cling to the most rudimentary understandings of life and existence."

Nick's curiosity was piqued despite himself. "You know of the Artifact?"

Lucien shrugged and avoided the question.

"I ask you again, what is a self?" he asked. "When you label yourself 'Nick,' what is it you are labeling?"

"It's... it's me," Nick said, unsure and confused. His father had never been a philosopher. That'd been their mother's area of expertise. "My mind. My body. Everything that I am."

The imposter paced back and forth, and he seemed excited by Nick's answer.

"But your body is forever changing, its cells cycling through. Can you claim identity to flesh when your every organ and tissue is replaced over the course of seven years?"

"I still have my memories, my emotions, my personality."

Lucien wagged a finger at him.

"Chemical reactions amid a brain soup. Electrons firing signals across protein fibers. You cling to them, but they are processes, rigid and predictable. But I agree, Nick! Which is why the 'you' in front of me within Yensere is still real. It's valid. Those same processes happen, albeit in a different manner. Your emotions, though... they remain. As does your personality. And most importantly of all, your memories."

His father loomed closer, and Nick trembled.

"I am everything I always was. Built of the same signals and processes that currently re-create you. And I have those same memories, too. If I am not real, then why are you?"

In answer, Nick twisted his fingers to point at Lucien and let loose his lightning. It streaked into Lucien's face and then swirled into his chest. Nick poured his mana into it, refusing to let the lightning end so it burned twice. He gasped when the spell ended, his head throbbing.

"You're a fake," Nick shouted at the burnt, smoking abomination trembling before him.

Lucien slowly stood. The smoke about him faded. His OPC uniform healed away its burns. If he was angry at the attack, he did not show it. Instead he gently placed his hand on the side of Nick's face. Nick hated just how much love and tenderness he sensed in the move. The other hand closed about the fingers of Nick's left hand and steadily, one by one, broke them.

"When you were five, you ran face-first into a picnic table at a park on Taneth's surface," he said, twisting the knuckle.

"It cost you one of your baby teeth." The next finger. "When you were nine, you split your leg open at a farm you were distinctly ordered to stay away from during our vacation." The next. "When you were thirteen, your advances on a girl you liked, Francine, were soundly rejected. I bought you ice cream and sat with you while you cried in a park. Every time, I cared for you, watched over you, and cherished you amid both your mistakes and your achievements."

"Stop it," Nick whispered, hating Lucien, hating this *thing*, more than anything in all his life. He couldn't even concentrate well enough to burst another bolt of lightning from his mutilated hand.

"You wish to embrace me, don't you? You wish, deep down in your heart, for me to be all that I say I am. But something holds you back."

"I said stop!"

Lucien grabbed Nick's face, swallowing it within his grasp. His hazel eyes held Nick prisoner. There was light in them, red and savage, and it was growing.

"Show it to me," Lucien said. "Let us live it together."

Nick slammed into the chair of the escape pod, and despite the firm padding, the impact left him dazed. He sank into the seat, hands shaking, vision swimming. The alarm. It was so loud. So loud.

"Rescuers will come for you, I promise," his father said, standing at entrance of the pod. Red lights flashed off and on behind him, another method of alerting people on the research station that something was terribly amiss. "Just wait and hold faith."

"No, don't," Nick said, unsure of what exactly he was protesting. He was sixteen years old. This was too much for him. Just moments ago, he'd been in his room, reading one of his favorite saga books. That felt like a different life, one that ended when the alarms blared and a sudden jolt shook the entire station.

"I have to stay," his father said as he hit a button on the outside of the pod. "I'm sorry, Nick, but I have to see if I can stop this."

Nick finally regained his senses, and he pushed out of the chair. The door of the pod was sealed shut, and though he beat his hands against it, it would not open. Through the thick double pane of glass in the center of the door, he met his father's gaze.

Lucien placed one of his large hands on the lower section of the door.

"Nick," he said, shouting to be heard. "The—"

The words. Nick never understood the words. The alarm kept blaring. Nick was screaming. Another explosion rocked the station, adding a screech of metal to the cacophony. One sentence, lost to Nick as the pod was ejected into space. Lost to Nick, as he collapsed into his chair and watched the stars swirl around him.

Lost forever, when four minutes later, distant Research Station 68 erupted into a brief flash of fire. There had been no noise. No sound.

LEVEL: UNKNOWN

Just Nick, sixteen years old, sobbing.

───────────●───────────

Sobbing as his father loomed over him, lit by the light of two torches flickering above the grotesque statue. No, not his father. Lucien. He did not deserve that title. Nick had to remember that if he was to keep from breaking completely.

"Amazing, isn't it, the gifts Yensere offers?" Lucien said, withdrawing his hand. "If only I could have studied them much earlier in life."

"You're dead," Nick said, shaking his head in an attempt to banish the lingering memories and force himself into the here and now. He saw his mana bar drop significantly, the sight unnerving. Just what was this abomination doing to him?

"You can't be him," he insisted, pouring his resolve into those four words.

Lucien leaned closer, his look one Nick had never seen on the face of his father. It was cold and cruel, and in those eyes Nick was a small, pathetic thing.

"If you believe I am, and I believe I am, does it even matter?"

Before Nick could answer, his father's hand was back on his throat, fingertips digging into his jaw. The red light bloomed once more in Lucien's irises. Nick's mind raced.

───────────●───────────

A research station, breaking apart from a damaged reactor.

Blaring alarms demanding all inhabitants flee.

An empty escape pod and a sealed door, his father's face on the other side of the glass.

Unheard final words before the cold silence of space.

———•———

"Accept the truth before you," Lucien said, his grip tightening, plunging Nick again into the unwanted past the instant he came to.

A research station, breaking.

Alarms, blaring.

An escape pod, empty.

Words unheard, then silence.

———•———

"It is my face you see within the memory."

A station.

Alarms.

Escape pod.

Unheard words.

———•———

"It is my face you see outside the memory."

Station.

Alarms.

Pod.

LEVEL: UNKNOWN

Face.
Words.
Silence.

───────●───────

"The same," Lucien said, his deep voice rumbling amid the blackness swamping Nick's consciousness. He couldn't remember where he was, why he was. Chains. He hung from chains. Red shone before him. Eyes. A memory.

───────●───────

Stationalarmspodfacewordssilence

───────●───────

His father.
His father was abandoning him.
His father was *hurting* him.
A nearby door opened as Nick hung, imprisoned and weeping.
"Lord Frey," said his father / Lucien. "My son is ready for your knife."

Chapter 39

GARETH

Gareth knelt beside Yuni's bed, gently cleaning her forehead with a cloth.

"Just hang in there, Beans," he told her, curling a bit of wet hair from her face and tucking it behind her ear. "You're strong enough to kick this, I know it."

He set the cloth down in the bucket beside him. Yuni's room had been a small servants' quarters inside Astarda's keep, cleared out so she might rest and recover. Except she didn't seem to be recovering.

"Your foster parents are waiting for you, you know," he said, resting his arms on the bed and leaning back on his haunches. "I haven't told them the blight is gone. I want you to be the one to tell them." He flashed a false grin no one could see. "So stop worrying them over nothing, Beans. Wake up so we can go visit them together, all right?"

She stirred, but only briefly. He'd seen it plenty before, a tilt of her head and a soft moan of pain. Every time, his hopes

LEVEL: UNKNOWN

soared, just to be subsequently dashed. Her eyes never opened. Whatever dream imprisoned her, it remained locked tight.

We don't know the full nature of the blight, Gareth told himself as he stood. *Nor the damage that will remain upon its cure. Hold faith, Gareth. The girl will recover.*

Gareth dared not ponder what it would mean, to her, to his own faith, if she did not.

He exited the room, hesitated at the door, and then sighed. An unwelcome desire squirmed in his belly, and despite his best efforts, he could not dismiss it. He set his jaw. No putting this off. No remaining a coward. Gareth would accept Lord Frey's methods with his eyes open and his conscience clear.

Halfway down the steps to the secret room, Gareth was surprised to find Lady Jeanne climbing up toward him, her son cradled against her chest. He tipped his head and shifted so she might pass on the cramped steps, but instead she kept in his way. Her pale fingers tightened their grip on the blanket that swaddled baby Gestolf.

"Sir Gareth," she said. "It is...good to see you, actually. Might I ask you a question?"

His chest constricted.

"Of course you may," he said. "Though oaths and vows may keep me from answering as you desire."

Her yellow eyes stared into his with surprising fierceness.

"Yes, I suppose that should be expected," she said. "But I will ask, nonetheless. My husband...there is a room, in the depths of the castle at the end of these stairs, that he visits near daily now. Despite all my attempts, he refuses to explain where it leads, nor does he allow me entry."

This was exactly what Gareth feared her question would be about, and he fought to keep his face perfectly passive. The expression of a proper, orderly knight.

"I have tried to afford my lord his privacy," she continued, starting to gently rock Gestolf in her arms. "But that has not halted my curiosity. I have descended those steps as far as the soldiers guarding the entrance will allow, and from within I hear...screaming." Her face paled, her expression hardening. "So much screaming."

Gareth straightened, hating how easily the words came to him. It was not his place to reveal what Lord Frey deemed should be hidden, even from his own wife.

"Your husband's secrets are his own," he said. "But I assure you, all that he does, he does because he believes it best serves Vestor."

Jeanne shook her head. "I am not oblivious to the grim tasks expected of a ruler. I just wish he would trust me with the burden."

Gareth risked putting a hand on her shoulder. His careful, neutral expression slipped into a practiced smile.

"It is because he loves you that he seeks to lessen your burdens and bear them on his shoulders. He is a strong man, and capable. Accept that act of love."

"Love," she said, and the word sounded bitter on her tongue. "You hold a strange definition of 'love,' Gareth." She dipped her head in return. "Pleasant nights to you, good sir."

When Gareth arrived at the pit of the castle keep, he did not hear screaming through the door. Not because there was no screaming, only that it was too weak and pathetic.

LEVEL: UNKNOWN

"Have you come to join me, Gareth?" Lord Frey asked, not turning around. He stood before the imprisoned demon, who hung from the stone wall from four short chains. He was naked from the waist up, his shirt and leather armor in a pile in the corner. Numerous wounds bled from cuts all across his chest, neck, and abdomen. Gareth shivered at the sight.

He's so young, he thought as Nick's head gently lolled from side to side. *And he looks so weak. Where is the strength that let him challenge me?*

The stolen reflection, Lucien, waited patiently beside the wood table, his arms crossed behind his back. The Sinifel artifacts had been pushed aside, making room for a selection of cruelly twisted and hooked knives with which Lord Frey did his work.

"This demon has proven a crafty one," Gareth said, realizing he had not answered his lord's question when Frey glanced back with a cautious expression. "I wished only to check on you, and ensure there is no chance for the monster to escape."

Nick's laughter interrupted the both of them.

"Monster?" he said, lifting his head. Blood dripped down his face from cuts expertly laced into his forehead just underneath his hairline. "Right. I'm the monster." He grinned, revealing teeth stained with drying blood. "Isn't it obvious?"

Lord Frey backhanded Nick across the mouth.

"I pause your purification for only a moment, and already your tongue drips acid. I fear there is no finding the good in you, demon, no matter how deeply I cut."

Nick spat blood but said nothing as he hung from the chains. Frey seemed almost disappointed. He offered his current dagger to Lucien, then wiped his hands with a cloth he kept in his trouser pocket. Once clean, he approached the wood table and grabbed Nick's discarded weapon. The obsidian blade seemed to shimmer a black darker than the shadowed corners of the room, while the writing on its blade glowed a frightful crimson.

"Pain may provide no cleansing of the sins within you, but you may at least prove useful." Frey held the sword's edge against Nick's rib cage. "I ask again, demon, what is the secret to awakening the blade? I know this weapon. It is one of the judgment blades, weapons wielded by the Sinifel Empire's most faithful and worthy, and yet it will not grant me its power."

"Then you must not be worthy," Nick said. "Don't blame me. Ask Sorrow. Maybe he thinks your knife work is too crude. All these shallow cuts in straight lines? So boring. Maybe draw a picture instead? If you're going to leave me scarred, you could at least cut me a bird, a pretty flower, maybe a teardrop right under my—"

The lord silenced him with a punch to the stomach, robbing him of air.

"I am tired of your japes," Frey snarled. "'Ask Sorrow,' you say, as if a blade could answer. I will not be denied my rightful weapon. I am heir of the ideals and memory of the Sinifel. That sword you stole is mine, demon. I do not care how long it takes, or how stubborn your refusal. Whatever prayer, spell, or ritual is required, you will tell me the secret to unleashing the weapon's power."

To Gareth's surprise, Nick laughed, the sound ragged and uneven as he fought for each breath.

LEVEL: UNKNOWN

"You stupid, stupid man," he said. "You think I'm stubborn? Have a chat with Sorrow. Oh wait, you can't, because for reasons beyond me, I think he *hates* you." Nick's eyes shone with a feverish light. "You're not the heir to the Sinifel. You're just a petty lord playing pretend."

Frey pressed the blade harder until blood dripped down Nick's ribs. The demon grimaced but showed no reaction beyond that. Frustrated, Frey pulled the weapon away and slammed it back down on the wood bench. He remained before it, his head bowed and his hands trembling. It was not until his composure had returned that he turned away and addressed Gareth as if he were perfectly unbothered.

"My work here is taxing," he said, shaking his head. "And the hope within it dwindling. I need a drink. Would you come with me, Sir Gareth?"

"Forgive me, my lord, but I had hoped to have words with the demon. We have...business between us."

Lord Frey grinned at him.

"After Meadowtint and the Hulh estate, I suspect you do." He gestured at the table. "My knives are yours to use as you see fit. Just do not kill him. I will not let the fiend use death as an escape from the needed pain."

Sir Gareth said nothing, only crossed his arms and nodded. Once Frey was gone, he turned his attention to Lucien.

"Will you not escort him?" he asked.

"I am to keep watch over my troublesome son, to ensure he does not escape," Lucien said. "Do not worry. It is a burden, yes, but it is *my* burden."

This was decidedly unwelcome. Gareth sought privacy

with Nick, and he felt certain whatever he said and did in front of Lucien would make its way to Frey.

"I said leave," Gareth insisted. "I will not have my privacy invaded."

"Do you not trust me, Gareth?"

At least here, he could be honest. He grinned wide at the vile reflection.

"No," he said. "And I wish Frey did not, either. But while I am here in Castle Astarda, I am assuming command of Lord Frey's safety, as well as the safety of that which is most important to him. Consider your station here permanently dismissed. I'll have a guard replace you. A *human* guard."

Lucien shrugged. "So be it. It is your head if you do something foolish or anger our lord."

The reflection opened the door, then paused.

"And do not worry if the demon somehow escapes," he said over his shoulder. "I would merely find him again. We are forever linked, my son and I."

The door closed. Within the dim room, lit only by the torches on either side of the statue, the demon laughed.

"Have you come to fulfill your promise?" he asked. "Is my true death here at last?"

"I will not be baited," Gareth said. "Death will not claim you. Imprisonment while alive is the safest method to deal with your cursed kind."

"And Frey's torture? What is that? Just a fun game to help pass the time?"

Gareth grabbed Nick by the throat and shoved him against the stone. His neck felt so thin between his fingers. One squeeze, and he could snap bone. A large part of him wished to do so, if only to watch the life leave the demon's eyes one last time.

"He seeks to find goodness within you," he said. "A goodness as likely to exist as a snowflake beneath the summer sun."

"Goodness? Like when I let you live?" Nick fought back against Gareth's grip to bring his grinning face closer. "But I guess that wasn't goodness, was it? Just me being a fool. It's the one thing I've gotten quite good at here in Yensere."

"Do you think that one moment of mercy makes up for what you've done?"

The grin faltered. "No, but I made that clear already, didn't I?"

Gareth released him, and he rubbed his hand against his side as if it were stained. All the while, Nick eyed him carefully.

"Why are you here, Gareth?" he asked.

"As I said, I wanted to—"

"No," Nick interrupted. "Don't lie to me like you did to your lord. Aren't we friends? I deserve the truth from you. Why did you come down here? What did you expect to find, if not me chained and suffering?"

For reasons that baffled Gareth, he found himself wanting to be truthful to the imprisoned lad. As hard as he tried to cling to his hate, it felt like gripping a squirming fish. Nick looked weathered, his eyes bloodshot, his ribs exposed, and his shoulders sagged to the extent his chains allowed. If he was a demon, then demons were a pathetic lot once broken and bleeding.

Remember Meadowtint, he told himself. *Do not let your eyes be deceived.*

"I don't know," he answered. "I have forsaken the god-king and turned my heart away from the Alder. Yet my faith in Eiman is infantile, and my feet unsteady beneath me on this new road I walk. There is much I do not know, much that Frey does. And so I came to see. To learn. To understand."

Nick did not mock. He did not insult. No, he did the one thing that shocked Gareth by how badly it affected him: He acted disappointed.

"Your lord finds pleasure in torturing those he has imprisoned," Nick said. "What more do you need to learn than that?"

"It is because you are a demon," Gareth argued.

"Right," Nick said. "And I'm sure all those knives over there, those tools and these chains that bind me, have never been used before. I'm the first, and the last." He leaned his head back against the stone and sighed. "If you believe that, Gareth, then you're an even bigger fool than Frey."

Gareth clenched his fists. He wanted to scream, but what was there to say? All arguments turned to ash in his mind. His heart yearned to pray to Vaan, to beg for guidance, but he stood beneath the sightless gaze of Eiman. To even think those words made his blood chill and his skin crawl. His impotence turned to rage, and he struck Nick across the face. He'd hoped the blow would earn him a curse, a glare, anything, but Nick endured it in silence, his eyes closed.

"Never have I hated a day more than I hate the one on which you set foot in Yensere, and into my life," Gareth said as blood trickled down Nick's split lip.

"And I miss when I thought none of this was real," Nick

said, his head tilted back to the stone. "Because then I wouldn't pity you like I do now."

Fury overcame Gareth anew. He grabbed the two torches burning above the statue of Eiman, ripping the sconces out of the stones as if the nails meant nothing to his strength. He snuffed them out with his gloves, not caring for the heat.

"Suffer in darkness, demon," he said, dropping both torches to the cold stone floor. "And think on what little your pity has given you."

When he slammed the door shut, there was no screaming, no protesting.

Just bitter, broken laughter.

Chapter 40
FROST

Frost: Level 16 Human
  Agility: 14
  Physicality: 12
  Endurance: 10
  Focus: 13
  Archetype: Spellblade
  Special Classification: Ice Caster
  Armor: Augmented Chain Mail, Tier 5
  Mana: 91

Frost stared at the outer walls of Castle Astarda, studying them for the hundredth time. The night was deep and dark, with the moon momentarily hidden behind the ever-present orb that was the black sun. It would reemerge within a few hours. Frost was hoping to be long gone from the city by then.

"You don't have to come with me," she said as Violette joined her side. The pair were in a shallow dip of the plains stretching out toward the gateway through the Frostbound

Mountains into the lands beyond, known as Inner Emden. They were far from the road, lurking in the dark recesses of the northernmost wall at the exact point where the wall ended and the sheer ascent began.

"But you need my help," Violette said, as if it were simple.

"If I die, I'll come back. You won't."

Violette crossed her hands behind her back. "It's not so easy as that, is it? There's no pain from your dying, no suffering?"

Frost pushed away a memory of lying on a cold tiled floor, vomiting blood.

"It doesn't matter," she said. "I'm strong enough to endure. But what about you? You don't like killing, but there's no avoiding that, not if we're to rescue Nick."

The other woman nodded toward Castle Astarda and the soldiers patrolling its western wall.

"You and Nick are the first people I've met who aren't frightened of saying and doing things that might be considered heretical. Neither of you is beholden to any gods or kings, not of Alder, nor the Sinifel or Majere. Whatever you are, visitors or demons or something worse, it means nothing compared to how you've helped me. And call it crazy, but I think you two are destined to accomplish something wondrous in this frozen, decaying world of Yensere."

"And you really think that's worth risking your life for?" Frost asked. "That it's worth killing for?"

Violette watched the patrols, their faces lit by the torches they held.

"The two of you are special," she said. "I have to see just how special. Yes. I think it is."

The strength of Violette's resolve surprised Frost, and as if on instinct, the woman's truncated stats appeared above her head.

Violette: Level 10 Human
Archetype: Scholar
Special Classification: Fire Caster

Potent as her fire magic could be, Violette would be hard-pressed in a prolonged battle. Did she know that? Without numbers and statistics from Cataloger, did Violette sense that power disparity? And if she did, did she care?

Frost clenched her left fist, a bit of ice sealing around her knuckles.

Her foes were a higher level than her as well, and yet she was still about to leap into the heart of their keep. So what if the challenge wouldn't be fair? It was the right thing to do. Despite waiting and hoping Lord Frey would execute Nick, unknowingly freeing him from his prison, two days had passed without its happening. Cataloger had shown her the nearest ring of stones, and Nick had never stepped forth. He was trapped somewhere in Castle Goltara, and if the treatment he'd endured at Baron Hulh's hands was any indication, he was suffering tremendously.

Which meant that tonight, she and Violette were going to break him out.

Frost knelt before her travel pack, which she'd set on the ground beside her. A quick riffling through it and she found two thin vials, their containers crystalline, their contents a pale blue liquid. The topper was shaped like a dove, for reasons Frost did not remember.

LEVEL: UNKNOWN

"Here, take this," she said, handing over one of the two bottles.

"What is it?" Violette asked.

"Think of it like a bottle of sleep. Drink it, and your head will feel clear and all your spent mana will return to you."

"Sleep in a bottle?" Violette gazed upon it like it was a miracle realized. "If only we had such things during my time at Silversong."

Frost winced, remembering how much it had cost at a market far, far from Yensere.

"They're not cheap, nor easy to get," she said. "Use it only if you must, but given how badly the numbers are stacked against us, we're going to need my ice and your fire to even the odds."

Violette pocketed the vial, stood to her full height, and then nodded. Frost almost told her to remain behind. She could throw her life away several times trying to rescue Nick, whereas Violette had but the one. Only...there was something about the look in Violette's amber eyes. This was a woman who had undergone hardship and given up so much of her life to pursue knowledge in defiance of censorship and accusations of blasphemy. No matter her easy smile or the joyfulness of her personality, a strength lurked within her. How else could she be so defiant to the cruelties of the world?

"All right," Frost said, wrapping her arm around Violette's waist. "Stay still, and keep your trust in me. Kill any soldiers who see us."

"I will."

No more waiting. Time to do this. Frost pointed to her feet and let her magic flow.

Spell: Ice Pillar

The pillar grew beneath their feet, flat on the top and perfectly circular on all sides. It shot them into the air as it rose, carrying them above the outer wall of Castle Astarda. Two guards, one stationary near the mountain rise, another walking a lazy patrol from the south, both saw and froze in place upon the ramparts. Frost did not waste the opportunity. An **<ice lance>** shot from her palm, its aim true. The jagged edge punched into the guard's throat, and he dropped, easily slain. Violette struck the other, a wave of her hands summoning a spurt of fire directly underneath the feet of the baffled soldier.

Spell: Fire Burst

The fire charred into his flesh and melted portions of his armor, easily taking his life.

Frost prayed the soldiers protecting the inner keep were as low-level as these outside guards, who were mostly levels 4 and 5. She knelt on the pillar, picturing the desired effect of her next spell.

"Ever ridden a slide before?" she asked, magic building underneath her fingertips.

"What do you mean?"

As answer, she enacted the spell **<icy path>**.

The ice connected the pillar to the wall, the surface gently curved and sloping downward. Frost went first, straightening her cloak so its smooth surface would slide instead of her chain mail. A half second later she landed atop the wall and spun to catch Violette. The other woman landed clumsily in her arms, then grinned.

LEVEL: UNKNOWN

"My thanks."

"That's the easy one," Frost said. With a thought, she banished both the pillar and the slide. The ice shattered without the slightest noise, instantly melting into vapor that faded to nothing. That done, she focused her gaze on the inner keep.

Nick is in there somewhere, isn't he?

I cannot answer

Frost expected as much from Cataloger. Useful when it didn't matter, a helpless bystander when it did. She glanced to her right, checking the wall. In the distance, she saw another soldier sprinting toward them with his torch held aloft.

"Time to go," she said. It was foolish to think they could reach the keep without attracting attention. Her hope was to outpace the alarm and, by the time reinforcements arrived, have already completed their rescue.

Frost eyed the keep doors, two thick slabs of oak reinforced with iron. Hands touching the bricks of the rampart, she envisioned a second slide and used her magic to make it real. Ice shot out, crackling and hardening across the thousands of feet between her and her target. Thin little supports of ice stretched down from underneath the slide, connecting to whatever was below, be it the street, walls, or rooftops.

"Incredible," Violette said when Frost finished.

"Hold nothing back," she said, shaking off a bit of ache in her head and drawing her sword. "Overwhelming power is our only hope."

Frost hopped onto the slide, whose angle was much sharper than the last. She sped feetfirst toward the entrance, her sword lying flat upon her chest and clutched tightly. Halfway there, she extended her left hand and unleashed an enormous **<ice boulder>**. It was condensed to be as heavy as possible, its surface rugged and chipped as if it had been carved from the side of a glacier. The boulder struck the center of the doors, and with such weight and momentum, it blasted them apart, breaking the hinges along with them.

The ice slide pitched sharply at the end, and Frost grabbed her sword and readied for battle. Two soldiers stood guard on either side of the door, and they pointed and shouted in a panic. Their levels hovered over them: 7. Higher than those on the wall. Worrisome. How could regular soldiers without magic be so threatening?

The ice slide ended in a sudden pitch, and the moment her feet touched ground, she kicked, propelling herself straight at the guard to her left. He wielded a sword in two hands, his face half covered by his helmet. A torch burned above him, casting light on his pale red tabard. She noted these details clinically, analyzing her foe as she sought to cut him down. Her sword led the way, its tip aimed for his throat. Not worth striking his ring-mail armor, given how solid it looked.

Tier 3, to be exact

Thanks, Cataloger, she thought as her sword was parried aside. The soldier's weapon was heavier than hers, and he threw all his weight into that parry so her sword went flinging wide. A grim smile stretched his lips as he pulled his weapon back. He thought her vulnerable. Cocky fool. His slash aimed to cleave her in half at the waist. Her own blade was too far out to block in time, but she did not need the protection of steel.

LEVEL: UNKNOWN

Ice would be enough.

Frost pivoted, her left hand punching toward his arms. Her palm struck his forearm and enacted the magic of her spell.

Spell: Shatter

Both parts of the spell happened near instantly. The first was a layer of ice built around the soldier's forearms, spreading out from her touch. The second was a slamming impact, as if her palm were a massive piston. Ice, flesh, and bone shattered. One of the soldier's arms was severed with the blow amid a spray of blood. His health dropped by half, again confusing Frost. Such a blow should have killed an average man.

Her foe's sword went flying, released from his grip so it sailed behind her. She continued her pivot, putting her back to the wounded man so she could face the other soldier rushing to stab her. Her sword shifted the soldier's weapon aside, then came up to block the immediate overhead chop that followed. Their weapons interlocked.

"Eiman give us strength!"

Frost gasped as her sword rattled and his own blade drew nearer. So that was why they were so high-level. They were blessed with accursed Sinifel magic.

Blessed or not, it meant little to a sudden barrage that smacked his face and sides.

Spell: Flame Darts

Four fiery little darts thudded into him. He screamed, staggering away from Frost. Another barrage of darts struck him in the back as Violette came sliding down to join them at the broken entrance. The darts made a mockery of his ring mail as their heat sank deeper to char flesh unseen. Frost twisted again, instincts screaming warning. The soldier she had disarmed attacked with a frenzy, no plan, no hope, just pain and panic driving him to try to bash his helmet toward her head.

A quick slash of her sword across his throat ended his pain—and his life. She turned to the broken door and saw four more darts char away the other soldier's remaining health. He dropped, a burning corpse in the keep entryway. Beyond him was the opening hall of the guardroom. Doors on either side opened, and soldiers in various states of disarray emerged.

"Where to?" Violette asked, fire building across her hands.

Show me the way to Nick, Frost ordered Cataloger.

Doing so is an invasion of a fellow visitor's privacy

"Then ask him!"

Frost leaped into the room, knowing that with her armor and sword, she would need to take point over Violette. The other soldiers charged while screaming for help, the ruckus certainly waking other portions of the keep. Frost flung another <ice lance>, the brutal shard embedding deep into the throat to strike her foe's spine, and then gripped her sword in both hands. She'd already used 31 of her 91 mana. Time to let her steel do a bit of work.

As much as she liked to pretend with Nick, her skill with a sword was still fairly new, and born of only six months of training before coming to Yensere. These soldiers, though, had spent years learning to wield their weaponry, and it showed as she engaged the nearest. Their swords clashed, both her initial slashes easily blocked. Frost kept up the attack, for she had two advantages these soldiers did not: One was that the systems of Yensere, and of the Artifact empowering it, had come to believe her strength was far beyond what should have been humanly possible.

The other was that her sword was blessed with magic from a faraway land.

Two more good blocks, and the soldier's sword cracked along the edge. Her own blade continued, striking his shoulder and puncturing through his ring mail. Frost pivoted closer, painfully aware of the other soldiers nearing, and struck his chest with her palm. **<Ice shatter>** enacted, the magic pouring into his body to crush his ribs and turn his lungs to mush, far beyond what was needed to bring him down.

Nick has granted me permission to lead you to him

"Thanks," she muttered, parrying another hit, retreating two steps, and then waving her hand. A **<frost nova>** burst around her, encasing the legs of all three remaining soldiers. She'd hoped to keep them pinned, but it seemed they, too, possessed Eiman's blessing. The ice cracked as they stumbled forward, their strength crossing the required threshold. That momentary pause, however, was enough for Violette's spell to arrive.

Spell: Flaming Whip

The whip lashed across all three of them, moving with such speed and accuracy it seemed like a living thing. The first soldier cried out, burned across his chest by a lash. The other two suffered far worse, the whip curling around their faces and necks. The damage came in rapid succession, continuing to burn away at their health until they collapsed, their health bars fully depleted. Seeing it made Frost shudder. Violette might dislike killing, but she was exceptionally good at it.

"Frost, behind us!"

She spun at Violette's warning to see soldiers rushing toward the entrance from outside the keep. On patrol, perhaps, or brought running by the alarm sounded by the guard on the outer wall? Didn't matter. They needed to be dealt with.

"Sorry, door's closed," she said, lifting her left hand and pretending her head wasn't a pounding cacophony of sharp pains. Her <ice wall> spread across the entire entrance, sealing out the reinforcements. Deciding it was not enough, she cast it two more times, strengthening it so it would endure the attacks of the Eiman-blessed soldiers. They'd make it through in time, though. She had to move fast.

"Lead on, Cataloger," she muttered. Cataloger obliged by creating a faint gold outline around one of the doors near the far end of the guardroom.

But before that…

Frost pulled her mana vial from a small pouch on her hip, popped the winged cork, and then drank. The pale blue liquid slid down her throat, lighter than air and colder than ice. It was deeply foul to the taste. There was an acrid feeling to it, and she had to fight off an immediate desire to vomit. It was like swallowing bitter moonlight. The momentary unpleasantness was worth it, though, for her head cleared, and all her 91 mana returned.

"All right, let's go," she said, darting for the door while beckoning to Violette. "Follow me!"

One of the side doors burst open when they were halfway across the guardroom. Two soldiers dashed out, heavy swords clutched high above their heads. Frost spun, her panic rising. They were so close to Violette, and the scholar had no armor, no weapons, just her fire to wield on foes bearing down on her.

"Violette!"

Frost need not have worried. In a panic, Violette flung **<searing wrath>** directly at her own feet. Its fury roared about her, yet she went untouched by the flames. The same could not be said for the two soldiers who thought her vulnerable. The fire encased them, caring not for their armor. The sudden erasure of their health bars down to zero was terrifying, even to Frost.

"I've never tried that before," Violette said in the sudden silence that followed. "I can't burn myself. Good to know."

Frost blinked in shock, then burst into grim laughter.

"Indeed, good to know," she said. "But let's not try that on me or Nick."

"I won't be trying anything until after this." Violette reached into one of her many pockets, withdrew Frost's mana vial, and opened it. She sniffed it quickly, then took a drink. Her face made clear her opinion of its taste.

"Better," she said, coughing once. "Lead on."

The door revealed a slender stairway leading downward, its steps lit by little lanterns, half of whose candles had burned out. Frost dashed down them and their gentle curve, until they ended at a plain door guarded by a lone man in ring mail. He pressed his back to the door and lifted his sword in both hands, his eyes wide with fear.

"Begone, both of you," he said. "This room is off-limits by Lord Frey's decree."

"Is it, now?" Frost asked, angling her sword. The two attacked simultaneously, moving as if given a secret signal.

His sword scraped across her chain mail, drawing blood along her side. Her sword struck the center of his breast and punched inward in retaliation. He screamed, then again, louder, when she shoved the sword in deeper. When Frost ripped her sword free, she bashed aside his attempt to cut her legs off at the knee and then kicked him in the face. He staggered, his head snapping back to strike the closed door. His eyes crossed, and amid his daze, she shoved her sword right into his mouth.

The soldier collapsed, and Frost pushed his body aside so they could check the door. Locked.

"Can you open it with your ice?" Violette asked.

"Don't need to," Frost said, pulling a key off the dead guard's belt. "Got to conserve a bit of that mana for the dramatic escape."

She slid the key in, turned it, and entered the pitch-black room of Nick's imprisonment.

"A moment," Violette said, lifting her hand. Soft flame wrapped about it, granting them light. The room was dark, foul, and cursed with a statue of Eiman lording over all, casting his cruel, faceless gaze. Nick hung from chains bolted to the wall. He was naked from the waist up, his body covered with angry red wounds carved by a slender blade. Blood stained his skin. When his health bar appeared above him, she could barely see the faintest hint of red within it. His head sagged low, his eyes closed as he hung there.

"Nick," she shouted, rushing toward him. His head rose.

LEVEL: UNKNOWN

Even given how broken and tired he looked, he still gave her his best, most sincere smile. She shoved the door key into the slot of one of his wrist manacles and was immediately relieved to see it pop open. She undid his ankles so he could stand, unsteadily, then finally unlatched the other wrist, freeing him.

"Hey, Frost," Nick said, his words slurred as he collapsed. She caught him and gently lowered both of them to the ground, his head and upper body cradled in her lap. His pathetic health bar failed to adequately convey how weakly he moved, nor how shallow his breaths. She stroked strands of his brown hair away from his face.

"Lesya," she corrected, and smiled back despite the dark, the threat of soldiers, and the looming statue of Eiman. "My name's Lesya Koval."

Chapter 41
NICK

Nick leaned his weight against her, cherishing the warmth of her arms around him.

"Lesya," he said, working to commit it to memory. "That's a pretty name."

"Yeah?" She smiled, a mixture of kindness and sorrow. "My mother thought so, too."

She gently stroked his back with the soft portion of her mailed glove, and he closed his eyes and allowed himself to laugh.

"This is twice, now," he said, his voice raspy and weak. "I owe you double."

Lesya gently slid him off her, glanced to the door, where Violette was keeping watch, and then retrieved his leather chest piece from where it lay on the floor.

"Tell you what, Nick," she said as she wrapped it around him to hide his bare chest and its many scars. "If we get out of here with all three of us alive, you can consider that debt repaid. But that means walking and, worse, climbing some stairs. Can you manage?"

Nick accepted her help to stand.

"I can," he said, only half believing it himself. "Or maybe you should just give me a quick one-way trip to the nearest circle of stones?"

Lesya punched him in the shoulder.

"I didn't break in here just to kill you," she said, and then her grin softened. "Besides, what you've just endured... it's taking its toll on you in the real world. Isn't it?"

Nick winced at half-remembered fevers, feeding tubes, and his brother's frightened expression after Sir Gareth ambushed the mourning song. The torture Lord Frey inflicted, it wasn't real, he knew that... but did it matter if his body behaved as if it were?

"I haven't been the healthiest lately," he admitted. "All right. No dying, only escaping. Lead the way."

"Not yet." She hurried to the table of Sinifel artifacts, frowned at them in disgust, and then grabbed Sorrow.

"Not going anywhere without your sword," she said, thrusting it into his arms. "Now, follow us. We're getting out of here via the rooftop."

"Why the roof?"

"Because the gates will be guarded and the streets filled with soldiers. We're taking my special way out instead."

Lesya dashed ahead, sliding past a lingering Violette. The scholar stared at Nick, her expression unreadable.

"Hey," he said, grinning at her and pretending he was far healthier than his paltry life bar insisted.

"I don't care if you're a demon," she suddenly said. "You need to live, all right? You need to live, and explore, and take me everywhere interesting that you go. Promise me."

"That will just put you in danger, too," he said.

"Do I look like someone who cares about danger?"

Her clothes were splattered with blood, some hers, most from others. Fire had singed a tiny portion of her sleeve. Her hair was disheveled and slightly pulled out from her normal ponytail. She was serious, she was dangerous, and she was beautiful.

"It's a promise," he said. "How could I ever refuse?"

The seriousness passed, and she winked. "You can't."

The climb up the stairs was brutal on Nick's legs. It felt like he'd hung forever from those chains, and the movement awakened sore muscles he didn't know existed. He huffed in air as he ascended, trailing behind Lesya and Violette. Sorrow warmed to his touch when the stairs ended at a wide hall. The way higher was on the opposite side, and guarded by four soldiers pressed shoulder to shoulder with their heavy shields leaving no gap in their defenses. Several more soldiers lay dead, their bodies scattered across the battle-scarred room, though he suspected they had died during the initial break-in.

Nick slumped against the wall, furious that he felt so powerless to help. Lesya danced before the guards' formation, testing it with quick slashes. No magic, he noted. She must be trying to preserve what mana she had left. Violette hovered just behind Lesya, flinging <fire darts>, which placed little strain on her mana reserves.

Do you fear to aid them? Sorrow asked.

LEVEL: UNKNOWN

"I'd be a distraction," he said, and turned his thoughts to the sword. "Why didn't you serve Frey? He worships your god."

Sorrow's hilt warmed underneath his touch.

We did not worship Eiman. The Beast of a Thousand Mouths was the ruination awaiting us if we remained stagnant in our lives. He was the rot, and the breaking down of order, if we did not succumb. He was worth less of our prayers than the sun, the wind, or the rising tide. Frey's heart is twisted. He is a callous man who kneels before Eiman seeking power and domination. There is no surrender to the cycle, no humility and understanding that time will claim even our greatest accomplishments.

*He **is** unworthy.*

Lesya scored a lethal hit on one of the four when two more soldiers came rushing in from a side door.

"Behind you!" Nick shouted. Violette heard and spun, fire bursting about her hands as she readied a defense of their flank. Only one of the two soldiers rushed her, though, for the other saw a far easier target. Nick stepped out into the hall and lifted Sorrow in shaking arms to meet his foe. His heart raced. His forehead throbbed with pain, and there was no hiding the weakness in his grip, nor the pulsing red bar of his health and the lowly few percentage points that remained.

Sorrow's voice floated in Nick's mind as the soldier approached.

My people are lost, but my hate remains. Will you embrace it for me, Nick? Will you wield it against Lord Frey and end the life of he who insults the name and honor of our memory?

"I will," Nick whispered.

Then stand tall before your foe and strike him down.

Nick straightened his spine. He had no lightning, his mana having been steadily depleted over the course of his torture, and his left hand was still a broken mess. A single blow would kill him, but he would not die without a fight. Sorrow burned hot in his grasp, the power of the ancient weapon awakening. Feeling it, Nick grinned despite all his exhaustion and trauma.

Sorrow's modified damage returned to baseline

The soldier lunged toward Nick, his sword swinging from above. The man's fear was ruining his poise, and he attacked as if Nick were a wild animal. Nick waited the briefest moment to ensure the man committed to the strike, then lurched aside, grimly amused by his own lack of grace, and then thrust. A crimson light shimmered across Sorrow's obsidian surface, the tip easily punching through the man's ring mail as Sorrow's voice thundered in his ears.

My blessing is yours.

Special Attribute Unlocked

The deep black hiding the final ability peeled away, revealing a single word:

Vampiric

Nick gasped at the sudden strength flooding him. It felt like a tremendous weight slid off his shoulders. The pains in his chest reduced. The bones in his left hand mended. His health increased, as did his mana, by half that. Ripping Sorrow free, he pivoted slightly to properly square his hips and then swung again. The wounded soldier positioned his sword in the way, but it lacked any strength. Sorrow smashed it aside and continued onward to strike his neck. The obsidian blade sank deep down to touch vertebrae.

The ache in Nick's mind subdued, the pain in his chest easing as the ribs that were broken knitted together.

"Unbelievable," he muttered as the corpse dropped.

I am a judgment blade of the Sinifel, Sorrow exclaimed, all his pride and fury let loose. *Believe.*

Nick charged the nearest soldier, who was being held at bay by a steady barrage of **<flame darts>** bursting from Violette's hand. His shield absorbed the brunt of it, his health being chipped away tiny fragments at a time. His back was turned, easy prey for Sorrow to slip underneath his ring-mail chestpiece and then jab upward, severing organs and puncturing a lung. The soldier's entire body went rigid, and he gasped out once before dying. As he collapsed, Nick slowly breathed in and out. The last of his health bar had filled, as had most of his mana. All of Lord Frey's torture felt a lifetime away.

"Nick?" Violette asked, looking concerned.

Instead of answering, he rushed past her to where Lesya struggled against three soldiers who had gained the courage to advance from the stairwell. She'd layered the floor with **<icy ground>**, hampering their approach, but her slender sword struggled against their heavy shields.

Nick blasted their center with a **<lightning bolt>** so that it leaped among all three. The pain and shock of it made them stumble, and into that mess, Nick flung himself like a madman. One of the soldiers saw him coming and thrust over his shield. Nick impaled himself against it, enduring agony to stab Sorrow straight into the man's face. The obsidian edge punched through his mouth and out the back of his skull in a burst of gore. When the soldier dropped, his sword slid from Nick's chest, and it left not a scratch, all its damage healed away by Sorrow's vampiric kiss.

The other two turned, trying to crush him from either side. Nick summoned his **<lightning shield>** for his left hand to block. It sparked into his foe as it held the sword at bay. The other soldier's attack fared better, the edge of his blade carving into Nick's side with a splash of blood and a brief exposure of ribs. Nick pivoted and cut him down, Sorrow chopping through both blade and armor. Life drained from the corpse, healing Nick's torn flesh.

The final soldier, wounded twice by lightning, tried to retreat. His heavy boots slipped on the ice, and when he fell, Lesya was there immediately. Her sword slashed his thigh, then stabbed his chest, the two hits more than enough to end his life.

A wave of Lesya's hand, and the frost on the ground vanished. Blood still dripping from her sword, she turned to Nick, her eyes wide and her expression baffled.

"You look...recovered," she said.

Nick grinned back at her, and he lifted Sorrow as explanation.

"Save your magic," he said. "I'll take the lead."

He dashed into the stairwell, barely having time to take three steps before encountering another soldier rushing down them. The man shouted and thrust his sword. Nick tried, and failed, to parry it. The blade sank into his shoulder, bleeding him. Grinning through the pain, Nick hoisted Sorrow up and over his head as the soldier's eyes widened.

LEVEL: UNKNOWN

"My turn."

He chopped, burying Sorrow through the soldier's collarbone and deep into his chest, making a mockery of his ring mail. He felt the pain vanish from his wounded shoulder. He saw the body of his foe collapse, blood pouring from him as he rolled limply down the stairs.

"To the rooftop," Nick said, pounding up the steps and trusting the two women to follow.

The cold air felt refreshing on Nick's sweat-soaked skin as he exited the stairwell onto the wide, flat space at the very height of the castle keep, its wall crenelated and waist-high. Little fires visible through windows mixed with the lit streetlamps to create a pleasant yellow star field below. If only the castle keep was as peaceful as the rest of the city.

"What now?" Nick asked as the other two joined him.

Lesya circled the rooftop, her gaze to the distance.

"Here," she said, sheathing her sword and then clapping her hands. Blue light swelled between her fingers as she cast her **<icy path>** spell. Ice latched on to the side of the rooftop and spread outward, little support pillars dropping beneath it as it traveled beyond the homes and workshops of Castle Astarda. It continued onward for thousands of feet at a gentle slope until connecting with the top of the far eastern gate.

"There's our way home," she said, stepping away while clapping her hands.

A trio of **<dark orbs>** smashed the side of the bridge, two pummeling the initial support beam while a third struck the drop. The ice shattered, huge portions of the slide collapsing to fall like jagged snow upon the courtyard. The trio spun, weapons and magic readying when they saw who had chased them to the rooftop.

Sir Gareth, and with him, a furious Lucien Wright.

"Can you two handle the knight?" Nick asked, cold fury holding his growing fear at bay.

"We can just run," Lesya argued. "Make another bridge, a much shorter one, while you keep them occupied."

"No running. Lucien will always find me. I have to end this here and now."

Lesya exchanged a look with Violette as their two foes slowly approached with their weapons lifted.

"He's strong," Violette said, her expression darkening. "But not strong enough. Have your duel, Nick."

And then, as if to punctuate her assertion, she flung a **\<fire meteor\>** Gareth's way. It burst harmlessly upon his shield. Gareth was keeping extra cautious after his previous defeats. Or perhaps he knew time was on his side.

"Good to see you, Lucien," Nick shouted as he separated from the two women so he was on the opposite side of the keep's rooftop. "We've unfinished business between us."

It seemed their foes were all too happy to separate for their own individual skirmishes. Sir Gareth weathered a storm of ice as he marched, while Lucien cocked his sword across his right shoulder and moved with a swagger that was strange and unfamiliar on the body of his father.

Lucien: Level 13 Human
Archetype: Administrator
Special Classification: Reflection
Armor: Natural, Tier 10

LEVEL: UNKNOWN

"You are determined to be a problem, aren't you?" Lucien asked.

Nick flashed a grin. "Seems like what I'm best at lately."

Lucien shook his head, his disappointment familiar and biting with the strength of memory.

"You are drunk on freedom, but do not worry. Our chains will render you sober."

He dashed forward, his sword swinging in a wide overhead chop. There was no subtlety to it, no finesse. It reminded Nick of when his father had taught him how to throw a handball, and the sudden, stark memory nearly robbed him of his defense. His father could not hurt him. His father would never hurt him, but this thing would, and only at the last moment did he position Sorrow to block the strike. Steel and obsidian collided, and Nick gasped at the strength of his foe.

Remain calm, Sorrow insisted. *You are stronger than him, Nick. Now is the time to prove it.*

Nick pushed Lucien's sword away, only to see it swing back in immediately. He retreated, held back a scream as it cut across his shoulder. Blood sprayed, and the ensuing pain threatened to cloud his mind further. Instead, he fell into instinct, recalling one of Frost's positions and forcing his body into it. Her training was an advantage he held over this monster wearing his father's face. He had to use it.

Lucien's next swing came in strong, but Nick's feet were better positioned, his sword lifted and held in both hands. Their weapons collided, and without even thinking, Nick moved into the next position. His hands turned. His sword slashed the space before him, and he hadn't even thought of it as an attack but a mere movement of his body. Lucien was too busy pulling back his sword for another overhead swing, leaving himself exposed. Sorrow sank eagerly into Lucien's stomach, then cut across him from side to side.

No blood from the cut. No severed flesh. Instead, the simulacrum of humanity broke to reveal shards of mirror glass, neatly stacked and pressed. Sorrow cracked their surfaces and ruined their reflections. The damage, though, was real enough, taken from Lucien's red bar and siphoned into Nick to partly heal the bleeding wound on his shoulder.

"Do you see?" Nick said, gesturing to the wound he'd inflicted as Lucien retreated several steps. "No more lies. No more pretending. I can see you for what you are, Lucien. You are nothing."

"I am your *father*," Lucien seethed, his sword a blur in his hand as he swung. He was strong, but he had little training. He struck as if his weapon was a hammer, and Nick a stubborn nail. Sorrow met it each and every time. The sound of their colliding weapons pounded louder than his heartbeat in his ears.

"I raised you. Protected you. Did my duty to shape you into something good, something greater than all your faults and failures would have you remain."

Nick sidestepped the next overhead swing, pivoted, and then swung. Sorrow slashed across Lucien's stomach. No blood, just another shimmer of glass that sparked and cracked. Lucien elbowed Nick in the face, then cut across him with his sword. It was a vicious wound, and Nick staggered in retreat as he bled.

"Yet this is what you would become?"

LEVEL: UNKNOWN

"And what is that?" Nick asked, trying to shake off the pain. "What am I that is so horrible?"

Lucien did not answer. Instead he doubled the intensity of his assault with wild, untrained swings that carried so much more strength than he ever possessed in his former life. Nick tried to block the first two, and he paid for it with the impact. His elbows wrenched awkwardly, and his shoulders and hands ached. Fighting off panic, he parried the third and then brought Sorrow slicing in faster than Lucien could defend himself. The obsidian blade cut across his abdomen, and if he'd been a real human, his innards would have spilled out to the brick. Instead his clothes and flesh cracked and became twisted, broken glass. A fatal blow to a real human, an annoyance to this reflection.

Halfway there, thought Nick, glancing at the health bar.

Nick's reward was a blow to the head from Lucien's fist. He rocked backward, lifting Sorrow to defend against a strike that never came. Lucien slowly stalked forward, his wounds refusing to heal so that each shone with jagged sparkles.

"Curse the potter given such poor clay," he said, pulling back for a thrust. "Never could I be more disappointed as your father."

"Then prove it," Nick said, spitting blood. "What were your final words?"

Lucien hesitated. "Explain yourself."

"Your final words," Nick said, slowly approaching with Sorrow held at the ready. "When Station 68 was in danger and the pod doors were closing, what did you say?"

This abomination in the shape of his father glared but said nothing. Nick bared his teeth as fury surged through him.

"You don't know because *I* don't know," he said. "You're not my father. You're just a pale shadow."

Lucien lunged, his sword aimed straight for Nick's heart. No more pretending. No more keeping him alive. Nick smashed it harmlessly aside, planted his back foot, and then held firm as Lucien impaled himself upon Sorrow's blade. It sank in all the way to the hilt. Crystal and glass hardened around the wound as Lucien struggled closer, his mouth bared like a wild animal's.

"You're my memories of him, stolen and twisted and made wrong. Made *hateful*."

Nick ripped the sword out, already feeling stronger, and not only from the power stolen through Sorrow's vampiric blessing. He chopped with all his strength, cleaving Lucien's hand off at the wrist. It fell with a shatter of glass, his sword falling with it. Lucien swung a punch with his other hand, and when that missed, he tumbled closer, mouth open and biting. Nick sidestepped, this time cutting low so his sword sliced through one of Lucien's knees. The impostor collapsed, howling in mindless fury.

A slash across the jaw silenced him. Nick knelt so he could place his left hand upon the face of his father, who gasped and struggled to maintain form.

"I loved my father," Nick said, his voice falling to a whisper. "And when you're gone, I will love him still."

Lightning exploded from his palm and into Lucien's forehead. The blast was more than enough to claim the last of him. Skin turned to glass. Organs turned to powder. Amid one final death scream, Lucien shattered, scattered across the rooftop stones as jagged, cracking shards, and lived no more.

Chapter 42
NICK

Nick stood over the broken remains of the thing that had worn his father's face. He wished he could spend the time to stomp each and every piece of broken glass with his heel, but Lesya and Violette were still locked in battle with Sir Gareth. Nick turned their way, readying his sword, but a newcomer up the stairs stole his attention first.

Lord Frey stood dressed in red-and-black finery at the exit of the stairwell. Despite the late hour, his every hair was in place, his clothes immaculate. In his left arm he cradled a young girl in a plain white shift, her body limp and her eyes closed as if she were asleep. In his right hand he held a cruel knife Nick recognized all too well.

"Enough!" the older man shouted, carrying an undeniable air of authority. Nick retreated to join Lesya and Violette, all three keeping back as Sir Gareth separated from them, his enormous sword held up in the defensive.

"Lord Frey?" he asked. "Why is Yuni here?"

The lord ignored the question, his gaze locked on Nick. The knife shook in a trembling hand.

"Is there no end to your depravity?" the lord asked. "No price you will not force us to pay? You cannot be let loose upon our lands. I will not fail in my duty."

Lightning crackled around Nick's fingers as he readied his power. He had experienced the lord's madness, and he feared for the life of the girl he held.

"Put her down," Nick said. "Whatever you're planning, it's just between us."

It seemed even Gareth was unnerved by the man's arrival.

"Frey..." he said, his attention split between Nick and the lord of the castle. "I asked, why is Yuni here?"

Lord Frey smiled, an act so sad, so bitter.

"I sought to heal this world through kindness and mercy," he said. "But this world is one of cruelty, not kindness."

He plunged the knife into the girl's chest. Nick screamed, but there was no blood, only darkness that blossomed outward like smoke billowing from a fire. It curled around them both, hungry and eager. Yuni's eyes finally opened, wide and fearful, but she said not a word before the shadows swallowed her. From within the darkness, unseen, he heard her scream once, and only once.

"I am the final thread of faith," Lord Frey bellowed.

The darkness withered, revealing Yuni's corpse, rent and torn with her rib cage blooming outward through her flesh as if something had ripped its way free from within. Her body was void of color, her eyes, of life.

Nick fought back vomit. Lesya gasped. Sir Gareth screamed

LEVEL: UNKNOWN

a wordless protest, his voice drowned out by Frey's triumphant proclamation.

"I am the true hope of a broken empire."

The last of the shadows imploded, and from their curling, wispy darkness stepped a monster. Frey's fine clothes ripped and tore to make room for his enormous bulk. Four muscled arms stretched from his sides, the higher two ending in scorpion pincers, the lower two human hands, only with feline claws the color of coal. Black chitin covered his chest and waist. Silver fur wrapped his arms. His legs bent backward like a goat's, and they ended in hooves. Unlike a goat's, they were covered in scales that glistened crimson in the moonlight.

His face, though, was the worst. His flesh was veined and textured like exposed muscle, only it was colored a deep gray. His lips were gone altogether, revealing a smile full of jagged daggers. Of his eight eyes, the inner two were human, the other six solid black and bulbous like a spider's. Instead of hair, two horns curled up from the sides of his head, spiking toward the stars like the antlers of a deer.

When Frey opened his mouth to speak, his tongue hung low to his waist, and it forked halfway down.

"Behold godhood."

Frey: Level 45 ▊▊▊▊
Archetype: Paragon
Special Classification: Deity Blessed (Eiman)
Special Attribute: Fire Resistant
Armor: Natural, Tier 6

Sir Gareth dropped to his knees upon witnessing what

Lord Frey had become. His sword hit the stones and rattled in a clatter of steel.

"This is the price you would demand?" Gareth cried. "This is the blood you would shed in the name of your freedom? Yuni... Yuni!"

Clouds darkened in the sky above. It was as if the stars themselves hated to bear witness to the wretched monstrosity born of bloody sacrifice. That hate paled in comparison to the rage billowing off Sorrow into Nick's veins.

A champion of a god unworthy of worship, the blade seethed. *Eiman is to take his due when the world is reborn, never before. To sacrifice an innocent life is blasphemy of the highest order. We must slay him, Nick. I demand it.*

An order Nick was all too happy to fulfill. Lesya joined him, and her voice held the faintest quiver.

"I've never seen anything like it," she said.

"Which means it needs to die," Nick said. He glanced her way. "Are you with me, Lesya?"

"I am," she said.

"As am I," Violette said, fire curling around her fingers. Despite her bruises and her bleeding lip, she grinned eagerly. "But if he does kill us all, make sure you two come back to avenge me."

"No one's dying," Nick said, and he pointed his sword. "No one but him."

Nick sprinted at Frey, ignoring the staggering difference in their levels. They had numbers, they had magic, and they had lives depending on them. He feared to imagine what Frey would do to the people of Castle Astarda while in such a form,

LEVEL: UNKNOWN

especially if the populace did not acknowledge his supposed "godhood."

Victory would be theirs. It had to be.

Lightning blasted from Nick's hand, a **<lightning bolt>** striking the center of the chitin plates. The lightning swirled into Frey's body, seemingly only tickling the monster's enormous amount of life. A **<fire orb>** followed, which Frey batted aside with one of his scorpion pincers. The ball erupted, struggling to burn the hard exoskeleton. It served more as a distraction for Nick's and Lesya's arrival, the two splitting at the last moment, each cutting hard toward a side. Lesya's sword carved a slash through the crimson scales about those goatlike legs. Sorrow cut deep across the thigh, and Nick could feel the weapon's eagerness as it drained Frey's life.

That hit earned him a brutal kick straight to the chest. Nick landed in a sprawl, Sorrow momentarily clattering free of his grasp. Nick fought off panic. One hit, and he was down three-fourths of his total health.

"Leave him alone!" Violette shouted. Fire burst from her hands, the **<fire plume>** washing over Frey, charring him twice. Resistant though he might be to fire, it was still enough to enrage him. He charged straight at Violette, the castle rooftop trembling with his every step. Lesya reacted first, her left hand swinging wide as she cast **<icy ground>**. The ice spread underneath Frey's intended path, but it failed to slow him down. His hooves smashed straight through the surface, leaving indents in the stone to grant him traction. Violette crossed her arms as both pincers closed in on her, ready to snap her into pieces.

Spell: Fire Wave
Flames erupted outward from Violette, forming a tremendous wall of fire twice her height rolling in all directions. Frey rocked backward from the blow, and it was only the resistance of his chitin and scales that kept the damage to a minimum. The flames ended once they passed over him, sparing the rest from their fury. During Frey's momentary confusion, Violette staggered, looking exhausted and drained from the powerful spell. Lesya aided her retreat by conjuring a thin **<ice wall>** whose sides were spiked.

Frey smashed it away in his fury, the hard chitin of his pincers suffering not a hint of damage. Nick clenched his left fist, summoning his lightning. Two quick blasts of **<lightning bolt>** struck Frey across the head and shoulder.

"Hey," Nick said, grabbing Sorrow and twirling the weapon in his hand. "I thought I was the evil needing purification."

Nick got what he wanted, even as it spiked fear in his chest as the gargantuan Frey lumbered toward him with claws and pincers eager to tear his body apart. In return, Nick braced his left arm and summoned his **<lightning shield>**.

With his legs planted, Nick blocked a reaching strike from a clawed hand. He thought he could endure, as he had against Sir Gareth. He thought wrong. Though lightning crackled in retaliation, swarming Frey's body, it was far from worth Nick's pain and exhaustion as the claws punched through the lightning shield to scrape along his arm. Minimal damage to his health, but a massive drain of 20 of his mana, leaving him with only 9.

"Okay, let's not do that again," he gasped as he retreated a step. He had little health left, and he felt it, every part of his body aching and blood soaking his clothes. With shaking hands, he readied Sorrow, expecting Frey to push the assault. Instead, Frey stood to his full height. He sucked in a great inhalation through his nostrils and then opened his mouth. Deep within his throat, Nick saw dark fire swirl, growing in power. Panic struck him, but he did not know the nature of the attack, nor how he might avoid it.

Eiman's power was always meant to serve, Sorrow screamed, his deep voice piercing through Nick's paralysis. *Swing true!*

Nick lifted the ancient weapon high above his head. The shadow erupted from Frey's throat, blasting toward him like a beam of purest darkness whose width was greater than Nick was tall. Before such a thing he felt small and pitiful, but he held faith in Sorrow and swung his sword with all his might.

The obsidian edge cleaved the beam in half.

The darkness blasted to either side of him, tearing apart bricks to carve grooves into the keep's rooftop. An invisible shock wave of Nick's swing traveled the space between him and Frey, all the way to Frey's open throat to end the blast. Meanwhile, black fire swirled into the empty gap of Sorrow's blade, the power of the beam gathering and eager for use.

Now release my vengeance!

Nick swung, and just as before, the length of Sorrow's edge seemed to grow and grow, a searing, burning, wrathful blade to slam Frey's chitin chest. The monster howled as the hit seared a crack into his exoskeleton.

"You would turn a judgment blade against its own god?" Frey rumbled. He stepped closer with a crack of stone. "Is there no limit to your blasphemy?"

A solid **<ice lance>** blasted one of his scorpion arms, then shattered into shards.

"You murdered a girl to become what you are," Lesya said, flinging two more **<ice lances>**. "And you want to talk about blasphemy?"

Frey crossed all four of his arms, weathering the blows with the aid of his toughened hide and chitinous plating. Nick took advantage, dashing in to carve a gash along Frey's left knee. Enough to bleed him, and heal a bit of Nick's wounds, but his follow-up dodge was slow, and what health he'd recovered was lost when the edge of a pincer barely clipped his shoulder, tearing flesh and soaking his body with blood. Frey roared, shadows swelling within his throat for another fiery blast.

"Your sword can protect *you*," Frey said. "But what of your friends?"

His tongue lashed out, suddenly the length of his body, to strike Violette in mid-cast. The fire vanished from her fingertips, her spell broken as she flew several feet backward to land in a heap upon the hard stone.

"Violette!" Nick screamed, panicking. Lesya reacted faster, sprinting three steps toward where Violette lay before leaping into the air. A flash of her fingers, and **<icy ground>** formed a path along the ground toward Violette. Lesya landed on her right hip and then slid at a wild pace to the path's end. She skidded off it to her knees, bloodying them as she spun about while slamming her palms to the castle rooftop.

The ice hardened, thicker and thicker, to form a protective **<ice dome>** just in time for the beam of fiery darkness to strike it. Cracks spread along the sides, but when the shadows faded, the dome remained strong, Lesya and Violette safely protected within.

It won't hold long, Sorrow warned. *We must bring the monster low.*

So much easier said than done. Despite the aches across his body, despite the dangerously low stamina left in that little green bar in the corner of his vision, he charged Frey. Two human fists swung at him, and though he dodged, one smashed him across the side. It felt like slamming into a wall, and he feared the pain meant bones had broken in his ribs or arm. Nick struck Frey's arm in retaliation, Sorrow easily parting the silver fur. Immediately the pain in his ribs lessened.

Trust my power, Sorrow insisted. *Trust the strength of your enemy to be your boon. I will not let this blasphemy endure.*

Nick wished he could share in Sorrow's confidence. One good strike with those scorpion claws would snap him in half, and he doubted any healing magic would be enough to save him. Still, the flow of power was intoxicating, mixing with his fear to fill him with a frantic energy, to which he fully succumbed. He swung twice more, wild and savage. Despite Frey's enormous size, he was the one to retreat, his arms flailing and pincers lashing. Twice they exchanged blows, but Sorrow's fury was too great. What health Nick lost was made up by the gruesome carnage he hacked into goatlike legs. The blows refreshed his mana, though he held his lightning back, wanting to reserve it for when he needed it most.

At last, his greed cost him. Nick chopped once more into Frey's leg, dropping the enormous monster to his knees. Thinking he had the advantage, he thrust for Frey's belly, but the hideous thing lowered his head so the hit deflected off the antlers. Frey lunged, and though Nick retreated, it was not enough to gain separation. The antlers struck him, three different points sinking into his body. He screamed as blood flowed, nearly all his health spilling away in the blink of an eye. He flailed with Sorrow, but the weapon could not cut the antlers, which seemed composed of the same obsidian that made up Sorrow's blade.

A twist of Frey's head, and Nick flew several feet, landing on his back. He gasped, struggling to catch his breath. He had a sliver of health left, and hardly anything remained of his stamina. If only Sorrow's vampiric magic could aid him there.

Get up, Sorrow raged. *Get up or be slain, you damned fool.*

Nick pushed to his knees, but he already knew he would be too slow. Frey crawled closer on his four arms, the blood-soaked antlers eager and ready. Nick braced for the killing lunge... but when it came, it was slow, and he easily dodged it as he stumbled to his feet.

Spell: Time Slow

Nick's bafflement was immediately removed by that flash of words from Cataloger, followed by the proud voice of a furious knight.

"I am the blade of the god-king," Sir Gareth said, approaching with his sword held wide to one side. Divine magic sparked about him as his left hand reached toward Frey.

"I am the shield of Goltara."

Gold light shimmered across his fingers. Matching light lashed Frey, taking the form of linked chains wrapping about his vulgar body.

"I am Vaan's beloved knight, and I will not be moved."

LEVEL: UNKNOWN

Spell: Time Imprisonment

Frey squirmed against those chains, but his movements were slow and lacking strength. Even his guttural roar sounded lacking. Gareth lifted his arms high, all his strength flooding into the spell as he screamed at Nick.

"Strike this monster down!"

Nick crossed the space in a sprint, his bare left hand closing about the naked blade. He gritted his teeth to endure the pain as Sorrow opened the flesh of his palm to coat its obsidian edge with his own blood. His legs flexed, and he leaped into the air while lifting his sword high above his head.

Sorrow sank into Frey's chest, piercing the gap between two chitinous plates. A good hit, but still a small percentage of the gargantuan beast. Yet this was just the start. Nick's left hand gripped the edge tighter, and he screamed in defiance of the pain, his voice joining Frey's agonized roar. The blood flowed thick, the wound on his palm opening and closing repeatedly as Sorrow's vampiric trait attempted to undo the damage with the life siphoned out of Frey. Lightning crackled about that same hand as Nick readied his magic. He did not ask Cataloger to confirm his plan. Yensere and its rules would bend to him, to his belief, and to his certainty.

Blood and water were the same, so far as electricity was concerned.

A **<lightning bolt>** streaked down Sorrow's length, flowing through a mixture of blood from Nick's hand and that which spilled from the wound in Frey's chest. It sank deep into the monstrous body and then crackled outward, searing through Frey's limbs for a massive release of power.

Gareth's magical chains broke, the imprisonment spell run its course, but Frey trembled in place, muscles locked by the coursing lightning. Nick clung to the sword and howled, giving Frey all his rage, his pain, and the last remnants of his mana, blasting **<lightning bolt>** after **<lightning bolt>** in a frenzied display.

When all was spent, Nick yanked Sorrow free, and at last, he let go of the blade with his injured hand. His head ached, his heart pounded in his chest, and his every breath felt shallow and weak, but still he stood. Gareth joined him, his fine golden sword held at the ready.

"You will bow," Frey bellowed, his voice wet and his words punctuated by blood spilling out across his lips and chin. He staggered back to his full height, still clinging to the last quarter of his life. "You will break. My faith has granted me godhood!"

Sorrow burned in Nick's grasp.

We bow to no one. End him, pillager.

Nick and Gareth charged together, as behind them, the ice of Lesya's protective dome shattered. A volley of **<ice lances>** shot overhead, joined by a **<searing wrath>** flung by a recovered Violette. The last of their magic led the way, an explosive greeting of fire and frost.

Lances of ice smashed Frey's chest.

A ball of flame exploded against his throat to burn the many eyes of his face and melt the ice still embedded in his chitin.

Blood flowed with Gareth's hacking into Frey's right thigh, peeling off crimson scales and severing tendons.

And last was Nick, plunging Sorrow straight into Frey's

LEVEL: UNKNOWN

abdomen, twisting the hilt, and then ripping it free in a spray of blood.

Strength flowed into him, clarity returning to his mind as his diminished mana pool stole power from the monstrous lord. Frey slammed Gareth away, a brutal swipe with two arms that left his armor dented and his health flickering with but a scrap left. A similar swipe of a scorpion claw lashed for Nick, but he spun underneath and away. When he came out of the spin, he extended his left hand, his palm raised high.

"Fuck your godhood," Nick said, and flung a **<lightning bolt>** straight into Lord Frey's hideous face.

That last quivering percentage of red crackled away from the health bar and left it empty. Frey collapsed, his legs going limp and his arms splaying out at awkward angles. Nick closed his eyes as the rest of the dead lord's body landed upon the keep's rooftop with a wet thud. He slowly exhaled as the level bar flashed into view, filling and restarting multiple times.

Reassessment
Level: 13 (+3)
Statistical Improvements
Agility: 10 (+4)
Physicality: 7 (+2)
Endurance: 11 (+5)
Focus: 10 (+2)
Mana: 60 (+11)
Archetype Changed—New Categorization: Spellblade

When Nick opened his eyes, Sir Gareth stood before the

body with his sword held in shaking hands. Nick noted the knight had also gained a level, going from 17 to 18.

"You did the right thing," Nick said, sliding Sorrow into his belt.

"Did I?" Gareth asked, and turned. His bloodshot blue eyes seemed to stare straight through Nick. "I abandoned my faith for a lie. I served a monster. Now my lord is slain, and a demon stands before me, unchallenged and stronger than ever."

Nick stood tall. "I am no threat to Yensere. I stand by my promise."

Gareth sheathed his own sword.

"I must seek God-King Vaan's forgiveness," he said. "Will you do the same, demon Nick? Will you bend your knee to the true god of Yensere?"

Nick glanced over his shoulder to see Lesya and Violette approaching. Violette had also gained in level, from 10 to 12, and he suspected Lesya had as well. The pair moved gingerly, both exhausted beyond measure.

"No," Nick said, turning back. "Vaan means nothing to me, Gareth. But you? You, I'll trust. When it mattered most, you did the right thing. Your forgiveness is the only forgiveness I will accept for the crimes I have committed. Yours alone."

Sir Gareth approached the corpse of the young girl whose sacrifice had spawned the behemoth.

"You have your sins," he said, gently lifting her body into his arms. He cradled her to his chest and turned away. "And I have mine. Farewell, Nick. May we never meet again."

Chapter 43
NICK

The city was in chaos when Nick, Lesya, and Violette crossed the eastern wall on Lesya's **<icy path>**. Word of Lord Frey's death spread like wildfire throughout the city, as did confusion about who would take over. Whoever it might be, Nick prayed they were smart enough to leave Nick and his friends alone. Beyond the wall, the trio walked the grass, staying off the road for the time being. The sun rose, and in its blossoming light, Nick looked over the lands of Inner Emden.

"Beautiful," he whispered.

It felt like stepping into a completely new land from Vestor. Gone were the swaying meadows of ryegrass and occasional fields of wheat. Replacing them were gentle hills wreathed with flowers running a spectrum from white to a violet so deep they appeared almost black. Instead of tall forests, he saw a wide lake in the distance, its calm surface reflecting the rising yellow sun. A river ran southward, knifing through the hills. Deer drank from it, normal deer, not ones twisted and mutated and eager to kill him. In the distance, the hills rose higher, and he saw villages built atop them, smoke rising from chimneys to form dozens of little gray lines.

"We've all had a long few days, but you especially," Lesya said, patting Nick on the shoulder. "Let's get you home. Cataloger, care to show us to the nearest ring of stones?"

The nearest ring of stones is one thousand three hundred yards away

A golden arrow appeared, pointing in the proper direction. The trio followed it, skirting closer to the downward slope of the mountain to the north. Where the ground grew rocky, the grass not quite so healthy, there waited a simple ring of stones, imperceptible if one was not looking for it... or didn't have a glowing arrow leading the way.

"I'm starving here," Nick said, pausing at the edge. "I can't imagine how hungry I'll be out *there*." He winced. "I hope my brother isn't too mad at me. It's going to be hard convincing him none of this was my fault."

Before Nick could enter the ring of stones, Violette flung her arms around him and held him tight.

"Promise you'll come back?" she asked, the side of her face pressed to his chest.

"I'm not sure I have a choice," Nick said, and he smiled at her. "But even if I did, yes, I promise I would."

Lesya lingered behind Violette, her arms crossed over her chest.

"You've had a long few days," she said, grinning. "Enjoy a break from Yensere. You need it."

"What of you?" Nick asked. "Will you be waiting for me?"

LEVEL: UNKNOWN

A rattle of metal as Lesya shifted in place.

"I still need to find Irina. And since you seem capable of handling yourself in a fight, your help is welcome."

Nick laughed. "Good to know I'm finally earning my keep. I still have quite a ways to go before I catch up to your level, though."

Her blue eyes sparkled. "As if you ever will."

Violette pulled away from him, and Nick took a deep breath. Exiting Yensere was never easy, but it was certainly easier through the rings of stones than through a brutal death. He waved goodbye to both of them, then closed his eyes and stepped inside.

Send me home, Cataloger.

Departure requested and approved—oh, and Nick

Yes?

I am glad you are safe

Before Nick could respond, the darkness deepened, Cataloger's voice receding into the distance.

Visit terminated

This time Nick knew what caused the gagging sensation in the back of his throat. The knowledge helped, but only a little. His eyes fluttered open, and to his surprise, his brother was not beside him, but Dr. Haley. She had her tablet in her left hand, its glow lighting her face in the somber room. Her right hand stroked the Guidance emblem hanging from her neck, quick and nervous.

"Hey," he said, grabbing her attention. She lowered the tablet, and he saw fear—fear that was quickly hidden behind a practiced, professional expression.

"You're finally awake," she said, quickly sliding her Guidance emblem and chain back underneath her shirt.

"How..." He paused to fight off a gag. "How long was I out?"

"Two days," she said, folding her tablet closed and setting it on the little side table. "Do you think yourself capable of eating?"

Nick swallowed. His stomach hurt, a mixture of cramps and a strange bloated sensation.

"I don't know," he said. "But I'm willing to try."

"That's good enough for me. Lie back and keep still."

She removed the oxygen from his nose first, then unhooked the IV. Last was the feeding tube. He endured the removal, holding back a retch until she finally pulled it free of his left nostril.

"What about the, uh..." He gestured toward his crotch. "You know."

"We're getting there." She lifted the blanket off his legs, then pulled back the thin medical gown he'd been changed into at some point during his adventures in Yensere. "You'll feel a gentle pulling. Take a deep breath for me, then slowly exhale."

Nick did as asked. As he breathed out, he had to hold back a bitter chuckle.

Behold the legendary hero and his triumphant return home.

When finished, Haley put away the supplies, washed her hands, and then tapped her watch.

LEVEL: UNKNOWN

"Director Simon should be here shortly," she said curtly.

"Is something wrong?" Nick asked, his worry growing. He'd never seen Haley frightened before, and even now, she seemed remarkably tense.

"That's for the Director to say. Relax for now. Don't push yourself too hard. Once you've had something to eat, we'll see if we can get you washed up and then do some stretches while you're lucid. The last thing we want is bedsores."

"Of course," Nick said, sitting there awkwardly in his med gown. "Whatever you think is best."

Haley seemed to flinch at that.

"Indeed," she said, and left without elaborating. Nick drummed his fingers on his thighs, then pushed off the bed. This was his room, and if he was going to be exercising and eating in the mess hall, he wasn't going to do it in a paper-thin gown. He removed it, then quickly changed into a loose pair of sweats and a long-sleeved shirt. He was just finishing pulling the shirt over his head when the door opened and Simon stepped inside.

"Well, there's a fine sight," he said, shutting the door behind him. "The med gown doesn't suit you."

"I'm not the one who chose it," Nick said, sliding his arms through the shirtsleeves. He used the delay to study his older brother. Simon's eyes were bloodshot, with thick bags underneath. He looked like he hadn't slept in a week. Nick suspected he looked similar and could confirm it if he was brave enough to find a mirror. Again he sensed tension, if not outright fear.

"What's going on?" he asked. "Something is wrong, I know it. What is it? Is it about my health? The Artifact?"

Simon frowned, but his hesitation lasted only a moment. "Come with me."

They exited Nick's room into the main corridor, but instead of going anywhere, Simon immediately approached the opposite door. It belonged to Dr. Gharda, their astrophysicist. Simon hesitated a moment, then muttered something to his watch. The red light on the handle flicked to blue, and he pushed it open.

"Don't worry, it's empty," Simon said. "Come on."

Gharda's room was nearly identical to Nick's, only without all the medical equipment. Simon crossed the space to the windows, whose metal blinds were closed to keep the room dark. A touch of a button, and they lifted, exposing the sweeping starfield above Majus.

"It can't be," Nick whispered.

A black hole of nothing hovered in the sky, denying the light of the stars. It perfectly resembled the frozen sun of Yensere except for the blue fire lining its edges. In Yensere, the edges were frozen and still. Here, they gently swirled and rotated, with fragments of the fire's light drifting inward, adding to a curling sensation within the black sun. The sight of it put a brick in Nick's already tightened stomach.

"It appeared six hours ago," Simon said, staring out the window. "Just like the Artifact, it messes with our scanning tech. We're not sure how far away it is, nor how big. We'll send a shuttle to it soon, unmanned, of course. But for now, we're in the dark."

"Not entirely," Nick said, mesmerized by the swirling blue fire curling around the edges. "It's the same as the one on Vasth, and in Yensere."

LEVEL: UNKNOWN

"I suspect so," Simon said quietly. "But Vasth went dark, and as for Yensere? We've seen what remains of the planet Majus. What little of it."

Nick clenched his fists, his resolve growing as he glared at the black sun.

"We may not know what it does, but I know how to find out," he said. "Get me more sedatives, and put the feeding tube back in if you must. I have to return to Yensere."

"Return? Nick, this is the most lucid I've seen you in weeks, and you spent two days completely catatonic."

"It doesn't matter. Something terrible is coming, and we have a way of finding out exactly what. It's struck Yensere repeatedly, and if I can trigger it again, then I can bear witness. Maybe even figure out how to stop it for real."

Nick turned away from the window, Simon trailing after him as they returned to his bedroom.

"Nick, please, you're talking insanity. You're going to trigger a worldwide catastrophe within the Artifact? How?"

The audacity of it brought a smile to Nick's face. It seemed impossible, but then again, he'd come a long way from bashing farmers in the head with rocks. He sat on the edge of his bed, closed his eyes, and offered his vow, one he suspected Sorrow would be thrilled to aid him in keeping.

"By taking the life of the one holding back the apocalypse," he said, closing his eyes. Despite his hunger, his thirst, and the adrenaline pounding through him from the sight of the swirling black sun, he felt the call of Yensere sliding like a fog over his mind.

"I'm going to kill the god-king."

The story continues in...

Level: Ascension

Book TWO of Level: Unknown

A NOTE FROM THE AUTHOR

This might make me sound a little crazy, but I swear it makes sense, so just stick with me here.

When starting this LitRPG, I knew there'd be growing pains. Stepping into any new genre is going to have them. And many of the ones I expected were there, such as getting used to integrating statistics in a meaningful, fluid way without going overboard (which I very much did the first time around). Dabbling in some sci-fi was another, though one I enjoyed given that, despite all my fantasy novels, my first few published short stories were either sci-fi or horror. No, what ended up throwing me off infinitely more than expected was a seemingly impenetrable barrier: I did not see Yensere as real.

Now, the reason this sounds insane, at least to my own ears, is that *none* of the worlds I write are real. Thanet and Dezrel and Kaus are all just make-believe locations, silly hallucinations of my mind. But they *felt* real to me. When I imagined characters living and acting within those worlds, I was able to treat them with gravitas, and as if the actions my characters took *mattered*. But when I tried to imagine Nick running

A Note from the Author

around Yensere, and I started to build the world around him...I couldn't get it to work. I knew, in my head, that it was a digital simulation. It wasn't "real." And for a good long while, I honestly thought I would abandon this project entirely because of it.

And then I wrote Gareth's first POV chapter. I realized that if I was to see this world as something more than a strange place Nick would dip into like the starting zone of a video game, I needed to see the people there. I needed to feel like Meadowtint was a real village, with people under siege by this strange, terrifying entity known as "Nick." I was hesitant to write such a chapter, given how it would not include any stats or levels, but I needed it. And by the time I finished, I felt grounded in a way I hadn't before. Now...now I had something. Now the world was starting to fill out around me. When Nick killed someone, there were people to grieve, mourn, and burn the bodies. And when I had Gareth meet Beans, who in truth started out as little more than a nod to a friend's *Final Fantasy XIV* character, I realized I had so many more ways to make Yensere real to me...even if some of those ways got rather dark.

All right, time for some quick thanks. Thanks to my editor, Brit, for being so eager to grab the kind of story you've been dying for over at Orbit. Thanks to my agent, Michael, for guiding me through yet another transition in my career. A particular thank-you to Steph, *Level: Unknown*'s main editor, who helped guide this whole project through its weird creation...and, more importantly, was there for every single complaint and grumble as I realized I made a math error and

A Note from the Author

needed to do five chapters of corrections. I would not have stayed sane without you.

Last, but most certainly not least, thank you, dear reader, for making it this far. I hope you enjoyed this story, or at least got enough out of it to have a mostly entertaining time. Should you continue with Nick and Lesya's story, I'll be right here, waiting for you at the end of *Level: Ascension*, with another Note from the Author. I've got some crazy stuff planned to really push the ideas of the kind of world the Artifact can contain, and maybe, just maybe, I'll do it justice.

David Dalglish
April 26, 2024

MEET THE AUTHOR

DAVID DALGLISH graduated from Missouri Southern State University in 2006 with a degree in mathematics. He has self-published more than twelve novels, as well as had seventeen books traditionally published through Orbit Books and 47North.

He also has a lovely wife and three beautiful daughters, with all four being far better than he deserves.

Find out more about David Dalglish and other Orbit authors by registering for the free monthly newsletter at orbitbooks.net.